PRAISE FOR
Original Sin

"From the moment you begin reading *Original Sin* by D.P. Lyle, M.D., you'll know you're in the hands of a master of the medical thriller. Disorienting and riveting, *Original Sin* finds retired police officer Sam Cody embroiled in a series of puzzling homicides in which heart surgery patients turn into killers – but then, sometimes modern medicine is so high-tech it can seem almost supernatural. Bristling with rich detail and smart repartee, *Original Sin* is indeed an original. You don't want to miss it."

—Gayle Lynds, *New York Times* bestselling
author of *The Book of Spies*

"Retired Detective Samantha Cody returns to face her greatest challenge in D. P. Lyle's superb new thriller, *Original Sin*. Cody. She is called upon to help her heart surgeon friend, Lucy Wagner, whose professional and personal life turns chaotic after she operates on a snake-charming evangelist. Deftly plotted and expertly executed, Lyle is at the top of his game in a heart-pounding thriller. Sam Cody is a protagonist worth rooting for. Find a comfortable chair, and plan to stay up late. Highly recommended."

—Sheldon Siegel. *New York Times* Best Selling Author of
the *Mike Daley/Rosie Fernandez Legal Thrillers*

A Samantha Cody Mystery

ORIGINAL SIN

A Samantha Cody Mystery

ORIGINAL SIN

D. P. LYLE

REPUTATION BOOKS

ORIGINAL SIN

Published by Reputation Books
www.reputationbooksllc.com

Book design by Lisa Abellera

Library of Congress Cataloging-In Publication Data (TK)

ISBN-10: 0-9740222-2-5 (paperback)
ISBN-13: 978-0-9740222-2-2

ISBN-10: 0-9740222-5-X (e-book)
ISBN-13: 978-0-9740222-5-3

First Edition: July 2014

10 9 8 7 6 5 4 3 2 1

Reputation Books

Acknowledgements

A very special thanks to my wonderful agent, Kimberley Cameron of Kimberley Cameron and Associates. Another special thanks to all the wonderful people at Reputation Books for making this book possible. To my dear friends Glenna Hearn, Madison Fife, Teri Raines, Rankin Sneed, and Peter Elia, and my sister Melinda Martin for graciously allowing me to co-opt their names.

And these signs shall follow them that believe; In my name shall they cast out devils; they shall speak with new tongues; They shall take up serpents; and if they drink any deadly thing, it shall not hurt them; they shall lay hands on the sick, and they shall recover.

Mark 16:17-18

CHAPTER 1

Lucy Wagner knew exactly when she would hold the heart in her hands, its hard muscle churning against her palm, its moist heat warming her fingers. Knew when its rhythmic twisting would stagger and fall silent as the drugs brought it to a standstill. Frozen in time.

She just didn't know it would be this heart or under these circumstances.

John Doe changed everything. John Doe couldn't wait. John Doe bumped her 7:30 elective coronary bypass until later. Probably much later.

Thirty-five minutes earlier, Doe had been found down, face down, on the ER entry ramp at the Remington Medical Center. Purple, breath coming in shallow gasps, pulse barely palpable, and spiraling toward death. Circling the drain in medical slang. The heroic efforts of ER Director Dr. Jeffrey Dukes and his staff, pumping Doe full of fluids and blood, restoring just enough blood pressure to feed Doe's weak but tenacious spark of life, somehow stabilized him long enough to reach Lucy's operating table in OR Suite 3.

Now, the scalpel she held in her rock-steady hand hovered near the old man's flesh. Tinted reddish brown by the hasty pre-op Betadine scrub, the parchment-thin skin and its underlying age-wilted muscles were all that separated the blade from the torn aorta and the massive pool of blood she knew waited within Doe's abdominal cavity. A cardiovascular surgeon's worst nightmare. The elderly man had little chance of getting through this alive but absolutely none if Lucy didn't jump right in. As one of her fellowship mentors at Vanderbilt had been fond of saying, "They're are times to contemplate and times to slash and grunge."

This was slash and grunge time.

Prayer wouldn't hurt.

Scrub nurse Rosa Lopez adjusted the round bank of overhead lights to better illuminate the surgical field. Across the table stood Dr. Herb Dorsey, Remington's oldest and most respected general surgeon. He had been in the OR, waiting for his elective gall bladder case to begin, and had volunteered to help.

"How's he doing, Raj?" Lucy asked anesthesiologist Dr. Raja Singh.

Raj peered over the curtain of surgical drapes that separated his little world of monitors, anesthetic gas and oxygen canisters, and whooshing ventilator tubes from the sterile field that was Lucy's domain. "BP up to eighty, heart rate one-thirty, sinus tach. Four units of blood in. Two more on the way." He shrugged. "Not too bad considering."

Lucy smiled into her mask. Typical Raj. Always understated, always unflappable. She looked at Herb. "You ready to dive in?"

He nodded.

Rosa picked up the suction cannula, an angulated plastic nozzle connected by a clear plastic tube to a suction bottle near her feet. "Crank this baby up all the way," she shot over her shoulder to the circulating nurse. "It's going to be a gusher."

Damn right, Lucy thought. John Doe's atherosclerosis had finally caught up with him. His hard and brittle aorta had cracked and split and ripped and pumped nearly his entire blood volume into his abdomen, swelling it to pregnant proportions. He was, as the locals say, "As swollen as a chigger on a blue-tick hound."

It was going to be bloody.

God, she loved this. Always had. The adrenalin rush that had enticed her into surgery in the first place. As far back as high school she had thought being a surgeon would be cool. Even the word surgeon was cool. When she shared these dreams with her classmates, most nodded politely and told her that was a wonderful ambition. But she knew they believed she'd never do it. She was a marginal student, interested in athletics and boys more than academics. Track and softball were her sports. Things changed in college where she majored in chemistry and focused on her grades. Straight A's opened the door to medical school.

During med school, she tried to keep an open mind, accepting of all medical and surgical specialities. Until her junior year surgical rotation. Trauma surgery. Run and gun. Do first, think later. She was hooked and dropped all pretense of considering another branch of medicine. As she climbed the medical food chain from student to intern to surgical resident, cardiac surgery stepped to the forefront. So here she stood, ready to dive elbows-deep into John Doe's belly.

Lucy drew the scalpel blade down the center of the Doe's belly, dividing the skin and subcutaneous tissues. She extended the incision from the lower end of his sternum to his pubis. Dark blood leaked from the slash.

"He looks a little desaturated," she said. "What's his O2 sat?"

"Eighty-four percent," Raj said. "He's on sixty percent O2. I'll bump it to a hundred."

Lucy continued dissecting downward through the old man's tissues until she reached the peritoneum, the membranous sac that lined the abdominal cavity.

She glanced up at Herb. "Here we go."

The blade punctured the membrane. Liquid blood erupted through the breach, dragging with it thick maroon clots that looked like over-fed leeches. The suction cannula jerked, squealed, and gurgled as it drew blood from the distended belly. The clots swirled down the plastic tube and into the collection bottle beneath the table.

This was the critical time. With the lessening of the tension inside the abdomen, the pressure on the torn aorta would fall. Pressure, which like the proverbial thumb in the dyke, had held the bleeding in check. At least somewhat. Now the flow of blood from the ruptured vessel would dramatically increase and Doe could bleed out in a minute. Literally.

In two swift motions Lucy elongated the incision in the peritoneum, first north and then south. Herb scooped up the intestines and tugged them aside, giving Lucy access to the deeper regions where the aorta lay along the back wall of the abdomen. She dipped both hands into the blood pool, her experienced fingers quickly finding the aorta. The squealing of the suction cannula grew louder.

"Jesus," Lucy said as she located the tear. "He blew out the lateral wall and it's extended superiorly." Her hands worked upward along the vessel. Blood welled in the abdomen faster than the suction cannula could remove it. Lucy's fingers painted the picture for her. "Left renal artery is trashed." He hands worked higher. "It's dissected up through the diaphragm."

She exhaled heavily. Doe's chance of survival had just dropped to near zero. An acutely ruptured abdominal aorta carried a mortality of 95% or more, but if the breach extended up and into the chest, that figure rose to near 100%.

Lucy looked across at Herb. The narrowed eyes that stared back from above his surgical mask and the sweat that stained the front edge of his cap said it all. Herb had performed thousands of surgeries and knew when things were going sideways. His look reflected that. Not fear, experienced surgeons being immune to that emotion, but a healthy dose of anxiety.

"BP is down to 60," Raj said. "I'll up the Dopamine and the Epinephrine."

"We're going to have to open his chest," Lucy said. "I've got to get above the dissection and cross-clamp the aorta if we're going to stop this bleeding."

"Some ectopic beats," Raj added.

Lucy glanced at the cardiac monitor. The blips that indicated the cardiac rhythm, which before had raced across the screen in a rapid but steady pace, now showed irregularity. Then an angry burst of wide and rapid complexes appeared.

"And salvos of V-Tach," Lucy said. "Give him some lido, Raj."

"Got it." He shoved the needle into the IV port and depressed the plunger. "Lido one hundred milligrams on board."

"Scalpel," Lucy said.

Rosa slapped it into her open palm. Lucy divided the skin over the chest down to the sternum. Herb handed her the sternal saw. Lucy fitted the knob, designed to protect the heart and lungs from the blade, into the sternal notch and flipped on the saw. Its high-pitched whine cut through the room and echoed off the tiled walls. The scream of the saw blade slowed and dropped an octave or two as she drew it along the length of the sternum, dividing it cleanly. The acrid smell of burning bone filled the room.

Rosa had the sternal retractor ready. Lucy hooked it beneath each half of the divided sternum and Herb twisted the crank. The chest yawned opened. The exposed heart churned rhythmically. At first. Then it gave several spasmodic jerks and fell into a fine quiver.

"V-Fib," Raj said.

Lucy examined the monitor again. The EKG no longer showed the blips of cardiac electrical activity, but rather the fuzzy, wavering line of ventricular fibrillation, the most lethal of all cardiac rhythms. Beneath that, a second line, the blood pressure monitor, was now flat.

"Let's rock and roll," Lucy said.

She wrapped her fingers around the heart. A normal, strong, blood-filled heart is firm and churns and grinds against your hand. Not Doe's. His was flabby and soft, indicating that the muscle was diseased and weakened and that his heart was nearly empty. Most of Doe's blood now resided in his abdomen. Wouldn't do much good there.

This was going badly.

Lucy began the cadenced squeezing motion of internal cardiac massage. The blood pressure monitor now displayed a weak pulse in time with Lucy's compressions. Enough to keep him alive, but not for long.

"Defib paddles," Lucy said.

Herb took them from Rosa, grasping the handles and fitting the business ends, flat metal discs, against opposite sides of the heart.

"Charged to thirty watt/seconds," Raj said.

"Clear," Herb said.

Lucy released the heart and withdrew her hands.

Herb depressed the paddle's buttons, delivering an electric jolt directly to the heart. The monitor indicated a brief moment of cardiac rhythm, but quickly returned to V-Fib.

"Again," Lucy said.

Herb fired the defibrillator a total of seven more times, Lucy continuing compressions between each while the device recharged. Raj injected more lidocaine, along with procainamide, metoprolol, and amiodarone. None of this restored a viable rhythm. Lucy continued to squeeze the heart, her hand serving as Doe's only means of survival. With each compression, the heart became softer as blood continued to leak into the abdomen.

Sweat trickled into Lucy's eye and she blinked it away. "Let's cross-clamp the aorta. Maybe control some of this bleeding."

"You think that'll help?" Herb asked.

"No, but we're running out of options."

Lucy stopped her massaging efforts and snatched a curved vascular clamp from the surgical tray. In the tight quarters behind the heart and the left lung, she managed to slide the clamp around the thoracic aorta. So far so good. But when she attempted to squeeze the fragile vessel between the instrument's jaws, the brittle tissues cracked, disintegrated. She resumed the cardiac massage and looked across the table at Herb. "Any other suggestions?"

He shrugged. "Call a priest."

"Anyone else have any ideas?" Lucy asked.

Silence, a few heads shook.

Lucy nodded. "I guess that's it."

As she started to release her grip on Doe's flabby heart, a cold sensation surged through her fingers as if she were holding a ball of ice. Her hands ached and the chill flowed up her arm and into her chest. A wave of nausea and dizziness racked her.

Somewhere in the distance she heard Raj say, "Time of death is eight twenty-four a.m."

A flood of sweat popped out on her forehead and trickled down the side of her face. The lights dimmed and closed in. She wavered.

"You okay?" Rosa asked, her voice tinny and muffled.

Another wave of dizziness. Lucy took a deep gulp of air, another, shook her head, but she felt as if she were sinking and sensed her legs folding beneath her. Her world went black.

The next sensation she had was a cold hardness against her cheek. A bright, irritating light seemed to come from all directions. She felt shadows moving across her and heard voices, but couldn't make out what they were saying. Several smudges of light blue shuffled before her. She heard someone call her name but couldn't tell who or where it came from. Someone shook her shoulder. Her vision began to clear. The blue smudges became three pairs of surgical booties, each speckled with blood droplets. Again she heard her name, closer now, more distinct, and felt something clutching at her shoulder, shaking her again.

She rolled to her back. Three angels stood over her, their faces framed by bright haloes. They reached for her. One of the angels was Herb.

"Lucy. Lucy," he said.

"What...." she began.

Someone said, "She's coming back."

Lucy looked up into Herb's face, and then Rosa's, each backlit by the overhead surgical lights. She looked around. She was on the floor of the operating room.

"What happened?" she asked, attempting to sit up. She realized someone had removed her surgical mask and cap.

Herb pushed against her shoulder. "Just lie there for a minute."

"What happened?" Lucy asked again.

"You fainted," he said. He reached behind her neck, untied the top of her surgical gown, and pulled it over her arms, taking her bloody gloves with it. "Just relax and take a few breaths."

CHAPTER 2

Lucy sat on the worn green sofa in the OR doctor's lounge, where she often cat napped between cases. Never a comfortable place to recharge the batteries, the old sofa seemed even more saggy and lumpy than usual. She finished a second cup of orange juice, and then peeled the top of her sweat-soaked surgical scrubs away from her chest and flapped it, creating a welcome cool draft. The dizziness and nausea had subsided and she almost felt normal again.

Herb stuck his head in the door and then entered. "You feeling better?"

She nodded.

"At least your color's back." He settled into a nearby chair.

She offered a weak smile. "I feel like an idiot."

He turned his palms up and gave a one-shouldered shrug. "It happens to all of us at some time or another."

"Not to me. Not even my first day in anatomy lab as a freshman." She didn't mention the single other time she had hit the deck. Her first surgery as a junior med student. Not a good thing for a female intent on becoming a surgeon. She had taken the teasing in stride but had promised herself it would never happen again.

So much for promises.

"Anatomy lab's when it happened to me."

"You? You're the Rock of Gibraltar."

"Some members of the surgical staff might take issue with that."

Lucy nodded. She knew he was referring to Dr. Gilbert Birnbaum, neurosurgeon, Chief of Surgery, President of the Remington Medical Center Foundation, and all around prick. Two years earlier, when Lucy completed her training and set up shop here in Remington, he had tried to block her appointment to the medical staff, largely to protect the turf of his close friend, Dr. Elliott Meeks, the only chest surgeon on staff. Lucy being a fully-trained cardiovascular surgeon was a threat to Meeks' turf.

The politics of medicine never sleeps.

Birnbaum had also used his political connections and more than few sleazy deals to wrest the Chief of Surgery position from Herb, who had served as chief for two decades. Herb had graciously stepped aside rather than enter a long and potentially destructive war, saying it was time for a change anyway. Lucy knew otherwise. She knew the loss of his position to Birnbaum, a man he held in little regard, had been painful and humiliating. He had noticeably aged in the past two years. Hair a bit thinner and grayer, face lined a little deeper, and shoulders carrying an even larger invisible weight.

"I'm just glad Gil wasn't around to witness this," Lucy said.

"Oh, he'll find out soon enough," Herb said. "You can bet on that."

As if to prove the point, the door swung open and Birnbaum walked in. His surgical scrubs struggled to contain his round body and a mask hung loosely beneath his three chins. "I heard what happened." He sat next to Lucy. The sofa sagged further. He lay a pudgy hand on her shoulder. "You okay?"

"Yeah."

"Any idea why this happened?" He looked from Lucy to Herb, then back to Lucy. "You aren't ill, are you?"

"Just a hectic schedule lately." She forked her fingers through her short, spiky, blonde hair. "And with the emergency triple-A, no time for breakfast this morning."

"Any more cases scheduled today?" Birnbaum asked.

Lucy wanted to smack the smugness off his face. He knew damn well she had a case today. He constantly hawked the surgical schedule and always knew who was doing what and when. Of course that's one of the duties of the surgical chief, but for Birnbaum it wasn't anything chiefly that drove him. It was simply another way of keeping his thumb on everyone in the department.

"A triple bypass at one."

"Are you up to it?" A false fatherly concern laced his voice.

"I'll be fine," Lucy said.

He struggled to lift his round body from the sofa and looked down at her. "As long as you're sure." He glanced at Herb. "We do have a responsibility to make sure our doctors are capable and healthy."

Capable? You arrogant shit.

Lucy stood. At five-ten she was two inches taller than Birnbaum. "I'm okay. And if I think I'm not, I'll cancel or delay the case myself."

"Of course," he said. "Good thing that congenital case wasn't scheduled for this morning. Hate to see you fall ill during that one."

You'd love it, you jerk.

The case, one she had been planning for six weeks, would be the first congenital heart case at the medical center. "It isn't scheduled until Tuesday."

"I know." He turned toward the door, but stopped. "If you're coming down with something, a bug or whatever, you could push it back a few days."

And give you another chance to block it? I don't think so.

"I'll be okay. It's been a very hectic couple of weeks. A string of long and difficult cases and not enough sleep. Too much coffee, too." She nodded toward the ancient coffee pot on the counter next to the sink. "In fact I was just telling Herb a couple of days ago that with the work load I felt like I was a surgical resident again."

"Wait until you get my age. It doesn't get easier." Birnbaum cleared his throat. "Well, I have a case starting. Another tough one. A deep glioma in a young woman. I'd better get to it." He left, the door swinging closed behind him.

"I don't like that guy," Lucy said.

Herb raised an eyebrow. "I can assure you, the feeling is mutual."

"I've never done a damn thing to him, but every time I turn around he's trying to sabotage me."

"You're a threat to him."

"I try to avoid him as best I can."

"He came along in the days when neurosurgeons were the top guns. The fighter pilots. That's all changed. Now, it's the heart surgeons."

"Not my fault."

"True. But Birnbaum was and is the only neurosurgeon on staff. That put him at the top of the food chain. The most specialized surgeon around. Until you came along. Hearts are sexier than brains."

"Sexy?" Lucy laughed.

Herb shrugged. "Then there's his buddy Meeks. You are definitely a threat to him. I imagine you've already eroded his referral base for chest cases."

"Still not my fault."

Herb smiled. "The main thing I suspect is that Birnbaum's ego won't let him be second string. Especially to a woman."

"You mean like he believes the doctor gene is on the Y chromosome?"

Herb smiled. "Something like that."

"But..." Lucy started to protest, but stopped when the door swung open again and Glenna Hearn, the ER charge nurse, stuck her head inside.

"We got a name on Doe," she said. "It's John Scully."

"The preacher?" Lucy asked.

"That's the one."

"Family here?" Lucy asked.

"Yeah. Came to the ER. I was going to take them to the OR waiting room but then I heard things didn't go so well. No surprise with what he had. I put them in the chapel room."

"Thanks."

"They know he didn't make it. Dr. Dukes spoke with them." Glenna gave her look. "You okay?"

Like AC current the hospital grapevine moved with lightning speed.

"I'm fine."

Glenna nodded and let the door ease closed.

"You ever met John Scully?" Herb asked.

"No. Just heard the name. Doesn't he have a small church just north of town?"

"Sure does. Up in the hills. Strange cat."

"How strange?"

"Very. He's one of those snake handlers."

"You're kidding. I hate snakes."

"Want me to talk with them?" Herb asked. "So you can rest."

Lucy shook her head. "I'll do it."

CHAPTER 3

B efore Lucy went to see the Scully family, she thumbed through the old man's chart. While she was elbow deep in the then John Doe's chest, two family members had arrived at the ER and filled Glenna Hearn and Dr. Jeffrey Dukes in on the background information that hadn't been available from Doe. She read through their notes.

John Scully had been 82. Father of two, grandfather of three. Long history of hypertension and diabetes. MI five years earlier. Smoked for 60 years. Now dead, a victim of his genes and bad habits. Lucy closed the chart and massaged her temples. Losing a patient was never easy. Even if he was 82. Even if he had one foot in the grave from his diseases and both feet when he collapsed outside the ER. Talking to a family after an unexpected, or at least sudden, death was one of the very few things she hated about her job. Necessary, and in her field not all that rare, but she still hated it. Never seemed to get easier.

When she entered the hospital's small chapel room, a man and a young woman sat on the single sofa, silhoutted by a light box with a plastic mosaic of a praying Jesus on the wall behind them. They didn't look like snake handlers, whatever snake handlers should look like. Crazed and wild-eyed? Foaming at the mouth or writhing on the floor or twisting and gyrating is some wild dance? But these two seemed normal. The man appeared to be fifty or so. He wore jeans and an untucked white shirt. The girl, late teens, Lucy guessed, wore a light-blue, calf-length dress with a white lace bodice, shoulder-length brown hair tied back with a white ribbon. No way Lucy could picture her with a rattler, twisting around her arm or neck.

Lucy had also expected to see tear-streaked, pale faces, reddened eyes, trembling lips, wringing hands, all the signs that a grave loss had occurred. Audible sobbing wouldn't have been unusual. Instead, their eyes lit up and they smiled when she entered. Her first thought was that this wasn't the right family. Maybe John Scully's family had gone outside to collect themselves and another family had come to the chapel to pray or reflect on a loved one's illness.

Lucy hesitated at the door. "Are you with Mr. Scully?"

"Yes," the man said as he stood, extending his hand. "I'm his son, John, Jr. This is my daughter, his granddaughter, Felicia."

Lucy shook the offered hand and then eased into a chair opposite them. John, Jr., like his father, was gaunt with a prominent Adam's apple and pale blue eyes; Felicia thin, attractive, and with the same blue eyes.

"I'm so sorry for your loss," Lucy began.

"It's okay," John said, returning to his seat. "This day was expected." He smiled and gave a slight nod.

They must be in shock, Lucy thought. She had seen it all too often. Traumatic news often spun people into a foggy, trance-like state and their reactions were at times inappropriate. "Still, I'm sure it's hard."

"No," Felicia said. "It was prophesied. This is a good day. Grandfather would not have wanted it any other way."

They both stared at her, smiling, as if studying her. Lucy adjusted her posture, sitting more upright as her discomfort with the situation grew. "He ruptured his aorta. The large artery from his heart. There was little we could do."

"Please, don't blame yourself," Felicia said. "It is exactly as it should be."

"We know you did all you could," John said. "My father knew this day would come. He knew when it would come. His work here is finished so, you see, this is a glorious day."

Religious nuts. That must be it. They weren't in some shock state. They were full of Jesus. Or whoever. She had seen this before, too. The glazed-over look of religious contentment.

"Still, I'm sorry."

"We know you are very good at your work," John said. "We have followed your career quite closely."

This was getting even weirder. "You have?"

"Oh, yes," he nodded. "You're quite the celebrity."

Lucy felt the flush of embarrassment creep into her face. "You're very kind."

John leaned forward, his face showing a fatherly, comforting smile. "My father knew your grandmother," he said. "Your mother's mother."

"Martha?"

"That's right."

"Really?" Lucy felt off balance. Her grandmother? John Scully?

"Yes. Long ago. And I knew your parents. Remember when you were born. Attended your parents' funeral," John's lips tightened, face drawn, gaze dropping to the floor as if remembering. "Very sad day."

Lucy's parents had died in a fire when she was nearly five. She had little memory of them, only a single charred and faded photo. And now this guy, who knew them, sat here casually talking about them only minutes after his own father had died.

HIs gaze returned to her. "They were wonderful people."

"Did you know them well?" Lucy asked.

He nodded. "For many years." He inched forward so that he perched on the front edge of the sofa. "If you ever want to talk about them just let me know."

Lucy's heart rate increased to a gallop. She felt as if she were floating on a cottony cloud. This was all too bizarre. She was telling them about the tragic death of their patriarch and somehow the conversation had come around to the parents she had barely known. Her throat felt dry. She couldn't speak, so she nodded.

"I'm the pastor at Eden's Gate Church of God. Took over from my father a year ago." He smiled, his eyes deep and penetrating. "I meant what I said. If you ever want to talk about your parents my door is always open."

"Thank you," Lucy said.

"Your grandmother?" he asked. "How is she?"

"Not well," Lucy said. "Her memory isn't what it once was."

"And the schizophrenia?"

How did this guy know all this? "Comes and goes."

"I'm so sorry to hear that. She is such a special lady." His face seemed to express genuine concern. "Do you see her often?"

"Every chance I get."

"I'm sure my father would have wanted to say hello."

"I'll tell her when I visit," Lucy said. Her heart slowed somewhat.

"Good," he said. "Is there anything else you need from us?"

"No. I'm sorry for your loss."

John stood. "Every door that closes opens another. The body may depart this world, but the spirit remains." He smiled. "His essence lives on within us." He laid a hand on Lucy's shoulder. "All of us."

CHAPTER 4

What was the deal with John and Felicia Scully? What lay behind their blank stares and fixed smiles? Their relief, even joy, at the death of the older Scully seemed macabre. Inheritance? Maybe they stood to get a bundle. Revenge or retribution? Maybe he was an abusive jerk and they were glad to be rid of him. Maybe they were simply weird. But that would probably go for anyone that handled snakes on a regular basis.

God, she hated snakes. Had ever since she walked up on one in her own back yard. She was maybe five. It was shortly before her parents died. She froze, some deep DNA instinct telling her this was not something to mess with. Her father freaked. Came running from the kitchen and killed it with a hoe, chopping it to pieces. Odd that her memory of the snake was so vivid yet she couldn't recall what her parents looked like. Other than that single old photo. But no real memory of their faces.

She had heard of these snake-handling churches but thought they were a thing of the past. A relic of history. For the most part anyway. She remembered reading an article about a preacher dying from snake bites in some church up in West Virginia. When was that? Several years ago at least. But here in Remington? Right here in her own backyard?

These questions continued to perplex Lucy even now as she worked in William Nevers' chest. Lucy pushed the images of John and Felicia aside and continued suturing the last of three bypass grafts into place. She tugged the final suture tight, securing the graft to the circumflex coronary artery, and then stretched the suture tags upward, as scrub nurse Rosa Lopez snipped them with a pair of Metzenbaum scissors.

"Good job," Rosa said.

Lucy nodded. "I love it when a case goes smoothly."

"Better than this morning," Rosa said.

Lucy laughed. "Don't remind me. That was embarrassing."

"Seen it before," Rosa said. "Of course, usually with med students."

"Funny," Lucy said. "But never harass a surgeon when sharp instruments are nearby." She nodded toward the tray stacked with scissors, scalpels, probes, all the tools of surgery.

Rosa raised her gloved hands before her, her smile, hidden behind her mask, reflected in her eyes. "Point taken."

Lucy slid her experienced fingers over the unmoving heart and along each of the grafts. She inspected every suture line, lifting the heart slightly to examine the circumflex graft.

"Looks clean." she said. "Let's reverse the cardioplegia and start warming him up."

To perform most heart surgeries, the heart and lungs are "put to sleep" and the job of circulating and oxygenating the blood falls to the cardiopulmonary, or heart-lung, machine. It's called cold cardioplegia. A large dose of potassium chloride stops the heart and the body is cooled so that the heart and other bodily tissues slow their activities and require less oxygen.

The pump tech made adjustments to the heart-lung machine, raising the temperature of the blood it pumped through William Nevers and washing the heart-stopping potassium from his body. Soon, Lucy felt the heart quiver, then spasm, and finally begin its rhythmic contractions. She glanced up at the cardiac monitor. Sinus rhythm.

"All systems are go," Lucy said.

For the next twenty minutes they went through the process of disconnecting the heart-lung machine. Mr. Nevers was again flying solo.

Lucy lifted the now beating heart and made a final inspection of each graft, searching for leaks. Finding none, she settled Mr. Nevers' heart back into its place.

She felt it first in the center of her chest. An icy sensation. As if she had wolfed down too much ice cream. The feeling crept outward into her arms and legs. A wave of dizziness and nausea swept over her.

Not again.

Her hands seemed frozen to the churning heart. The dizziness increased, her visual filed darkening around the edges. She heard voices but they seemed far away. She looked at Rosa who stared at her, eyes wide above her mask.

"You okay?" Rosa asked. Her voice seemed to waver, like a distant, weak radio signal.

Lucy felt her legs tremble. She took a deep breath and pumped her knees back and forth, as she concentrated on remaining upright. With great effort, she pulled her hands free and took a step back from the surgical table.

"Lucy?" It was Raj. Concern crinkled the corners of his eyes and etched his forehead.

The dizziness softened, the chill dissipated, and Lucy's vision and hearing began to clear. "I'm fine." She shook her head. "I'm such a wimp."

"You sure you're okay?" Raj asked.

"I'm fine." Lucy stepped back to the table. "Let's close up."

৶

Lucy downed a glass of orange juice, a fully-sugared Coke, and a chocolate chip cookie at the nurse's station while she scribbled a note and post-op orders in the chart. By the time she finished dictating her operative report and retreated to the OR doctor's lounge, she felt better. Maybe a little residual shakiness but the dizziness and cold feeling had long since evaporated. She filled a Styrofoam cup with over-cooked coffee and sat on the sofa. She tugged off her surgical shoe covers and tossed them into the trash can in the corner.

The coffee tasted bitter, but no more so than any other day. She placed the cup on the floor near her feet, leaned back, and ran the fingers of both hands through her short blonde hair. What the hell is wrong with you, Lucy? She looked up as the door swung open and Jeffrey Dukes came in.

"You okay?" he asked.

"I wish people would quit asking me that?"

"A little bitchy today?"

"I'm sorry. Tough day. But yes, I'm fine."

"I know about what happened this morning." He sat next to her. "I hear it happened again during your bypass case."

"Ah, yes. The hospital grapevine."

"Faster than Twitter."

"You got that right."

"So, what is it? You coming down with something or what?"

"I haven't had any time off call for a couple of weeks. I've had half a dozen tough surgeries. I guess I'm just tired."

"Any symptoms?"

Lucy frowned at him. "You can quit playing doctor now."

"I thought you liked playing doctor?"

Her frown morphed into a smile. "Not the brand you're selling."

"Humor me. I'm just worried about you."

Lucy yanked the surgical mask that still hung around her neck, snapping its ties. She waded it and tossed it into the waste basket. "What would I do without friends like you?" She patted his hand and then picked up her coffee. "Maybe it's this stuff. I'm sure it's poisonous."

"Why don't you run down to the lab and get a couple of blood tests."

"Jeffrey, I don't need any blood work. I'm just tired."

"If you won't go to the lab, I'll have them come here."

She shook her head and rolled her eyes. "Okay, okay. If it'll make you happy."

"It will. And as a bonus I'll quit bitching at you."

"No you won't."

"You're probably right."

She stood. "I'll go after I check on Mr. Nevers in recovery."

"Promise?"

She nodded.

"And pee in a cup."

She frowned. "I'm not pregnant."

"You sure?"

"Unless it's the second immaculate conception, I'm sure."

"Are you sure you're up for the shindig tomorrow?"

"Don't baby me."

"It's what I do."

"Yes, I'm going. Wouldn't miss this for anything." She finished the coffee and tossed the empty cup into a nearby trash can. "You're going aren't you?"

"Of course. I can't think of anything better than seeing you receive some much deserved recognition."

"That part I'm definitely not looking forward to."

"Come on, Lucy. You earned it. We didn't do open hearts until you got here. You put us on the map."

"That's me. Google Earth."

He laughed. "When is your friend coming in?"

"Anxious to meet her?"

He shrugged. "You said she was hot."

"She is. And she can whip your butt."

"I can outrun her."

"Don't be so sure. Sam is a stud."

"You make her sound like a truck driver."

Lucy laughed. "Not exactly. You'll see. She's got model looks and a left hook that would take out most truck drivers."

"She sounds down-right charming."

"Not sure Sam would be considered charming. She tends toward sarcasm."

"Hmm. Now I am intrigued."

"Cool your jets, Buck Rogers," Lucy said. "And get back to the ER and do something useful."

Jeffrey stood, walked to the door, and turned back toward her. "And you get your butt down to the lab."

She saluted. "Yes, Sir."

CHAPTER 5

The town of Remington, Tennessee had sprouted and grown along the western edge of Crockett Lake and straddled Remington River, which flowed east, bisecting the town before turning south to the Tennessee River. Two bridges jumped the river, connecting the town's north and south regions. The Veteran's Memorial Bridge, or the Vet Bridge as locals called it, crossed closest to the lake, the Crockett Bridge downstream a dozen blocks.

Samantha Cody guided her SUV along Main Street toward the Vet. The town hadn't changed much since she was last here. When was that? Two years? No, closer to three. She had visited Lucy for Christmas. Lucy was in her last year of CV surgical training at Vanderbilt.

She and Lucy had met years ago when Lucy was in med school at UCLA and Sam was ensconced in the LAPD Police Academy. One of her instructors had set her up on a blind date with a medical resident who turned out to be a friend of the surgical resident Lucy was dating at the time. A double date to a high-dollar, Hollywood-star-studded Beverly Hills restaurant. What was the name of that place? She couldn't remember but it was outstanding.

Her blind date was less stellar. A dud in the truest sense of the word. No personality and less sense of humor. She couldn't remember his name either. Not that she wanted to.

But she and Lucy hit it off. Instantly. They became close friends and hung together every chance they got until Lucy completed her internship and returned to Tennessee for her residency and Sam headed home to Mercer's Corner as a deputy under Sheriff Charlie Walker.

A job she no longer had.

When Charlie retired, Sam had been the logical choice to take his job but politics reared its head in the form of Lanny Mills. A dirt ball who controlled the city council and county commission. He and Sam never got along and he rigged the election. She never had a chance. So with Lanny as the new sheriff in town, Sam folded her tent and left.

Not really left. Her home remained in Mercer's Corner but she had taken this *period of unemployment*, as she liked to call it, to see parts of the country she had never visited. First order of business: dump her old Jeep, it being near end of life. Then she splurged on a new Lexus GX 470 SUV. Not exactly new, but new to her. It had 28,000 miles on the odometer when she drove it off the lot. That was two months ago. She had crisscrossed the Pacific Northwest and the Great Plains, before finally turning south, adding another 4,000 miles to the SUV's mileage. The past two days she had been in Memphis, staying at the famous Peabody, home of the equally famous Peabody Ducks, eating ribs at the Rendezvous, and roaming Beale Street to listen to the blues at BB Kings Blues Club, Silky O'Sullivan's, and Mr. Handy's Blues Hall.

She had slept in this morning, grabbed a final dose of BBQ for lunch, and hit the road. She avoided the interstates and roamed the state and county roads as she wiggled her way toward Remington.

The one thing that had changed in Remington was the Vet bridge. Where the Crockett Bridge was newer, the Vet had been built before World

War Two. Three years ago, its metal frame had been faded and rusted but now it was a bright red-orange. According to Lucy the city council had decided to make the bridge a center piece and chose the color. International Orange. The same paint used on San Francisco's Golden Gate. The town had apparently been divided, some folks wanting the traditional gray, but the orange fans won out.

Lucy had warned Sam but now seeing it rise before her was shocking. Vermillion was the word. Sam slowed as she crossed the bridge not sure how she felt about the color. It would definitely take a little getting used to.

She continued up Main a couple of blocks, leaving the downtown area behind, and hung a left on to Crockett Lake Boulevard, Lucy's street. The road hugged the lake's northern shoreline and, like charms on a bracelet, was strung with lake front houses. The homes weren't little cabins as was the south shore norm. This was the high-dollar neighborhood. The houses were large, mostly brick, mostly two-stories. Sam turned into Lucy's tree-shaded drive. Before she could step out Lucy came through the front door and across the lawn toward her.

She hadn't changed in the nearly three years since Sam had last seen her. Still lean and fit. She and Sam were of similar builds and people often confused them for sisters. Except Lucy's hair was blonde and short with that spiky thing going while Sam's was more to the strawberry side of blonde and shoulder-length, most often pulled into a ponytail, as it was today. Lucy's eyes were blue; Sam's green.

"It's so good to see you," Lucy said as she hugged Sam.

"You, too. It's been too long."

"Come on in."

Lucy had only lived here a year and Sam had never seen it so Lucy showed her around. The house had three bedrooms, a large living room with a deep, curved sofa and a stone fireplace, and a spacious, open kitchen and dining room. A wall of French windows and doors looked over a broad wooden deck. Beyond, a tree-shaded lawn sloped down to the lake, where a short wooden pier and an aluminum boathouse extended into the water.

The walls in the living room and the hallways held two dozen or more paintings by Martha Ackers, Lucy's grandmother. Martha was famous with works displayed in galleries around the South and even in the Smithsonian American Art Museum. Martha's ability to capture mood and movement was amazing. Lucy led Sam down a hallway, Sam examining each painting. Many of which she had seen before. She stopped before a portrait of a young girl in a white summer dress, gazing over a lily-pad strewn, willow-shaded pond. The water appeared liquid, the hovering dragonflies alive, and the girl sad and wistful.

"I love this," Sam said. "Is it something new?"

Lucy sighed. "An old one I found among Martha's things. It was wrapped in canvas at the bottom of a trunk."

"You're kidding?"

Lucy shook her head. "Don't you love it though?"

"It might be my new favorite." Sam turned from the painting and looked at Lucy. "How's she doing?"

"Not well. A couple of years ago her schizophrenia quit responding to drugs and then her dementia kicked in. She got worse seemingly week by week."

"I'm so sorry."

Lucy took a deep breath and exhaled slowly. "Not much to do about it."

"Does she still live here with you?"

"No. She became so confused she couldn't be by herself. I tried to find someone to stay with her during the day but that really wasn't practical. I get called out at night too often. So she's in an extended care facility."

"Does she like it?"

"Probably not. Can't really tell since her contact with reality is sporadic at best."

"That bad?"

"Unfortunately. We'll go see her tomorrow or Sunday."

"I'd like that."

"Let's get your stuff out of the car and get you settled and then go grab some dinner. Hungry?"

"What do you think?"

"That was a stupid question." Lucy laughed. "Never saw you when you weren't hungry."

Sam shrugged.

"Wish I could eat like you and still stay lean and mean."

"Take up running. Or boxing."

"I thought you gave the boxing up?"

"I did. Professionally anyway. I still do the same workouts though."

"I've been bad. Haven't been to the gym in three weeks."

"You have a day job."

"And unfortunately all too often a night job."

"There you go."

"With you here to inspire me, maybe I'll be a little more diligent."

CHAPTER 6

JT's BBQ sat smack in the middle of downtown on Main Street at Elm, diagonally across from the northwest corner of the square. A square that embraced an eighty-year-old, two-story brick courthouse that was topped with a white copula, round, Roman-numeraled clock dials aimed at the four compass points. A dozen fifteen-foot-tall lampposts lit the surrounding sidewalk. Two broad oak trees, easily as old as the building, dappled the light as it fell on the stone walkway that led to the wide granite entry steps. Several black iron hitching posts, relics of a bygone era, flanked the walkway.

"I love this old building," Sam said as she and Lucy walked past.

"Me, too," Lucy responded. "And you're going to love JT's."

"I can smell it already,"

"Best barbecue in town."

JT's possessed a darkly-stained, knotty-wood front facade and a large picture window and glass front door, each emblazoned with gold script that announced: JT's BBQ, The Planet's Best Food. Sam pulled open the door and she and Lucy stepped inside. Eclectic would be the word that best described the interior. One wall brick, another paneled, both covered with an array of photos and knick knacks: a yellow life preserver, a parking meter, a pair of ancient wooden skis with cracked leather bindings, a rail crossing marker, and other signs from feed companies to chain saw manufacturers. A red, yellow, and green traffic signal hung from the ceiling in one corner, its lights cycling slowly, and in another stood an old red and white Fire Chief gas pump.

"It's only been open a couple of years," Lucy continued, "and it's the most popular place in town."

The mostly filled tables and elevated noise confirmed Lucy's contention. Sam noticed that the decibel level dropped a fraction as a few furtive looks and the occasional open smile and nod came in her direction. Strangers always attract attention in places like Remington.

Sam and Lucy grabbed an empty four top along the brick wall, beneath a movie poster for The Doctor's Dilemma. Sam was sure she had never seen the movie, a romantic comedy from the way Leslie Caron and Dirk Bogarde happily nuzzled one another. Before Sam could settle her purse into an empty chair, a waitress appeared.

"Welcome, Dr. Wagner," the perky redhead said.

"Julie, this is my dear friend Sam Cody. She's visiting from California."

Julie's eyes lit up. "California? Hollywood?"

"No," Sam said. "I live out in the Mojave desert."

Julie had no comeback for that but did appear disappointed. Probably hoped Sam would have some Hollywood gossip. Or maybe an offer to make her a star. From BBQ to to the big screen. Just the kind of mostly mythical story Hollywood liked to promote.

"Well, welcome to JT's," Julie said as she tapped a pen against the pad she held. She turned to Lucy. "You having your usual?" When Lucy nodded, she looked at Sam. "What can I get you to drink?"

"What's the usual?" Sam asked.

"Makers Mark, neat," Lucy said.

"Make it two."

Julie turned, her short red ponytail whipping around, and headed toward the kitchen.

"I take it you come here often?"

"Everybody does."

"Sure looks that way."

"It's like this every night. Not just Fridays."

Julie returned with the drinks. "Know what you want?"

"I haven't even looked at the menu," Sam said.

"Pulled pork," Lucy said. "You want the pulled pork."

"I do?"

"You do." Lucy smiled. And then to Julie said, "Maybe some turnip greens and corn muffins, too."

Julie scribbled on her pad. "Have it out in a sec."

Lucy raised her glass to Sam. "Welcome back."

"Seems like it's been forever. Christmas three years ago? Right?"

"That's right."

"You know what I remember most about that week?" Lucy looked at her waiting. "The three of us—Martha, you, and I—sitting by the fireplace with hot chocolate and Martha telling stories from her childhood. That was special."

"It was," Lucy said and then she sighed. "That seems so long ago. Now, more often than not, she doesn't recognize me when I visit. And when she does it's fleeting."

"I'm sorry."

Lucy shrugged. "Circle of life."

"Still, I know it's not easy."

"True."

"Lucy?"

The voice behind her was gravelly and deep. Sam turned to see two men. One was older and thick and wore a uniform, badge on the pocket, gun hanging from a wide leather belt. The other younger, tall, and rangy. Handsome with a mop of dark brown hair over his forehead. He wore jeans, a dark blue golf shirt, and a gray sports coat.

"Chief." Lucy said.

Lucy introduced Sam to Police Chief Bump Whitworth and Ty Everson, who Lucy described as "our one and only homicide detective." They each shook Sam's hand.

"Join us," Lucy said.

"Wouldn't want to intrude," Bump said.

"You're not. Sit."

Bump took the chair next to Sam; Ty beside Lucy.

"How'd you get the name Bump?" Sam asked.

"Everybody's got to be called something," he said, then smiled. "But it's better than Burton, my real name."

"The story goes that when his mother was pregnant she called her ever expanding belly her bump," Ty said. "It stuck."

"Young folks," Bump said. "They think they got the answer to everything."

Ty laughed and raised his hands. "Just giving Sam the local lore."

"Sam's a cop," Lucy said.

Bump twisted toward her, his wooden chair creaking. "Really? Where?"

"Not anymore," Sam said. "I was deputy in my home town. Mercer's Corner."

"Where's that?"

"A place in California you'd never find. In the desert. Sort of off the beaten path."

"But you're not a cop anymore?" Bump asked.

"Long story."

"Sounds political."

Sam nodded. "Exactly."

"How do you two know each other?" Ty asked.

Sam told the story. As she was finishing the food arrived.

"Chief, Ty," Julie said. "Can I get you guys something?"

"That looks fine to me," Bump said, nodding toward Sam's plate. "And some sweet tea."

"I'll have sweet tea, too. And the catfish," Ty said.

"Burned as usual?"

Ty laughed. "Let's say extra crispy."

"You got it." Julie said, giving Ty a sly look and a flirty grin. "Pulled pork and one charred catfish coming up."

Bump looked across the table at Lucy. "You okay?"

"Of course."

"I hear tell you had a little problem over at the hospital this morning."

"Jesus." Lucy shook her head. "Small town gossip."

Bump smiled. "You know don't much go on around here me and Ty don't know about."

"What happened?" Sam asked.

"I fainted in surgery."

"You? The iron maiden?"

"Funny." Lucy forked some pork into her mouth. "Let's talk about something else."

"Let's don't," Sam said. "What exactly happened?"

"I was doing a difficult case. Actually it was over. I got woozy and the next thing I knew I was on the floor."

"Really?"

"Oh yes, really."

"Why?"

"Fatigue. Too much work and not enough sleep."

"That'll do it," Ty said.

"I hear it was Pastor John Scully on the table. Something bad?" Bump asked.

"As bad as it gets. He didn't make it."

"I heard."

"Who's John Scully?" Sam asked.

Bump folded his hands before him. "A local preacher. Odd fellow. Handles snakes and all that."

For a second Sam wasn't sure she had heard him correctly. "Really? People still do that?"

"That was my reaction, too," Lucy said. "I had heard his name before and knew he was a preacher but I'd never heard about the snake part. I thought that was old folklore and that no one did that anymore."

"Sure do," Ty said. "I'd bet we have half a dozen snake handling congregations within fifty miles of here."

"And Scully's church is one of the oldest," Bump said.

Sam shook her head. "Unbelievable."

"Your grandmother used to go to his church," Bump said to Lucy.

"What?" Lucy asked. "You're kidding?"

"Nope. Your parents did, too."

"Scully's son John, Jr. told me that his dad knew Martha and my parents, but he didn't mention they were church members."

"They were," Bump said. "For a while anyway."

"Why didn't I know this?" Lucy asked.

Bump shrugged. "I assumed you did."

"This is the first I heard of it."

"Anyway, after your parents' accident Martha quit the church," Bump Said. "Not sure why, but I know old John Sr. wasn't happy about it."

"Not happy in what way?" Lucy asked.

"Not rightly sure. But I suspect that having someone famous like Martha as a member was a big coup for old John. Course back then Martha was more a local celebrity. Not what she became. But a celebrity just the same."

Lucy placed her fork on her plate and leaned back in her chair. "This has sure been one hell of a day. It wasn't enough wimping out in surgery now I learn that Martha and my parents congregated with a bunch of snake handlers."

"Have another bourbon," Sam said. "That helps everything."

Waitress Julie was walking by and must have heard what Sam said. "Another round?"

"Sure," Lucy said. "Why not? I'm not on call tonight."

"Back in a flash." And she was. Seemed like it took about ten seconds to grab a pair of fresh Makers.

"John Senior'd been ill for at least a year so John, Jr's taken over the congregation," Ty said.

"The snakes, too?" Sam asked.

Ty laughed. Easy and relaxed. "Yep."

"Ah, nothing like the family business," Sam said.

Ty laughed again. Maybe a little too hard this time. Sam had noticed him checking her out. Of course she had been doing the same. He was interesting in a ruggedly handsome, Marlboro man sort of way.

Down girl.

"I hate snakes," Lucy said.

"Don't everybody?" Bump asked.

"No. I really hate them. Can't stand to be around them. Makes me all queasy."

Sam looked at Lucy. "You sure you're okay?"

Lucy took a slug of whiskey. "Better now. A little Makers makes everything better."

"So you're not a deputy anymore," Ty said to Sam. "What are you doing?"

"Seeing the country. Visiting Lucy."

"You coming to the big shindig tomorrow?" Bump asked.

"Wouldn't miss it."

CHAPTER 7

S am's shoes padded softly on the asphalt as she hugged the side of the two-lane road. She had awakened at 5 a.m. and tossed and turned for a half hour before concluding she wouldn't be able to go back to sleep. Might as well go for a run.

Hoping not to disturb Lucy, she quietly slipped on shorts, sports bra, tee shirt, and her New Balance shoes and headed out the door. A loop through the neighborhood led her to a road that spurred north and wound its way through a thickly wooded area. Up and over several hills before it broke out of the shadows and into open farmland, where it bent west, the rising sun now behind her. Sweat lacquered her skin as she fell into a comfortable rhythm.

The sky was clear but a faint cool mist hung low to the ground in broken patches. The fertile soil that flanked the road looked as if it had been recently planted and the aroma of freshly turned dirt was thick and sweet. Not like back home. There the air would be hot and dry, the wind pushing against her, the constant dust irritating her eyes and nose. Here, everything smelled rich and alive.

She encountered very few vehicles, mostly farmers in their pick ups beginning their day's work. Those that passed nodded or waved, one man touching the brim of his frayed straw hat. After a half hour, a good four miles or so based her usual seven-and-a-half-minute mile pace, she turned back into the sun and retraced her path. A squadron of crows, fussing and cawing, flew past her and settled into a field a hundred yards to her left. No doubt beginning their early morning feeding on the grubs and insects unearthed by the plow blades.

She heard a vehicle approach from behind and moved to her right off the asphalt and on to the grassy shoulder. The vehicle, a black dually Chevy pickup, slowed. Two guys. Both wore caps and sweatshirts, sleeves scissored off at the shoulders. The passenger had one arm dangling out the open window.

"How you doing little lady?" he asked as the truck slowed further and matched her pace.

"Fine," Sam said. "How're you guys doing?"

"Need a ride?"

"No, but thanks anyway."

"Come on," he patted the seat between him and the driver. "Got plenty of room."

"I think I'll just finish my run."

"We can party a little."

"I think not."

"You ain't from around here," the driver said. It was more a statement than a question.

"Nope."

"We got some good weed," the passenger said. "Mellow you right out."

Sam stopped. The driver braked. The passenger's eyes brightened and he started to open the door, obviously thinking Sam's stopping was an indication she'd accepted their invitation. Sam pushed the door back closed before he could step out.

"There's something you boys need to know," Sam said.

"What's that, darling?"

"Make that two things. First, I'm not your darling. Second, and most important, I'm a cop." Now four very wide eyes looked at her. "So offering me party favors probably isn't very smart."

The driver recovered from his shock quickly. "You ain't no cop. We know all the cops around here."

"I imagine that's true."

"What's that supposed to mean?"

"It means this is a small town and everyone knows everyone else."

"That's right," the passenger said. "It's a friendly town. And we're friendly guys. Come on and hop in and we'll show you how friendly we are." He reached out the window as if to grab her arm. Sam stepped back.

"Maybe you guys should move along."

He laughed. "Feisty. We like feisty."

He started opening the door again. Sam took another step back, her brain calculating options. Run or fight. She doubted these guys were athletes but they had a truck. And from what she saw there wasn't much but blacktop roads and open land, which gave them an advantage. Best option would be a left-right-left to take out the passenger before the driver could react. Hopefully.

Just as the passenger got the door open and a boot on the ground, a black Tahoe, light bar across its roof, rounded a curve a hundred yards ahead. Didn't take a heart beat for the passenger to jump back inside and pull the door closed.

"It's fucking Ty," he said. "Let's go, Elvin."

The truck accelerated and left her standing there.

Ty Everson's Tahoe came to a stop and the window came down. "Sam? You alright?"

"Fine. But I'm glad you came along."

"I see you met Eric and Elvin."

"Not sure I'd call it that."

"Oh?"

"They were looking for a party girl."

"Which I'm guessing you ain't."

"Not their kind. Partying to me is a good workout and a couple of beers."

Ty laughed. "Or maybe a whiskey?"

"That, too." Sam looked up the road and saw the pickup disappear around a curve in the distance. "I see the criminals start early around here. Where I come from they usually come out after dark."

"The Watson brothers probably can't tell time," Ty said. "Odds are they've been up all night."

"Well, I'm glad you start early, too."

He brushed his hair from his forehead. "I'm definitely an early riser. Always have been. Comes from growing up on a farm."

"You must be a local boy."

"Pretty much. We have a few acres up near Lynchburg. My dad still lives there but doesn't farm it anymore."

Sam flapped her tee shirt to create a bit of cooling breeze.

"Did you run from Lucy's place?" Ty asked.

"Yeah."

"That's a ways. It's what? Maybe three, four miles?"

"That's what I guessed. Each way."

He nodded. "Lucy mentioned you'd been a boxer. That right?"

Sam shrugged. "I played at it."

"That's not what Lucy said. She said you never lost."

"True. But I only had fourteen fights before I decided it wasn't a healthy pursuit."

He stared out the windshield as if thinking and then said, "I tried it. Back in high school." He looked back at her. "I found football easier. Less painful."

"Then you needed to learn to duck."

He laughed. "Maybe that was it." He glanced back over his shoulder. "Want to grab some breakfast?"

"Maybe after I finish my run."

"You heading back to Lucy's I suspect?"

"Yeah."

"Hop in. I'll take you."

"Sort of defeats the purpose, don't you think?"

"But safer than dealing with the Watson boys."

"I think I could out run them if I had to."

"Still?"

"I'll be fine. But breakfast later sounds good. Unless you have somewhere else to be."

"Nope. Not much happens around here. Murders anyway."

"I was wondering why a town this small had their own homicide detective."

He laughed. "Me, too. I worked homicide up in Knoxville for a couple of years before moving back here. Bump gave me the title of Homicide Investigator. Said it sounded more important than simply officer."

"Have you had to use that title?"

He shook his head. "Just once. And then I have one cold case I inherited. That's the sum total of homicides in this neck of the woods. The past decade or so anyway."

"That's more or less the way it was back home. Except for a couple of instances."

"Mostly fights, robberies, car theft, that kind of thing?"

Sam nodded. "And drunks tear-assing along the freeway."

Ty laughed. "Ain't that the truth." He again swiped his hair from his forehead. It didn't stay. "Why don't you go ahead and finish your run and then meet me over at Gracie's Kountry Kitchen?"

"Will do. I'll drag Lucy along."

By the time Sam returned home, Lucy was up and in the shower. Sam stuck her head through the bathroom door into a cloud of steam and asked what Lucy's WiFi password was. She then grabbed her laptop, sat at the kitchen table, answered a couple of E mails, and then Googled Ty Everson. There were a ton of them. She added "Remington, TN" and he popped right up.

Tyson Charles Everson. Native of Lynchburg. High school football star. Played halfback and set a bunch of county records. College up in Knoxville at the University of Tennessee, majored in Criminology, and then the police academy. Two years on the Knoxville force in Homicide and then here the past four years. Just as he had said.

"What are you doing?"

Sam jumped. She hadn't heard Lucy come into the kitchen.

Lucy stood behind her, looking over her shoulder. "Nice picture." She nodded toward the image of Ty on the screen. He was in uniform. Buttoned down, hair combed, a half smile on his face. "Are you stalking him?"

Sam laughed. "Something like that."

"Stalking a homicide detective? Doesn't sound very smart to me." She punched Sam's shoulder. "Want some oatmeal?"

"Actually, I ran into Ty during my run and he invited us to meet him at Gracie's. You up for that?"

"No time. Got to go make rounds."

"You need breakfast though."

"Oatmeal works, And I'll leave you and Ty to your courting."

"Courting?"

"Okay, stalking." Lucy moved to the counter and flipped on the coffee maker. "Want some coffee before you go?"

"Maybe a shower instead."

"Good idea."

CHAPTER 8

·

The aroma of fresh coffee grabbed Lucy's attention as she entered the surgical floor. She didn't like to admit her caffeine addiction, but in truth she didn't know any surgeons that weren't similarly addicted. Came with the territory. A byproduct of med school. During the first two years, when information was shoveled into eager brains at an alarming rate, it helped students hit the books until well past midnight. Then from the junior year on, eighteen-plus hour days became the norm and coffee an indispensable tool to remain upright and functional. This became especially acute during internship where your entire world revolved around ERs, ORs, and hospital wards, sleep coming in three to four hour blocks, for the entire year. Not for the weak of mind or heart.

Lucy detoured toward the nurse's lounge where the pot sat on a pale yellow Formica-topped counter. Finding coffee in a hospital was easy. It was everywhere. But fresh coffee? That was a different story. Most hospital coffee smoldered in the pot for hours, converting it into a bitter stomach-eating acid. Still it was hot, black, and caffeine-loaded and often that's all it needed to be. But fresh coffee was a gift from the gods.

She poured a cup and carried it into the dictation area where she sat down and flipped open the chart of a patient she'd been asked to see in consult. A sixty-three year old male with an abdominal aneurysm. His aneurysm wasn't like Scully's. His was intact. Swollen, but not torn and leaking his life into his belly. Whole different kettle of fish. She read his medical history and then scanned the testing that had been done. Since the man was having no symptoms and the aneurysm was only 3.0 by 3.5 centimeters by ultrasound it wasn't likely he needed surgery but rather observation for now. Good news for him.

After she talked with the man, examined him, reassured him that all was okay, and arranged for a follow up ultrasound in six months, she returned to the nurses station, dictated her consult, and called his physician to discuss her findings.

Next on her list was Clarence Levin, a pleasant eighty-two year old man with an odd sense of humor. He was one of her favorite patients. Lucy had performed a left carotid endarterectomy on him three days earlier. She had done the right side a year ago.

Clarence was sitting up in a bed-side chair reading the paper, the remnants of his breakfast on a nearby table. He folded the paper and tossed it on to his bed. "Dr. Wagner, how are you today?"

"I'm supposed to ask you that."

"I'm great. Anxious to get home."

"Let's take a look." Lucy examined the healing wound on his neck. "It's healing nicely."

"So you're going to spring me today?"

"You make it sound like prison."

"It is." He flashed a mischievous smile. "Foods the same, I suspect."

Lucy nodded toward the empty plates. "Looks like it wasn't too bad."

"Hard to screw up scrambled eggs and toast."

Lucy laughed. "I'll write the discharge order. The nurse will go over all your meds. Call my office Monday and set up a follow up in about ten days."

"Will do."

"And maybe use some common sense in the meantime."

"Whatever could you mean?" Another grin.

"No water skiing for at least five weeks."

Clarence had been a competitive waterskier in his youth and at 82 he could still burn it up. Sort of a local legend. Many a day during the summer you could see him cutting wakes behind a boat and a churning Evinrude.

"We'll see."

"Clarence." Lucy frowned at him. "Don't mess with this. Just because I cleaned out the plaque it doesn't mean it's well yet. This takes time to heal."

"You win. Just get me out of here."

As she left Clarence's room, she bumped into Birnbaum.

"Lucy." he nodded to her. "A brief word?"

This would be fun. No doubt he wanted to hammer her again for fainting in surgery. She wanted to scream "not a chance," but instead followed him down the hallway out of earshot of the nurses.

"How are you?" Birnbaum asked.

"Fine."

"You sure? I heard about your second case yesterday. Nearly fainting again."

"But I didn't."

"Still . . ."

"Gil, I'm fine. I really am."

"Good. Good." His brow furrowed. "As Chief of Surgery I have to make sure the staff is healthy and not impaired in any way."

Egos. Everybody had one. It was just that Birnbaum's knew no bounds.

"And we all appreciate what you do," Lucy said.

You arrogant prick.

He stared at her for a beat and then nodded. "I guess I'll see you this evening."

"I'll be there."

"You know I truly do think this is a well-deserved honor. You've been a great asset to our community."

"Thanks."

Another curt nod and he turned and walked away. Lucy watched him go wondering what he would dream up next to sabotage her career. Seemed as though he came up with something new every month. Protecting his buddy Dr. Elliott Meeks. Meeks had been the only vascular surgeon before Lucy showed up. Wasn't really trained in it but no other surgeon took on these tasks so he did. Things like aneurysm repairs and carotid endarterectomies. Things Lucy was trained to do, which meant she had taken over most of those cases, costing Meeks an income stream.

Like Mr. Levin. Both the endarterectomies she had performed on him were procedures that Meeks would have done before her arrival. Such cases became a sore point between the two of them, the soreness infecting Meeks' buddy Birnbaum.

The conflict began the minute she applied for staff privileges. Even though she meticulously filled out every form and supplied every document and letter they requested, there was always something else. Reminded her of the old Columbo series. Just one more thing. The process took months when it should have taken weeks. Then when she started doing cases, Meeks was her proctor. It was standard procedure in every hospital for a new doc to be monitored by an existing staff member for a series of cases. Until the new doc proved to be competent. Good medicine and it kept some incompetent physicians off the staff. Usually it was easy, a mere formality, but when the new doc threatened the old doc's turf, it could become contentious. Lucy had weathered Meek's nitpicking her every move and after three months finally garnered full privileges. Birnbaum and Meeks didn't let up though. The second guessing and snide innuendos continued. And her fainting had started a new fire she would have to deal with.

With her scheduled to perform the hospital's first ever congenital heart case next week, a new war with Birnbaum and Meeks was the last thing she needed.

More coffee and then she headed to the surgical ICU to check on William Nevers. He was stretched out in bed, the ET tube now out, but two chest tubes, one protruding from each side of his chest, were still in place.

"How's he doing?" Lucy asked Madison Fife, one of the ICU nurses.

"Great. His BPs have been in the one-twenty range. No arrhythmias. Chest tube drainage minimal."

"Good." Lucy leaned over the bed and examined Nevers' mid-line chest incision. "This looks good. How are you feeling?"

"I'm a little sore. Well more than a little. It feels like a truck hit me."

"That truck would be me," Lucy said.

"And you look so nice," Nevers said.

"It's a facade." She smiled and then turned to Madison. "Let's get a portable chest x-ray. If his lungs are fully inflated maybe we can get those chest tubes out."

"Okay." Madison left.

"Once we get the tubes out we'll get you up in a chair."

"That'll be nice."

"Other than the chest discomfort how's everything else?"

"Fine. Except for the dream I had last night. It was a doozy."

"What kind of dream?"

"I don't remember a lot of it. I was in a desert. At least I think I was. Except it wasn't that hot and there were trees. But the soil was sort of sandy." He looked over toward the window, unfocused, as if recalling an image.. "It was night but I think the sun was up." He shook his head. "Doesn't that sound crazy?"

"Dreams don't often make sense."

"And there was something moving through the trees and the sand."

"What was it?"

"I never saw it. It was always behind the leaves or just under the sandy surface. It did seem to wriggle along. Like a snake might do."

"Anesthesia," Lucy said. "It makes some people have wild and incoherent dreams."

"You think so?"

Lucy nodded. "We see it from time to time. Don't worry, the dreams will go away."

"They weren't really scary, just odd."

Lucy heard a commotion behind her and turned. The x-ray tech maneuvered the portable machine into the cubicle.

"Let's get this done and if it's okay I'll come back and pull those tubes out."

"Sounds like that'll be fun."

"Not too bad."

"For you or for me?"

Lucy smiled at him. "Both."

Lucy left Nevers to the x-ray tech and headed to the ER. Jeffrey Dukes, sitting in the nurse's station, scribbling chart notes, looked up as she came in.

"How's the queen of hearts today?" Jeffrey said.

"Funny."

"You look fine."

"Cut to the chase, Dukes. Where's my blood work?"

"All normal." He pulled several folded pages from the pocket of his white coat and handed them to her. "And you're not pregnant."

Two of the nurses laughed.

Lucy shot them a glance. "Don't encourage his juvenile behavior."

One of them said, "He doesn't need encouragement. He's adept at high school humor all by himself."

Jeffrey leaned back in his chair, lacing his fingers behind his head. "It's good to be loved."

"It's not love," Lucy said. "It's tolerance.

CHAPTER 9

Gracie's was packed. And noisy. Conversation, laughter, the clinking of forks and knives against plates, and the aroma of bacon and hot cakes hit Sam as she pushed through the front door. The din of conversation sank a notch and she felt more than a few eyes turn her way. Not hostile, merely curious. A stranger had entered, disrupting the normal breakfast rhythm, so the regulars took notice.

Sam spotted Ty at a table near the far wall and headed that way. Gazes followed.

"What? No Lucy?" Ty asked.

"Making rounds." Sam slid back a chair and sat across from him.

"She works too much."

"Always did."

A waitress appeared, coffee pot in hand. "Want some coffee?" she asked Sam. "Maybe OJ?"

"Both," Sam said. "And some water."

She flipped over the cup in front of Sam and filled it. "What about you, Ty? Ready for a refill?"

"Sure, Claudell" He nudged his cup in her direction.

"So I'm curious," Ty said after Claudell had walked away "About this boxing thing. What got you into that?"

"I was a tomboy. Had more than a few fights in school. Even with some of the boys."

"You sound like Scout Finch."

Sam laughed. "I never thought of that, but I guess it fits. I did roll around inside my share of old tires. And my Dad was a lot like Atticus. No nonsense. He didn't mind me fighting but he had a problem if I lost. So he taught me a few moves. But what would really chap him is if I was the one who started it."

"Did you? Start them?"

"Not really."

"That's a qualified no."

"Maybe a few." She smiled. "But like Scout, I quickly learned that the boys weren't so tough if you smacked them in the face."

"Ouch. Glad you weren't my prom date."

"That was Billy Westerling. Nice guy. He didn't need any discipline."

Ty laughed. Sam had noticed last night that when he laughed or smiled his eyes narrowed to the point of near closure and deep crow's feet appeared at their corners. His teeth stark white against his olive complexion. He was one of those guys who wore handsome easily.

"Besides he was terrified of my father." Sam continued.

"Your folks still live in California?"

"Both gone. Many years ago."

"I'm sorry."

"It's been a while. What about you?"

"I still have my Dad though he's showing his age now. I lost my Mom to breast cancer eight years ago."

"Mine, too. My Mom had breast cancer."

"What can I get you?" Claudell was back. She plopped a glass of OJ and another of water in front of Sam.

Ty nodded in Sam's direction.

"I'll have the country boy special." She saw Ty's eyebrows lift slightly. She had seen the look many times. People were always amazed at her appetite. Apparently it had been that way since birth. Her mother had often said she couldn't heat the bottles fast enough and her father constantly teased her about eating them out of house and home.

"How you want your eggs?" Claudell asked.

"Over easy and the bacon crisp."

"Grits or pancakes?"

"Pancakes."

Claudell looked at Ty. "The usual?"

He nodded. Claudell left.

"What's the usual?"

"Oatmeal and an English muffin."

"Sensible."

"Like you?"

Sam shrugged. "What can I say? A girl's got to eat."

Ty laughed that easy laugh again. "Back to the boxing. So you beat up all the boys at school?"

"Not all of them. Just the ones that picked on me." She gave him another smile. "Or needed it."

"Bet that was a dwindling number."

San shrugged. "Some were slow learners."

"You don't look like a boxer," Ty said.

"What does a boxer look like?"

"Not like you. Busted noses, cauliflower ears. That sort of thing."

"Those are the ones that lose. When you win you tend to absorb less punishment than you dish out."

"So how did you jump from the school yard to the professional ring?"

"Back home in Mercer's Corner we don't have much but one thing we do have is an excellent gym. One of the owners was an ex boxer named

Jimmy Ryker. He added a heavy bag and a couple of speed bags to the usual mix of weights and aerobic mats. He taught me."

"Must have been a good teacher."

"He had a fairly simple philosophy. He preached two things. In boxing second place is last place and hit first, hit hard, and keep hitting until they don't move anymore."

"Did most of your fights end in KOs?"

"Eleven of the fourteen."

"I'm impressed." He took a sip of coffee. "A little scared but impressed."

"You don't look very scared to me."

Another easy laugh.

The food arrived. Claudell placed the plates before them and said she'd be back to check on them shortly.

"Sure you can handle that?" Ty asked indicting the platter in front of Sam.

It was huge. Three eggs, four strips of bacon, crisp, two sausage patties, a slab of ham, three pancakes, and two biscuits.

"You're welcome to help," Sam said.

"I have enough here to deal with." He sprinkled brown sugar on his oatmeal.

"Doesn't look like much to me."

"Can't eat the way I did when I played ball."

"I understand you were pretty good. What is it? Six county records?"

A look of surprise fell over his face.

"Google," Sam said. "You can find anything on Google."

"You Googled me?"

"I'm a cop. I'm curious." She took a bite of sausage. "You telling me you didn't Google me?"

Ty grinned. "Not yet. I was going to when I got back to the office."

"Let me know what you find out. I'll correct any mistakes."

"Will do."

"Did you and Lucy ever date?"

"What'd she say?"

"I didn't ask."

He hesitated a beat and then said, "Fifth grade. We were sweethearts for a couple of months but sort of outgrew it. Then in high school folks tried to put us together. I was the football dude; her the cheerleader, homecoming queen, smartest person in the school. And the prettiest. But we were more friends than anything else."

They ate quietly for a minute until Ty finally said, "I bet you're a good cop."

"I think so. The city council and county commission thought otherwise."

"There's a story there."

"A jerk named Lanny Mills. Sat on the council and the commission. Totally unqualified but he's the new sheriff."

"City politics. Nothing quite like it."

"No argument there."

"I take it the job was supposed to be yours?"

Sam shrugged as she bit into a strip of bacon. "I was Sheriff Charlie Walker's deputy for years. Before he retired he made sure I was ready to step in. Didn't happen. Charlie was furious. Me? I took a more fatalistic approach"

"How so?"

"I decided not to shoot Lanny."

"Or beat him up?"

"That, too. I resigned and took off to see the country. And here I am."

Ty lifted his coffee cup. "I'm glad you are."

Sam felt a warmth rise in her face. Hoped it wasn't visible. She had no comeback for that so they ate silently for a few minutes. A few awkward minutes. Finally, Sam said, "Tell me about the two homicides you have."

Ty settled the cup onto its saucer and leaned back in his chair. "The old one is from seven . . . no eight years ago now. An elderly man. He was sixty-nine. Named Pete Grimm. Shot and killed in his home. Over near the lake."

"Any suspects?"

"None. Looks to me like it was a robbery. Based on the reports anyway. I never saw the scene since it was before my time."

"And the other one?"

"Marvin Purdy. About six months ago. Owned a farm just up north of the city. Sort of isolated and he lived by himself so we had no witnesses. He was forty-two. Stabbed six times and his throat was cut."

"Suspects?"

"Not a one. The best Bump and I could come up with was that some transient or druggy did it."

"Another robbery?"

"Maybe. His wallet was missing but the house wasn't ransacked or anything like that."

"I take it his credit cards were never used."

"Nope. Folks who knew him well said he always carried a few hundred in cash so the killer might've known that."

Sam nodded.

Ty lifted his cup and tilted it toward her slightly. "So you can see we aren't too busy around here."

"You shouldn't have said that," Sam said.

"You mean like I might've jinxed myself?"

"Something like that."

Ty smiled and shrugged, then his gaze elevated past her, his eyes narrowed, and his jaw set.

"Who's the new bitch?"

The voice came from behind her and almost immediately a woman stepped up to the table, ignoring Sam, glaring at Ty.

"Go away, Darlene," Ty said.

The woman carried all the markers of a meth addict: painfully thin, sunken eyes and cheeks, sores in various stages of healing peppering her face, trashed teeth, dark, dilated pupils, and an obviously bad attitude. Dirty, frayed jeans swaged from her hips, looking as if that might have fit at one time. Before meth killed her appetite. A faded lime-green t-shirt hung from her boney shoulders, pale, spidery arms falling from each sleeve.

"You fucking her, too?" the very pleasant Darlene asked.

Ty's jaw tightened further, pulsing slightly. "You want to put it in reverse and back on out of here or do you want me to arrest you?"

"For what? It's free country. I can say anything I want." She looked down at Sam. "I'd stay away from this bastard. He'll fuck you and dump you."

"Darlene, knock it off."

"Fuck you, Ty. You, too, bitch."

Sam raised her palms. "You obviously have me confused with someone else."

Darlene sniffed and swiped the back of one hand across her nose. "Not likely. Old Ty here will fuck anything. Even a nasty piece like you."

Sam slid her chair back an inch. "I suggest you leave. Now."

"Or what? You think you can fuck my husband and get away with it?"

Sam looked at Ty.

"Ex," he said. "I think it's pretty obvious why things didn't work out."

"You sanctimonious prick. It didn't work out because you screwed everything that didn't run away."

"Is there a problem here?" a man in back pants, white short-sleeved shirt, and narrow black tie, concern on face, said as he walked up behind Ty.

"It's fine, Lester," Ty said. "Darlene was just leaving."

Darlene propped a fist on each hip, chin extended. She started to say something, but hesitated as if she couldn't quite form the thought, and then suddenly turned and marched toward the door, firing, "We ain't finished," over her shoulder.

"Sorry about that, Lester."

Lester sighed. "I understand. Ain't your fault. If it wasn't you it'd be someone else. She comes in here and rants from time to time."

Ty introduced Sam to Lester Goodson, the manager of Gracie's.

"You okay?" Lester asked Sam.

"No problem."

Lester nodded. "Let me know if you need anything." He navigated through the tables toward the rear of the restaurant.

Sam felt eyes boring into her back. Made her feel like "the other woman." "That was fun."

"Sorry. She can be a handful."

"Ex-wife?"

"She wasn't like that when we got married. She was actually attractive and a very nice person. She hooked up with the meth about a year into the marriage."

"Ran with the wrong crowd?"

"Yeah, but not like you might think. She worked over at the bank and started hanging out with one of the other women there. An assistant manager. Turns out her new friend was plugged into the meth world. Darlene went along." He sighed and rubbed one temple. "Didn't take long for her to slide down that road into oblivion. I tried to get her help but . . . " He turned his palms up. "Like butting my head against a brick wall. Ultimately all I could do was divorce her and walk away. She kept my name though. Can't say I'm thrilled about it, but there it is."

"Can't you make her change it?"

"Nope. I gave it to her so she can keep it as long as she wants."

"Meth will steal your soul and more often than not there's no way back," Sam said.

"That's for sure," Ty said. He took a sip of coffee. "And for the record, I never cheated on her. She accused me all the time, but I never did."

CHAPTER 10

Lucy insisted on driving; Sam countered that Lucy was the guest of honor, that she should simply sit back and relax, that Sam would be the chauffeur. Lucy said she might have to leave and go to the hospital at any minute; Sam replied that Lucy wasn't on call so that was unlikely to happen and even if it did Sam would drive her there, too. Lucy said that the good old boys in their pick ups could make for dangerous driving for the uninitiated; Sam responded with a roll of her eyes, saying, "Give me a break," that pick ups were common in Mercer's Corner, too, and that she had just driven across the entire country without a scratch, not to mention that she had lived in LA so a few trucks weren't really a concern.

Lucy gave in and climbed into the passenger seat of Sam's Lexus.

"Where to?" Sam asked as she backed from the drive.

"That's why I should drive."

"You can be the navigator."

"I thought I was the guest of honor."

Sam laughed. "You are but if you want to get there a little guidance would help."

"You can be such a bitch," Lucy said, smiling.

"Something you'd never be."

"You win. The best way is to head west. When the road ends, take a left and I'll show you the turn off when we get there."

Lucy lowered the visor and examined her hair in the mirror, picking at the blonde spikes in a futile effort to bring them under control. It was times like this that she missed the long mane she had had in med school. That ended about half way through her junior year. Tired of wasting precious minutes blowing it dry; fed up with it falling across her face when she started IVs, dressed surgical wounds, or peeked into a microscope; and weary of stuffing it beneath a surgical cap. Practicality ultimately won out and one day she hacked it away with a pair of Metzenbaum scissors. Now it was a short-cropped, tousled mess that looked like a machine-harvested corn field. She finished her examination with a swipe of her fingers through her short bangs.

"You can quit primping. Your hair looks fine," Sam said.

Lucy flipped the visor up. "Nothing I can do with it anyway."

"Nervous?" Sam asked.

"A little. They'll probably make me say something."

"Probably."

"I don't like speaking to crowds."

"Just pretend they're all naked. That'll take care of the pressure."

"I'll pass. Seeing Birnbaum in the buff would probably vapor lock my brain."

"Ty will be there."

"I'll let you work on that mental image."

"But he was your fifth grade love."

"He told you that, huh?"

Sam shrugged.

"Still, I think I'll opt for a glass of champagne instead."

"That'll help."

"Turn here," Lucy said pointing to the left. Sam did. "In a half mile you'll see the drive on the left. You can't miss the house."

The tree-shaded drive led to a massive antebellum home. Stark white, with thick, scroll-topped ionic columns, dark green shutters, and a gray slate roof. Lucy could see Sam's eyes widen as she took it all in.

"Wow," Sam said. "Who is this guy?"

"General Adam Fallbrook. He was in the Air Force for over thirty years. Did a stint as attaché to the Chairman of the Joint Chiefs. Then got into real estate. Made a fortune. He and his wife Ann are big donors to the hospital. The biggest from what I understand. I heard he's given upwards of three million dollars to the medical center so far."

"And this shindig is to get others to pony up?"

"The General can definitely twist arms."

The drive ended in a circle centered by a three-tiered fountain surrounded by a multicolored blanket of flowers. A squadron of young men dressed in black pants, white shirts, and red bow ties greeted them. One approached and pulled open the passenger door, holding it as Lucy stepped out.

"Welcome," he said and then led them through the house and to the broad rear patio.

The party was set up on the rear grounds, a broad expanse of green grass and oak trees that sloped down to the lake. Off to the right was a white guest cottage and to the left a pool complex--an Olympic-sized pool with two diving boards, jacuzzi, and a pool house. Two dozen round tables, each with a ground-length white table cloth and a centrally-placed vase of red roses, settled in the shade of the oaks. Waiters and waitresses in black pants, white shirts, and red bow ties, apparently the uniform of the day, passed trays of champagne and finger food among the crowd that easily numbered a hundred and fifty. A tux-clad string quartet added background music from a large, white, ornate gazebo near the water.

"This place is out of control," Sam said as she lifted a champagne flute from the tray thrust her way by one of the waitresses.

"Anne and the General always do things up right."

"I take you've been here often?"

"Only a couple of times. For fund raisers. They do a lot of them."

"Lucy? Sam?" Ty Everson's unmistakable voice came from behind them.

Lucy turned. Ty stood with Bump, both wearing suits and ties.

"I'm so glad you guys could make it," Lucy said.

"Wouldn't miss it," Ty said.

"Me, neither," Bump said, giving his tie a tug as if it was too tight around his neck.

"You both look nice," Sam said.

Bump shoved his hands into his pockets and rocked back on his heels. "Not many people could get me into a suit, but for Lucy? That's a different story."

"You look dashing," Lucy said. "Maybe you should scrub up more often."

"Not likely," Ty said. "The only time I see him in a suit is at a funeral."

Lucy laughed. "Is that what this is?"

"That didn't come out right," Ty said, his face reddening a notch.

"I know what you meant," Lucy said. She then nudged Bump with an elbow. "But I do appreciate the effort."

Bump tugged at his tie again as he launched into a story about his childhood, about his mother dressing him for church and how Bump had hidden his only tie in hopes that she wouldn't make him go.

As he talked, Lucy gazed over the crowd, seeing many of her colleagues in small groups, talking and laughing. A few glanced her way and nodded. Then her gaze landed on Birnbaum, in the distance, down near the water and the gazebo, his back to her. He was huddled with Elliott Meeks.

Probably cooking up a funeral for her career. Not that she was paranoid or anything. Not that she had a right to be. Through the grapevine she had learned that most of their plotting took place in closed offices and over drinks in one of the local bars, but why not here in broad daylight, at an event to honor her? She had no doubt that this event inflamed every nerve each of them possessed.

"Here's our guest of honor."

Lucy turned to see Adam and Ann Fallbrook. Behind them stood Joyce and Charles Whitworth.

"Thank you for throwing the party," Lucy said to Ann. "Everything is so beautiful."

"It's for a very worthy cause," Ann said.

"And to honor a very special person," Adam added.

Lucy felt her face redden. "You're both too kind." Lucy rested a hand on Sam's shoulder. "I want you to meet my dear friend Samantha Cody. Sam, these fine folks are our hosts. General Adam Fallbrook and his wife Ann. And this is our mayor Joyce Whitworth and her husband Charles."

"Nice to meet you." Sam shook hands with each of them.

"You're the boxer aren't you?" Adam asked.

"Not anymore," Sam said. "Gave it up about six months ago."

"Undefeated, I might add," Lucy said.

"I'm impressed," Adam said.

"Remind me to never make you mad," Charles added.

"She's a pussycat," Lucy said. "Right up until she's not."

That drew laughter from everyone.

"You're way too pretty to be a boxer," Adam said.

Sam shrugged. "It helps if you win."

"So it's the other guy that doesn't look so good?"

"That's more or less how it works, isn't it?" Sam said. "Inflicting more damage than you receive?"

"Hmm," Adam said. "You could say that about many things in life."

"Not that Adam's competitive or anything," Ann said.

Adam laughed. "What was it J. Paul Getty said? Something like the meek might inherit the Earth but not the mineral rights."

Ann rolled her eyes and then tugged on Adam's sleeve. "Come along, General. We better circulate." She smiled to Lucy and Sam. "Please make yourself at home and enjoy this wonderful weather."

᭡

After an hour of doing their own "circulating," Lucy introducing Sam to many of her friends and colleagues, Sam feasting on the shrimp, mini-quiches, and other foods offered on silver trays, Lucy downing two and half glasses of champagne, the event kicked off. The quartet fell silent and repositioned itself toward the back of the gazebo. Lucy climbed the four steps, entered the gazebo, and turned to face the gathered guests, Adam and Anne to her right, Birnbaum her left.

Adam stepped up to the microphone, adjusting its angle slightly, tapped on it to make sure it was live, and then said, "Ladies and Gentlemen, may I have your attention?" The crowd noise waned to a murmur. "Thank you all for coming. Over the years, many of you have given generously to our hospital. As a result we have a wonderful medical center that is the envy of most communities of this size in the state. And today, I'll be picking your pockets again for the new Cardiac ICU beds we have planned." Laughter rippled through the crowd. "As you know, the Remington Medical Center unveiled its cardiac surgical program just over a year ago and next week will embark on its new pediatric cardiovascular surgical program. This means that those unfortunate children afflicted with cardiac defects and in need of surgery will no longer have to leave home to receive such care. Our very own Dr. Lucy Wagner is responsible for this development."

He smiled at Lucy. "Lucy?" He extended a hand toward her and she stepped to his side.

Applause rose from the gathering.

Adam raised a hand to quiet them. "We are here today to honor her for her amazing accomplishments." He rested a hand on her shoulder. "It has been a long and arduous journey for our Lucy to become Dr. Lucy Wagner and to return here to us. She's a local girl, having grown up right here in Remington. Tragically, her parents died in a fire when Lucy was very young. After that, her grandmother, a wonderful person and world-renowned artist, raised her. According to Lucy's teachers, her brilliance revealed itself at a very early age and her aptitude for anything scientific was readily apparent. Academic scholarships aided her education at UCLA and then Vanderbilt University. She returned home to establish our heart program."

Again, applause welled up.

Adam continued. "Lucy is the only trained CV surgeon in the area. Several of you have personal knowledge of her skills in that area." He laughed. "Including yours truly." He tapped his own chest.

Lucy had introduced Adam to her operating table and had installed a quadruple bypass just eight months earlier. Didn't slow him down a step. True to his macho attitude about everything, the General had been out of the hospital in three days and back to his many projects, mostly speaking engagements and fund raising, in less than two weeks. As if nothing had happened. The man was as hard as tempered steel.

Anne stepped forward and Adam moved aside.

"Lucy," she said. "In honor of your outstanding achievements and your tireless service to our community, Adam and I want to take the first step in establishing a much needed expansion of our ICU to care for your heart patients."

She motioned toward Birnbaum, inviting him to join them. Birnbaum gave Lucy a stiff, perfunctory hug. Lucy knew this entire event wound his gut into a knot. She knew she should feel at least some guilt over taking pleasure in his discomfort, but then again, karma's a bitch.

Anne continued. "Dr. Gilbert Birnbaum is director of the Remington Medical Center Foundation and Chief of Staff for the hospital." She turned to Birnbaum. A check appeared in her hand. "Dr. Birnbaum, Adam and I want to give the foundation this check for one million dollars for the establishment of the Dr. Lucy Wagner Cardiac Intensive Care Unit."

Oohs, aahs, and applause rose from the gathering.

Lucy couldn't hide her shock. She knew the unit was going to be built but had no idea it would bear her name. She looked at Sam who gave her an excited smile. She felt her eyes moisten.

Birnbaum accepted the check and stepped closer to the microphone. He nodded toward Adam. "We gratefully accept this most generous gift from two people who have been incredibly gracious and supportive over the years." He then turned to Lucy, his face frozen in a forced smile. "Our medical staff is extremely lucky to have a physician with the skills and dedication that Dr. Wagner displays and we are honored to accept this check to begin the establishment of an ICU in her name." He stepped back and waved Lucy toward the microphone.

Her heart rate ticked up a couple of notches. She felt moisture collect on her skin followed by mild dizziness. The incident in surgery the previous day popped into her head. She looked toward Birnbaum, an expression of concern on his face.

Not now. Not here. Not with Birnbaum watching. Everyone watching.

She imagined waking up on the floor again. She could almost hear the collective gasps that would follow. Fortunately the extended applause that erupted from the gathering gave her time to settle her nerves. She took a deep breath, swallowed, and stepped up to the mic.

Get a grip, Lucy.

Her mouth felt dry but thankfully she sensed the dizziness receding. Seeing Sam looking up at her helped.

She cleared her throat. Sort of. "I'm speechless," Lucy said. "This was truly unexpected. I'm deeply honored and more than a little humbled." She smiled to Adam and Anne. "This is the culmination of a lot of hard work by many people and would not have been possible without the efforts of Dr. Gilbert Birnbaum and the generous support of many of you. Thank you."

More applause.

"Thanks to the hospital administration and all the dedicated staff, our heart program has grown and improved. We have to date done over one hundred and fifty cardiac procedures and just next week will perform our first congenital heart repair at the Medical Center."

Even more applause.

"Thank you all so much."

Adam gave her a hug and took the mic. "Thank you all for coming. Now, let's party."

As she descended the steps, Birnbaum clutched her arm.

"You okay?" he asked.

"Fine."

"Are you sure? You look a tad wobbly."

"Public speaking. Not one of my favorite things."

He gave her shoulder a paternal squeeze. "As long as you're sure everything is okay."

"It is. Thanks for your concern."

He released his grip, nodded, hesitated a beat, and then turned and walked away.

Just perfect. Like he needs any more ammo.

CHAPTER 11

The icy fingers that touched her arm caused Lucy to flinch. She hadn't herd her approach but when she turned an elderly woman stood before her. Thin, fragile-looking, with spider-like arms, liver spotted hands, a white mist of thinning hair, and clear, sharp, and ice blue eyes.

"I'm sorry," the woman said, her voice raspy with age. "My hands are always cold."

Earlier, Lucy had left Sam, Ty, and ER Director Jeffrey Dukes huddled at a table, laughing and talking, and went searching for the ladies room. She had only been in the mansion a couple of times and wasn't sure where to look, its massive size and multiple wings not making her search any easier. She finally located a small, stark-white restroom near the end of a long hallway. She then explored that wing, moving from room to room. Some were bedrooms, other sitting rooms, each filled with impressive antiques and artworks. She couldn't help wondering what it would be like to live here. How would you decide which room was best for curling up with a good book? Which would be comfortable for chatting with friends? There were simply too many to choose from. Not to mention that walking from here to the kitchen or the garage was an aerobic endeavor.

Her meandering brought her into a large library. Books filled each of its soaring walls, rolling ladders offering access to the higher shelves, its pressed-copper ceiling age patinaed. A massive, dark, oak desk faced her from the far end. The rich, thick aroma of aged books reminded her of the old stone library of her childhood. Now gone and replaced by a more modern structure, she missed the old Carnegie one. It had been a big part of her history so she had always resented its destruction.

She found a shelf filled with ancient leather-bound medical texts. She lifted a heavy volume of Gray's Anatomy and opened it to the title page. It was an 1859 First American Edition. The editor had been Richard James Dunglison. Lucy knew that Richard's father Robley Dunglison had been one of Thomas Jefferson's physicians.

What would something like this be worth? How does one go about even finding such an edition?

She felt like an intruder but couldn't keep herself from carefully thumbing through the pages, the illustrations inside mesmerizing. The heart and coronary arteries crystal clear, the kidney opened, each calyx beautifully rendered, the bones and muscles and tendons breathtaking in their detail. And this book was a century and a half old. Amazing.

She was lost in the images when the woman seemingly materialized from nowhere.

"It's okay," Lucy said. "My mind was somewhere else."

"It's such a thrill to see you." Her eyes penetrated Lucy. "After all these years."

Lucy carefully closed the book and slid it back into its space but before she could ask the woman what she meant by "all these years," the woman went on.

"Thank you for taking on this tremendous burden," the woman said.

Lucy laughed. "It's no burden. Not really. Sometimes my practice does get a little hectic, but I love the work."

Lucy hadn't noticed the woman before. Not during her mingling with the crowd outside or during the presentation ceremony. The woman's simple, floor-length, blue dress seemed out of place among the cocktail-attired gathering. In contrast to that worn by most guests, the woman's only jewelry was an age-tarnished gold wedding band that settled loosely against the wilted flesh of her finger.

"Life is filled with burdens," the woman said. "Many we do not realize until much time has passed. Many that we are not prepared for. Many that are not of our own choosing."

Lucy nodded, unsure exactly what to say.

The woman's gaze never broke from hers. "Our deeds, our useful acts, often go unnoticed, even by ourselves." Again, she reached out and placed her cold fingers on Lucy's arm. "You're one of us now. It pleases me that the soul of our community is in such capable hands."

Lucy felt off balance. The woman had such an odd way of expressing herself. Burden? Soul of our community? "Who are you?"

"I'm Miriam Scully. You operated on my husband John."

And he died, Lucy thought to herself. Yesterday. "Yes. I'm so sorry for your loss."

The woman smiled, her blue eyes deep and calm. "It is as it should be."

Lucy flashed on John Scully, Jr. and his daughter Felicia and their unusual affect, almost joy, when she spoke with them at the hospital. This woman reflected that same joy.

"You said you were pleased to see me again. Have we ever met?"

Miriam smiled. "You were a mere child. I hardly suspect you'd remember."

Before Lucy could respond, she heard footsteps behind her and turned as Joyce and Charles Whitworth approached.

"There you are," Joyce said. "We have to take off. Another event. Fund raiser for the school district. We wanted to say goodbye and congratulate you again."

Lucy smiled. "I'm so glad you came. It's not everyone who has the mayor come to their party."

Joyce took Lucy's hand in both of hers. "Wouldn't have missed it for anything. Lucy, you're so important to this community. We're lucky to have you."

"I'll see you at the next hospital board meeting," Charles said.

Past Charles' shoulder, Lucy saw Miriam Scully slip through the library door and disappear into the hallway.

"I think it's in a couple of weeks," Lucy said.

"That's right." He hooked his arm with his wife's. "We better run."

Lucy followed them into the hallway, looking both ways, but Miriam Scully was gone.

CHAPTER 12

Lucy knelt in the morning shadow of the gnarled oak tree that stood like a sentinal over her parents' grave in Shady Hill Cemetery. Sam stood quietly behind her. The city's oldest and largest and the final resting place of over 1,200 departed souls, Shady Hill's ten, tree-dotted acres draped over a hillock just northeast of town. A single, broad, gray-marble headstone marked the graves of George and Lynette Wagner, their engraved names and the dates of their births and shared death flanking a faded, glass-encased photo of the couple, her father in a suit and tie, her mother in a trim, black dress, each smiling as if sharing a joyful moment. The photo, a copy of the original she kept on her dresser, was all that remained of them, virtually all she knew of them. Her vague recollections of them as living, breathing people had all but faded.

She often stared at the print, its edges charred by the fire that took them days before her fifth birthday, and wondered what they had been like. What their dreams had been, and what joy they were sharing at that captured moment. She struggled to hold their memory close, but year-by-year it slipped from her grasp. Now, she was unsure which memories were true and which were merely melancholy fabrications.

After placing a red rose on each grave, she stood and blew a kiss to them, a ritual that her grandmother Martha had begun a week after her parents' death. As a child she had cherished the Sunday morning walks through the cemetery, Martha holding one hand, letting her clutch the roses in the other, showing her how to center them on the graves just so, telling her that her mother watched over her every day. The ritual fell to her alone a year ago as Martha's mind faded into the gauzy world of dementia.

"You okay?" Sam asked.

"I miss sharing these mornings with Martha." Lucy turned and gazed down the slope, over the collection of graves and headstones that reached to the stone wall that embraced the cemetery. "I hope she remembers them." Lucy sighed. "But somehow I doubt it."

"I'm sorry." Sam laid a hand on Lucy's shoulder.

Lucy reached up and squeezed her hand. "Thanks."

༒

Twenty minutes later, Lucy parked near the entrance to Wellstone Manor Guest Home, the nicest elder-care facility in the area. Fortunately, Martha didn't need specialized care, just comfort and companionship, which made Wellstone perfect. Most residents had private rooms and Lucy found the staff to be kind and skillful and very attentive to Martha. Though the guilt she felt for abandoning her to care of strangers was never far away. Not that it wasn't necessary, but still, the guilt clawed at her on those nights when sleep came slowly.

Lucy pushed through the double front doors, greeted by the astringent smell of cleaning agents laced with the odors of age. Luther, the bent-shouldered, white-haired janitor nodded to her and Sam as he swiped a mop across the floor.

"Watch your step, Dr. Wagner" he said. "Just mopped the hallway there."

"We will," Lucy said, her shoes squeaking across the linoleum floor.

Before heading to Martha's room, they stopped by the duty nurses' office. Sue Cramer, a pleasant woman of fifty or so, who had once worked the medical ward at the Medical Center, dropped the Sunday paper and smiled as Lucy stuck her head in the door.

"Morning, Dr. Wagner," she said. "I figured that was you I heard coming down the hall. Coffee?"

"Thanks, Sue." Lucy said. "That would be nice." She nodded to Sam. "I want you to meet my friend Sam Cody. She's visiting from California."

"California? I got a cousin out there. In Fresno."

"I live down south. In the Mojave desert area."

Sue laughed. "Sounds hot and dry."

"It can be. And cold and wet in the winter."

Sue stood, filled a Styrofoam cup with coffee from the ancient pot on the counter behind her, and handed it to Lucy. "Sam? What about you?"

"I'll pass. Thanks."

Lucy took a sip. "Good. How's Martha?"

"Fine. She's mostly calm and manageable today. Not like yesterday." She rolled her eyes. "She was on Mars. She's back on Earth now. More or less. And she did eat all her breakfast this morning."

"See you later."

"If you need anything, just give a shout."

Martha Ackers, had been a nationally renowned artist, a frequent guest on TV talk shows, and had given a least a dozen college graduation speeches. Lively, witty, and more than a little feisty. That changed five years ago when schizophrenia wormed its way into her mind. While Lucy was deep into her surgical training at Vandy. At first, an assortment of drugs kept the demons at bay, but ultimately, the battle was lost. Hallucinations, nonsense babbling, and the occasional paranoid outbreak reduced her to a mostly catatonic shell. To add to her misery, senile dementia joined hands with her schizophrenia so that now she passed her days staring out the window, talking to herself, and succumbing to fits of crying and the occasional psychotic outbursts.

Today, she sat in her padded, wooden rocker, facing the window, back to the door. The woven, purple shawl Lucy had given her for Christmas last year hung from her boney shoulders. Lucy scraped a chair over beside her and sat. Martha didn't seem to notice. Her eyes appeared glazed and occasionally her head gave a slight nod. An extended index finger pecked at the air in front of her as if she were embroiled in some internal argument and was attempting to make some point.

"Good morning," Lucy said. "I hear you had a good breakfast."

No response. A trickle of saliva dampened one side of Martha's chin. Lucy snatched a tissue from the table next to her and dabbed it away.

"Look who's here. Remember Sam?"

Sam stepped into her line of vision. "Hello, Martha."

No response.

Lucy looked at Sam and shrugged. "That's mostly what I get, too," she said, and then to Martha, "I went by the cemetery today. I left roses and blew kisses for both of us."

Martha's finger pecked more frantically at the air and her head bobbed a few times. She must have been winning whatever argument was unfolding in her head.

This had become their routine. Lucy would talk and Martha would offer no response. Occasionally she would utter something, a word or two, that rarely made sense.

"It was a wild week," Lucy continued. "I fainted in surgery. Haven't done that since I was a neophyte. Embarrassing, but I survived."

Lucy continued for another quarter-hour, jabbering about this and that. Martha seemed to hear none of it but apparently did finally win her imaginary argument and folded her hands in her lap, a contented look on her face. Lucy sipped her coffee, now cold.

"Oh, I almost forgot," Lucy said. "I met someone who knows you. Well, I didn't actually meet him. I operated on him but he didn't make it. His son says he knew you years ago."

Martha's gaze rose toward the window. Unfocused, face placid.

"His name was John Scully. Apparently he knew Mom and Dad, too."

Martha began to wind the edge of the shawl around one boney finger. Lucy placed one hand over Martha's. They felt cold and tense and took on a slight tremor. She felt the tendons on the back of Martha's frail hands tightened into thin cables as she entwined the shawl more tightly.

"Are you cold?" Lucy asked.

Sam lifted a blanket from the bed. And handed it to Lucy who draped it over Martha's lap, tucking it on each side.

"That better?"

Sue stuck her head in the room. "You guys need anything?"

"We're fine," Lucy said.

"Just making morning rounds," Sue said and headed down the hall.

Lucy stood and walked to the window. "Anyway, according to his son, Mr. Scully thought a great deal of you." The sun was beginning to burn off the scattered morning clouds, exposing clear blue sky. "It was during his surgery that I fainted." She laughed. "I think everyone thought I must be pregnant. Can you imagine that?"

She turned toward Martha who was now shaking uncontrollably. Lucy knelt next to her.

"What is it?"

Lucy had seen Martha have these spells before. In fact, they were becoming more frequent with each passing month. That didn't make them any less unnerving. She could be dispassionate when patients did such things, but when it was Martha, it was too close to home. She became a granddaughter, not a doctor.

Lucy clutched Martha's hands, which felt even colder, and automatically felt for a pulse at her wrist. A little fast, but strong and steady. Tears slid down Martha's cheeks and she convulsed with heavy sobs. Her head shook back and forth.

"No...no...no...no," she repeatedly said with a galloping rhythm. Another strong shiver racked her body. She began rocking back and forth, and then threw back her head and screamed, "No...no...no." Over and over. Her body jerked back and forth. Lucy grabbed her by the shoulders for fear she might fall from the chair.

Sue hurried into the room. "What's going on?"

"This is bad one," Lucy said.

"Jesus...Jesus...Jesus," Martha screeched. "Help me. Help me." Her face took an anguished look Lucy had never seen.

"Ativan?" Sue asked and when Lucy nodded she darted from the room.

"Anything I can do?" Sam asked.

"Hold her up so she doesn't slide out of the chair."

Sam stood behind Martha and circled the chair back and Martha's shoulders in a bear hug. Martha tried to twist away but Sam held her tightly.

Sue returned. "Two milligrams?" She began to fill the syringe.

"We'll start with that," Lucy said.

Sue nodded and drew up the liquid. She held the syringe toward Lucy. "You want to do the honors?"

"Go ahead," Lucy said.

While Sam leaned Martha up onto her left hip, Lucy pulled the blanket and nightgown out of the way, exposing the upper portion of her right hip. Sue quickly injected the Ativan.

"Let's get her into bed," Sue said.

The three of them lifted Martha and eased her onto the bed. She continued to jerk and shriek, mostly nonsense. And then . . .

"Scully. No, no, Scully."

She clutched at Lucy's blouse, crushing it in her fist, sending a button skittering off the bed to the floor.

"Stop it. Stop it." Spittle collected at the edge of Martha's mouth. "Kill it. You must."

Lucy managed to pry Martha's fingers open and release her grip. Her hand kept opening and closing as if searching for an anchor.

"Another two milligrams," Lucy said.

After Sue administered the drug, Martha's shaking and the rolling of her head from side to side gradually diminished. He eyes fluttered closed, her body relaxed, and she murmured, "No Scully," before mercifully drifting to sleep.

CHAPTER 13

Earlier, on the drive home, Lucy had been quiet, her eyes glistening with tears, stress lines around her eyes and lips. Sam had asked once if she wanted to talk about it but Lucy simply shook her head so Sam dropped it. Once home, Lucy headed to her room "to lie down for a while." Sam caught up on her e mails and then read until she dozed on the sofa. She awoke when she heard Lucy in the kitchen and detected the aroma of fresh coffee.

Sam rolled off the sofa and walked into the kitchen where Lucy was removing dishes from the washer and placing them overhead cabinets. "Need some help?"

"I'm almost finished," Lucy said over her shoulder. "Want some coffee?"

"Sure."

Lucy handed her a pair of clean cups and Sam filled them.

"You still take it black?" Sam asked.

"Absolutely."

They went out on the the rear deck where Lucy settled into one of the two lounge chairs that faced the lake. Sam stood at the rail looking out toward the water. A soft, warm breeze rustled the leaves of the maple trees that shaded the deck.

"It so peaceful here," Sam said.

"I'm sorry," Lucy said.

Sam turned. "Sorry for what?"

"For the way I acted. For locking myself in my room."

Sam sat on the other chaise. "Not without reason."

"Still."

"You didn't hurt my feelings if that's what bothering you." She added a soft laugh.

Lucy nodded, her gaze toward the water. "It's just so hard."

Sam sat in the other chair and waited quietly, letting Lucy formulate what she wanted to say.

Lucy took a couple of sips of coffee, her gaze never leaving the lake, her eyes moistening. "Martha was always so bright. So witty and funny. It kills me to see her sink this way."

"What she did today? Is that typical?"

Lucy placed her coffee on the deck and forked her fingers into her hair, elbows on her knees, gaze directed toward her shoes. "I've never seen her like today. Confused, sure. But she seemed . . . I'm not sure what she seemed."

"Scared. She looked scared to me."

"I agree." Lucy straightened her shoulders and looked at Sam, "But there was something else. Something deeper. Like an anguish. Does that make sense?"

"Absolutely. That's the exact word I'd use."

Lucy's gaze moved back toward the water.

"It seemed to me that your mentioning Scully is what set her off," Sam said.

Lucy nodded.

"Why would she react that way?"

Lucy picked up her coffee and took a sip. "I have no idea."

"Other than Martha going to his church for a while, what's their relationship?"

"None that I know of. I just learned that she and John Scully knew each other from Scully's son two days ago. And then you were there when Bump confirmed that. And that Scully also knew my parents."

"Did Martha ever mention him?"

Lucy traced a finger around the lip of her cup. "Not that I remember."

Which meant no. One thing Sam knew for certain was that Lucy never forgot anything. Had what her father had called a steel-trap mind.

"Maybe it's just the church thing?" Sam said. "Maybe she was simply shocked that Scully had died?"

A sip of coffee. "You don't believe that anymore than I do."

"True." Sam shrugged. "Martha didn't seem to be sad or grieving."

"One thing I do know for sure is that the Scully clan is an odd group."

"You mean the snake handling thing?"

"That would be enough, but it's more than that."

"In what way?"

"Talking about not grieving. When I told his son John, Jr. and his granddaughter Felicia that he had died they weren't upset at all. At first I thought it was just shock but that's not it."

"People behave oddly under stress."

"This was different. It was as if they expected it. And were happy about it."

"Maybe an inheritance."

"Maybe. Then I ran into his widow yesterday. In General Adam's library. She had the same odd affect. Spoke in a very odd way."

"Ever met a preacher or a preacher's wife that didn't talk in circles?"

"Not many."

"Then there you go."

Lucy shook her head. "This was something else. Not sure what but it wasn't just preacher talk."

"Before all this? Did you know any of the Scullys?"

"Not really. Just by name and reputation. I knew they had a congregation. Just north of here. Up in the hills. I didn't know anything about snakes or anything like that until Ty mentioned it the other night."

"Hmmm."

"Hmmm what?"

"Maybe I'll look into Mr. Scully."

Lucy laughed. "Sure you will."

"What does that mean?"

"It means you're Samantha Cody and you always will be."

∾

Lucy had an early morning surgery so after an afternoon of reading and napping, she ordered in pizza and she and Sam ate on the deck. They watched TV and chatted about the old days, staying up until midnight, later than Lucy had planned. Finally Lucy fell into bed and immediately fell asleep. A deep and much needed sleep.

That lasted until 4 a.m.

Lucy jerked awake, gasping for breath and kicking at the snake that wound itself around her legs. She twisted and turned and kicked and somehow managed to break free. She sat up, a cold chill rippling through her.

The snake turned out to be the bed sheet.

She dropped back on her pillow and lay there, staring at the ceiling, letting her heart rate settle.

What the hell was that?

Lucy tried to recall the dream but got nothing. No images or feelings or sounds or smells. Nothing. Not unusual for her. She rarely dreamed, at least she didn't often remember them if she did. And she hadn't had a nightmare since she was a maybe eight. After her parents death, after she moved into Martha's home, she had off and on nightmares for a couple of years. Mostly ones where she was alone. Sometimes lost in the woods, sometimes abandoned on the side of a dark highway, cars whipping past, dropping a strong wind in their wake, none ever stopping despite her pleas. But never was anyone else, much less a snake, in these nocturnal adventures. But these gradually evaporated.

She flashed on the post-op dreams William Nevers and Ronnie Draper had had. Both said they dreamed of snakes. And now this.

Jesus, Lucy, what the hell is wrong with you?

There it was. The question that had niggled around in the back of her mind. The one she refused to say out loud. Was something wrong? Was she ill? Crazy? Were her dizziness and fainting, and now this wild dream, the first warnings that she had inherited Martha's schizophrenia?

She swung her legs off the bed and stood. A wave of dizziness followed and she sat back down.

Get a grip.

Again she stood, and waited a beat to make sure her legs would support her. Sort of. She oscillated to the bathroom using her armoire and the doorway and finally the sink for support. Damp hair clung to her scalp and sweat slicked her face, neck, and chest. She splashed cold water on her face, toweled herself off, and returned to bed. Now the sheets felt cool. She pulled them up to her chin.

She stared at the ceiling and for the next half hour again tried to recall her dream but it remained elusive. The only images she finally managed to pull from the mist were those of a long, thick snake and trees that drooped with some heavy yellow fruit she couldn't identify, each perfectly round orb dripping with moisture that collected in pools in the shadows cast by the tree.

She glanced at the digital clock on the nightstand. Ten till five. Might as well get the day started. She rolled out of bed.

CHAPTER 14

Lucy had parked in her slot in the doctors' parking are near the ER at 5:30, two hours before her scheduled triple coronary bypass. She walked to the medical office building next door and climbed the stairs to her second floor office. She spent the next hour catching up on chart work and dictating letters before entering the hospital. First stop, the cafeteria where she downed two cups of coffee, scrambled eggs, a a pair of biscuits. She then stopped by the pre-op holding area to see Mr. Joseph Finch asking if he had any final questions about the procedure. He didn't, saying he was ready "to get this done."

Now she stood over Finch's open chest, finishing the second of his grafts.

The feeling, deep and cold, germinated in her chest. She fought it, willing it to resolve, but it increased, becoming a tight, heavy aching as if an icy hand gripped her heart. It reminded her of the times during her childhood when she had eaten ice cream too quickly, Martha telling her to slow down, she ignoring the advice and charging ahead until her chest burned from the cold. Though similar, this sensation carried a more ominous undercurrent.

It had begun as she secured the final suture of the saphenous vein graft to Finch's obtuse marginal coronary artery into place. It progressed as she dissected the Left Internal Mammary Artery free. The LIMA, as it was called in medical jargon, branched off the left subclavian artery, ran down the inside of the chest, and was the perfect artery for bypassing blockages in the Left Anterior Descending Coronary Artery, the LAD for short. While she freed it from the tissues that bound it, the coldness threatened to spread into her back and arms but she resisted, keeping it locked deep in the center of her chest, near her own heart. As she began suturing the LIMA to the LAD, the sensation began a slow, rhythmic throb and spread across her chest, digging its way into her back, near her shoulder blades. She felt sweat collect on her upper lip and a trickle escaped down her back.

Come on, Lucy. Keep it together.

She worked quickly, part of her brain focused on making each suture even and snug, another part fire-walling the icy feeling. She tugged the final suture tight, quickly knotted it, and stretched it so that scrub nurse Rosa Lopez could snip the tags with a pair of Metzenbaum scissors. Lucy released the clamp from the LIMA and inspected the suture line for leaks. None.

"Good job," Dr. Herb Dorsey said.

Coronary surgery required two surgeons. Two pairs of skilled hands and eyes were essential if all was to go smoothly. Simply too much to do, too much to keep an eye on. Two CV surgeons would be ideal, but since Lucy was the only CV surgeon on staff, she had to enlist one of the general surgeons to scrub in on her cases. She had a group of six that were always willing to help, but Herb was the one she most enjoyed working with. Skilled and laid back, he was perfect for the assistant surgeon job. Often a thankless job but Herb never let his ego get in the way of playing second fiddle. Not like Eliot Meeks. As the only other surgeon on staff that had any experience with chest and vascular cases, Meeks would have been the logical choice as assistant but his ego wouldn't allow it. Besides, his sniping and second guessing didn't make for an happy OR. And a happy OR was also essential.

Lucy nodded. "Let's take a last look and then we can get out of Mr. Finch's chest."

Her inspection showed that each graft had good flow, each suture line tight and dry. As she settled the heart back in place the frozen knot in her chest seemed to liquify and flow into her arms and hands, freezing them to Mr. Finch's heart. A wave of nausea and dizziness swept over her and her vision tunneled, then blurred.

Get a grip.

"A few PVCs."

Anesthesiologist Raj Singh's voice seemed to come from far away. She looked toward him, his eyes aimed back at her over his mask.

"Lido?" Raj asked.

Lucy tried to speak but couldn't seem to form even a simple yes.

Herb stepped in. "One hundred milligrams IV and the start a drip."

Raj went to work as Herb turned back to Lucy, his eyes narrowed with concern.

The cold feeling was now so intense that Lucy's fingers ached. She attempted to pull her hands away from Finch's heart but her fingers refused, maintaining their grip. It was as if her hands and Finch's heart were locked inside a ball of ice. Finally, she took a step back, her hands came free, the coldness evaporated, and a wave of heat descended over her. A last wave of dizziness and then, other than the sweat that soaked her scrubs beneath her surgical gown, she felt normal again.

"Let's get him off bypass and close up," Lucy said.

An hour later, Mr, Finch had been packed off to the recovery room, Lucy had talked with his wife and son, their relief that the surgery had been successful apparent in the relaxing of their facial stress lines, and now she sat in the surgeon's lounge completing her chart notes.

Herb came in. "What was that about?"

"That what?"

"Lucy. Don't bullshit me. What happened in there?" His tone wasn't accusatory but rather soft and fatherly.

"Nothing much. Just a little fatigue."

"You sure that's all it was?"

"Mostly."

"Mostly?"

"I saw Jeffrey Dukes and all my labs are normal. I'm fine."

Herb hesitated as if he had something else to say but then simply nodded and left. Lucy stared at the door as it closed. Was she fine? Her brain conjured up a long list of diagnoses: cardiac arrhythmia, seizure disorder, brain tumor, hypoglycemia, vasovagal syndrome, panic attack. Panic attack? Her? Not possible. She had been in so many dicey situations in the OR and had never experienced even the slightest rise in her blood pressure. She was too well trained, too professional for panic to even be a consideration.

Still, it must be something. What, she had no idea, and she didn't have the time to deal with it right now.

She carried the chart to the recovery room, checked on Mr. Finch, finding all was well, and then headed off to make rounds. Her day was back to normal.

CHAPTER 15

S am ducked into the drug store, looking for someplace to hide without looking as if she were hiding. She rejected the magazine rack, too low, and the shelf packed with cold remedies and vitamins, also too low, and finally settled behind a revolving rack of cards, keeping it between her and the front window.

"Can I help you?" the clerk behind the counter to her left asked. She was a middle-aged woman with gray-streaked brown hair, half glasses perched near the end of her nose, and a pleasant smile.

"No, thanks," Sam said. "I'm just looking for a birthday card."

"We got a bunch of them so take your time. If I can be of help just let me know."

"Will do."

Sam let her fingers idly play over the cards while focusing her attention between a pair of them and through the broad front window to the street. An elderly couple strolled by followed by a kid with stringy blonde hair wagging back and forth on a skateboard, but then nothing. No Darlene. A few minutes earlier she had seen Darlene Everson, Ty's ex, walking up the street toward her and rather than chance another encounter had decided to take cover. So here she was, hiding from a woman who was . . . where?

Maybe she went into another store or turned up one of the side streets. Sam started to leave her hiding place when Darlene appeared. On the sidewalk, at first seeming to move past but then stopping and looking at the window display of children's toys, household knick knacks, and a rack of tee shirts. Sam flexed lower, now face to face with a card that had a half dozen cartoon cats dancing around a birthday cake, "Happy Sweet 16" written across the top in bright red script.

Please don't come in here.

The soft chime of the front door dinged, a good morning from the counter clerk, and a good morning back from a female voice. Sounded older than Darlene. An elderly woman walked past, nodded a hello to Sam, and continued toward the back of the store. Sam felt foolish lurking here behind a card rack but the woman didn't seem to notice.

Sam returned her attention to Darlene, who now rummaged in the oversized purse she had slung over one shoulder. She finally removed a tube of lipstick, and using the window as a mirror, swiped it across her lips. She returned the tube to her purse, made one last inspection, touched her hair, and then continued up the sidewalk and out of sight.

"Find anything you like?"

Sam jumped and then turned to see the clerk standing behind her. "Not yet." She glanced at her watch, not really looking, and said, "I'm a little late. I'll have to come back"

The clerk smiled. "We're open until seven."

Outside, the foot traffic along the sidewalk was meager and she saw no sign of Darlene. She felt like a wimp for hiding from her, but she didn't relish locking horns with that psycho again. The woman obviously wasn't bashful about making a scene and Sam could only imagine her launching a verbal assault her way right there on the street. Avoidance seemed the best option regardless of how silly she felt.

A half a block later Sam entered the Remington Police Department, the secretary who greeted her responding to her request to see Ty Everson with a wave her hand and a, "Go ahead on back."

Ty sat with his chair, which was spun to the side, one leg propped over the the corner of his desk, looking out the window.

"I see Remington's finest is hard at work," she said.

He slid his leg off the desk and swiveled toward her. "At least you didn't find me asleep."

"Maybe I should have waited a few more minutes." She sat in the chair that faced him.

"Funny. What brings you here?"

"Hiding from your wife."

"Ex-wife."

"Somehow I got the impression she hasn't bought into that concept."

He nodded. "True. But fortunately the court is on my side."

Sam told him what had happened.

"So the big bad boxer hid from the little brain damaged druggie?"

"You know the old saying: never fight a crazy person."

Ty laughed.

"I had visions of her screaming at me and then painting me with scarlet letter."

"She'd do it if she could. She ain't got no brakes that's for sure." He rearranged a stack of papers on his desk. "So to what do I owe the pleasure of your visit?"

"Maybe I just came to see you."

"I'd like that. If it was true."

Sam shrugged. "Well, that's part of it but I want to know more about John Scully."

"Any particular reason?"

Sam told him of she and Lucy visiting Martha and Martha's reaction to hearing Scully had died, finishing with, "It really shook Lucy up."

"Lucy? Heart surgeon Lucy?"

"I know. She's unflappable. But this was different. I know Martha's decline has been tough on her. But this outburst seemed to rock her back a bit."

"You sure Martha's reaction was real and not imagined? I mean, isn't Martha pretty much out of it?"

"Definitely out of it."

"Maybe she was simply having a spell."

"Spell?"

He laughed. "For lack of a better word. You've seen it before, I'm sure." Sam shrugged but didn't respond so Ty continued. "We had an old boy who was like Martha. Very confused and senile. Maybe three, four weeks ago. He escaped from a nursing facility by crawling out a window. We found him over behind the bank, hiding behind a Dumpster. Thought aliens were cooking his brain with death rays."

"Maybe they were."

Ty stared at her for minute as if deciding if she was being serious or not but then she smiled and he did, too.

"Sort of like Richard Earl Garrett?" Ty asked.

Richard Earl Garrett. A child murderer. Claimed to be Satan's right hand dude. Back in Mercer's Corner. She and her boss Sheriff Charlie Walker had had to handle that can of worms.

"So Google is your friend, too?"

Ty shrugged. "Just trying to keep up."

"Garrett was a real piece of work. Completely psycho. Murdered three children in a ritual killing."

"So I read. But what about all the other stuff? Him controlling other people? Was that true or was it mass hysteria as some claimed?"

Sam had spent many hours contemplating just that. And she had no idea. Her pragmatic mind said it was indeed some form of mass hysteria that had made seemingly normal citizens, people she had known all her life, people absent criminal backgrounds, people who were pillars of the community, kill other community members in bizarre and brutal manners. Just as Garrett had done. And the other consideration? That Garrett did indeed possess some supernatural, unexplained power. Power that controlled not only the murdering citizens but also Charlie. And her.

"I honestly don't know," Sam said.

"Sounds very woo woo to me."

"You had to be there."

Ty stared at her as if he was judging her sanity. Probably was. Understandable since she had done the same thing back then, back when Garrett's madness descended over Mercer's Corner, when good people like Walter Limpke committed horrific acts or murder, when Charlie Walker himself fell victim to the . . . what? Garrett's control? A community's shared madness? Hadn't she also been sucked into that same madness? Probably best not to bring that up.

"The stuff I read, particularly the articles by Nathan Klimek in *Straight Story,* made Garrett seem like a monster from hell."

"Nathan's a tabloid journalist. Not sure I'd buy his word as gospel." Even if she had had a brief affair with him. Better to leave that part out, too. "He was there to stir things up and sell a few newspapers."

Ty folded his hands on his desk. "So, you want to know about John Scully. Junior or Senior?"

"Both."

"I can tell you some of it but Bump's the one who really knows all the history."

"He around?"

"Went fishing today. I'm meeting him for dinner later. Why don't you and Lucy join us? We can talk about it then."

"I'll check. Lucy's schedule changes from minute to minute."

"Ain't that the truth." Ty stood. "Want to take a ride?"

"Where?"

"I'll show you Scully's church."

CHAPTER 16

Lucy's first stop on rounds was to see William Nevers. He was out of the ICU and in the PCU, the Progressive Care Unit, a monitored and well-staffed ward whose level of care was sandwiched between the ICU and the regular surgical ward. Nevers was dozing but woke up when Lucy walked in.

He stretched and yawned. "You caught me napping."

"Nothing wrong with napping. Especially after a big surgery."

"And not much sleep."

"Too noisy?"

Hospitals are terrible places to sleep. Too much activity, day and night. Too many people—nurses, various techs, the cleaning crews—coming and going, checking vital signs, giving meds, drawing blood, taking x-rays, mopping and polishing floors, hauling away trash. Not to mention the incessant chirping of cardiac monitors, the whooshing cycles of ventilators, and the never-ending stream of overhead pages.

"That and these wild dreams."

"You had another one?"

"Oh yeah. Even more intense than last night."

Lucy's heart rate ticked up a notch. She thumbed through his chart until she found his med page. "Looks like you only needed the morphine twice yesterday."

"That's right."

"And you had the sleeping pill at eleven."

"Correct."

Lucy closed the chart. "Sometimes narcotics and sleeping meds can do odd things to the brain. As can anesthesia and being on the bypass machine. Not uncommon to have sleep problems and nightmares afterward."

"That's what I figured."

"Well, you figured right. I'm not saying don't use these meds if you need them but be aware they can make for some very colorful dreams."

"Colorful and scary."

"More snakes?"

"Lots of them. And these were even bigger and badder. At one point I was wrapped in them. Like a snake mummy."

Lucy flashed on her own dream. Her bed sheet-snake had tried to wrap her like a mummy too. "Sounds scary."

"More like terrified and panicked. I couldn't move and it was like they were pulling me down into a dark hole or something. I woke up wrapped in my sheet, sweaty, short of breath."

Lucy continuing thumbing through the chart, not really looking at the pages, buying time, while trying to sort this out. Nevers' dream echoed her own.

What is going on?

Nevers pulled her attention back to him. "If you hadn't already patched me up I'd of sworn I was having a heart attack."

Lucy closed the chart and forced a smile. "You didn't."

"I just really hate snakes."

"Me, too," Lucy said.

"I think anyone in their right mind does."

"True. But I really hate them. Even looking at pictures of them makes me all squishy."

"Squishy?"

Lucy shrugged. "Maybe not the best word."

"Somehow I don't see you as squishy."

"Not a good quality in your heart surgeon is it?"

"My point exactly."

"Walk as much as you can today," Lucy said. "The nurses will help you."

"When do I get out of here?"

"When you can walk to the front door," Lucy laughed.

"Well let's get at it. I want to go home."

"That's the attitude. I'll stop by later."

Lucy snagged a cup of coffee, old but not too bad, and sat at the nurse's station next to the rotating chart rack, Nevers' chart before her. As she was finishing her progress note and updating the orders, a shadow fell over her left shoulder. She turned. Birnbaum. Chart in one hand and a scowl on his face.

"Lucy, can I have a word?"

"Sure." She handed Nevers' chart to one of the nurses and then back to Birnbaum, "What's up?"

"In private?" He dropped the chart he held on the counter and waved a hand toward the hallway.

She followed him down the hall, not wanting to, preferring to tell him to mind his own business, to leave her alone and let her do her job, but knowing he was not someone you could simply blow off. He was too powerful and too deeply entrenched in the old boy network for her to take him on. Didn't mean she didn't wish she had a gun and could shoot him right here, right now.

Ah, the little fantasies that get you through the day.

She squared her shoulders and prepared for what she was sure would be a one-sided and very unpleasant discussion. The one thing you could say about Birnbaum and his buddy Elliot Meeks is that they were consistent. And persistent. Both had tried to sabotage her career on many occasions and she knew this would be another salvo. No doubt related to her episode in surgery this morning.

Birnbaum stepped into an empty, glass-encased cubicle in one corner of the PCU. He turned to her, arms crossed over his chest, and fixed her with his narrow-eyed gaze.

"Want to tell me what happened this morning?"

No. I don't want to tell you a damn thing you jerk.

"Nothing to tell. My case went well."

"That's not how I heard it." His chin came up and he glared down his nose at her. "I heard you had another episode. That you nearly fainted again."

"That's not exactly true. I'm a bit tired but that's it."

He stared at her, accusing, but saying nothing.

"You know I've had a very hectic couple of weeks. A lot of long and complex cases. Many late into the night. You know how that is. When you have a stretch like that you work too much, worry too much, and don't eat or sleep right. It catches up."

"So maybe you should take some time off."

And show you weakness? Not a chance.

"After the case tomorrow things are a bit slower," Lucy said. "I don't have much else scheduled right now."

"Are you up to the case tomorrow?"

"Of course."

He nodded. "It'll be long and stressful."

"Not really. It's a fairly straightforward VSD repair. Shouldn't take long."

"But the staff. It's their first. It'll take a little extra to get them up to speed."

"They're pretty good. I don't think they'll have any trouble."

"It's you I'm worried about. This makes three cases now where you've had . . . issues."

"Not issues. Fatigue. And I'm fine."

"You're sure?"

"All my labs are normal and Dr. Dukes said I'd live." She smiled. Birnbaum didn't.

"You don't think it might be wise to delay tomorrow's procedure?"

"Not at all. I'm okay."

He seemed to study her for a minute and then said, "I just want to be sure. I have a responsibility to protect our patients. All our patients."

"I know what your responsibilities and duties are. Mine, too. Like I told you before, if I thought I couldn't do this procedure I'd cancel it myself."

"I'm sure that's true."

Of course it's true, you condescending prick.

Birnbaum continued. "Herb Dorsey scrubbing in with you?"

"Sure is."

He nodded. "Good. Good. It'd be a shame for anything to go wrong with that case. Particularly after that big shindig on Saturday night."

It was all Lucy could do to rein in her anger. And not punch him in the face. She wrestled the impulse under control and said, "It'll go well."

Birnbaum hesitated a beat and then walked to the door of the cubicle before turning back toward her to fire his closing salvo, "I'm sure it will, and if not Herb will be there to help."

CHAPTER 17

A series of sharp raps on the window.

Sam flinched.

She was sitting shotgun in Ty's truck, twisted slightly toward him, watching him snap his seat belt into place and crank the engine to life. She turned to see that the rapping came from the knuckles of Darlene who stood next to the truck, scowling. Ty lowered the window. A waft of alcohol-laced breath hit her.

"What do you want, Darlene?" Ty asked.

"Where are you and your new whore off to?"

Sam started to say something. Something like, "Do you like your teeth? Want to keep them in place or would you rather I knocked them into your lungs?"

Ty beat her to it. "You drinking already? It's not even noon yet."

Darlene leaned both palms on the door and leaned down, looking past Sam toward Ty. "None of your goddamn business."

"Actually it is. If you make a scene I'll run you in. Might be wise for you to stagger on home and sleep it off."

"You'd like that wouldn't you. Leave you alone to daly with your new toy."

"Have a good day, Darlene." Ty raised the window and pulled from the curb. "Sorry about that."

"Not your fault."

"I'm not sure anymore whether it's the alcohol and drugs or she's just generally insane."

"The two aren't mutually exclusive."

"True." He sighed. "You wouldn't know it to see her but there was a time when she was actually pleasant."

"Drugs and alcohol change everything. Especially meth."

Ten minutes later they were north of town, winding up a two-lane blacktop into the hills. Sam watched the lush greenery and thick stands of trees, broken by expanses of open farm land and several creeks, roll by.

"Scully's congregation isn't far up here."

"How do the locals feel about having a snake handler in the neighborhood?"

"Some aren't happy but most just take it in stride. Part of the local color."

"As long as they don't bring their snakes to town, right?"

He laughed. "We have an ordinance against that."

"That's good to know."

"Scully's church ain't the only one that handles snakes up this way," Ty said. "There's a couple of others just in this county and I'd suspect a few others on up the road."

"I honestly thought all that was a thing of the past. Maybe a hundred years ago."

"You'd think. But it's alive and well. Most of the congregations are small. Less than forty or fifty people each. Scully's I think is a little bigger. Not much but some."

"So what do they do? I mean with the snakes?"

"Handle them." He smiled.

"Don't be a smart ass. You know what I mean."

"I only know they use them during the ceremonies and that only certain members are allowed to handle them."

"Allowed? They'd have to hold a gun to my head."

"Me, too."

Ty hung a right onto another, even narrower road that dipped down, twisted through a thick stand of gum trees, and crossed a wooden bridge over a rock-strewn creek, before rising again. As they exited the trees and burst back into the sunlight Sam saw a white clapboard building ahead. Rectangular with an A-frame, green-shingled roof topped by a white cross. Two thick round poles held a white sign with black lettering that read "Eden's Gate Church of God." It indicated that Reverand John Scully, Jr held services on Sundays as well as Tuesday and Thursday evenings.

"Is this it?" Sam asked.

"The one and only."

"Doesn't look like anyone's here."

"I suspect noon on Monday isn't a busy time for them."

Ty swung into the gravel lot and came to a stop near the three steps that led up to the double front doors. Sam stepped from the truck. She shaded the sun from her eyes with one hand while she inspected the church. Seemed to be locked up tightly.

"They've been in this location only a couple of years. Before that they were several miles on up the road in a smaller building."

Sam heard the crunch of tries and turned to see the Chevy dually pickup that belonged to Eric and Elvin Watson. They pulled up next to Ty's Tahoe. Sam detected the distinct aroma of marijuana as the doors popped open and Eric and Elvin climbed out.

"Can we help you?" Eric asked.

"I was just going to ask you the same thing," Ty said.

"We're here to do some work for Reverend Scully."

Sam saw that the pickup's bed held a stack of two-by-fours and a roll of wire mesh.

"You do maintenance for the church?" Ty asked.

"Naw," Elvin said, "We're building some new snake cages for him."

"New cages, huh? Why would he need new ones?"

"Didn't ask."

"He wouldn't be bringing in more snakes would he?"

Eric and Elvin glanced at each other, hesitated a beat, then Eric said, "We wouldn't know anything about that. We're just doing the building."

"Wouldn't be legal to transport snakes into or out of the county. You might want to make sure he remembers that."

"Maybe you should tell him," Elvin said.

"Maybe I will."

Eric looked at Sam and then to Ty. "She a new cop here?"

Ty shrugged. "Not yet, but I'll work on her."

Elvin snickered and punched Eric in the arm. "I bet that's the truth."

"Watch your mouth," Ty said.

"Didn't mean nothing," Eric said. "Besides it's a free country. I can say pretty much what I want."

"Within reason," Ty said.

Eric stared at him but said nothing. Elvin lowered the back gate of the truck and lifted a roll of chicken wire, settling it on one shoulder. Sam and Ty climbed back in his truck. Ty cranked the engine.

"Have a nice day," Ty said. He pulled away, circled their truck, and turned on the black top, aimed back toward town.

"Is everyone around here either drunk or stoned?" Sam asked.

Ty shrugged. "Some are."

"And you don't arrest them?"

"Wouldn't do much good. They'd pay a fine and head to a bar." He smiled that relaxed smile again. "Bet you have a few like them back home."

"True."

"Then there you go."

They rode quietly for a few minutes, Sam taking in the tree-crammed hills and rolling farmland. Then she said, "Let me get this straight. It's okay to own snakes but illegal to transport them?"

"Pretty much. It's a lot like the marijuana laws. You can possess up to an ounce but you can't grow, buy, or sell it."

"Which never made sense to me. If you have it you must have either grown it or bought it."

"I don't make the laws."

Sam laughed. "Maybe you should. They'd probably make more sense."

"You know how it goes, laws are never made by those who have to enforce them. Or those that have to live with them for that matter. They're made by people trying to buy votes."

"Nice to see Tennessee and California have so much in common."

"Except we don't have Hollywood or Disneyland. Beaches and surfers neither."

"Count your blessings."

"Wouldn't mind the beaches. The rest, maybe not."

"How many members does Scully have in his church?"

"Not sure but I'd suspect maybe sixty to eighty. Something like that."

"Who are they? Who joins a snake-handling church?"

"You'd be surprised. Farmers, business owners, even a school teacher from over at the middle school."

"Do you know many of them?"

"Some. Mostly fairly normal folks."

"I'm not big on churches anyway but if someone pulled a snake out in the middle of a service I'd be out the door."

Ty laughed. "Smart move."

"You ever attended a service there? Been inside?"

"Not a service but I've been here. Remember the guy I told you about? Marvin Purdy? The farmer that was murdered?"

"Yeah. One of your two unsolved cases."

Ty nodded. "He belonged to the church."

"Really?"

"Yeah, so I had to talk with Scully, Sr. about him. Came out here and met him in his office."

"Was Scully a suspect?"

"No more than everyone else in the county." He smiled. "I just thought he might know something about Purdy's acquaintances. As I said, Purdy was somewhat of a loner so I didn't know much about him."

"Did Scully help?"

"Not really. He didn't know him all that well either."

"You believe that?"

"Why not?"

"Small church. Seems to me the pastor would know his congregation well."

"You'd think. I actually asked Scully that."

"What'd he say?"

"That he was only interested in his soul not who he knew or didn't know."

Something about that made Sam uncomfortable. A preacher not knowing the ins and outs of one of his followers? Not knowing his family and friends? Even a snake-handling preacher. Maybe she was too cynical, particularly where religion was concerned, never bought into the whole church-preacher deal, mostly seeing them as a money-making scheme. Wouldn't Scully want to know about Purdy's business so he'd know how much to hit him up for? Wouldn't he want to know who his friends were, new members being the life blood of any church? Probably more so for one with a small congregation. She started to voice her view but hesitated, not wanting to dump a bunch of her baggage on Ty.

"I guess looking after their souls is what he's supposed to do," she said.

They were now back in town and Ty guided his Tahoe over the Crockett bridge. Sam saw the courthouse and downtown square ahead. She glanced at her watch.

"Buy you lunch? Sam asked.

"I was just fixing to ask you the same thing."

"My treat."

"A liberated woman, I see."

"Just consider it payback for a pleasant drive in the country."

"Even if we didn't see any snakes?"

"More like because we didn't."

CHAPTER 18

Ty was right. Gladys Johnston did know everything about everything. And then some.

Earlier, while she and Ty woofed down a pair of pulled pork sandwiches piled with a rich mustardy cole slaw, Sam had asked where she might start her research of Scully's church. Ty didn't hesitate, saying, "The library. Ask for Gladys Johnston. She's the head librarian and knows everything there is to know about Remington. She's been there forever. In fact, I think she came with the building."

Finding Gladys is exactly what Sam did. Wasn't hard. She stood behind the main desk and greeted Sam when she walked in. She was exactly as Ty had described. White hair, thin, animated, and with sharp blue eyes. She wore an unconstructed blue denim dress over a white long-sleeved pullover, cuffs pushed up to her elbows, a gold cross on a thin gold chain dangling from her neck, a yellow pencil perched over her right ear.

"I'm Sam Cody. Ty Everson said you might be able to help me."

"He did now did he? Well I just bet I can." She inspected Sam for a beat then said, "You're that friend of Lucy Wagner's that's visiting from California."

It was more a statement than a question but Sam felt obligated to answer. "That's right."

"The cop who boxes." Another statement. Sam must have appeared surprised because Gladys went on, "I'm sort of nosey in case you haven't figured that out yet." She laughed. "Librarians are that way, I suspect. Especially in small towns."

Now Sam laughed. "I understand. I live in a small town."

Gladys nodded. "So how can I help you?"

Sam told her she was looking into John Scully and his church.

"Mind if I ask why?"

"Cops are like librarians. We're nosy too."

That brought a burst of laughter and a clap of hands from Gladys. "I got some stuff on that." She came around her desk. "Why don't you take a seat over there I'll get it together for you." She pointed toward an empty rectangular table that sat in an alcove just off the main reading room. "It'll only take a quick minute."

It took more than a quick minute but less than three.

"Here are a stack of articles on the church," Gladys said, a single boney finger tapping a blue folder she dropped on the table before Sam, Eden's Gate Church of God neatly handprinted on the side tab. Gladys flipped it open. "Don't you just love our filing system?" She smiled, a twinkle in her bright blue eyes.

"Judging from the two or three minutes it took you to locate it, I'd say it works," Sam said.

"For now. We've been trying to get all these loose pages and folders scanned into the new computer so someone will be able to find what they need once I kick the bucket. Which could happen any day now." Another twinkling smile.

Sam suspected Gladys would live well beyond a hundred. Maybe even end up being the oldest person in the country. She seemed to have more life in her than most people 20 years her junior.

"Look through these," Gladys continued. "I'm going to check in our photo files. I know we have some old pictures of John Scully when he was a young preacher." With that she turned and left.

The file consisted of loose type-written pages and letters, old news clippings, pages ripped from magazines, and even a menu from a place called Joe's Shrimp House. Someone had scribbled a Biblical passage on the back of the menu in pencil.

And he said unto them, Go ye into all the world, and preach the gospel to every creature.

He that believeth and is baptized shall be saved; but he that believeth not shall be damned.

And these signs shall follow them that believe; In my name shall they cast out devils; they shall speak with new tongues;

They shall take up serpents; and if they drink any deadly thing, it shall not hurt them; they shall lay hands on the sick, and they shall recover.

So then after the Lord had spoken unto them, he was received up into heaven, and sat on the right hand of God.

And they went forth, and preached everywhere, the Lord working with them, and confirming the word with signs following. Amen.

Mark16:15-20

Even with what had apparently been a dull pencil and the coarseness of the paper, the script was clean and elegant as if it had been written by some monk in an isolated monastery.

She laid the menu aside and began reading through the other pages. The most interesting and complete seemed to be a newspaper article from the *Remington Post Herald* written by Tommy Jenks, the editor. It was yellowed with age and when Sam checked the date she saw it was from nearly 30 years earlier. The article, titled "New Church Forms in County," told of John Scully and several others leaving Pastor Bill Whitehurst's Pine

Valley Church of God to form the Eden's Gate Church of God. Apparently Scully thought snake handling was a good thing but Billy didn't. A dispute over this and the theological direction of the church jammed a rift between Scully, then an assistant pastor, and Whitehurst.

She found an article on the murders of Marvin Purdy and Pete Grimm, the articles simply saying that they had at one time been church members but had left the congregation, no reason given in either case. Sam remembered Ty saying that Purdy had been a member but not Grimm. She made a mental note to ask him about that.

Gladys returned with a brown envelope and from it pulled out a stack of photos. She spread them on the table and shuffled through them, finally selecting one.

"Here's Scully's church today." The photo showed the church she and Ty had just visited. She selected another photo. "This is the original church. Maybe thirty years ago." It was little more than a patio cover. Four thick wooden poles topped with a slanted piece of corrugated metal. "Ain't much to look at is it?"

"They held their services outdoors?"

"More or less. You'd be surprised how many congregations up here started that way. I think old John only had about a dozen followers back then."

"And they were doing the snake thing even back then?" Sam asked.

"Oh yeah. Old John thought the Lord sent serpents to help man. Make him more self-reliant."

"How does that work?"

Gladys picked up the menu and laid it in front of Sam. "Tommy Jenks, used to be our newspaper editor before he passed, I suspect a dozen years ago now, interviewed old John for an article."

Sam indicated the article she had read. "This one?"

"That's it. They met over at Joe's. Not there anymore. Closed after Joe died and his son didn't want to be in the restaurant business. Anyway,

Tommy told me that John wrote out this verse for him. Right from memory. Said this was the Lord telling all to worship the serpent as mankind's savior."

"Okay," Sam said. "I'll bite . . . no pun intended . . . how does a serpent save mankind?"

"I've spoken to John about this more than a few times over the years. Seems that he believes that if there had been no serpent Adam and Eve would have forever lived in Eden and would have become worthless slobs. All was provided. They didn't have to do or think or create. Simply be."

"But the serpent ended all that?" Sam asked. "How?"

"According to Scully it was like that movie *The Time Machine.* Remember the Eloi?"

"The folks that did nothing. Didn't help the drowning girl? Let the library books disintegrate?"

"That's them. John said that if the serpent hadn't enticed Eve to eat the apple, breaking God's commandment, we would all be Eloi today. But since God showed them the gate so to speak, tossed them from Eden, they had to fend for themselves and mankind is better for it."

"Thus Eden's Gate."

"That's right. John always said that it was okay to worship Christ and all the other Christian beliefs but that none of that would have come to be without the serpent."

Sam shook her head. "Amazing that people bought into that."

"People'll buy all kinds of things. If they need something to buy into. Abraham was ready to kill his own son. Those muslims believe there are seventy-two virgins waiting. But for the life of me I don't see what the women folk would do with them. Menfolk yeah, sure, but the women? And then there's that whole resurrection thing."

"I take it you're not all that keen on religion?"

"I'm a Baptist I reckon. Mostly. Don't mean I lost my common sense."

Sam liked Gladys. She was feisty and didn't seem to worry what other people thought, just plowed ahead through life. "Amen to that."

Gladys laughed. "Amen is right. The way I see it is there either is a god or there ain't and either way is astounding. But I guess one day pretty soon I'll find out which it is."

"As will we all."

"It'll just be a bit sooner for me than for you, I suspect."

Gladys slid another photo from the stack and pushed it toward Sam. "Here are the original members of Eden's Gate."

Sam studied the old black and white photo. It showed a group of twelve people standing in front of the patio-cover church, an Eden's Gate sign above their heads. The women wore simple dresses, the men dark suits, white shirts, and thin black ties, all with solemn expressions. A single child stood next to one of the women, head resting against her leg, the woman's hand on her head.

"The tall guy there in the middle is John Scully," Gladys said. "The woman next to him, on his right, is Martha Ackers, Lucy's grandmother, and the couple here," she indicated the woman with the child and the man next to her, are Lucy's parents. And this young lady is Lucy."

Stunned wasn't exactly strong enough for what Sam felt. "Really?"

"I think Lucy was about four then. A year later her parents died in a fire."

Sam picked up the photo and examined it more closely. "This is amazing." She looked at Gladys. "Lucy never knew Martha or her parents belonged to the church."

Gladys' brow furrowed. "Are you sure?"

"She just found out a couple of days ago. John, Jr. told her after his father died in surgery."

"My goodness. I always assumed she knew." A wicked smile appeared and she tapped her index finger against the side of her head. "Guess I need to update my files."

❧

Sam stepped out into the sunlight, an envelope stuffed with copies of the articles and photos Gladys had made for her sticking out of the top of her purse. She checked the street, looking both ways, but saw no sign of Darlene. Didn't want to run into that psycho again. She rummaged inside her purse, found her sunglasses and slipped them on, and then extracted her cell phone. She called Lucy.

"How's your day going?" Sam asked.

"Hectic. You?"

"Found some interesting stuff on the church."

"Like what?"

Sam hesitated, not sure she wanted to talk about this over the phone. Better face to face so Lucy could read it for herself. And see the photos. "It's a lot so I'll tell you later. When are you heading home?"

"Not sure. I still have a few patients to see here in the office and then evening rounds. Maybe six or six-thirty."

"I told Ty we'd meet him and Bump at JT's around six. That work for you?"

"Ty, huh?"

"Don't go there."

"I'm just saying . . ."

"Say something else."

Lucy laughed. "I better meet you there."

Sam closed her cell, dropped it back in her purse, walked to her Lexus, and headed toward Lucy's. She needed to digest everything she'd learned today.

CHAPTER 19

"**D**id either of you know that Pete Grimm was a member of Eden's Gate?" Sam asked Ty and Bump.

They were sitting in a corner booth at JT's BBQ, Sam sipping whiskey, Bump and Ty long-necked PBRs, Ty seated next to her, Bump across the table. The place was already filling with people and noise.

"What?" Ty asked.

"You mentioned that Marvin Purdy had been a member but not Grimm."

"I never knew that," Ty said, casting a glance at Bump.

"Me neither," Bump said. He scratched his chin. "You sure?"

"Gladys Johnston over at the library said so."

"If Gladys says so, it's a fact," Bump said.

"She also has some old pictures of Grimm with John Scully . . . the older John Scully . . . at the church."

"That never came up," Ty said. "His only relative was a daughter. Named Melinda Martin. Lives over near Lynchburg. I talked with her on several occasions and she never mentioned him being a member."

"Probably didn't think it was important," Sam said.

"And I never asked her," Bump said. He ran a finger around the lip of his beer bottle. "Should have."

"Not really," Sam said. "Twenty-twenty hindsight and all that. It might look important now, but back then. . .eight years ago, right?" Bump nodded. "Back before Purdy's murder, it wouldn't have made a blip on the radar."

"You're a pretty smart young lady," Bump said. "I'd bet a good cop too."

Sam shrugged. "I have my moments. Bet you two do too."

Bump took a long pull from his Pabst Blue Ribbon, the bottle almost disappearing in his large hand. "Intermittently. Me more than Ty." He gave a sly grin.

"Funny," Ty said as he tipped his PBR toward him. "But that sure puts a whole different spin on things. We never had anything to link Grimm and Purdy. Other than both being random B&Es."

"The fact that they went to the same church ain't exactly a link," Bump said.

Sam nodded. "But it is a small church."

"Maybe I'll have another chat with his daughter," Ty said.

"That's what I'd do," Bump said.

"Mind if I tag along?" Sam asked.

"Tag along where?"

It was Lucy. Sam had been so involved in the conversation she hadn't seen her come in. Lucy sat next to Bump.

"Talk to a witness," Ty said.

Lucy laughed. "You can tell she's on vacation."

"Actually she uncovered some things that just might help out," Bump said.

Lucy rolled her eyes. "Why am I not surprised? What kinds of things?"

Sam told her about Grimm and Purdy belonging to Eden's Gate. As she finished, their waitress returned, took food and drink orders, and left.

"So your two cold cases were connected to Scully's church?" Lucy asked.

"Looks that way."

"There's more," Sam said. She pulled the envelope from her purse and took out the pages and photos. "Here is an old newspaper article. An interview of John Sr. She handed the page to Lucy, Bump leaned over to read it along with her.

"It was done by Tommy Jenks," Bump said.

"Haven't heard his name for a while," Ty said. "What does it say?"

"That Scully had been the assistant pastor under Billy Whitehurst," Sam said. "I assume you knew him?"

"Sure did," Ty said. "Good man. Ran the Pine Valley Church of God for decades."

"Well, it seems that about three decades ago he and Scully had a falling out. Over snake handling. Scully left with about a dozen members and formed Eden's Gate."

"I remember that," Bump said. "I was just out of school and had joined the force about that time. Never knew what the fuss was about though."

"Apparently Scully believed the serpent, the Garden of Eden one, was the true savior of mankind."

Lucy and Bump stopped reading and stared at her. Sam related what Gladys Johnston had told her and what she had read in the various articles. She then handed them a copy of the scripture-scrawled menu and waited while each of them read it.

Lucy shook her head. "Amazing."

"There's more," Sam said.

"Well, you're just full of news, aren't you?" Bump said.

Sam help up the copy of the photo of Scully and the original congregation in front of the original meeting place, the carport-looking one. "Recognize anyone?"

"The tall guy in the middle is John Scully," Bump said. He squinted. "Is that? Hand me that." Sam did and he inspected it for a minute. "Well,

I'll be shot in the butt." He looked at Sam and then Lucy, a finger tapping the picture he now held out toward Lucy. "That right there, next to John, is Martha. There's your parents on the end there." Lucy's eyes widened. "And that little tyke right there, hugging on your Mama's leg, is you."

Lucy took the photo and studied it. "Are you sure?"

"As sure as I am of anything."

"That's what Gladys said, too," Sam said.

Lucy's fingers trembled and tears welled in her eyes. "The only picture I have of them is the charred one that survived the fire. And I don't have any of me at that age."

"Now you do," Sam said. "There are a few more over at the library."

Lucy's eyes seemed to glaze over. "Martha and my parents were original members of Scully's church?"

"Sure looks that way," Sam said.

Lucy dabbed her eyes with the corner of her napkin. "Can my life possibly get any weirder?"

CHAPTER 20

.

Fuck me.

Lucy wasn't sure if she actually said that out loud or not, but she definitely thought it. What she did know is that she was prone, right cheek pressed firmly against the hard tile floor of the OR, and several pairs of bootie-covered shoes shuffled back and forth through her field of vision. Then, as her brain cleared out the cobwebs, she heard voices, distant and hollow, calling her name.

She was screwed. Getting dizzy was one thing, fainting again another thing altogether. What the hell was going on with her?

She had been elbows deep in young Ronnie Draper's chest, completing his VSD repair. She remembered that much. Actually she remembered more. She had completed the repair, closed up the young man's heart, and was doing a final inspection before beginning the exacting process of weaning him from the bypass machine. What was different from the other events, what scared her the most, was that there was essentially no warning this time. No creeping coldness and approaching dizziness, coming in waves, allowing her time to react. This time it came as a blinding flash of deep cold pain that raced from her chest and down her arms to her hands in literally a heartbeat. And in another heart beat all went black.

With the Nevers' case, when she fainted the first time, there was a warning, a prodrome. She knew something was wrong and had tried to stay upright. Not successfully but at least she felt it coming. This time it hit like a rogue wave, literally knocking her to the floor.

The distant voices seemed closer, clearer now.

"She's coming around." It was scrub nurse Rosa Lopez. "Lucy? Lucy? You okay."

Lucy rolled to her back and looked at Rosa, who was now kneeling beside her. "I'm fine." Lucy sat up. She did an inventory of her body parts and all seemed to work.

"I'll finish up," Dr. Herb Dorsey said. "You go lie down."

"I told you, I'm okay. Just get me a fresh gown and gloves and we'll get Ronnie here off the bypass." Lucy stood.

"You sure?"

"I'm sure."

Ten minutes later, Lucy had re-gowned and gloved and was repositioned beside the surgical table. "That was fun."

"Not for us," Raj said.

"I lied," Lucy said. "It wasn't fun for me either." She again examined Ronnie Draper's heart. "Everything looks good here. Raj?"

"Vital signs are stable and O2 sats are normal. Ready to rock."

Forty-five minutes later Ronnie was flying solo, the pump lines removed, and his chest closed. Lucy then talked with the young man's family, telling them the surgery had gone well and that the VSD was closed and would no longer be a problem for him. She avoided the fact that she had ended up on the floor.

When she walked into the doctor's lounge, Herb was sitting on the sofa, a chart open in his lap.

"What are you going to do? Herb asked.

"About what?"

"Lucy?"

She slipped off her surgical cap, snapped the mask strings from around her neck, wadded them into a ball, and tossed them in the trashcan. She flopped onto the sofa next to Herb, leaning back, messaging her temples. "I don't know."

"Yes you do. You want to do it or do you want to leave it to Birnbaum and the Credentials Committee?"

"I don't have any more cases this week. I'll cancel my office appointments and except for daily hospital rounds will take a mini vacation."

"You think that'll fly?"

"Probably not. But I'll give it a shot."

"You need to find out what's wrong."

"I'm just tired and stressed."

"Stress and fatigue? You going to go with that?"

"I have to." She shoved her fingers through her hair. "Anything else I don't want to think about."

The other things? Tumors, aneurysms, seizures, cardiac arrhythmias, cerebral emboli, the list goes on. And it's a long and nasty list. Things that end careers. Things that end lives. Lucy couldn't go there.

This was exactly why doctors and nurses make terrible patients. Know too much. Know all the nasty, even if rare, things that can go wrong with the human body. Know all the signs and symptoms. And when they sense them in themselves, they either ignore them or more often conger up the worse case scenarios. Starts in med school. While learning about the massive array of diseases that plague the world, any symptom, real or imagined, becomes a deadly disease. A headache is a tumor, nausea stomach cancer, and back pain a dissecting aneurysm. Junior year, the first year of actually taking care of sick folks, is the worst. By internship this syndrome tends to fade. Too busy to worry about minor aches and pains.

"Let me ask you this," Herb said. "If one of your patients had suffered two syncopal episodes, like you have, would you let them drive a car?"

"Probably not."

"Definitely not."

Lucy stood. "Let me think about it. Right now I need to make rounds."

"Don't leave this in Birnbaum's hands or the outcome won't be pretty."

CHAPTER 21

"I need to get some gas," Ty said as he turned into the dirt and gravel area that fronted a white clapboard grocery store, sliding up next to the gas pump. "How about a Moon Pie and an RC?"

"How'd you know I was hungry?" Sam asked.

"Didn't. But I am."

"Doesn't sound like a very nutritious lunch."

Ty laughed. "A Moon Pie's about the best lunch you could have. Ain't cookies, marshmallow, and chocolate the three basic food groups?"

"Don't forget sugar."

"That's a given."

Now Sam laughed. "You're on."

After Ty pumped the tank full and purchased a pair of Moon Pies and RC's they were back on the road.

"Can't remember the last time I had one of these," Sam said, using a moistened fingerprint to collect the crumbs that had fallen on her dark blue tee shirt.

"I'd of never made it out of childhood without them. And peanut butter of course."

"I hear you. For me it was peanut butter and banana sandwiches."

"Like Elvis?"

"My mom didn't fry them in a pound of butter though."

"Probably a good idea."

"How much further? Sam asked.

"Couple of miles. We'll turn off the highway up here and then her place is just a bit further."

Earlier Ty had called Melinda Martin, asked if he could drop by for a chat about her father. She had agreed so long as it was after one. Her farm was near Lynchburg, home of the Jack Daniel's Distillery. The fact that Moore County was a dry county never deterred the folks at Jack Daniel's from churning out one of the most popular and largest selling alcoholic concoctions in the world. Daniel's, as most folks call it, wasn't labeled as bourbon, even though technically it was, but rather Tennessee Sipping Whiskey. Don't believe there's difference? Try telling one of Lynchburg's 6000 residents it's bourbon and you'll get a earful. It would go something like: "Where the hell you think you're standing? Kentucky?" That about covers it.

The road that split off the highway and led to Melinda Martin's farm proved to be a pair of dirt and gravel stripes divided by a grassy center, wads of battered Johnson grass standing the tallest. Sam could hear their long blades flapping against the undercarriage. The road wound through stands of maple and pine and rolling grass land, divided into sections by barbwire fences, the round, wooden support poles hugged by even more Johnson grass. As Ty's Tahoe crested yet another rise in the road, a white clapboard house came into view. Its small porch was embraced by a white railing and shaded by a short roof and a mature maple tree. A suspended two-person swing and a pair of oak rocking chairs flanked the front door. A woman, who Sam assumed was Melinda Martin, sat in one of the rockers, magazine in hand. As Ty pulled to a stop near the front steps, she dropped the magazine to the floor and stood.

Ty introduced Sam, explaining that she was a cop, visiting from California. Melinda offered sweet tea, but Sam and Ty declined. Melinda offered them the rockers, while she moved to the swing.

"Sorry to bother you," Ty said.

"No problem."

"We . . .actually Sam . . . was doing some research on John Scully and turned up the fact that your dad had belonged to his church. Did you know that?"

"Sure did."

"I know I didn't think to ask before, didn't really have a reason to, but I don't remember you mentioning it back when I was looking into your father's murder."

Melinda parked a stray strand of hair behind her ear. "I didn't know then. Just found out a couple of years ago." The swing began a gentle back and forth motion. "My aunt, Dad's younger sister, lives up in South Dakota so I don't see her much. She was down visiting . . .let's see . . . I guess it's been more like three or four years ago truth be told. She mentioned it then. I was surprised that Daddy would have anything to do with a snake handler."

Ty nodded. "I wish I'd of known that before."

"I didn't think it was important. At least not to what happened to him."

"Probably it isn't."

Her eyes narrowed and she leaned forward, stopping the swing's motion and tilting it slightly. "But maybe it is?"

Ty shrugged.

"Which is it? Yea or nay?"

"There was another fellow murdered a few years ago. Somewhat similar to Pete. Someone broke in, at night, and killed him. Looked like a robbery gone bad." Ty leaned forward, resting his elbows on his knees. "He was a church member too."

"You telling me these two murders was related?"

"Don't know. Possible. Or it could just be a coincidence."

Melinda's gaze turned toward a weathered red barn, maybe a hundred yards away, down a gentle grassy slope. She said nothing for a minute as if absorbing the possibility. "Daddy always said that coincidences were things that you just hadn't connected up yet." Her gaze returned to Ty. "Is that what we got here?"

"Maybe."

She nodded, leaned back, the swing falling back into its gentle rhythm. Then to Sam she said, "That how you see it too?"

"Sure is."

"How'd you come up with on all this?"

Sam told her about Martha Ackers and Lucy's parents. How they had been members but Lucy had never known that.

"I've heard of both of them. Martha of course is known by everyone and I hear tell Lucy is a hot shot heart surgeon over in Remington."

"That's true."

"Sounds like she and I have a lot in common. Not the surgeon part, of course." She cast a brief smile. "But neither of us knew our parents had fallen under old John Scully's spell."

Sam nodded. "Did your aunt say anything about your Dad and Scully?"

"Just that they had a few disagreements. That Dad finally left the church."

"She give you a reason why?"

"Not specifically. I suspect he didn't care for the direction things were going is all."

"So they didn't have a big blow up or anything like that?" Sam asked.

"Not that she said."

"You think maybe I could give her a call?" Ty asked. "See if she remembers any of the details."

"It'd be long distance. Real long distance. She passed November was a year ago now."

CHAPTER 22

"How's Mr. Nevers doing today?" Lucy asked his nurse, Amy Barton.

"Great. He walked twelve laps this morning and had a good lunch."

Nevers was now housed on the surgical floor and had been cut loose from the cardiac monitors, oxygen tubings, and IVs, now wearing only a heparin lock and a telemetry box dangling around his neck. The surgical floor's twenty-four rooms lined a square of hallways that embraced a central nurse's station, doctor's dictation room, break lounge, and a locked medicine closet. Laps around the unit were the measure of a post-op patient's progress. Nevers twelve loops put him right on the expected recovery pace.

Lucy and Amy stood in the lounge, Lucy pouring a not-so-fresh cup of coffee and eyeing the picked-over, stale muffins in the pink box next to the coffee pot. Breakfast leftovers. Probably brought in by one of the nurses, maybe one of the docs, or even a medical products rep. Food of any kind was always welcome. Never knew when a lunch or dinner break wasn't going to happen, patient care always taking precedence. The muffins were no longer very appetizing, but breakfast seemed eons ago and Lucy hadn't made time for lunch. Her stomach growled in protest. Maybe she'd have the half blueberry that seemed to stare at her.

His eyes were wild, pupils dilated, head on a swivel as if looking for an escape route, or perhaps fearful of a blindside attack. He looked like a cornered animal. Frantic, fearful, and capable of anything. In full fight or flight self-preservation mode. Finally his gaze locked on the window and he shuffled in that direction.

"Mr. French," Lucy said. "Look at me."

HIs gaze flicked around the room before finally landing on her again.

"Let her go and we'll talk about this."

"Go away."

"We're here to help you."

"You put something inside me."

"No we didn't."

"You did. You did. You did." His screaming was now shrill, panic filled. Sweat dotted his face and chest and his breaths came in great gulps. "You put something inside and it's eating me up."

Lucy mentally ran through the differential diagnosis: too early for ICU psychosis but hypoxia, hypoglycemia, stroke, sedative and pain med reaction, or, most likely, post-pump psychosis, each remained a possibility.

"You're just confused right now. Let's get you back in the bed so I can examine you and we'll see what the problem is."

"It's you. You did this."

Then things happened rapidly. French charged toward the window, pushing Madison ahead of him. The two young security guards rushed past Lucy. French screamed. Madison stumbled and fell against the wall. The guards took the kicking and screaming French to the floor, one wrapping him in a bear hug, the other locking his arms around his flailing legs. A plaintiff wail rose from the French's throat.

"Versed," Lucy said. "Two milligrams"

Fifteen minutes later, a sedated and restrained Joseph French lay in bed. The reconnected cardiac monitor showed sinus tachycardia at

Amy saved her.

"I have a couple of granola bars in my locker," Amy said. "Want one?"

"I'd love one. If you let me pay for it."

"You can have it. Just don't eat those stale old things." She nodded toward the muffins.

Simple gym-like lockers for the staff to store personal items while at work lined one wall of the lounge. Amy worked the combination on hers, pulled it open, and retrieved the bar from her purse.

"Here you go." She tossed it to Lucy and then snapped the locker closed.

"Thanks."

"I have some meds to give," Amy said. "If you need anything else let me know." She left.

Lucy settled at the nurse's station and washed the granola bar down with the coffee while thumbing through William Nevers' chart. All looked good. She walked down to his room, where she found him sitting in a chair, reading.

"How are you doing?" Lucy asked.

He closed the book and placed it on the table next to is chair. "Great. Do I get to go home today?"

"Let's make it tomorrow."

"All Amy and the other nurses are doing is baby sitting me. My wife can do that. Besides, I sleep better at home."

"You mean our accommodations aren't top drawer?"

"You know what Dorothy said—there's no place like home."

Lucy laughed. "True."

"And then maybe these dreams will go away."

"You had another one?"

"A real doozy. Thought my heart was going to jump out of my chest. If you hadn't put all those wires in there it just might've."

"Tell me about it."

"Same thing as before. Only more so. Like before it was sandy but this time there weren't any trees and it was definitely night. Like I was trying to cross a desert in the dark. Then the sand starting moving like a nest of snakes was writhing beneath my feet. Seemed I almost fell a couple of times but knew if I did they'd have me." He shook his head. "Damnedest thing. Then one of them grabbed my foot. Not with its mouth but with its tail. Tried to pull me right under. Got down to where only my chin was above ground. That's when I woke up. All sweaty and my heart doing its thing."

"Any pain in your chest?" Lucy asked. "With the dream."

"Just a lot of pounding and flopping around."

"You feel okay now?"

"A little tired but otherwise fine. You still think this is from the anesthesia?"

"That and the bypass machine. Like I told you before, it can do some odd things to the brain."

"Do I have to live with these?"

"No. These symptoms will resolve in a few days. And getting home, back to familiar surroundings, might help."

Doctor Strong to ICU Stat. Doctor Strong to ICU Stat.

The urgent operator's voice came through the ceiling speakers. Doctor Strong meant that security was needed. Usually meant some disturbance that required authority and muscles.

Lucy hurried down stairs and into the ICU. Several wide-eyed nurses stood outside one of the cubicles. Mr. Joseph French's cubicle. Lucy's CABG patient from yesterday.

"What happened?" Lucy asked,

"He just went crazy. Ranting and raving. Threw a chair through the window and now has Madison in there."

The nurses made a path and Lucy stepped inside the cubicle. French, who had discarded his gown and was completely naked, had his arms wrapped around nurse Madison Fife, holding her as a shield against the two security guards who faced him. Madison's eyes were wide with fear. The window behind them was gone, only a frame of jagged glass remaining. The chair rested half in and half out on the sill. Blood trickled down French's right arm from where he had ripped out his IV. The IV pole, fluid bag, and IV lines lay in a pile in one corner. Wires dangled from the electrode patches on his chest, now disconnected from the cardiac monitor, which pulsed its shrill warning.

"Relax Mr. French," one of the guards said. "Let her go and we'll talk about this."

"Stay back," French screamed. "I'll jump. I swear I will. And I'll take her right out of this window with me."

"Mr. French," Lucy said, her words a short, sharp bark.

His gaze snapped toward her as if he had just realized she was there. Took his glazed eyes a beat or two to locate and focus on her. "You." His voice now high-pitched. "You did this."

Lucy walked around the bed to the cardiac monitor and flicked it off, silencing its strident beeps. The room seemed suddenly still, as if all the air had been sucked out.

"Did what, Mr. French?" Lucy tried to sound calm and clinical. Her racing heart told a different story.

"This." He twisted Madison away from him, still clutching her with his left arm around her neck, and pointed to the surgical wound down the center of his chest. "You did this."

Lucy casually walked around the bed and stood not ten feet from him. He pulled Madison tightly against him.

"That's right," Lucy said, "We fixed your arteries. Remember?"

twenty. The oxygen sat monitor clipped to his finger revealed his O2 sat was ninety six percent and a finger prick blood sugar was acceptable at one eighteen, ruling out hypoxia and hypoglycemia as causes for his confusion.

At the nurse's station. Madison sat in chair, shaken but apparently uninjured.

"You okay?" Lucy asked.

She nodded. "I'm fine."

Lucy turned to Amy. "Call Dr. Jenner and tell him we need a neuro consult."

Amy picked up the phone.

Lucy sighed. First Nevers' dreams and now this. What the hell is going on?

"What's the problem here?"

Lucy turned to see Birnbaum standing behind her.

"I think a bit of post-pump psychosis," Lucy said.

Birnbaum nodded. "I see." He frowned. "Can I have a word?"

Sure it would be more than a word, Lucy followed him into the dictation room, Birnbaum closing the door behind them.

"I heard about what happened this morning. In surgery."

"Nothing happened."

"Really? I understand you had another one of your spells."

Spells? You arrogant prick.

"It was nothing," Lucy said.

"I'm afraid that's too easy an answer." He hesitated a beat and then said, "And I'm afraid I'll have to remove your surgical privileges until this is resolved."

"Don't you think that's a bit of an overreaction?"

"You know as well as I that I'm responsible for everything that goes on here. If there is even the slightest possibility that you're impaired, I have to take action." He tried to soften it. "I don't like it, but I must."

"I don't have anything scheduled until next week anyway."

"I want you to see Aaron Jenner. When he clears you I'll reconsider."

"Look—"

"Lucy, I'm afraid this isn't negotiable."

The door opened and Jenner stuck his head inside. "Lucy, you wanted to see me."

Confusion showed on Birnbaum's face.

"I asked Aaron to see Mr. French," Lucy said.

Birnbaum nodded and excused himself.

჻

Lucy waited until Jenner had completed his consult, he agreeing with her assessment that it was likely some form of post-pump psychosis, and then she followed him to his office. She told him the entire story, almost. She excluded her nightmares.

Jenner performed a complete neuro exam and then said, "I don't see anything amiss."

"Tell Birnbaum that."

"He can be a bit difficult."

"That's not exactly the word I'd use."

Jenner smiled. Aaron was one of the good guys. Good doc, good friend, and one of the older staff members. Old guard. Silver white hair and mutton chops of the same hue. His dark eyes were both piercing and friendly, narrowing when he smiled.

"Let's schedule an EEG and a MRI for tomorrow."

"Is that necessary?"

"If you want me to get Birnbaum off your case, I'll need some hard evidence. Besides, isn't that what you'd do if one of your patients exhibited these symptoms?"

Lucy had no argument for that.

❧

The power of suggestion comes in many flavors. Someone yawns, you do too. Someone says they feel queasy after eating the same food you did and queasiness worms its way inside. Someone says they're coming down with the flu and suddenly your throat feels scratchy. Or maybe, someone tells you about a dream, and you have a similar one.

For Lucy, when she finally fell asleep that night, not an easy thing with all the crap swirling around in her head, the snake dream returned. This time, rather than wrapping around her legs as it had the other night, it more closely matched William Nevers's dream. Sand and wind and snakes under her feet, grabbing at her, trying to pull her beneath the surface. When she jerked awake, wrapped in a sweat-soaked sheet, she escaped the covers and planted her feet on the floor, elbows on her knees, head hanging, a trickle of sweat working its way down her nose.

It was three thirty.

Get a grip, Lucy.

Chapter 23

An MRI is like being stuffed into a claustrophobic metallic tube while someone bangs on the outside with a hammer. A big hammer. The clanging palpable and deafening, even through the music-filled headphones Carla Knowles, the radiology tech, had settled over Lucy's ears. Add to this, her shoulders wedged against the sides, gray metal only inches from her face, and the realization that left to her own devices there was no escape. No wiggle room. No way to extrude herself from either end of the tube. Panic hovered in the periphery of her mind.

And her mind raced.

What if the radiology department caught on fire?

What if there was an earthquake?

Or a tornado?

What if Carla, who ran the test from a separate room while peering through a plate glass window, dropped dead?

What if all the oxygen was suddenly sucked from the room?

Stop it, Lucy.

She tried to ignore the confinement, the noise, the feeling of complete helplessness and concentrate on remaining still. No easy task. She wanted to scream. She wanted to end this nonsense. There was nothing wrong with her and she didn't need to go through this. Her symptoms were due to simple stress and fatigue. Nothing more sinister. She was here only to get Birnbaum off her ass.

Don't be a candy ass. It'll be over in a minute.

It wasn't. She gritted it out for twenty minutes until, finally, Carla shut down the magnet and slid her from the tube.

"That wasn't so bad now was it?" Carla said.

"Piece of cake," Lucy said, refusing to admit she would never do this again. Never. "But we really need to get an open MRI. This one's too small."

"I know. Our patients complain about it all the time. Especially the noise."

"That can be a little nerve racking." Lucy swung off the cradle and stood.

"Tell the board to pony up the million we need for an open one and everyone will be happy."

"Only a million?"

"For a used one."

Lucy laughed. "A well used one."

"True. I'll get the images prepped and Dr. Jenner will go over them with you."

"Is he still here?"

"He went back to his office but said for me to call him as soon as we finished."

Twenty minutes later Lucy stood next to Jenner as he examined the images through half glasses that rode low on his nose. Not that she was very good at reading these studies but it looked good to her. Jenner took his time, running a finger over each image as if touching them gave him a better picture. Patience wasn't a strong point with Lucy but she stood quietly, waiting for him to finish.

He pulled off his glasses and turned to her. "Well you have a brain." He smiled. "Not that I doubted that."

"Maybe you should mention that to Birnbaum."

"I'll let you. When you tell him it's completely normal."

"That probably won't make his day."

Jenner shrugged. "Probably not. But don't let that ass get you all worked up."

"Unfortunately, that ass has a lot of power around here."

"Let's get your EEG done and when that's normal too, as I'm sure it will be, you can go wave the reports in his face."

"That'll make my day."

The EEG was indeed normal.

Took Lucy a few minutes to wipe and brush the EEG electrode paste from her hair and another five minutes to track down Birnbaum. He had just finished a case and was in the OR doctors' lounge, dictating his op report. Lucy waited for him to finish and then told him all her testing was normal and that Jenner had given her clean bill of health.

"That's wonderful news," he said.

"So am I off restrictions?"

His brow furrowed and he hesitated as if deciding the issue. Or maybe he was simply torturing her. Wouldn't put it past him. Finally, he said, "Well there are possibilities other than the physical ones."

She knew where this was going but cut him off before he could say anything else. "It's like I said. Too much work and not enough sleep."

"Stress does a lot of us in this business in."

"It's part of the job. You know that. And you know I can handle it. I always have."

"But it does tend to add up as the years go by."

"Look, I'm fine. I don't have any surgeries until next week and I'll be rested by then."

Again, he hesitated. "You're sure?"

"Of course. If I wasn't, I'd take myself off the schedule."

He stared at her for a beat and then nodded. "Okay. Since Jenner said you were okay I'll take his word for it. You're cleared to go back to the OR on Monday."

"Thanks."

"But if you feel anything—anything at all—I want to know about it. Deal?"

"Deal."

Deal my ass, Lucy thought as she walked from the medical office building that snugged against the east side of the hospital and up the stairs to the surgical floor. Birnbaum would continue to sniff around for some way to undermine her. And if he could somehow get her booted off staff—it wouldn't be the first time he had maneuvered a physician out the door—he and his buddy Elliot Meeks would again be at the top of the heap.

Why was all this happening now? Birnbaum on the warpath, patients going all goofy and psychotic, Martha doing the same, not to mention the crazy dreams she'd been having. With the launch of the new congenital heart surgery program and the development of the new cardiac surgical ICU, the timing couldn't really be worse. Cliches like when it rains it pours were cliches because they happen all too often. Just not to her.

જી

By the time Lucy looked over William Nevers' chart and walked to his room, it was just past nine a.m. Nevers was sitting in a chair, dressed in street clothes, an overnight bag on the floor near his feet.

"Anxious to get out of here?" Lucy asked.

"No offense but I'm ready to hit the streets."

"Any problems?"

"I feel great."

"Let's take a look." Nevers unbuttoned his shirt. Her exam showed that all was going well: lungs clear, heart normal, chest wound healing nicely. "Everything looks great."

"Told you."

"Anymore dreams?"

"If I said yes would you make me stay?"

"Probably not."

"Then yes. Last night was another doozy. Kept coming and going. Must've woke me up three or four times."

Lucy could relate to that. "Maybe they'll be better at home. In your own bed."

"I'm sure they will."

"I'm going to give you a pain med and something to help you sleep. Use them only if absolutely necessary since they could make your dreams more vivid."

"I don't rightly see how that's possible. What's more vivid than snakes?"

Lucy laughed. "True. Let me know if they aren't resolved after a couple of days."

After she dictated the discharge summary, wrote prescriptions, and signed Nevers' discharge orders, she walked down one flight to the ICU. Ronnie Draper was sitting up sipping water through a straw. He too was doing well and his exam, labs, and hemodynamics were all normal—for someone only twenty-four hours post-op.

"His chest tube drainage is down to practically nothing," ICU nurse Madison Fife said. "Only a hundred ccs the past twelve hours."

After most thoracic surgeries, including cardiac procedures such as Ronnie's VSD repair, chest tubes were left in place for at least the first twenty-four hours, and were removed only when the drainage of the residual post-op blood and tissue fluids had decreased to acceptable levels. The two clear plastic tubes that fell away from Ronnie's chest and connected to the wall-mounted suction device were clear, indicating that all was well inside the young man's chest cavity.

"Let's get them out then," Lucy said.

"How do you do that?" Ronnie asked. "Another operation?"

Lucy smiled. "Simply clip a couple of stitches and yank them."

"That sounds painful."

"Only for a second."

Once the tubes were out, Lucy ordered a portable chest x-ray to make sure his lungs remained inflated, she walked down a couple of cubicles and found Joseph Finch sitting up in bed, watching TV.

"I see you're back to earth," Lucy said.

"What happened?"

"You had a little bout of post-op psychosis. But it looks like the Haldol has settled that down."

"I don't remember much. The nurses said I was pretty out of it."

"You might say that."

"Does that mean something went wrong?"

"Not really. Just that your brain didn't care for the anesthetics and the bypass machine. Don't worry, it's temporary."

"Is that why I had such wild dreams last night?"

Lucy felt a knot grow in her gut. "What dreams?"

"Crazy stuff."

"Any snakes involved?"

He gave her a look. "No. Should there be?"

Lucy laughed. "No. Tell me about them."

"I don't remember much. A feeling that something was inside me eating away." He shook his head. "Guess that sounds strange."

"Dreams are always strange."

"It didn't hurt. I simply felt all cold and empty inside."

Cold and empty. The words rattled around in Lucy's head as she exited the hospital through the ER and into the doctor's parking area. That's exactly what she had experienced. Like a block of ice had settled in her chest. But not simply ice. More than that. Something cold, numb, and dead. Even evil and soulless.

When she reached her car, she hesitated and lifted her face to the sun, eyes closed. Its warmth felt good.

CHAPTER 24

"She had a rough night," Sue Cramer said as she led Lucy and Sam down to Martha's room. "We had to sedate her a couple of times."

As usual, Martha sat in her chair, facing the window. Lucy dragged a chair up next to Martha and sat down. She automatically checked her wrist pulse but Martha seemed not to notice.

"She ranted about all sorts of things. Said she needed help but of course couldn't tell me what. Her vital signs were all okay and she didn't seem to be in any discomfort."

Martha began to rock back and forth slightly, her face adopting a grimace, her eyes wide and glazed.

"No, no, no," Martha repeated in a steady rhythm.

"What's the matter, grandma?"

"No, no, no." She tightly waded the edge of the blanket that lay across her lap, her knuckles blanching. "No Scully. No Scully."

"She went off on Scully a few times, too," Sue said. "That seemed to wind her up the most."

Lucy glanced at Sam and then back to Sue. "Anything specific?"

"She just kept chanting his name over and over. I figured it was part of her perseveration."

"Perseveration?" Sam asked.

"It's when a patient keeps repeating the same word or phrase over and over," Lucy said.

"Like a mantra?"

Lucy smiled. "Sort of but we most often see it in dementias and some types of brain injury. Even in obsessive and autistic disorders."

Lucy slid from her chair and knelt in front of Martha, taking both her hands in hers. Martha's fingers were cold and her unfocused gaze remained aimed at the window as if she was unaware of Lucy. He eyes were moist and she began to rock back and forth. Her breathing deepened. Then her eyes widened and she dropped her gaze to Lucy. Her bony fingers tightened their grip.

"No Scully."

"What about Scully?"

"Scully. Scully. Scully." Her gaze drifted away, toward the wall, then the window again.

"Martha?" Lucy said, shaking her hands. "Look at me."

Martha actually seemed to focus on her. "MIne. Mine. Not yours. Mine."

"Your what?"

"Mine. Mine. Mine." Her gaze drifted again.

"Martha, look at me."

She did. "I'm sorry," she said. That sounded almost lucid. "Sorry. Sorry."

"About what?"

Martha leaned forward, her face now near Lucy's, her eyes now glistened with tears. "Give it to me. Me. Mine. Not yours. Mine."

"Give what to you?"

Martha collapsed back into her chair, eyes closed, sobs wracking her. "Give it back." Her voice now a wail.

"Martha, give what back?"

But Martha was gone. Receding again into her own world.

❧

Sam flung an arm around Lucy's shoulders as they walked out into the parking lot. "You okay?"

"Not even close."

"Any idea what that was about?"

"No. But I think it's time we had another talk with Scully."

"Why?"

"I'm not sure. But he seems important to Martha."

"Assuming she knows what she's saying."

Lucy sighed. "True. But something's changed. Ever since Scully the elder died on my operating table there have been a lot of odd things going on."

They climbed into Sam's Lexus.

"Okay," Sam said. "Let's take a spin by the church."

"My thoughts exactly."

"Want to call Ty and see if he wants to go with us?"

"No." Lucy shook her head. "I don't want Scully to feel threatened. I want some answers."

CHAPTER 25

"**I** knew you'd come back to us," John Scully said as Lucy and Sam walked into the church. He and Miriam were standing near the pulpit.

"Back?" Lucy said.

"Back to the church."

"That implies I was ever here."

"You were," Miriam said. "From the moment you breathed your first breath."

"You're not making sense."

Scully smiled. "You have always been a part of us. Martha and your parents saw to that."

Lucy glanced toward Sam. "Am I missing something here?"

"Doesn't make sense to me either," Sam said.

"You were baptized into the church when you were only days old."

"No offense, but I don't remember that. And no one ever bothered to tell me."

"But deep inside you know it's true," Scully said.

"I don't think so."

Felicia walked in, carrying a wooden box. She placed it on a table to Scully's left. The unmistakable buzzing of snakes rose from the box. Scully raised the lid and casually removed a fat rattlesnake. Its buzzing now adopted an angry tone.

Lucy and Sam each took a step back.

"I don't think that's a good idea," Sam said.

"Don't worry. I'm immune to the poison."

"I'm more worried about me and Lucy," Sam said.

"He's been bitten a dozen times," Miriam said. "His faith protects him."

"That and a little strychnine," Scully said.

"Strychnine?" Lucy asked. Her attention never drifted from the snake that now waved its head around as if looking for a suitable target. She felt perspiration gather along her back as her heart rate clicked up a notch. God, she hated snakes.

"A little sip neutralizes the poison," Miriam said.

"I must have missed that day in med school," Lucy said.

Miriam offered a maternal smile. "Can't learn everything from man's books. Only from the word of the Lord."

The snake coiled around Scully's arm, head raised. Lucy felt as if it was watching her. She took another half step back, Actually, she wanted to run out the door, but fought the impulse.

"Why snakes?" Sam asked. "What do they have to do with Jesus?"

Lucy knew Sam was playing cop now. Ty and Bump had told them about Scully's insane beliefs. And Sam had told her that Gladys Johnston had said the same thing. Sam was merely asking questions she already knew the answer to. Seeing if Scully changed his story in any way.

Now it was Scully's turn to offer a a paternal smile. It faded and his gaze seemed to glaze over. He spoke.

And he said unto them, Go ye into all the world, and preach the gospel to every creature.

He that believeth and is baptized shall be saved; but he that believeth not shall be damned.

And these signs shall follow them that believe; In my name shall they cast out devils; they shall speak with new tongues;

They shall take up serpents; and if they drink any deadly thing, it shall not hurt them; they shall lay hands on the sick, and they shall recover.

So then after the Lord had spoken unto them, he was received up into heaven, and sat on the right hand of God.

And they went forth, and preached everywhere, the Lord working with them, and confirming the word with signs following. Amen.

The quote Sam had shown her. The one Scully had written on the back of a menu.

"Mark Sixteen," Felicia said.

"I'm afraid I don't understand," Sam said. "This is the scripture that tells you to play with snakes?"

Scully gaze hardened. "It's not play. But you wouldn't understand."

"Explain it to me," Lucy said.

The snake worked its way up Scully's arm and around his neck, its triangular head continuing its wagging, its slitted eyes seeming to never leave her.

"Most Christians believe that Eden was perfection. That it was the place man was supposed to live. That if you lived a Christian life you would eventually return to Eden in Heaven."

"That's the way I remember it," Sam said.

"But it's not true. You see, man had to leave Eden before he could reach his true potential. In Eden, all was provided. There was no death or pain or loss. And no growth. No expansion of his understanding of himself. Or of God."

"Seems backwards to me," Lucy said.

"Remember the movie The Time Machine?" Felicia asked.

"Sure."

"The Eloi basically lived in Eden. And they did nothing, and knew nothing."

"So man needed to commit the original sin to be fulfilled?" Sam asked. "And I thought sins were bad things."

"But you see," Scully said. "It wasn't a sin to eat from the tree of knowledge. It was this that gave man the capacity to think. To appreciate all that God had created. To deserve his love."

"Let me see if I have this straight," Lucy said. "The serpent, the one that enticed Eve to eat the fruit, is actually mankind's savior?"

"Exactly," Miriam said. "And now that you have returned to us, you will come to know this truth."

"I'm not here to join your church. I'm trying to discover what the relationship between John Senior and Martha was."

Scully glanced at Miriam for a beat and then said, "Your grandmother and my father had a very special relationship."

"And that would be what?"

"There was great love between them. Martha had a unique understanding of our principles."

"You're saying Martha handled snakes?"

"No. Only a few blessed men get that honor."

"Like you and your father?"

"So far. But we have a couple of trainees now." He removed the snake from his neck and returned it to the box, stirring up a chorus of buzzing from the others inside. Sounded like a hundred to Lucy.

"Even if it's illegal?" Sam asked.

Another paternal smile from Scully. "There's man's law and then there's God's law."

"So what was Martha to the church?" Lucy asked.

"She was a true believer. She understood these beliefs very deeply."

"But she left the church."

"Faith can be lost just as it can be found."

"So why did she leave?"

"I think only Martha knows that."

"What about Pete Grimm and Marvin Purdy?" Sam asked. "Did they leave the church too?"

Scully's face hardened, his eyes cold, narrowed. "They lost their faith."

"And their lives."

"Yes. Tragic but true."

"You know anything about what happened to them?"

"Why are you asking?"

"I'm a cop. I tend to ask a lot of questions."

"You are in a house of God," Scully said. "I don't think you should be making allegations in such a place."

"Like you said, there's man's laws and then there's God's laws. I'm more interested in the former."

His jaw twitched and then his face softened and he flashed yet another fatherly smile. "Perhaps you should join our church too. It might soften your heart."

"Don't see that happening."

"Often the Lord enters our lives when least expected and transforms our souls. I've seen it many times."

"Don't hold your breath here," Sam said. "Me and the Lord had a falling out when he saw fit to give my mother cancer."

Scully recoiled slightly, more a twitch of his shoulders and a straightening of his spine. This was escalating into a true verbal duel. Lucy started to say something to diffuse it but from the corner of her eye she saw Felicia, eyes wide, studying Sam. As if she couldn't believe she would stand up to her father.

Scully's voice softened. "We aren't privy to the workings of HIs mind. He has a reason for everything He does."

"Just doesn't share it? Is that it?"

"One day it will all be revealed."

Sam shook her head. "Gee, I never heard that from a preacher before."

⁏

"You sure like to stir the pot, don't you?" Lucy asked.

They were back on the road, Sam winding down the hill toward town. Sunlight stabbed through the pines that flanked the road and through the open sunroof Sam could see that a few clouds dotted the otherwise clear sky.

"Always have. You know that."

"Do you really think Scully had anything to do with those murders?"

"How big is this county?"

"Not very. Why?"

"Only two murders in nearly a decade. Both under odd circumstances. Both victims former members of a small, snake-handling church. For a community this size it seems more than a little odd to me."

"When you put it that way."

"There's not really any other way to put it." Sam picked up her cell phone from the center console and handed it to Lucy. "Call Ty and put it on speaker."

"I don't have his number."

"Punch in seventeen."

"Really? You have him on speed dial?"

"Always a good idea to have the local police on speed dial."

Lucy laughed. "I'm sure that's it."

"Just call him."

Lucy did. Ty answered almost immediately. After Sam told him Lucy was with her and that he was on speaker and that they had been to see Scully, he asked, "Why'd you do that?"

"I wanted to know more about John Senior and Martha," Lucy said. "What her deal with that church was and why she left."

"What'd you find out?" Ty asked.

"Not much. He basically said I should ask Martha. Of course that's not really an option."

"Why'd you want to dig into all that?"

Lucy told him about their visit to Martha that morning and her repeating Scully's name over and over. "I think she was trying to tell me something."

"Isn't she completely out of it? How could she be telling you anything?"

"I don't know but she seemed to have flashes of lucidity. She was different. She looked at me. Actually spoke to me."

"I see."

"And Sam seems to think Scully might be involved in your two murder cases."

"She does have an active imagination."

"Whoa," Sam said. "It's my phone. Im sitting right here."

Ty laughed. "I know. I'm just poking a stick at you."

"I wouldn't recommend that," Lucy said. "She's like a coiled snake sometimes."

"Speaking of which," Sam said, "Scully had some of his snakes with him. One wrapped around his neck."

"He's a crazy son of a bitch," Ty said.

"No argument here," Sam said.

"What are you two up to now?"

"Do you know any church members who might be willing to talk with us?" Sam asked.

"They're a pretty tight-mouthed group. I'm not sure any current members would say a word without Scully's permission."

"He has that much control?"

"That's what I hear."

"Maybe someone who left the church," Sam said. "One that's still alive would help."

Ty laughed again and then paused a beat. "There's an old boy who might. Name's Gary Underhill. Owns a grocery store out on the county road toward Lynchburg."

"I know that place," Lucy said.

"He might talk," Ty said. "Want me to give him a call or maybe meet you there?"

"You might intimidate him," Sam said.

"I promise not to lay a hand on him. And I'll be polite."

Sam laughed. "But you have a badge. That might make him forgetful."

"Or make him talk."

"Maybe. But, I'd rather catch him off guard."

"Okay. You win. What about lunch afterwards?"

"I think we're headed to the gym," Sam said. "Lucy needs to work off some stress and I'm going all soft."

"Right."

"Maybe around noon?"

"Perfect. See you there."

CHAPTER 26

Felicia checked the latches on the snake box and then picked it up. "I'll take these guys back to their cages. Need anything else?"

"No, honey," her father said. "Do you have your Sunday school class ready yet?"

Felicia gave classes for the younger children every Sunday morning, before the services started. Had done so since she was ten.

"Almost."

"If you need any help, let me know."

"Will do."

Felicia used the corner of the snake box to push through the door that led down the hall to the storage area where the snakes were kept. As the door behind her eased closed she heard Miriam ask, "What are you going to do about this?"

Felicia stopped. She stood quietly, her ear near the door.

"About what?" Scully asked.

"John, don't play dumb. You know what I'm talking about."

"It'll be okay."

"You can't be sure of that."

"My father planned it perfectly. Everything is going according to his plan."

"Didn't seem that way to me. In fact, I'd say she is no where near returning to the church."

"Give it time."

"I have a bad feeling and you know when I have those they're always right."

"Not always."

"Don't get snappy. I'm still your mother."

"But you're wrong about this. She'll come around. It's inevitable."

"She's not ready. She was never prepared. Never trained in our ways. She can't be trusted with this power."

"But she's the perfect one. You know that. My father knew what he was doing."

"Not always. He was a good and righteous man but not infallible."

"No one is."

"But this was always a bad idea. I told him so."

"I know you did. Over and over."

"Don't you be smart with me. I have as much to lose here as you do. Maybe more."

The snake box was getting heavy but Felicia was afraid to put it down in case she had to move quickly. She didn't want to face her grandmother's glares or her father's temper, which she surely would if she were discovered eavesdropping. She wedged it between her hip and the wall, allowing her arms to relax a bit.

"He planned this," John said. "For years. Ever since she returned to town. Actually before that. Ever since she went up to Vandy. Ever since he knew she was returning. Which incidentally, he predicted she would. Years ago. Because of her position, her occupation, she is the perfect Keeper. I think what he did was brilliant."

"Not sure I'd call it that. And this whole mess has the potential to get out of hand. We can't afford to have that kind of power in the hands of a non-believer."

"She will become a believer. Father prophesized it."

"And if she doesn't?"

"Then we will deal with it."

"How?"

"We'll see. But whatever is necessary."

"Like Verna?"

Felicia took in an audible gasp. Her heart raced. Did they hear her? She eased the snake box away from the wall, ready to hurry away, but then Miriam spoke.

"Don't you think that might raise a few eyebrows? I mean another death from a snake bite would definitely attract attention. They might even take away all our snakes."

"They can't We're a church. We have a right."

"Don't mean they couldn't make trouble."

"Besides, simple elimination is not the answer in this case. We would have to retrieve what is ours."

"By you becoming the Keeper?"

"As I should have been anyway."

"So you don't agree with John's plan either?"

"That's not what I'm saying. I would have been the logical choice. The normal path of succession. I've been trained for it and would have willingly accepted it. But father felt otherwise and I accepted his authority in this matter."

"With no bitterness?"

"None. Once he explained the opportunity—the gift—that Lucy Wagner offered, I saw the wisdom in his choice."

Mariam sighed. "I hope you—and he—are right."

"She carries Martha's blood in her veins. She is in the perfect position to spread the word, so to speak. She is a brilliant choice."

"I 'spect we'll see."

༉

Felicia sat on her bed, trying to make sense of what she had heard. Her mother's death had been an accident. Everyone said so. But this?

Could her father have killed her mother? She saw no way that could be true. Could it have been her grandfather? He was definitely more . . . what was the word? . . . zealous. No that didn't sound right. Sounded so crazy, even cultish.

Was this all some cult? She had heard that before. Mostly from classmates. The ones that picked on her, picked on everyone. They accused her and her family of being in a cult.

She had also heard it murmured on the street, by people who thought she was out of earshot. Even read it in the newspaper from time to time. She remembered one headline blaring, "Eden's Gate A Dangerous Cult?" The reporter had gone on to say all manner of bad things about her church and her family. Things he knew nothing of. Things, like the snakes, that he had no way of understanding. Outsiders never seemed to grasp it.

The true word, anyway.

She guessed some of them were religious. Baptists, Methodists, Catholics, and the like. But if their religion was sacred to them, why shouldn't hers be just as sacred? Why shouldn't her father and her grandfather be just as devout and blessed as the preachers in those other churches? Why couldn't her church be just as good and pure as the next one? Even more so since the true word had been revealed to her grandfather.

But the real question was could a man, like her father, a man that led such a sacred group, commit murder? Kill his own wife. Kill another true believer?

No way.

Yet, how else could she read the conversation she had just overheard?

A knock at her door.

"Yes?"

"You going into town with us?" It was Miriam.

Felicia suddenly realized she had been crying. She rubbed the heels of both hands across her eyes.

"I think I'll stay here and work on my Sunday class."

"That's good. We won't be long."

CHAPTER 27

·

Underhill's Market sat just over four miles from town on the south side of a broad curve in a two-lane blacktop that eventually led to Lynchburg. Yellow cinder block with a tan, asphalt tile roof, its front lot occupied by a lone vehicle—a gunmetal gray Chevy sedan nosed up to the wall beneath a white sign with bright blue hand lettering that read "Ice—Meat—Vegetables." The glass front door and its two flanking windows were covered with multicolored lettering that boasted eggs for $3.99 a dozen, bacon $5.49 a pound, and milk $3.29 per half gallon.

Everything you needed for breakfast around here. Almost.

Sam wondered what grits went for as she and Lucy climbed out of her SUV.

Inside, a man, who Sam assumed was Gary Underhill, stood behind the counter. Painfully thin, with a prominent Adam's apple, and thinning gray hair, he wore gray slacks and a white short-sleeved shirt buttoned against his neck. He was ringing up purchases for a stout woman in baggy jeans and an untucked plaid work shirt. The woman held a child, a girl, maybe two years old, in one arm, the child facing over her shoulder, looking at Sam and Lucy with huge brown eyes.

The store reminded Sam of the market near her house in Mercer's Corner. Two central isles packed with canned and packaged goods, fresh vegetable bins along the right wall, cold cases with dairy products along the left, and refrigerated cases filled with ice cream, frozen dinners, and bags of ice against the rear wall. While Underhill finished helping the woman, Sam moved down one of the aisles. The canned goods were neatly arranged as were several shelves of soft drinks, bottled water, and beer. She came to a display of crackers and cookies and immediately saw a box of Moon Pies. Her stomach growled so she grabbed a couple, sure that Lucy would want one too. She then found a pair of RC Colas and walked to the counter.

"You need any help with that, Stephanie?" Underhill asked the woman as she hooked a grocery bag with her free arm.

"I got it."

"You take care now," Underhill said, and then to the child, "And Chrissy, you mind your mother."

The child immediately buried her face in her in her mother's neck. Stephanie nodded to Sam and walked toward the door.

Underhill looked at Sam. "Anything else?"

Lucy walked up. "What's that?" She indicated the items Sam had placed on the counter.

"I'm starving and I figured you were too."

"Good call."

"That'll do it," Sam said to Underhill.

He rang it up and Sam paid. She unwrapped one of the Moon Pies and took a bite. "I do love these things."

"And you're the California girl." Lucy peeled back the wrapper on hers.

"California?" Underhill asked. "What part?"

"Southern. The high desert. Place called Mercer's Corner."

He nodded. "Never heard of it."

"Neither has anyone else," Sam said.

Underhill had been studying Lucy and now asked, "Aren't you Dr. Wagner?"

"I am."

He extended a hand. "I've heard good things about you. Proud to make your acquaintance."

They shook and Lucy introduced Sam.

"What brings you here from California?" Underhill asked.

"Lucy and I are old friends so I came for a visit."

"Well I'm glad you did and I'm glad you stopped by."

"Mind if I ask a couple of questions?" Sam said.

"About what?"

"The Eden's Gate Church."

Underhill showed a flash of surprise and then looked toward Lucy before coming back to Sam. "What about it?"

"I understand you used to be a member."

"Yep."

"But you left?"

"Yes, I did."

"Why?"

He hesitated. "Didn't really have the time and after my wife died a few years ago, I sort of gave up on it."

"On what? Eden's Gate or religion in general?" Sam took another bite of Moon Pie.

Underhill scratched his chin. "A little of both."

Sam twisted the cap off her RC and took a sip. "I understand you had some sort of misunderstanding with the church. Or with the Scullys."

Another hesitation. "Why are you asking about this?"

Sam shrugged. "Just curious."

Underhill nodded but said nothing.

"My grandmother belonged to the church," Lucy said.

"I know."

"You know Martha?"

"Of course. At one time she was very active in the church but she stopped coming too."

"Any idea why?" Sam asked.

He glanced toward the front door and then back to Sam. "I don't feel comfortable talking about this."

"Why?" Sam asked.

"It's personal." Then to Lucy, "Why don't you ask Martha why she left?"

"I'd love to but unfortunately she has severe dementia and doesn't communicate much. At least not in a coherent manner."

"I'm sorry to hear that," Underhill said. He sighed. "She's a very special person."

"I think so too," Lucy said. "That's why I'm trying to understand why she left a church she had been involved with for so long."

Underhill's gaze softened and he took a deep breath, letting it out slowly. Another glance toward the door. "But this goes no further. Okay?"

Sam and Lucy nodded.

"Martha left many years ago. And the truth is I'm not sure why. I know she and John Scully—the older one—had a falling out. Not sure exactly why but I think it had something to do with the direction the church was moving. That's why I left anyway."

"What didn't you like?" Sam asked. "The snakes?"

"That was part of it. I was never into all that snake stuff but I still believed in John Scully. At first. But then he changed. He began talking about his God-given powers. How God had named him to carry on his word. How he alone understood the true message of God's words."

"So he had a direct line to the Lord?" Lucy asked.

"Said he did. Said the power to understand and decipher His words was passed to him by his old mentor." Underhill glanced up toward the ceiling for a beat as if in thought and then continued, "Can't recall his name. Some guy Scully studied under up in West Virginia. Apparently when the old boy died he passed along this unique power to John Senior."

"Sounds a bit culty to me," Sam said.

Underhill smiled. "Culty. I like that word. If it is a word. Anyway, that's exactly how I felt. He was grooming John, Junior to take over and from what I could see, Junior bought into that whole messianic message even more than the old man."

"So you split?" Sam asked.

"That's right."

"Did you know Peter Grimm and Marvin Purdy?"

"Yes."

"I'm going to ask an odd question," Sam said. "Do you think Scully had anything to do with their murders?"

"No. Not really."

"Not really?"

"I've got to admit it crossed my mind."

"Why?"

Another chin scratch. "John, neither of the Johns, liked to be challenged. Wanted their word to be taken as gospel. Both Peter and Marvin questioned a bunch of what they preached."

"And that made them angry?"

"Seemed that way to me."

"Did Scully, either Scully, make any direct threats to either of them?" Sam asked.

"Not that I know. But after they left he did remark on more than a few occasions that they had lost their faith and were doomed to hell." He flattened both palms on the counter and leaned forward, resting his weight on his stiffened arms. "Course he said that about anyone who wasn't a true believer—as he called the church members."

"Did you ever have a run in with either of the Scullys?" Lucy asked.

"Both. When I began to pull away, they weren't real happy."

"Did they threaten you?" Sam asked.

"Not directly. John Junior did tell me once not to bad mouth the church. He thought I'd said a few derogatory things."

"DId you?"

"Some. People wanted to know why I left my church and I wasn't bashful about telling them."

"He say what he'd do?" Sam asked. "If you trash talked the church?"

"Nothing specific. Just that the Lord was a vengeful Lord and didn't take kindly to folks talking about his disciples. Made ill things happen to non-believers."

"Sounds like a threat to me," Sam said.

"Maybe. Regardless, I decided it might be wise to keep my opinions to myself." He straightened and crossed his arms over his chest. "Truth is this is the first time I've talked about it in years."

"I appreciate it," Lucy said.

"You know anyone else that might talk to us?" Sam asked. "Anyone who left the church or had problems with the Scullys?"

"I'd rather not say."

"You afraid? Of the Scullys?"

He sighed. "Not really afraid, but I'd rather not stir them up."

Sam stared at him but said nothing.

Underhill stared back for a beat and then sighed. "You might try Dwight Doucet. He left shortly after I did."

"Any idea why?"

"Same reason I did. The Scullys were getting all crazy with power. Or so it seemed."

"Any idea where we might reach him?" Sam asked.

"He's got a farm on down the road here. I can give you his number."

"That would be great."

He opened a drawer beneath the counter, rummaged around, and came up with a scrap of paper. Using the pencil that lay on the counter, he scribbled on the paper and slid it toward Sam. Before he let go, he said, "But you can't tell him you got it from me."

Back in the car, Sam called Doucet's number. No answer. She cranked the engine, backed away from the building, and pulled on to the road. "What do you think?"

"I think Mr. Underhill's scared," Lucy said.

"Seems like a lot of people are."

"Let's go meet Ty at the gym and work off those Moon Pies."

"Sounds like a plan."

CHAPTER 28

It was a massacre. A word unfamiliar to the citizens of Remington, unless it was some news report from Atlanta, or Detroit, or New York, or some other large, dangerous urban area. But in this case, no other word fit.

Lucy couldn't believe that just ten minutes earlier she had been basking in the afterglow of an intense workout and a steaming hot shower. As she pushed through the door that led from the women's locker room to the lobby of the River Athletic Club, a two-story glass-walled facility that sat near the Crockett Bridge and overlooked the Remington River, her legs beginning to stiffen from her forty-five minutes laboring up the stair-climber, she saw Sam and Ty standing near the front door. Sam, gym bag on the floor near her feet, was pulling her still damp hair into a ponytail, securing it with a scrunchy hair tie, while Ty pressed his cell phone to his ear, concern on his face.

"What's happening?" Lucy asked Sam, nodding toward Ty.

"Don't know. Doesn't sound good though."

Ty snapped his cell closed. "Got to go."

"What is it?"

"I'm not sure. A shooting. Sounds like multiple victims. Or at least that's what Teri says she was told." Teri Raines, the police dispatcher. "Apparently a neighbor called it in."

"Where? Who?" Lucy asked.

Ty shouldered open the front door and hurried up the sidewalk toward his Tahoe. Sam and Lucy struggled to keep up.

"Caller said the shooter is William Nevers."

Lucy grabbed Ty's arm, yanking him to a halt. "Who?"

Ty stared at her. "Nevers. William Nevers."

"Jesus." Lucy let go of his arm and took a step back. "He's a patient of mine. He had surgery. Just got out of the hospital."

"I got to run," Ty said. "I'll call and let you know what the story is after I know."

"We're coming with you," Lucy said.

"No, you're not."

"I wasn't asking permission."

"Look. I don't know what the situation is. It could be dangerous."

"He's my patient. I'm going."

Ty looked at Sam. "Can you talk some sense into her?"

"Probably not. Wouldn't matter anyway. I'm coming too."

Now as Sam pulled her SUV to the curb behind Ty's Tahoe, Lucy saw three bodies, all bloody: two women crumpled in the front yard of the house next to William Never's home; a man sprawled in the middle of the street. Next to the man stood another man Lucy didn't recognize. A shotgun rested across one arm and he appeared pale and shaken. He looked at them as Ty climbed from his vehicle and walked toward him, Lucy and Sam following. A small crowd of neighbors had gathered on the sidewalk across the street, mostly wide-eyed, silent, disbelief etched on each face.

"I had to," the man said.

Ty had unholstered his gun, holding it at his side. "The gun." He nodded toward the shotgun. "Put it down."

The man bent and carefully laid it on the asphalt. "I had to."

"Had to what?" Ty asked.

"Shoot him. He pointed that gun at me." He indicated another shotgun that lay a few feet away.

Lucy now recognized the fallen man as William Nevers. She stepped forward and knelt next to him, checking for a pulse, finding none. She then hurried to the two women, again finding no pulses. She walked back to where Ty and Sam stood, shaking her head. "All dead."

"What happened?" Sam asked the distraught man.

Before he could answer, Bump pulled up and climbed from his truck. "What the hell is going on?" he asked as he approached them, adjusting his gun belt.

"Not sure yet," Ty said. "He was just fixing to tell us."

The man, Albert Headley, lived across the street and apparently heard several gunshots. He looked out his front window and saw William Nevers burst out his front door and head next door to the Tate house, the house with the two bodies out front. He kicked open their front door and Headley heard another gunshot. By the time he retrieved his shotgun from its rack in his den and stepped out on his front stoop, Catherine Tate and her daughter Katie ran from their home. Katie had been shot in the hip and Catherine was helping her flee. They only made it into the front yard before Nevers gunned them down with two shots from his twelve gauge pump.

"So I yelled at him," Headley said. "At first he didn't seem to hear me and just stood there over their bodies. So I yelled again. That's when he started right at me."

"And you shot him?" Ty asked.

"I tried to talk to him first. Told him to put his gun down. But by the time he reached the street he drew down on me." He fought back a sob. "I had to."

Ty laid a hand on his shoulder. "It's okay." He turned and looked back toward Nevers' house. "Did you go inside?"

Headley shook his head. "No."

Ty looked at Bump. "Let's check it out."

"I'll go with you," Sam said.

"Better wait here," Ty said.

"And I was just thinking another set of experienced eyes couldn't hurt," Bump said.

"Looks like I'm outnumbered," Ty said.

⤮

Lucy watched them enter the house, Ty and Bump leading with guns drawn, Sam close behind. She then asked Headley, "Any idea why this happened? Did he have issues with his neighbors?"

"Not at all. They were very close."

Lucy felt a growing dread well up inside. A dread that had reared up as soon as she learned that William Nevers was the shooter. Now it expanded, becoming an icy ball in her chest.

"In fact, Bill is Katie's godfather," Headley continued. He sighed. "This don't make a lick of sense."

"Have you seen him since his surgery?"

"Just last night. We sat on his patio and talked for an hour. Until he got tired and needed to go lie down."

"Did he seem okay?"

Headley hesitated a beat. "Yeah. Mostly."

"Mostly?"

"He was tired of course. And his memory wasn't what it usually is. But I figured it was just from what he'd been through."

That was common. Fatigue for a few weeks or even months after cardiac surgery was common and memory problems were essentially universal after being on the heart-lung bypass machine. No one knew exactly why, there were many theories tossed around, but the truth is that no one came off bypass as smart as they went on. Usually it was simply minor holes in memory, forgotten phone numbers and things like that. But Lucy, like every cardiac surgeon, had seen more than a few cases of significant memory problems, or difficulty remembering how to do even simple math. She had had a couple of accountants who could no longer do their jobs. Couldn't make the numbers behave. As if they developed some form of numerical dyslexia.

And sure some experienced emotional lability and angry outbursts, mostly due to frustration and depression. Some did indeed act out and do some fairly bizarre things. But this? A massacre of his neighbors? Maybe his family? Lucy didn't want to think about what might be found inside the Nevers' home.

Her brain was in full differential diagnosis mode. Running through what could cause such violent behavior. A stroke? A medication reaction? Post-pump psychosis? Sleep deprivation? Infections of various types?

"Memory deficits aren't uncommon," Lucy said. "But did you notice anything else?"

"Like what?"

"Confusion? Disorientation? Any change in his emotions?"

"He said he hadn't been sleeping well. That he was exhausted. Said he'd been having some wild dreams. About snakes or serpents or whatever."

The ice ball in Lucy's chest grew.

"But to me," Headley said, looking Lucy in the eye. "He seemed scared. Like maybe he thought something was wrong."

"Did he say what? Anything specific?"

Headley's gaze dropped toward his shoes, which now kicked at a loose pebble. "Not really."

"What was it, Albert? What did he say?"

"I'm sure he didn't mean it."

"Mean what?"

He sighed, glanced up toward a nearby Maple tree, obviously buying time, but then his gaze returned to Lucy. "Said he thought you put something inside him. Something evil." He looked away. "That's the word he used."

❧

Sam followed Ty and Bump through the living and dining room, and entered the kitchen. At first she saw nothing out of place but then a spray of blood on the refrigerator caught her eye. Ty rounded the short counter that separated the kitchen from the small breakfast nook. He suddenly stopped.

"Jesus."

Sam looked past him. A woman, half her face blown away, lay on the tile floor, a halo of dark gelatinous blood around her head.

"It's Pattie Nevers," Ty said.

Down a hallway they found Nevers' daughter Megan, in her room, lying on her bed, the book she had apparently been reading still balanced on her chest as if she had simply fallen asleep. Of course her destroyed face from what had obviously been a close range shotgun explosion and the blood, brain tissue, and skull fragments that peppered the bedding and the wall told a much different story. The pillow beneath her head had exploded and synthetic fibers of some type covered the bed and floor like fallen snow.

"Ain't this some shit?" Bump said.

"If it ain't, I don't want to see the real shit," Ty said.

"You guys sure have a way with words," Sam said.

Ty shrugged. "It is what it is."

"Let's get the crew out," Bump said. "Start gathering some evidence." He sighed. "Not that there's much doubt about who did what to who."

"I'll give Larry a call," Ty said.

CHAPTER 29

L ucy wanted to leave. Put distance between herself and the scene of so much senseless carnage. Away from the corpse of William Nevers, now, like the bodies of Catherine and Katie Tate, covered with blankets Bump had pulled from his truck, saying he felt the folks gathered along the street had seen enough and the dead deserved at least a slice of dignity. The three plaid wool mounds would have been comical if they weren't so— what was the word she searched for? Sad? Disturbing?

But Lucy didn't leave. Rather she waited until Dr. Larry Granville, the chief of pathology at the hospital as well as the county coroner, arrived. She wasn't sure why she felt the need to hang around. Maybe it was that part of her that felt she needed to pass off her patient, rather her late patient, to Larry. Not abandon William Nevers. Even though there was nothing she could do for him now. Nevers now belonged to Granville. A homicide statistic in a county whose murders could be counted on two fingers. Until now.

Sam was inside Nevers' home with Ty and Bump, doing the police thing. Fifteen minutes earlier, a couple of guys from the crime lab had appeared and they also went inside, each carrying a tackle box of supplies. Then Sam had come out and told her that Pattie and Megan Nevers had suffered a fate similar to the Tate women. Lucy was struck by how calm and clinical

Sam had been as she described the brutal murders. Yet she understood. She could do the same with even the most gruesome medical situations. Not that it didn't bother her, sometimes deeply, just that her training and experience had taught her how to look past the horror and do her job. Sam had the same capacity when dealing with the tragic events of her world.

Cops and docs shared that ability.

"Looks like we'll be here for a bit yet," Sam said. "If you need to leave take my Lexus." She handed Lucy the keys. "I'll catch a ride with Ty."

"I'll wait until Larry Granville gets here."

Sam nodded. "If you need to go, don't worry, I'll be fine." Sam turned and headed back into the Nevers' home.

While Lucy waited, leaning against Sam's SUV, arms crossed over her chest, she avoided eye contact with the throng of neighbors that now numbered several dozen. Each time she did catch someone's gaze, it seemed hostile and accusatory. Like this was her fault. Like she was some evil mastermind who with her own hands had created Frankenstein's monster in the form of William Nevers. She was sure she was just being paranoid and over-reading their gazes. She was sure the looks were more curious than accusing, but logic couldn't tamp down her feelings. So she kept her head down while her mind raced.

Was this her fault? Did she do something wrong? Pass something along to William Nevers? Ridiculous. Physiologically impossible. Yet—— how could she explain Nevers' nightmares? Her own nightmares? Joseph Finch's paranoid outburst?

Easy, she thought. Nevers had post-anesthesia, post-bypass nightmares. Not that uncommon. Her own crazy dreams were from stress. She had had the full neuro work up and all was okay. Stress was the answer. And Finch? A classic case of post-pump psychosis. She had seen it many times.

She glanced toward Nevers' house. But this? How could she explain this? What stress could push a normal and decent man to commit a massacre like this? Probably an extreme case of post-pump psychosis. Or so she wanted to believe. The logical half of her mind told her no other explanation was possible. Yet to the other half, the half where logic wasn't allowed, this felt like something else. She wasn't sure what, but this didn't fit any pattern she had ever seen.

Fortunately, before her mind could race down another scary corridor, Larry Granville pulled to the curb behind Sam's Lexus and stepped out.

"Lucy. What's the story here? I hear some folks got shot." HIs gaze traveled toward the three covered corpse. "Oh my goodness."

Lucy told him what she knew. As she finished, he eyed her, an eyebrow raised.

"You okay?"

"Of course."

"You look a little pale."

"William Nevers was my patient. I operated on him just a week ago."

"I'm sorry."

Lucy shrugged. "Life's a bitch sometimes."

He hesitated a beat, as if not sure how to respond, and then said, "I'd better get inside."

❧

Lucy parked Sam's SUV in the doctor's parking area adjacent to the ER and entered the hospital through a side door. Less chance of running into any of her colleagues that way. She was sure the news had reached the hospital grapevine by now and she was in no mood to be quizzed about it. Of course that would happen as soon as she reached the ICU but at least this way she could avoid having to repeat the story over and over.

A headache blossomed behind her eyes.

She pushed through the double doors and into the ICU. Madison Fife looked up from behind the nurse's station counter.

"Is it true?" she asked. "About Mr. Nevers?"

And so it begins.

Lucy nodded. "I'm afraid so."

A couple of other nurses walked up just as Madison asked, "What happened?"

Lucy told the story she didn't want to tell but knew she had to.

"My, God," Madison said. "He seemed so—normal—when we discharged him. Any idea why this happened?"

Lucy looked at the three faces that stared at her. Faces that wanted an explanation she simply didn't have. She could give them all the logical stuff, the post-pump psychosis diagnosis, but they already knew that. They too had seen it before. Somehow that seemed insulting. As if she were some politician trying to lie her way into office. The truth was she was asking herself the same questions she saw on their faces. Questions with no answers.

She sighed. "I don't know. It's beyond me."

Lucy walked around the counter and twirled the chart rack until she found Ronnie Draper's and then Joseph Finch's charts. She removed each and sat down, flipping open Finch's chart. The move was as much to avoid further questions as it was her need to do something ordinary. Something familiar. Something that would bring her world back to reality. She felt more than saw the two nurses slide away, heading back to their patients' cubicles, back to work, Lucy hearing one of them say, "It's awful. Just awful."

Awful hardly seemed strong enough.

"How's Mr. Finch doing today?" she asked Madison.

"He's back on planet Earth if that's what you mean. And his vitals are stable. He had a good lunch."

"Let's go see him."

Finch was sitting in bed, dozing but awoke and yawned as Lucy walked in. "Dr. Wagner. How are you today?"

"I was just going to ask you that."

"I'm fine. Aren't I, Madison?"

"Yes, you are."

Lucy stood beside his bed. "At least you recognize me today."

He shrugged. "I hear I was a little crazy yesterday."

"A little?" Lucy smiled.

"Sorry about that."

"Not really your fault. It happens from time to time."

"Madison tells me it was probably a combination of the anesthesia and the bypass pump."

"That'd be my bet."

"And the dreams too?"

Lucy felt the hair on her neck snap to attention. "What dreams?"

"Had them off and on all night."

"Tell me about them. If you can remember."

"Oh, I remember. Odd, crazy stuff. Like I was smothering or drowning or something. But I wasn't in the water or anything like that. I was in a wooded area. Not like around here though. I mean there were pine trees alright but also some tropical looking stuff. And thick vines. And then a snake would fall right out of a tree. Land right on me. Knock me down. Coil around my neck like it wanted to strangle me. That's when I'd wake up."

The ice ball Lucy had felt in her chest earlier reappeared. She did not want to hear this. Not now. Not today.

"Same dream? Every time?"

"Yep. Every time I'd fall asleep. Fact is, just now, right before you woke me, it was starting up again."

Lucy's hands felt as if they had frozen solid. As if they might crack and shatter like crystal dropped on concrete. She shoved them into the pockets of her white coat.

After she reassured Finch that all was okay, assurances she wasn't completely confident in, she moved down a couple of cubicles to see

Ronnie Draper. He sat in a chair, looking out the window. Only twenty-four hours after she had had his heart open, sewing a patch over his large VSD, he looked like nothing had happened.

"I feel great," he answered when Lucy asked how things were going. "A little sore, but otherwise great. In fact, I feel better than I have in years."

"Your heart is working a little more efficiently without a hole in it."

He laughed and then hugged the pillow in his lap to his chest. "Guess I ain't ready to laugh yet. And coughing sure ain't no fun."

"That's my fault," Lucy said with a smile. "But it'll get better day by day."

"So when do I go home?"

Lucy shook her head. "Cool your jets. You just had surgery yesterday."

"Well I feel like I could wrestle a warthog and win. Except for those crazy dreams I had last night."

Lucy didn't want to hear this either. "What kind of dreams?"

"I don't usually remember my dreams. My mom says she does. In great detail. But I've never been able to. But these I do. At least some of it. All I now is that every time I'd doze off I'd be surrounded by snakes or something like that. I mean, I couldn't see them well, just shadowy, slivery things. Scaly and rubbing all over me. Crazy, huh?"

"A little."

"Each time I'd wake up in a bit all sweaty and shaky. Not fun."

Chapter 30

"**G**ranville's going to do the autopsies tomorrow." Bump said. "Not that they'll tell us anything we don't already know."

Sam sat with him and Ty at a corner table at JT's BBQ. After three hours working the crime scene, they had been at JT's just long enough for the waitress to serve a beer to Bump and bourbon to her and Ty. They were waiting for Lucy to join them before ordering dinner but were munching on the roasted peanuts that sat in metal buckets on each table, shells tossed on the floor.

"Glad I don't have his job," Ty said.

Sam popped a couple of peanuts into her mouth and spoke around them. "I meant to tell you guys earlier, Lucy and I stopped by and had a chat with Gary Underhill."

"What'd he have to say?" Ty asked.

Sam told them about the conversation concluding with, "So, Underhill had a falling out with Scully. Not so much because of the snakes, though that would do it for me, but more because Scully began preaching about this new power to talk with God that he had gotten from some old dude up in West Virginia."

"If that ain't a cult I don't know what is," Bump said.

"My thoughts exactly," Sam said. She took a sip from her bourbon. "Underhill seemed reluctant to talk. He finally did when Lucy told him about Martha's dementia. Apparently he had a very good relationship with her."

"Reluctant?" Bump asked.

She ran a finger around the rim of her glass. "More than reluctant. He seemed scared."

"Of Scully?"

"Of something." Another sip. "Oh, that reminds me." She rocked up on one hip and tugged a scrap of paper from the back pocket of her jeans, unfolding it, glancing at the name and phone number Underhill had written on it. "He told us we might want to talk to Dwight Doucet."

"That's right," Ty said. "I forgot Dwight used to be a member."

"I called earlier but he wasn't home. Let me try again. Back in a sec."

Sam walked outside, cell phone in hand. As she dialed the number, Lucy walked around the corner.

"What're you doing?" she asked.

"Trying Dwight Doucet again. Ty and Bump are inside. Toward the back." And then into the phone, "Mr. Doucet?"

"Who's calling?" Doucet's voice was strong and clear.

"This is Sam Cody. I'm a friend of Dr. Lucy Wagner's and I, actually Lucy and I, wanted to talk with you about her grandmother Martha."

"What about her?"

"I understand that you know her."

"For many years. I hear she's not doing well. Dementia or something like that."

"That's right."

"I'm sorry to hear that. She's a special lady. So what can I tell you?"

"Both of you belonged to Eden's Gate Church at one time."

He hesitated a beat. "That's true."

"That's what we want to talk about."

Another hesitation. "Not sure I'm comfortable with that."

"Why?"

"Just not. Don't want to bring no trouble my way."

"What trouble could come from talking with us?"

"You ain't from around here, are you?"

"No."

"Then you wouldn't understand."

"Just between us. No one else need know."

"As far as you know."

"I beg your pardon."

"As far as you know no one will know. The Scully clan has ways of finding out all sorts of stuff."

"I don't see how."

"You'd be surprised what they can dig up."

"It'd be a big help if you'd just answer a couple of questions."

Sam could hear a deep sigh come through the phone. "Okay. But not on the phone."

"Where?"

"Can't be till tomorrow."

"That's okay. Tell me when and where and we'll be there."

"How about the parking lot behind the library? Say around ten?"

"Okay. See you then."

CHAPTER 31

"He isn't coming," Sam said.

"Let's give him a few more minutes," Lucy said. "Maybe he's just running late."

They were sitting in Sam's Lexus in the small asphalt lot behind the library. Only a dozen spaces, three others occupied.

"You mean like he's caught in a traffic jam?" Sam said.

"Funny."

"Yesterday, when I spoke with him, he sounded scared. Like if he talked to us something bad would happen."

"That's crazy. How could talking to us about Martha be a problem?"

"He said I'd be surprised what the Scullys could find out."

"Why is everyone so afraid of these people? They're just religious nut jobs."

"The most dangerous type," Sam said. "History's full of them. True religion gives you license to do all sorts of things. Sacrifices, genocides, even fly planes into tall buildings."

"Aren't you being a little dramatic here?" Lucy said. "I don't think Scully will fly a plane into city hall."

"Probably not. But he does have all those snakes."

"Don't remind me."

"Gary Underhill was scared," Sam said. "Martha, too."

A dark blue four-door Chevy pulled into the lot.

"Maybe that's him," Lucy said.

It wasn't. The car settled into an empty slot. A woman, cradling a baby in one arm and a stack of books in the other, stepped out and climbed the short steps into the library's rear entrance.

"Like I said, he isn't coming," Sam said. She opened her cell phone and dialed. "Is Ty Everson in?"

"Who's calling?"

"Sam Cody. I have a quick question for him."

Took only a few seconds and Ty was on the line.

"What are you up to today?" he asked.

"We're at the library."

"Doing more research?"

"Waiting for Dwight Doucet to show up. But he isn't going to. Do you have an address for him?"

"Why? You going to drop by and see him?"

"That's the plan."

"Want me to go with you?"

"No."

"No? I feel so rejected."

"While you cry over that little disappointment, do you have an address?"

"You're a hard woman, Sam Cody."

"So I hear."

She could hear his soft chuckle and then he said, "Dwight has a farm out off Pulgas Road. Pulgas turns right off the highway about a mile past Underhill's store. You'll see his place a couple of miles up on the left. First house you'll come to. White clapboard."

"Thanks."

"Sure you don't want company?"

"Maybe lunch when we get back to town."

"That'll work."

Sam cranked the Lexus to life.

"We'll probably miss him." Lucy said. "He'll be here and we'll be there."

"He's not coming." Sam spun out of the lot, hanging a left. She caught a green light, accelerated past the courthouse, and headed out of town.

"How do you know that?" Lucy asked.

"Instinct. Common sense."

"Really? That's your evidence? Your gut?"

"Don't you trust your gut? Everyday?"

"Of course."

"So do I. And my cop's gut tells me Doucet is too afraid to talk to us."

"But he agreed to."

"Maybe just to get me off the phone and buy him time to lay low." She glanced over at Lucy, who didn't appear convinced. "Besides, it's a nice day for a drive in the country."

It was. The sky was clear and cloudless, the temperature still in the 70s, and a soft breeze nudged the leaves of the trees that flanked the road to life. The turn off to Doucet's farm was a weather-worn two-lane blacktop that wound up over a rise and then flattened into a dark ribbon that cut through gently rolling fields. Soon, Doucet's house came into view.

He wasn't there. Or if he was he was hiding under the bed or in a closet. Sam knocked on the front and back doors, shouted his name, circled the house peering in each window. Dark and quiet.

"He's probably at the library, waiting on us," Lucy said.

They backtracked to the library, no Doucet, Sam saying, "I told you."

They headed to Wellstone Manor to check on Martha.

ॐ

"She was restless last night," Sue Cramer said over her shoulder as she led Sam and Lucy down the hall toward Martha's room. "The night crew said she climbed out of bed and crawled out into the hallway a couple of times."

"She didn't hurt herself did she?" Lucy asked.

"Nah. She's too tough for that. They said she was mumbling some stuff they couldn't understand. They finally gave her some Ativan and she slept through the night."

"What about this morning?"

"No problems. She had a good breakfast and has been in her chair staring out the window all morning."

They entered the room.

Martha's chair sat facing the window. No Martha.

"Where is she?" Lucy asked. Head on a swivel.

"There," Sam said pointing.

Martha's legs protruded from beneath her bed, one foot bare, the other with a pink fuzzy slipper.

"Jesus," Lucy said. She dropped down on all fours and peered beneath the bed. Martha didn't move. Her eyes were closed and her breathing slow and steady. "Martha?" Lucy grabbed her leg and shook it.

Martha jerked awake, withdrawing her leg. She looked back toward Lucy and then began frantically worming further beneath the bed. "No, no, no."

"Martha, look at me."

"MIne. It's mine." Her legs pumped but she couldn't get traction. She looked as if she were trying to swim.

"Relax. It's me. Lucy."

Martha kicked at her. "Mine. Not yours. Mine."

Lucy sat up on her haunches. "Can you help me get her out?"

It took a couple of minutes, seemed longer, Martha fighting them as best she could. Finally Lucy and Sam each grabbed a leg and pulled her from beneath the bed. Martha kicking and twisting and screeching that they wanted to kill her.

"I'll get some Ativan," Sue said and hurried out the door.

Sam and Lucy managed to extract Martha, having to break her grip on one of the bed's legs and then the frame edge, and finally got her up into the bed. Martha's struggles continued.

Lucy grabbed her shoulders, holding her down, while Sam struggled to control her flailing legs. Martha's screams took on a tortured, hysterical quality. Sue returned, syringe in hand, and jabbed Martha's hip, delivering the needed sedative. Sam and Lucy did not loosen their grips, waiting for the drug to take effect.

"Martha, it's me. Lucy."

Martha's now wildly opened eyes snapped toward her. With her one free hand she fisted Lucy's blouse.

"It's mine. Mine. Not yours. Mine."

"What's yours?"

"It's all mine. Give it to me."

Martha's struggles weakened as the drug began to take hold.

"Any idea what's she talking about?" Lucy asked.

Sue shrugged. "Nonsense. As usual."

Was it?, Lucy thought. She knew that demented people often spoke gibberish. Made no sense. Even became agitated and fearful, as Martha was now. But Martha rarely made any sense. Rarely spoke in sentences or in any coherent fashion. Usually just a string of meaningless words or sounds. But this? It appeared to Lucy that Martha recognized her and had to tell her something. Something Martha thought was important.

"What is it that's yours?" Lucy asked.

"MIne. Not yours. Always mine." Martha's eyes fluttered closed and her face relaxed. Her grip on Lucy's blouse weakened and then her hand fell away. She exhaled a long slow breath and as she drifted to sleep, her final mumbled words, "Give it back."

CHAPTER 32

Lucy was late for morning rounds, having slept until nearly eight a.m. Something she never did. Most days she didn't have the time to spare and even when she did she still awoke around six, climbed out of bed, and began her day.

Yesterday had been a welcome day off. She had made rounds early and then she and Sam walked all over downtown, shopping and chatting with friends. Something she never seemed to find time for. She had forgotten how tiring it could be. As the sun set, they grilled a pair of steaks, knocked back a few bourbons, and then watched two hours of mind numbing sitcoms. Around midnight Lucy crashed and slept hard. The first time in—she couldn't remember. At least last night had been nightmare-free.

"Want me to go with you?" Sam asked as Lucy came into the kitchen, Sam sitting at the counter, lap top open before her.

"You stay and enjoy the morning. I'll be back in a couple of hours, tops."

Sam closed her lap top and stretched. "Maybe I'll go for run."

"Then lunch?"

"Sounds good."

With only two patients to see, rounds didn't take long. Lucy found Joseph Finch, sitting in the chair beside his bed, wearing street clothes, a stuffed kick bag by his feet.

Lucy dropped his chart on the bed. "Looks like someone's anxious to get home."

"You got it. Just say the word and I'll call my wife."

"Let me take a listen."

Lucy pulled her stethoscope from the pocket of her white coat and gave Finch the once over. His heart sounds were crisp and strong, lungs clear, chest wound and right leg vein harvest site healing well. She folded her stethoscope and returned it to her pocket.

"So what's the verdict?" Finch asked.

"You look as good in the flesh as you do on paper, so you're good to go."

"Yes." He pumped one fist.

"One question. Any more nightmares?"

"Last night was a doozy. But I'm getting used to them. How much longer will I have them?"

"Hard to say. Maybe getting home will resolve them. We'll have to see."

"If not, I can wrestle snakes there just as well as I can here. Maybe better." He smiled. "My bed's more comfortable."

Lucy returned his smile even as her own tension rose. She had hoped that his dreams had evaporated. Like hers apparently had. At least for one night. One very welcome night of deep sleep. She felt recharged. And guilty that Finch still looked tired and a bit frayed—a faint darkness beneath his eyes and a relaxed face that seemed to sag with fatigue. Hopefully a few nights at home would take care of that.

"I'll write your prescriptions. The nurses will give them to you on the way out. Take it easy. No exercise or lifting for a few weeks. Call my office Monday and set up an appointment for about ten days."

"Will do."

"And if anything changes or if you have any questions, call me."

Her next stop was to see Ronnie Draper. He wasn't in his room but she tracked him down, walking his tenth lap around the unit. She ushered him back to his room and gave him a quick exam. All okay.

"Want to go home today?" Lucy asked.

Ronnie's eyes lit up. "Really? I thought I wasn't getting out of here until tomorrow."

"You're doing great so I see no reason you can't rest at home. Unless you'd rather stay."

"No way."

Lucy laughed. "Didn't think so."

"When can I leave?"

"Give me fifteen minutes to write your prescriptions and get the paper work done and you're out of here."

"Perfect."

"How about those nightmares? Any better?"

"Worse." Lucy raised an eyebrow. "Maybe not really worse. But definitely more intense."

"How so?"

"Before, the snakes seemed less interested in me. Less threatening. Now not so much. And the colors. Until last night everything seemed dim, muted. Washed out or faded might be better words. But last night was definitely technicolor."

"I see."

"And the snakes were bigger and more aggressive."

Lucy nodded but didn't say anything. She felt a cool fullness expand in her chest, upward until it settled in the base of her throat. She swallowed but the feeling remained.

"I've hiked these hills since I was ten. Maybe even younger. I've walked up on dozens of snakes. They always high tail it. Try to get as far away as possible. These guys—the ones in my dreams—don't run. They stand their ground. Last night, they did more than that. They chased me. Big fat rattlesnakes. Big around as my leg. Now a real rattler won't do that. He'll be shy. Unless you step on him or startle him or something, he'll give you a wide berth. The ones last night could flat out scoot. I had to run and run to get away." He laughed. "Listen to me. I'm talking like they're real."

"I'm sure they seemed so at the time."

"How long do you think they'll last?"

"Hard to say, but usually only a few days. Maybe a couple of weeks."

Ronnie yawned. "I'll be glad. I need a good night's sleep."

CHAPTER 33

The weather was perfect for a run. Cool with a clear blue sky, the morning dew glistening on the grass and pine needles, and patchy remnants of ground fog still hanging in the low lying areas along the blacktop road Sam followed through the rolling farmland. Out here, a couple of miles from town, the morning's quiet stillness was broken only by the sounds of her footfalls as they mingled with the chirping of small birds and the cawing of a squadron of crows that swept by overhead. She ran with an easy rhythm, everything all loosened up now, sweat plastering her dark blue tee shirt to her body.

She hadn't slept well last night, the Scully clan entering her head and waking her off and on. Each time, she laid there trying to figure them out until fatigue pulled her back under. They pried their way into her head again now. She always found running to be as much meditative as physical, the rhythm of her tap-tap-tapping shoes and her breathing serving as a quasi mantra, allowing her brain time to itself, to release stress or work out a problem. Today the problem was the Scullys.

The snake handling aside, this was an odd collection of characters. At least Sam found their beliefs to be odd. No, not odd. That would be an understatement. More like bizarre or maybe even insane. Of course she felt that way about virtually all religious dogma. Having been raised in the

Catholic church, she knew something about ritual and part of her could see the parallels between communion and snake handling. Humming mantras and bowing to Mecca five times a day too for that matter. At least on the most basic level.

Each was a ceremonial event, designed to bring the faithful closer to God, or Jesus, or whoever. Each was used to ritualize behavior and ingrain the church teachings into their respective congregations. Each was how the church tested the faith of its followers. Follow the rituals or the leaders of the faith will know you are not sincere in your beliefs. It was all crowd control.

Sam never saw a nickel's worth of difference in the major religions. Each had a God. Each had some kind of flood or Earth destruction story. Each had a method of salvation, this salvation depending on following the particular religion's teaching and performing the ritualistic behavior proscribed by the powers to be. Even though they were willing to fight and kill if necessary to prove they were the one true religion, the one that had found the true God and the path to His kingdom, they were each, in the end, simply mythology. Not much different than the Greek and Roman myths she had studied in school. To Sam, they were all the same song and dance.

After all, wasn't a hummed mantra simply gospel music?

The Scullys' belief that serpents were the doorway to God was, on the surface, strange and didn't pass the common sense test but then neither did the resurrection or Mohamed jumping to heaven from a rock or the multiple avatars of Vishnu. For Sam, none of these rang true.

She heard a vehicle approaching from behind so she veered to her right, off the roadway, and onto the grass shoulder. The vehicle slowed and came along side her.

"Look who we have here." It was Elvin Watson, leaning out the window of the truck, brother Eric driving. "You're looking mighty pretty today, Ms. Cody." He giggled.

Sam stopped. The truck did, too. She now saw Eric take an deep hit from a joint and pass it to his brother.

"You guys getting an early start today, I see."

"We're up early everyday."

"I meant the the pot smoking. Do you guys stay stoned all the time?"

"Why not? It's a free country."

"Not very smart to be behind the wheel of a truck though, don't you think."

Eric leaned forward to see her past his brother. "I actually drive better when I'm hammered. I'm more careful."

"That's comforting."

"Speaking of a free country," Elvin said, "those freedoms extend to religion, don't you think?"

"And your point is?"

"Why're you snooping around our church?"

"So, it's your church now."

That created a moment of confusion but finally Elvin recovered. "You know what I mean. What gives you the right to stick your nose in our business?"

"As you said, it's a free country."

"Don't allow for no harassment."

"Harassment? Doing a little research hardly falls into that category."

The pair apparently had no comeback for that. They stared at her with stupid, stoned expressions. Beavis and Butthead came to mind.

Sam propped her hands on her hips and gazed out over an undulating field, striped with rows of young bright green corn plants. A dense patch of ground fog had settled along a low lying dirt road that cut diagonally across the field before rising from the haze and disappearing into a wooded area.

"You see," Sam continued, "when a couple of church members are murdered and others seem intimidated by the leaders, not to mention a woman dying from a snake bite that probably wasn't an accident, I get suspicious. I'm funny that way."

"It's none of your business."

"You boys have a nice day."

Sam resumed her run. At first she thought maybe that was the end of it but then she heard the loping engine and the crunch of tires on loose gravel come up behind her. Better to ignore them, she thought.

"I was you I'd be careful," Elvin said as they pulled along side her.

"I'll do that."

Eric slammed down on the accelerator and the truck lurched forward, spraying gravel over her.

CHAPTER 34

Earlier, Lucy and Sam had grabbed a light lunch at Gracie's Kountry Kitchen, Lucy a Cobb Salad, Sam a double cheeseburger, and then headed home to do laundry, catch up on e mails, and rest up for Bump's BBQ. Around mid afternoon, Lucy stretched out on one of her deck lounge chairs with a book and the next thing she knew it was nearly five. She stood, stretched, and walked back inside. She heard the hiss of the shower in Sam's room.

After finishing her own shower, slapping on a little makeup, and spiking her short blonde hair with her fingers, she found Sam on the sofa, laptop balanced on her knees. Sam wore jeans and long-sleeved black pullover; Lucy the same except her pullover was dark green.

"Looks like we both have the same fashion consultant," Lucy said.

Sam laughed. It was a joke that went back to their time in Los Angeles, when Lucy was in school and Sam at the LA Police Academy. It seemed that they always showed up wearing the same, or at least very similar, outfits.

"Great minds," Sam said.

"Or telepathy."

"That, too."

"You ready to go?" Lucy asked.

"Just let me shut this down."

While Sam closed and put away her laptop, Lucy pulled two bottles of wine, a Cab and a Zinfandel, from her kitchen wine rack, sliding them into a paper bag. Sam nodded to the bag as she secured her ponytail with a black scrunchy.

"We brown bagging it tonight?"

"It's the best I could find. I thought I had a cloth wine bag around here somewhere but I couldn't find it."

"We can stop by a pick one up on the way."

"Trust me, Bump and Ty won't care."

"That's probably true."

⌘

The front door to Bump's house stood open. Lucy rapped a knuckle on the door frame saying, "Anyone here?"

"Come on in," she heard Bump shout from somewhere inside.

He was in the kitchen. Standing over the sink, washing a head of lettuce, which he placed on a folded paper towel to drain. He then dried his hands on a kitchen towel decorated with mallard ducks. The aroma of barbecue came through the open window above the sink.

"Smells delicious," Sam said.

"Thanks. One thing I do know is my way around a grill."

"We brought wine," Lucy said, extending the two bottles toward him.

"Thanks. Dinner won't be long. Go on out back. Ty's on the patio."

While Bump worked the cork out of the ZIn, Lucy and Sam walked out onto the flagstone patio. Like most properties along the shores of Crockett Lake, the house was ranch style, tree-shaded, and had an expansive back lawn that sloped down to a boat house and a short pier. The blue sky was cloudless and a soft breeze barely rippled the lake's surface. Near one end of the patio, Bump's black steel, barrel-shaped smoker pumped rich barbecue-laced smoke into the air, while at the opposite end, Ty sat beneath a market green umbrella that sprouted from the center of a round table. He wore jeans, an untucked blue work shirt, wrap-around sunglasses, and held a longneck PBR in his hand.

"How're you two doing today?" Ty asked as they sat opposite him.

"Not bad," Sam said. "You?"

He shrugged. "Still dealing with the aftermath of the shootings."

Bump appeared, handed Lucy and Sam each a glass of wine, and sat down.

"Anything new on Nevers?" Sam asked.

"Not really. It's just such a tragedy. Folks can't seem to get their heads around it."

"Understandable."

"Crap like this don't happen around here," Bump said. "Fortunately."

"You guys coming to the funerals tomorrow?" Ty asked.

Lucy felt tension rise in her shoulders. She dreaded the funerals. She actually dreaded all funerals but particularly these. She couldn't shake the feeling that she was somehow responsible. That she must have made some grave error in William Nevers' surgery. The she had been painted with a bright scarlet A. That everyone who would be there would know that this was all her fault. She could almost feel their accusatory gazes already. Not very rational thinking, but she couldn't shake that feeling.

"Aren't the Nevers' burials at one and the Tate's at two?" Sam asked.

"That's right." Ty worked the corner of the beer bottle label loose with his thumbnail. "Five burials in one day. Must be a county record."

"Hell, it might be a state record," Bump said.

"I'm sorry," Lucy said.

Ty looked up at her. "For what?"

Lucy sighed. "All this."

"How's this your fault?"

"William Nevers was my patient."

"How's that relevant here?" Bump asked.

A longer and deeper sigh. "Maybe I let him go home too soon. Maybe I should have paid more attention to his wild dreams. Maybe I should have seen that he was unstable."

"Don't you think that's a bit harsh?" Sam said. "How could you have predicted what he did?"

"By paying more attention, reading the signs."

"And those signs would be what?"

"I told you. His dreams."

Sam reached over and laid a hand on Lucy's arm. "Everyone has nightmares. Hell I used to dream about shooting Lanny Mills all the time."

Ty laughed. "The guy that took your job?"

"That's the one." She squeezed Lucy's arm. "Nothing about this is your fault."

Lucy shrugged, gazed out toward the lake for a beat, and then said, "He's not the only one. I had another patient go all psycho and a couple of others having very similar nightmares."

"So?" Sam said. "Doesn't that happen after surgery?"

"Rarely. That's why having all this happen at the same time is so disturbing."

"So how is it your fault?" Bump asked.

"I don't know. I just feel like something is off."

"With you?" Ty asked.

"I've been having crazy dreams too." She took a sip of wine. "Not much different than the ones that bothered Nevers. And the others."

"Really?" Sam asked. "You didn't tell me that."

"Because you'd worry."

"That's what friends do. Worry about each other."

Lucy smiled at her but it didn't last long. "And then there's Martha."

"What about her?" Ty asked.

"She's been acting out. More agitated than usual, crawling down the halls like she's trying to escape, talking nonsense."

"She's demented," Sam said. "You can't put much credence in anything she says."

"Normally I'd agree with you. But it's that sometimes she seems to make sense. Almost. All that stuff about Scully and about something being hers and not mine."

"And that means what?" Sam asked.

"I don't know. I just have a feeling she's trying to tell me something." Lucy took a healthy gulp of wine.

"Sounds to me like you're taking too much of this on your own shoulders," Bump said. "I don't see how someone's dreams and Martha's dementia is anywhere near your fault. Don't make sense."

Lucy laughed. "When you put it that way, I guess it does sound silly." A sip of wine this time. "Still."

"Still nothing." Bump stood. "Who's hungry?"

"Starving," Lucy and Sam said in unison and then they both laughed.

After Bump pulled a huge brisket and a dozen hot links off the grill, piling them on a platter, everyone ventured into the kitchen and loaded up a plate before returning to the patio table. Conversation died as everyone dug in.

"These hot links are amazing," Sam said.

Bump smiled. "Made them myself."

"You should patent the recipe."

"It's a combo of veal and venison with a touch of pork. Some onions and peppers—habaneros—tossed in for good measure." He smiled around a bite. "Adds a little heat."

"More than a little," Sam said. "But I love them"

"There's plenty so don't be bashful"

"Not one of Sam's basic qualities," Lucy said. "Particularly when it comes to food."

Sam shrugged. "A girl's got to eat."

While they ate they talked about the weather, the town, Ty's crazy ex-wife, Bump's long history as police chief, Sam's past, and eventually the conversion turned to John Scully and his church.

"We had a meeting scheduled with Dwight Doucet," Sam said. "But he didn't show."

"Maybe he got tied up," Bump said.

"We drove out to his place but no one was there," Lucy said.

"I think he was scared," Sam said.

"Why?" Ty asked.

"He was reluctant to meet with us in the first place. I suspect he got cold feet."

"Because of the church?" Bump asked.

"That's what he said," Sam said. "I told him no one would know he had talked to us but he didn't really buy it. How did he put it? Something like the Scully clan had ways of digging things up."

Bump nodded. "That they do."

"Want to explain?" Sam asked.

"Just that they seem to intimidate folks into silence. About the church and its doings anyway."

"Can't you show a badge or something?" Lucy asked.

Bump smiled. "Sure. I've tried that. When we were looking into the Marvin Purdy murder. But a badge don't make no difference. Everyone who might've known something simply wouldn't talk."

"Can't you make them?" Lucy asked.

"Not with all that separation of church and state stuff." He suppressed a belch. "There's a couple of them I'd like to water board but I don't think I can pull that off."

"Let me guess," Sam said. "Those Watson clowns?"

"That'd be a start."

Sam eyed him. "I ran into them again this morning. On my run."

"And?" Ty asked.

"Nothing. They were a little horsey but I managed."

"What do you mean horsey?" Bump asked.

"Jumped in my face about snooping around the church. Seemed to think I shouldn't do that."

A crease appeared in Ty's forehead and his jaw set. "Why didn't you tell me about this?"

"Didn't seem important."

"To be threatened by those two? You don't think that's important?"

Sam shrugged. "Nothing I can't handle."

"But that's what we're here for." He nodded toward Bump. "Next time you brush up against them I want to know about it."

"Yes, Daddy."

Ty rolled his eyes.

CHAPTER 35

To Sam, the funerals were almost surreal. As an outsider, not knowing any of the victims or the mourners, she thought she could remain apart from the pain that swept through the community. That she could simply watch the proceedings, remaining on the periphery, and not get entangled in the emotions of the day. That wasn't how it worked out.

The funeral ceremony for Catherine and Katie Tate was first, beginning just after one p.m. It seemed to draw the entire town. Must have been three hundred people gathered around the twin rectangular holes in the ground. She found herself near the front, where Ty and Lucy had settled just a few feet behind and to the left of Pastor Jeremiah Burgess, an elderly man who spoke with a tremulous voice. Across from them stood General Adam and Anne Fallbrook and Mayor Joyce Whitworth and her husband Charles. They each offered grim nods to Sam, Lucy, and Ty but mostly kept their collective gaze toward the ground. As did Sam.

The open graves reminded Sam of other funerals. Her mother succumbing to cancer and being buried on a densely clouded Sunday. Her father, also on an overcast day. The many people, including three innocent children, who had met their end during the Richard Earl Garrett madness. Though she fought it, didn't want to be part of it, the deep loss that now bound this community insinuated itself inside as if she had inhaled some narcotic or toxin. She felt tears press against her eyes but managed to hold them at bay. Mostly.

After the two caskets were lowered, the metal cranks squeaking softly as the gathering stood in tear-streaked silence, and the initial handfuls of dirt were tossed, and final prayers murmured, the crowd moved a couple of hundred feet away to where the Nevers family would be buried. Most of the crowd anyway. Many drifted away, some with hard scowls imprinted on their faces, obviously unable to forgive William Nevers for his heinous actions. More tears, murmured prayers, and moans followed as the Nevers family disappeared into the three rectangular graves dug to receive them.

As the crowd dispersed, Sam stood next to her Lexus, talking with Ty and Lucy.

"No, you're not," Ty said after Sam told him she and Lucy were going to go to the five o'clock service at Scully's Eden's Gate Church.

"I'm not sure we need permission to go to church," Sam said. "You know all that separation of church and state stuff."

"Funny. But that's not what I meant," Ty said. "I meant you two ain't going up there alone. I'm going with you."

"I think it might be better if you don't. We want to talk with Scully. I'm not sure he'll be very forthcoming with you along."

Ty hooked a thumb on his belt. "Sorry but you'll just have to work around that. I'm going. It's not negotiable."

"Jeez," Sam said. "You give some people a badge and they think they're in charge." She smiled. "Okay, you can follow us."

"I feel so honored."

"You should. We don't invite just any random dude along on one of our road trips."

"So I'm a random dude now?"

"More or less."

"What if I can get you a sit down with Billy Whitehurst?"

"The pastor at the Pine Valley Church of God?"

"That's the one. Would that make me a little less random?"

"It's a start," Sam said.

Sam remembered from her library research that the Pine Valley Church was the one the Scullys and Martha had attended. John Senior had been a deacon, and most felt he was in line to take over when Whitehurst retired. John Junior was an up and comer and would soon be a deacon himself. All was as it should be, line of succession intact, until John Senior took up snakes and became the one true fountain of Godly knowledge. Whitehurst leveraged them out the door, Martha going with them, leading to the Scully clan forming Eden's Gate.

"That might help get some answers," Lucy said.

"Your police department in action," Ty said with a smile.

Sam playfully punched his arm. "Protect and serve? Something like that?"

"You got it." Ty glanced at his watch. "We have a couple of hours before evening services at Eden's Gate. I'd bet Whitehurst is still at his church. I'll give him a call."

❧

"How is Martha?" Reverend Billy Whitehurst asked.

"Not well," Lucy said. "She's had dementia for a few years and now it's severe. She's out there most of the time."

"I'm sorry to hear that. She's a fine woman."

Lucy sat with Sam on the deep blue sofa that dominated the living room of Whitehurst's rectory house, which nestled in a tree-shaded corner of the church grounds, separated by a hedge row from the small private cemetery that held many former congregation members. Each held a glass of sweet tea, a frosted pitcher of the deep brown liquid sitting on a polished oak coffee table, the rich wood protected by an embroidered doily. Ty sat in a wingback chair to their left and Whithurst to their right in an identical chair. The aroma of the tea mixed with the perfume of roses that grew just outside an open window, giving a clean fresh feel to the room.

"So you have some questions about her time with our church?"

"That's right."

Whitehurst took a sip of tea and then placed his glass on the small table beside his chair. His gaze moved toward the window as he spoke. "Those were wonderful times. The church was growing, new members all the time. And Martha was a big part of that. Her celebrity aside, she was a wonderful advocate for our work."

"But she left. With the Scullys."

Whitehurst nodded. "She did."

"Why?"

"Didn't she tell you?"

"No," Lucy said. "In fact I only recently found out about all this. I never knew she belonged here or that she was with the Eden's Gate Church."

"You, too," Whitehurst said with a smile. "You were a tiny tot the last time you were here. Your parents and Martha brought you every Sunday."

"Don't remember that either."

"You were very young." His smile faded and a more serious look fell across his face. "Why are you asking about this now?"

"Let's just say that some odd things have been occurring lately and Martha, even through all her dementia, has said some some things that are—what's the word?—bothersome."

"Such as?"

"It started the first time I brought up Scully's name. You might not know but he died recently. On my operating table."

"Yes, I heard."

"That news seemed to spark something in Martha and she became hysterical. Mumbling his name over and over. She got so agitated we had to sedate her."

Whitehurst sighed, his face seeming to sag with fatigue, but he said nothing.

"Then later she began ranting about something being hers and not mine. And that I should give it to her. I'm not sure what she could mean but somehow I feel it's connected to Scully or the church or something like that. Any idea what she could mean?"

Now his shoulders joined his face in a leadened droop. "The trouble started when John Scully, the elder John, went off on a two month sabbatical to a church up in West Virginia. The pastor up there, I believe his name was Sneed. Rankin Sneed. An odd guy from what I understand. I never met him but I know he was into snakes and claimed to have some special healing powers. That kind of stuff."

"Is that when he got into snake handling?" Sam asked.

"Exactly. When Scully returned he had changed. Seemed to go against everything he had believed in before. According to him, Sneed passed while he was up there and in so doing handed off some special powers to Scully."

Sam nodded. "I take it these beliefs didn't exactly jibe with the tenets of the church."

"You might say that. It'd be an understatement of the facts though." He took another sip of his tea, carefully replacing it on the table. "Scully began to proselytizing about this new way of approaching religion. Caused a great deal of turmoil. So much so that he split the congregation. Infighting, open arguments in church. It was a trying time. Ultimately, he took about thirty members and formed his new church."

"The snakes?" Sam asked.

"That was part of it, but more so it was his insistence that Eve's original sin was what saved mankind. That being evicted from the Garden of Eden actually was good for man. Not the fall from grace that we believe. Made him more self sufficient. Less in need of God's blessings. In fact, he believed that the serpent, the trickster of Eden, was the true bearer of power." He shrugged. "Not exactly in keeping with the Bible or the teachings of Jesus Christ."

"He told us some about that," Lucy said. "What I'm having trouble with is Martha buying into this. She's the most intelligent, and for lack of a better word, most pure person, I've ever known."

"The forces of Satan are powerful. Very corrupting."

"So you view Scully's church as a force for Satan?" Sam asked.

"Not sure I'd go that far." He folded his hands in his lap. "Let's just say his teachings weren't in keeping with our beliefs."

"But Martha bought into it?" Lucy asked.

"She did. Not sure why. Like you said, she's a very intelligent woman. But in the end, she left with the Scullys. They hopped around to a few locations before buying the old church they're in now."

"But then Martha left Scully's church," Lucy said. "Do you know why?"

Elbows on his knees, he clasped his hands, steepling his index fingers, chin resting on their tips. "Not really. I asked her once but she didn't have an answer. At least not one that made sense. Said something about not having time to attend or some such. I got the feeling it was more than that."

"When was that?" Sam asked.

"A year or two after she joined. When Lucy was maybe five." Whitehurst now leaned forward and looked at Lucy. "Around the time your parents died in that tragic fire."

A thought suddenly blossomed in Lucy mind. Something she had never considered before. Never had a reason to. But now, here it was.

"This might sound crazy," Lucy said. "But do you think it's possible Scully had anything to do with that fire?"

Whitehurst sat up. He glanced at Sam, Ty, and then back to Lucy. "Why would you think that?"

"I'm not sure I do," Lucy said. "It just popped into my head when you mentioned her leaving Scully's church around that time."

Whitehurst stared at her for a beat. "No. I never considered anything like that."

"Might fit the Scullys' MO," Ty said. "Both of them strike me as the kind that would not take rejection well."

"And the former members we've talked to seem more than a little intimidated by Scully," Sam said.

Whitehurst shook his head. "I simply can't imagine that."

"What about John Scully's wife?" Sam asked. "I understand she died from a snake bite."

"Yes. John Junior's wife Pricilla."

"Did she handle snakes?"

"No. John never let the women do that. Only the Scully men, and a couple of other male members, handled the snakes. At least that's my understanding."

"So it was an accident?" Sam asked.

"That's what they say." Whitehurst glanced at Ty.

"We tried to look into it but got stonewalled," Ty said. "Seems she was cleaning out the cages and got hit by a rattler. John—both Johns—insisted she be treated by the church. From what I've heard with strychnine. Wouldn't take her to the hospital. So she died."

Sam shrugged. "Sounds like a good case for negligent homicide to me."

Ty nodded. "Me, too. But none of the witnesses would talk and we could never get a warrant to search the place. No judge would allow us to go sniffing around inside a church."

"What about you?" Sam asked Whitehurst. "Did you suspect this might not have been an accident?"

"I had my doubts. Wouldn't be the first time. There was an old boy, named Glen Summerford. Pastor at the Church of Jesus with Signs Following down on Sand Mountain in Alabama. He was convicted of attempted murder of his wife. She too was bitten by a snake and Summerford wouldn't take her in for treatment. She survived though. A reporter by the name of Dennis Covington wrote a book on it. It's titled Salvation on Sand Mountain. It's an interesting read."

"Do you think that's what happened with Priscilla Scully?" Ty asked.

"I have no way of knowing, of course, but it crossed my mind."

CHAPTER 36

S am stood just outside the entrance to Eden's Gate Church of God flanked by Lucy and Ty. Music, or something like it, more a cacophony of a banjo, guitar, tambourine, and what sounded like someone banging on a metal pot, along with voices that seemed to be more nonsense than words, came at them through the open door.

"Doesn't sound like we missed the service," Ty said.

"I hope they aren't playing with their snakes," Lucy said. "I hate snakes."

"Bet they are."

"Great."

Sam stepped inside, followed by Lucy and Ty. They planned to ease into the back row unnoticed but in a single room with only about thirty worshipers that didn't pan out. Several heads turned toward them before they could slide along the wall, behind the array of empty folding chairs. Empty because the entire congregation was up dancing and wailing in a chorus of nonsense syllables. Not a single word Sam could recognize.

John Scully stood before the congregation on a low platform, a microphone connected to a small floor amp in one hand. To his left, near the back wall, Eric and Elvin Watson stood behind the make shift band: an overall wearing guitar player, a plaid-shirted banjo player, an elderly woman banging a tambourine, and a young man blowing on a blues harp.

The Watson brothers swayed with the music while they sipped some cloudy liquid from a Mason jar they passed back and forth. Felicia Scully, her back to them, stood next to her grandmother, Miriam, in front of and facing her father, her body also swaying with the music. Miriam had her arms extended over her head, hands clapping in time with the music.

The curious members who had noticed their entry quickly lost interest and fell back under Scully's spell. The music shifted from a chaotic, over-distorted cacophony into something Sam recognized and Scully began to sing, his voice muddy through the cheap amp. The faithful dropped into "This Little Light of Mine," many spinning around, hands raised above their heads, necks lax, heads lolling from one side to the other, the spirit really taking hold now. Scully raised his other hand, revealing a wad of snakes, rattlers and copperheads, several waving their triangular heads perilously close to his face. He seemed unconcerned as he sang, the words punctuated with odd noises and grunts and groans that seemed to erupt from his throat like lava from a partially clogged volcano. Now, with the snakes held high, his head gyrated back and forth, eyes closed to the point that only thin strips of white were showing, really getting into it. The faithful adopted his posture and movements as they seemed to become a single organism, bound by some spirit that seemed to envelop them.

"Gimme that old time religion," Sam whispered, leaning close to Lucy so she could hear her over the noise.

"I hate snakes," Lucy replied.

"So you said."

"No I really hate snakes. I'm not sure I can stay in here."

"Don't worry. Ty's armed." She looked at Lucy and smiled. "So am I."

"I wish that was as comforting as it should be."

Felicia spun around several times and paused for a beat when her gaze locked with Sam's, a brief look of surprise on her face. And something else. Something just beneath the surface, visible only in her eyes. A sadness. As if she were lost and desperate for salvation. This struck Sam as odd since her father was sweating and gyrating and moaning and groaning and doing everything in his power to save every soul in the room.

Felicia quickly yanked her gaze away and returned to her spinning and gyrating.

Over the next half hour Sam witnessed behavior she thought only happened in psychiatric wards. And maybe horror movies.

A young girl, maybe twelve years old, began to shake violently, eyes rolled back, shoulders twisting right and left. The crowd stepped back, giving her room. She spun, arms extended, faster and faster, her long brown hair following her movements like a wind-blown banner. She suddenly collapsed to the floor, writhing, legs kicking as if she swimming the backstroke. Her blue calico bib dress flew up, revealing white panties. No one seemed to notice or care.

Scully stepped off the stage and waved the snakes over the girl. The music continued but softened, again shifting from music to what Sam saw as random noise.

"Let the spirit come on the child," Scully said, his voice adopting the sing song rhythm of all preachers. "Let her soul be purified, her sins washed away." The girls writhing intensified. "Lord take this child to your bosom and protect her."

The girls gyrations settled into tremors, her arms and legs shaking as if cold, eye lids fluttering. Then her movements ceased and she lay on floor, stone still. Miriam and Felicia knelt next to her, massaging her arms and legs. The girl seemed to come out of her trance, eyes now open, but still glazed. They helped her to her feet, her legs shaking as if they wouldn't support her. Several other women enveloped her and lead her to a chair against one wall. The girl sat, shoulders drooping as if fatigued from her efforts. Or maybe it was simply the weight of the holy spirit.

These people are full tilt looney, Sam thought.

Another woman limped forward. Elderly, white haired and frail. She dropped to her knees before Scully, her arms raised, palms up in supplication. Again the snakes were waved over her head, Scully speaking in random syllables and nondescript noises. The woman's arms swayed back and forth as if they were radio antennae searching for a signal. Scully turned toward the Watson brothers and waved them toward him. He exchanged his microphone for the Mason jar, touched its rim against the head of each of the four snakes he held, and then passed the jar to the woman. She clutched it both hands, immediately bringing it to her lips. She took a sip, then another, before passing the jar to Eric Watson.

Now Scully took back the microphone and spoke. "Oh Lord, let your strychnine do its work. Let it drive the afflictions from our sister. Let her legs regain their strength and let the potent cast her arthritic torment from her body. In the name of the serpent of the garden I command it."

The woman screeched and collapsed forward at her waist, head to the floor, as if praying. A few more waves of the snakes and Scully retreated to the platform. Miriam and Felicia helped the woman to her feet and then to a chair near where the young girl sat. The woman's limp was noticeably improved. Felicia again looked at Sam, holding her a little longer this time. The sad look remained but also there seemed to be a question hidden behind her eyes.

What is it? What do you want?

Felicia returned her attention to the woman, who was still glassy eyed with the Lord's salvation. She hugged her, one hand patting the old woman's back.

Two men came through a door along the back wall, each carrying a rectangular wooden box. They placed the boxes on the floor, unsnapped the locks, and flipped open the tops. Several snakes spilled from each, and began writhing on the floor. Lucy grabbed Sam's arm, squeezing tightly.

"I know," Sam said. "You hate snakes."

"Don't you?"

"Of course. Anyone in their right mind does. But I have a little more experience. Back home I run into them on my desert runs all the time."

"But these are poisonous."

"Like Western Diamondbacks and Sidewinders aren't?"

The two men began sorting through the snakes, nonchalantly, like two bargain hunters shuffling through a pile of socks at a yard sale. Each came away with a handful and raised them high. They took the stage next to Scully and the band began to play "I Saw the Light." Scully boomed out the lyrics, the two men and the congregation joining in.

For the next twenty minutes, the band played and the faithful sang and danced, Scully presiding over it all as if holding each member in the power of his presence. Sam had to admit he was a showman if nothing else.

Finally, exhaustion seemed to take its toll and the music fell silent. The band began to pack up their gear, while the Watson brothers gathered up the snakes. They then exited through a rear door, each carrying a buzzing box of snakes. The congregation streamed out the front door, most casting sideways glances at Sam, Lucy, and Ty on the way by.

John Scully approached them. He reached out and took one of Lucy's hands in both of his. "I knew the Lord would lead you back to us."

"Not exactly," Lucy said, extracting her hand from his.

Scully smiled. "Coming to our service is the first step. You'll see."

"We didn't come here to see Jesus," Sam said. "We have a few questions."

"Don't we all? And the Lord has the answers."

"Maybe not to these questions," Sam said.

An annoyed, almost angry, look flashed across his face but quickly faded as his fake smile returned. "The Lord can answer all. He is all."

"I want to talk about Martha," Lucy said.

Scully glanced around the room. Only a couple of stragglers remained. As did Miriam and Felicia, both of whom now walked to where they stood.

"What about Martha?" Miriam asked.

Scully laid a hand on her arm. "Just a sec, mother. Let's offer our guests a seat first."

Translation: let's wait for everyone to leave before getting into anything that might prove embarrassing. At least that's the way Sam saw it.

He glanced toward the stragglers, who now walked by, one of them saying, "A wonderful service tonight, Pastor Scully. We'll see you Wednesday evening."

"Go with God's graces," Scully said.

After the final few faithful exited, Scully asked, "What do you want to know?"

Lucy hesitated a beat as if deciding exactly how to start. Then she said, "Martha has severe dementia and doesn't often make sense but lately she's said some puzzling things. Things I don't understand."

Scully crossed his arms over his chest and stared at her. Sam guessed sitting down was no longer a priority.

"She brings up your name a lot," Lucy said.

"We were friends at one time."

"But in all the years I've known her, she's never mentioned you. Why now?"

"As you said, she is demented. If it's as bad as you say, I'm not sure I'd put much into any of it."

"It started when I told her your father had died during surgery."

"Then that must be it. She and my father were very close. The news of his death must have sparked some old memory. That might explain her sudden remembrance."

"She also keeps harping on something that I apparently have that she thinks is hers. She keeps saying give it back to her. That it belongs to her. Any idea what that might mean?"

Scully glanced at Miriam. "I'm afraid I don't know."

"I think you do," Sam said.

"Excuse me?"

"I think you know exactly what she's talking about. So let's have it."

"I'm not sure I like your attitude."

"I hear that a lot." Sam took a half step toward him. "Answer the question."

Scully stepped back and looked at Ty. "Are you going to stand their while she talks to me that way?"

"I don't see that she's breaking any laws. Just asking questions."

"She has no right to come to my church and make accusations."

Ty smiled. "She's a cop. Cops ask questions. And since she's armed I know better than to interfere."

Scully's face hardened as he returned his attention to Sam. "I have no idea what Martha could mean and neither do you. She's old and, as you say, demented."

"Okay," Sam said, "Let me ask you an easier one. What about your wife?"

"What about her?"

"I'm just wondering, since she wasn't a snake handler, exactly how she was bitten."

"She was cleaning out the boxes. It was an accident."

"And not taking her to the hospital? Was that an accident?"

"We don't take to doctors much around here." He offered an apologetic smile to Lucy. "The Lord takes care of us. I've been bitten a dozen times and I never died."

"Treated it with a little strychnine, did you?" Sam asked.

"What are you saying? That I let my wife die?"

"I don't know. Am I?"

Scully was now in full rage. Though he still plastered a half smile on his face, Sam saw the lines of fury in his face. He turned to Ty. "I don't like her coming in here and accusing me of these kinds of things. Do something?"

"Like what? Arrest her?"

"Why not?"

"Because she got the right to say whatever she wants." Ty hooked a thumb on his belt. "Besides I didn't hear her accuse you of anything."

"I see."

Scully was struggling so hard to keep his temper tamped down, Sam thought his head might explode. His breathing took on an audible rasp and his neck veins snapped to attention.

Just then the Watson brothers came in. Eric seemed to sense the tension.

"Anything wrong?" he asked.

"Not at all," Scully said. "Our guests were just saying that it's getting late and they had to leave."

Sam nodded. "We'll chat another time." As she headed toward the door, Ty and Lucy behind her, she heard Felicia say, "I'll walk them out."

∾

"I told you this was dangerous," Miriam said. "Told you she wasn't the right one. No training. No way to control it."

"But she's in the perfect position to help us," Scully said. "You know father had it all planned out."

"And he was wrong. I told him so."

"No, he wasn't. She can do more for our cause in a month than I could do in a lifetime. That's why I stepped aside. Gave to her what was rightfully mine."

"Which is where it should be. With you."

"Don't worry, Lucy will come back to us. You'll see."

"What about her friend? That Samantha Cody? She's trouble and you know it."

"If we have to, we'll deal with her. Not like we haven't had to clean up things before."

"But she's a cop."

"So. Cops bleed, too."

"Anything you want us to do?" Eric asked.

"Keep an eye on her. Maybe apply a little pressure. Give her an incentive to go home. Back to the Golden State."

❧

Felicia escorted them out to Sam's SUV and when Sam opened the door, Felicia said, "Thanks for coming."

"Not sure your dad feels the same way," Sam said.

Felicia stepped close to her, gave a quick glance back toward the church, and then handed Sam a folded piece of paper. Before Sam could say anything, Felicia turned and walked away. Sam watched her go. She couldn't shake the feeling that Felicia was a lost soul. Caught between the world of her father and the real world.

After the church's front door closed behind Felicia, Sam climbed behind the wheel and unfolded the paper. In block printing it read:

Meet me Wednesday. 3 o'clock. Parking lot next to Post Office.

CHAPTER 37

Lucy's first case, a fairly straightforward abdominal aortic aneurysm repair, went well. At least she didn't faint or anything stupid like that. In fact, she felt great, none of the cold clamminess rearing its head. Maybe it was all behind her. Maybe it was simply fatigue and a couple of nights of sleep had resolved it.

The second case was a different story. She had completed the distal anastomosis of the third and final bypass graft and was lifting the heart to give each graft a final inspection when it happened. The coldness in her chest, as it had the other times, began as a faint discomfort as if she had eaten ice cream or drank a very cold liquid too quickly. The deep-seated cold burning quickly became more intense, expanded across her chest, and then surged down her arms to her hands. Her fingers felt frozen and immobile. She tried to release the heart but her fingers wouldn't cooperate. A wave of vertigo swept over her. The room seemed to spin and fade away, everything dark and murky. Cold sweat popped out on her face, her knees weakening by the second.

Come on, Lucy, hold it together.

Her pep talk didn't help. Not completely. She felt as if she was going down so she dropped to her knees, her hands now free from the heart and gripping the edge of the surgical table. An empty feeling swelled in the pit of her stomach followed by a nausea. She took a couple of deep breaths and the feelings began to recede.

She stood, coming face to face with Herb Dorsey, his eyes wide above his surgical mask.

"Lucy?" he said. "You okay?"

"I'm fine."

The circulating nurse appeared at her side and mopped Lucy's forehead with a dry towel.

"Let's close up," Lucy said.

"Want me to finish?" Herb asked.

"I got it. Let's just get it done."

When Sam entered Gracie's Kountry Kitchen, she saw Ty sitting in a booth, sipping from a large glass of sweet tea. She slid in opposite him.

"Hungry?" he asked.

"Starving."

They ordered, Sam a double cheese burger, extra cheese and fries, Ty a meatloaf sandwich.

"I love a woman with an appetite," Ty said.

"I had a long run this morning and no breakfast."

"How was it? Your run?"

"Fine. Except for those two Watson clowns. They drove by again. Harassed me." Sam shook her head. "Don't know how they know my running schedule. I don't even know that."

"What happened?"

"They weren't thrilled with our visit to the church last night."

"Neither was Scully." He tilted his glass toward her. "Thanks to you."

Sam shrugged. "Just asking questions."

Ty smiled. "And stirring the pot."

"You don't know what's in the soup until you stir up all the stuff on the bottom."

"You seem to do that well."

"Complaining?"

"Simply an observation."

"Somehow I don't read the Watson brothers as church goers."

"Their daddy was," Ty said. "He was a mover and shaker in Scully's world."

"And I thought they were just the handymen."

"They do indeed do work for Scully but they also believe in his bull."

"I figured two plus two was over their heads. I don't see them grasping religious dogma. Even screwed up dogma."

"Go away, Darlene," Ty said.

"What?" Sam asked.

Ty nodded. Sam turned to see Ty's ex standing just off her left shoulder.

"Isn't this cozy?" Darlene said. "You two are becoming quite an item."

"I guess you didn't hear me," Ty said. "Go away."

"I've got business here. I'm picking up my take out order."

"Then maybe you should get to it."

Darlene ignored him and to Sam said, "You better watch out for this one, honey. He's a real bastard sometimes."

"Thanks for the heads up," Sam said. "But I already knew that." She gave Ty a brief smile.

"You think this is funny? Trying to steal my husband?"

"Ex isn't it?" Sam asked.

Darlene gave her a blank stare for a beat. "I'll be keeping an eye on you." She turned and walked toward the front counter.

"Sorry about that," Ty said.

"It's good to be popular. All these people looking out for me. Darlene. The Watson brothers. You"

"I'm not sure any of the others have your best interests at heart."

"Probably not. But I'm glad you do."

Sam thought she detected a slight blush rise in Ty's face. The awkward moment passed when the waitress appeared with their food. While they ate they talked about the Scullys and then about Lucy being spooked by the entire ordeal, Sam saying that Lucy had had a ton of baggage dropped on her in the past few days. Learning about Martha and her parents being members of Scully's church, the fainting in surgery and the professional pressure that followed, and the psychotic break William Nevers had obviously suffered.

"Lucy's tough," Ty said. "She'll be fine."

"Yes, she is. One of the toughest women I've ever know. But that's still a lot to deal with."

Ty's cell chimed. He picked it up from where it lay on the table and checked the screen. He stood. "I'll be back in a sec." He raised the phone to his ear as he walked through the front door and out onto the sidewalk.

Sam watched Darlene pay for her her food, grab the white paper bag from the counter, and walk out the front door. She stopped to say something to Ty, who waved her away, turning his back to her, and continued his conversation. Darlene disappeared from view and Ty began to pace back and forth, head down, a frown on his face. He seemed to be listening more than talking. After a couple of minutes he slipped the phone into the back pocket of his jeans, pushed back through the door, and walked toward her. "Let's go." He tossed a few bills on the table.

"What is it?"

"Some one has taken Pastor Ray Vance hostage. Over at the Mount Olive Church of God."

CHAPTER 38

After her near fainting episode, Lucy had finished the triple bypass without further problems and was nearing completion of her rounds when her cell buzzed. It was Sam.

"What are you doing?" Sam asked.

"Finishing rounds. What's up?"

"You need to get over here to the Mount Olive Church. Your patient Ronnie Draper has taken the pastor hostage and is demanding to talk to you."

"What?"

"I'll explain it when you get here. He's very unstable so get it in gear."

Lucy didn't bother to change clothes but rather jumped in her car still dressed in surgical scrubs. She did pull off her cap and snapped the mask that still hung around her neck free, wadding both, tossing them in the passenger seat. Ten minutes later she pulled into the gravel parking area in front of the church, crunching to a stop next to the white sign with black lettering that read, "Mount Olive Church of God, Founded 1958, Pastor Raymond Vance." The church was a simple rectangular, white clapboard building with a small steeple topped with a white wooden cross. It sat at the end of a spur off the county road on a couple of idyllic acres, dotted with rich green pines and pink and white dogwoods.

Today it wasn't so idyllic. Not even close.

Four patrol cars, Ty's black Tahoe, Bump's truck, and a paramedic van sat at haphazard angles in the lot just left of where she had parked. A half dozen uniformed officers milled around near the front door. One of them stopped her as she approached.

"Dr. Wagner. Wait here just a sec."

"I need to get inside."

"Detective Everson said he wanted to talk to you first." He nodded toward one of the other officers, who immediately disappeared inside the church. When he returned, it wasn't Ty who followed him but rather Sam.

"What's going on?" Lucy asked.

"Ronnie has killed two people and has Pastor Vance hostage."

"Two people? Who?"

"Apparently a young man and an elderly woman. Employees of the church."

"Jesus."

"He's got a very big butcher's knife and says he'll kill Pastor Vance if you don't *fix him*. His words."

"I don't understand."

"He's ranting about you putting something inside him. Says it's *killing his soul*. Also his words."

A chill ascended Lucy's spine and settled as a throbbing pain behind her eyes. "What do you want me to do?"

"Talk some sense into him."

"If he thinks I did something wrong why would he want to talk with me?"

"Crazy people rarely make sense."

"DId you call his parents?"

"No answer."

"Goddamn it. Where is Dr. Wagner?" Ronnie's voice, high-pitched and hysterical, came at her through the propped open door.

Lucy squared her shoulders. "Let's go."

She followed Sam inside. Ty stood half way down the center aisle while Bump and two uniformed officers loitered just inside the door, near the back of the chapel. Ronnie sat on the floor near the dais, Vance snugged up against him. Vance was shirtless and terrified, eyes wide, pupils dilated, sweat on his face and torso. A bloody gash slanted across his chest, another across his left bicep. Blood coated his chest, abdomen, and left arm. Ronnie pressed a long, thick-bladed knife against Vance's throat. To their left Lucy saw the corpse of the woman, the front of her dress soaked with blood, several deep stab wounds in her chest, a pool of dark blood on the floor to her left. Several chairs near the dais were overturned and a front pew was flipped on its back, a young man's bloodied corpse draped across it.

"I'll kill him," Ronnie screeched, his wild-eyed gaze locked on Ty. "I'll kill him right here."

"Take a breath, Ronnie, and relax," Ty said. HIs right hand rested on his still holstered gun.

"Relax? How do you expect me to relax with this . . . this thing eating me up?" His gaze shifted to Lucy who had walked up behind Ty, Sam right behind her. "You did this."

Lucy stepped forward, moving past Ty.

Sam grabbed her arm. "Wait a second."

"It's okay." Lucy pulled free from Sam's grasp and walked down the aisle toward the distraught Ronnie Draper. Sam and Ty followed, staying only a few steps behind.

"Not too close," Sam whispered.

Lucy stopped near the third pew. Now she could see the young man's corpse more clearly. He arched face down over the seat of the upturned pew. Dark blood had collected in the angle of the back. Several angry stab wounds gaped open the back of his tee shirt as well as the red flesh beneath.

"Are you okay?" Lucy asked Vance.

"No, he's not," Ronnie screamed. "And he's going to be a lot worse if you don't fix me."

"Ronnie, put down the knife and let Pastor Vance go."

"Yeah, right. So those two can shoot me."

"No one's going to harm you," Lucy said.

An explosive laugh followed. "You did. You did this to me."

"You're bleeding. Let me help you."

"This body isn't mine anymore. It belongs to . . . I don't know who it belongs to. Whatever devil you put inside me."

"It's the bypass machine. It sometimes scrambles the brain. Makes you think all sorts of strange things. But It'll pass."

"Like Bill Nevers?" He now aimed the knife tip at her, jabbing the air to make his point. "Yeah, I know about that. You did this to him, too."

"Mr. Nevers had a similar problem but it's not the devil or anything like that. It happens sometimes."

"Liar." His voice quivered with rage. "You're Satan. Pure and simple. You put something evil in him, too."

Lucy consciously tried to slow her own racing heart but wasn't very successful. "Does that make sense? Do you honestly think I could, or would, do that?"

"Who else could have? You opened my chest and put something in there. Something dark. Something that's eating my soul."

"Ronnie, you're not possessed. You're suffering a complication. That's all."

"A complication? Is that what you call this?"

"That's the truth."

"That's a lie."

"Ronnie, take and breath and . . ."

"Shut up. Shut the fuck up." He pushed Vance away, the man falling on his face on the floor. Lucy could now see that Ronnie had slashed himself, several deep, diagonal wounds across his bare chest. "If you won't cut it out, I will."

He plunged the knife into his own chest, again and again, screaming, not words but rather a series of unintelligible noises. Lucy rushed forward, Sam right behind her. Ronnie collapsed forward on the knife. Lucy rolled his now limp body to his back, the knife slipping part way out of his chest. His eyes were dilated dark black. She yanked the knife free, tossing it aside, and slapped her hands over the wounds, trying to slow the bleeding while beginning CPR. Blood gushed from the wounds and a bright red froth erupted from his mouth.

For the next twenty minutes Lucy worked on Ronnie, with the help of the paramedics Bump had ushered inside, but the young man was beyond saving. The deep stab wounds had obviously punctured his heart several times, making CPR an fruitless endeavor.

Finally Lucy stopped the CPR. "That's it."

She then turned her attention to Pastor Vance, now settled on one of the medic's stretchers. He had three deep lacerations over his chest, one into the muscles of his left bicep, and another across his right scapular area. The bleeding had stopped and the medic had applied loose gauze over each wound, Lucy having to lift the edges to get a look.

"These look worse than they are," she said to Vance.

"Don't feel that way."

Lucy offered him a weak smile. "I suspect that's true. But we'll get you over to the hospital and fix those up."

"Surgery?"

"No. We can do all this in the ER."

While the medics loaded Vance into the back of their rig, Lucy stood with Sam, Ty, and Bump near her car. Coroner Larry Granville and one of his techs were inside dealing with the corpses of Toby Parker and Maude Napier, the two slain church employees.

"I'll follow the medics over to the hospital," Lucy said, "and fix up Pastor Vance."

Ty looked at Bump. "You want to do the notifications or track down Ronnie Draper's parents?"

"Neither." Bump sighed. "But I've known Raymond and his wife Bertie for many years so I suspect it'll be best if she hears it from me."

CHAPTER 39

"What do you think?" Ty asked.

He and Sam stood next to his truck, now parked in front of Ronnie Draper's home. It was a simple brick structure with white trim and a three-step stoop flanked by small round junipers. A light-blue late model Chevy Impala sat in the drive, nosed up near the garage door, open, revealing a white Ford Explorer and clutter inside.

Sam knew the reason for Ty's concern was that they had called again on the way over and still no answer, yet the front door stood open.

"Maybe just catching a breeze?" Sam said.

"And not answering the phone?"

"Could be out back. Maybe doing yard work or something."

Ty tossed a skeptical look her way. "Maybe."

"I'll go that way," Sam said. "You take the front."

"So you're in charge now?"

She smiled. "Of course. Why do you ask?"

Ty nodded. "Good to know."

"But I don't like the feel of this."

"Me, neither."

"Want to bet we aren't going to like what we find inside?" Sam asked.

"After what we saw at the church? Not much of a bet, I'd suspect."

Sam crossed the yard and turned the corner as Ty stepped up on the stoop. She heard the doorbell ring and Ty shout, "Mr. Draper? It's Detective Everson."

She peered between the curtains that partially covered a side window. Living room. No one there, then Ty appeared as he stepped inside.

"Mr. Draper? Mrs. Draper? Are you here?"

Sam turned the rear corner and stopped. The concrete patio that stretched across the rear of the house was empty. Except for the bloody shoe prints that came directly toward her. She pulled her gun. Stepping around the prints she approached the rear door, which also stood open. She entered the kitchen.

Then she saw her. A middle-aged woman, face down on the floor next to an overturned chair. Congealed, maroon blood spread out from the body, a yellow halo of serum just beginning to form around the edges. Ty entered and froze, his gun now appearing in his hand. Sam knelt by the woman and checked her neck for a pulse. Nothing except cold flesh.

"She's cool and the blood's starting to separate," Sam said. "She's been dead an hour or so."

Ty nodded. "Let's check the other rooms."

Sam followed him down a hallway, the walls decorated with family photos. Happier times for sure. Two bedrooms and a bath proved empty but a third bedroom, now a home office, was another story altogether. A computer desk sat against a rear facing window, screen saver photos fading from one to the other. Long streaks of blood stretched across the screen, the desk, the window glass, and even the curtain that flanked the window. The desk chair was twisted to one side and on the floor lay who she assumed was Mr. Draper. On his back, his throat severed, blood soaking his shirt and the carpet. No need to check for a pulse here.

"Jesus," Ty said.

"Arterial spatter," Sam said, indicating the blood sprays.

Ty sighed and holstered his weapon. "I'd suspect he sneaked up on his father and did this first then took on his mother. Looks like she might've put up some kind of fight but he sure didn't."

"That'd be my guess."

As they walked back outside, Ty pulled his cell phone and thumbed in a number.

"Bump? The Draper's are dead. Both Hal and Sylvia. Looks like Ronnie used that knife on his parents before he went over to the church." He listened a beat. "Send a couple of the guys over here and let Granville know." Another silence. "We'll talk to the neighbors. See if they know anything."

The neighbors on one side weren't at home but those on the other side were. A woman answered Ty's knock.

"Detective Everson? What brings you here?"

The woman was young and carried a toddler propped against one hip. A strand of hair fell across her eyes and she pushed it back.

"Denise, sorry to bother you."

"No bother." Her eyes cut to Sam.

Ty introduced Sam to Denise Elia and then asked, "Is Peter home?"

"No." Concern furrowed her brow. "Something's wrong. What is it?

"Did you hear anything from next door at the Draper's?"

"Like what?"

"A commotion? Anything?"

"No. Lily and I just got up from a nap." She indicated the child and then stepped out on to the porch and looked toward the Draper home. "What's going on?"

Ty sighed. "The Drapers. They've been murdered."

Denise took a step back, wavering, color draining from her face. Ty grabbed her arm and steadied her.

"You want to sit down?" Ty asked.

"Murdered?" Her voice cracked. "When? Who?"

"Looks like it was Ronnie." He then told her about the events at the church. Not in any detail just that Ronnie had attacked Pastor Vance and killed two others before taking his own life.

Tears welled in her eyes and slid down her cheeks. "I don't understand. Here? In their house?"

"Afraid so."

"Maybe I should sit down."

She retreated into her living room, Sam and Ty following. She settled on a sofa, clutching Lily to her chest.

"You want me to call Peter?" Ty asked.

She sniffed. "Would you?"

"What's the number?"

She told him and he called, telling Peter he should come home, not to worry that Denise and Lily were okay but she needed him about now. He closed his phone. "You feel up to a couple of questions?"

She nodded, swiping the back of one hand across her nose.

"Tell me about Ronnie?"

"What's to tell? He's a very sweet young man."

"No outbursts? Anger? Anything like that?"

She shook her head. "No. Not that I've ever seen."

"What about since his surgery?" Sam asked. "Any changes since then?"

"I saw him Saturday. Just after he came home. He seemed fine. Maybe a little drawn looking and he seemed tired. I suspect that would be pretty normal after heart surgery."

"Was he stressed about the surgery?" Ty asked. "Beforehand?"

"Not really. He knew for the past few months that it was coming. If anything he seemed excited to get it behind him," She sighed. "This is just awful."

"So from what you saw he was more or less normal?" Sam asked.

She hesitated. "Yesterday afternoon I saw him in his backyard. He did seem a little out of it. I mean, I called his name and waved to him but he didn't respond. Just stared off into space. I assumed he didn't hear me . . . but now . . . with this . . . maybe something was off after all."

Something was definitely off, Sam thought.

Chapter 40

O nce Granville arrived with a pair of uniformed officers in tow, Sam and Ty turned the scene over to them, hopped in Ty's Tahoe, and headed to the hospital. While he drove, Ty called Bump and updated him on what they had found at Ronnie Draper's home.

As Sam listened to Ty's side of the conversation, she began to feel disoriented. As if the world had tipped slightly to one side. Four brutal murders and a young man stabbing himself to death in a psychotic fit will do that. She lowered the truck's shotgun window, letting the air flow flow over her. It didn't help much.

Weren't crazies and multiple murders the reason she left LA and returned to Mercer's Corner in the first place? Back to a quieter and more sane job than prowling the streets of Hollywood and South Central? Back where crime consisted of teenage vandalism and neighborhood spats and not automatic weapons, drug dealers, and gang bangers?

Though Remington was bigger than Mercer's Corner, it carried the same small town feel. Safe and quiet. Hadn't Ty said they had had only two murders in over a decade? And now what? Five deaths today, five others last week. Based on Remington's murder rate that should cover them for the next half century.

She turned from the open window and looked at Ty. "What the hell's going on?"

Ty ran a hand through his hair, sweeping it back off his forehead. "Wish I knew." He glanced at her. "You're the one with experience in this kind of stuff."

"Richard Earl Garrett?"

"From what I read and what you told me about that case, this does have some similarities."

Richard Earl Garrett was a Satanic killer that ritualistically murdered three children. The killings took place just north of Mercer's Corner, in an area of the Mojave known as Devil's Playground. Aptly named. Then the entire town went psycho. The effects of Garrett's madness seemed to sweep through the community like the Bubonic Plague. Normal people, people she had known all her life, got freaky and began killing friends and neighbors. It even affected her and her boss, Sheriff Charlie Walker. She could vividly remember her life-and-death, knock-down-drag-out with Garrett that night deep in the desert. There was a moment, actually several moments, that she thought she'd never survive the ritual Garrett had staged for her. Not to mention the feeling that she too had fallen under Garrett's control. A feeling she fought and ultimately won over but it was a disorienting experience. Not unlike the past few days.

"Didn't a bunch of the town's people go all crazy and hysterical?" Ty continued.

Including her, Sam thought. "I'm still not sure what happened. But yeah, some previously normal folks did do some very bizarre things."

"My point exactly."

"So you're thinking some viral madness has spread through Remington?"

"You mean like a zombie virus?"

Sam laughed. "Not sure I'd indict a zombie virus."

Ty shrugged. "There's something out there. In the air. Making all these folks go nutty."

"Except that these nutty folks are Lucy's patients."

Ty turned into the ER parking lot at Remington Medical Center. "Lucy ain't going like what we have to tell her."

"She's going to freak."

"More than she already is?" Ty asked.

He slipped into a parking space just left of the ambulance receiving ramp and they climbed out. Sam saw the paramedics who had transferred Pastor Vance to the hospital, cleaning the back compartment of their rig. They nodded as Sam and Ty walked by and entered the ER.

They found Lucy, standing at the counter of the nurse's station, chart in hand, talking with one of the nurses.

"His bed's ready on the surgical floor," the nurse said. "We'll transfer him up shortly."

Lucy handed her the chart and she walked away.

"How's Pastor Vance doing?" Ty asked.

"Fine. After forty or so stitches. He's lucky his wounds were mostly superficial. Nothing major damaged."

"That's good news," Ty said. "Something we can all use about now."

"Did you locate Ronnie's parents?" Lucy asked.

Sam glanced at Ty.

"What is it?" Lucy asked.

Ty told her what they had found at the Draper's house. As he related the story, Lucy paled, her eyes widening, then moistening.

"Jesus." She massaged one temple and swallowed hard. "What the hell is going on?"

"That's what I'd like to know."

Sam turned toward the voice. It was Dr. Gilbert Birnbaum, Dr. Herb Dorsey at his side.

"I heard about Ronnie Draper," Birnbaum continued. "What he did at the church. Not to mention his family," His eyes narrowed as he looked at Lucy.

"A real tragedy," Lucy said. Her voice was weak, barely above a whisper.

"You seem to be attracting tragedies lately."

"Gil," Dorsey said. "I don't think this is time."

"The hell it isn't." He took a step toward Lucy. "What's going on? All your patients are having these kinds of problems."

"Not all," Lucy said.

He smirked. "Just William Nevers and now Ronnie Draper. And let's not forget Mr. Finch's little psychotic episode in the ICU the other day."

Sam started to jump in and defend Lucy, but apparently Ty sensed it and laid a hand on her arm, stopping her before she could say anything.

"These are all cases of post pump psychosis," Lucy said. "And you know it."

"But so many?"

"It's like plane crashes," Lucy said. "They must come in threes."

"Well, I'm not going to give you the chance to increase that number."

"And what does that mean?" Lucy asked, her voice now clear and strong.

"It means your hospital privileges are suspended. Completely and immediately."

"Gil, aren't you over reacting?" Dorsey said. "These things happen to all of us."

"Really? Has this kind of thing ever happened to you? To anyone else on staff here?"

Dorsey sighed. "But I don't see this as being Lucy's fault."

"Then whose fault is it? Not only have her patients gone all crazy but she's fainted in surgery. Several times." He puffed out his chest. "As chief of staff I have responsibility to the hospital and to the patients to make sure each of our doctors is stable enough to care for the sick."

"But Gil . . " Dorsey began. That's as far as he got before Sam interrupted.

"Lucy's the best surgeon you have. You know it and I know it. Everybody knows it."

Again Ty grabbed her arm but she shook off his grip.

"I don't know anything of the sort."

"Well, you should. Being chief of staff and all."

"Who the hell do you think you are?" Birnbaum's face reddened, his neck veins popping into thick blue ropes.

"Apparently the only person around here with any common sense."

"I'm afraid I'll have to ask you to vacate the hospital. Now."

"You're a pompous ass. You don't give a rat shit about anything but your own turf. And that of your buddy Elliott Meeks."

Sam thought Birnbaum might have a stroke. His face went from red to purple. Then over his shoulder he spoke to the two nurse's who stood nearby, taking in the entire conversation. "Call security."

Sam shook her head. "Give a moron a title and he thinks he's King Kong."

"Get out," Birnbaum said through clenched teeth. Then to Ty, "I want her arrested for trespassing."

"Not sure being in the ER would constitute trespassing," Ty said. "Besides, she's leaving." He grabbed Sam's arm again, this time holding his grip, and directed her toward the entrance.

Sam didn't fight but rather turned and walked out into the parking lot. She leaned against the front fender of Ty's truck, arms crossed over her chest, gaze into the clouds, teeth clenched so hard her jaw ached. A few minutes later Ty and Lucy walked to where she stood.

"Well that was fun," Ty said.

"I thought so." She looked at Lucy. "I'm sorry. I know I didn't make things better but I couldn't just stand there and listen to that crap."

"Actually, I loved it" Lucy hugged her. "And I love you too."

""Even after I sabotaged your career?"

"I think Birnbaum beat you to it."

"I need to go catch up with Bump and the guys and see what the latest is," Ty said. "Dinner later?"

"Not me," Lucy said. "I want to go home, drink a bottle of bourbon, and go into a coma."

Ty nodded. "Can't say I blame you."

"I'll go with Ty," Sam said to Lucy. "Pick up my car and I'll be there in a few."

"I'll have a bottle and a glass waiting."

CHAPTER 41

S am found Lucy on her deck, settled into one of the Adirondack chairs that flanked a small table and faced the lake. Lucy knocked back the last of the bourbon she had and refilled her glass before passing the bottle of Knob Creek to Sam. Sam filled her own glass and sank into the other chair. The plastic seal from the now one third empty bottle sat on the table.

"You've made a pretty good dent in that," Sam said.

"And I'm going to make a bigger one before this day is over."

"Can't say I blame you."

The lake was glassy flat and a warm gentle breeze barely moved the tree leaves. It would have been a perfect evening, except it wasn't. No way anything could be perfect after the events of the day. Five people dead, Pastor Vance carved up and in the hospital, and Lucy's career literally hanging by a very thin thread. Sam searched for something comforting to say but drew a blank. What could possibly soothe such wounds?

""Wonder what I'll do next?" Lucy asked.

"Next? After what?"

"After my career is officially over."

"It's not."

"Really? I have no way to explain all these bad outcomes and Birnbaum will never let it go."

"He's a prick."

"True. But he's powerful and he's never liked me."

"Is that the bourbon talking?"

"You saw him. Heard what he said."

"Things like this have a way of passing."

"Not this."

"Sure it will," Sam said. "It's like a ship that leaves behind a wake. Soon it settles, the waters calm, and there is no evidence that the ship was ever there."

"That's very poetic of you."

"I try."

"The problem is that this is more like a glacier carving out a valley. Those tend to become national parks."

Sam laughed. "So they'll put you on Mount Rushmore or something?"

Lucy shrugged. "In case you haven't noticed, all those guys are dead,"

Sam looked at her. "Cheering you up isn't going to be easy, I see." She drained her glass and grabbed the bottle. "I better have some more of this."

"'Me, too." Lucy refilled her own glass.

They settled back in their chairs and for the next half hour sat quietly and drank bourbon.

Sam heard a dove cooing in a nearby tree and watched a orange-breasted Robin do its herky-jerky dance across the yard, stopping here and there to tug a worm from the ground. Soon she sensed the bourbon warming her insides and the tension in her shoulders ratcheted down a notch.

Lucy finally broke the silence. "You know what really pisses me off?"

"Lot's of things."

"True but right now I'm thinking Birnbaum might be right."

"How do you figure that?" Sam asked.

"This has to be my fault. Something I'm not doing right."

"Like what?"

"I don't know. But as a scientist I have to look at the evidence dispassionately." She placed her drink on the table, stood, walked to the edge of the deck, and leaned a shoulder against one of the roof's support poles, her arms crossed over her chest. "What's the common denominator here? Me. I operated on each of them. William Nevers. Ronnie Draper. Peter Finch."

"So? As you said, these things happen."

"But three in a row? Plus my little nose dives in surgery?" She sighed. "Something's not right but for the life of me I can't see what it is."

"Maybe because it has nothing to do with you. Maybe because some things can't be explained."

"Everything can be explained if you just find the key to understanding it."

"I wish that was true but I know it isn't. Some things have no rational explanation."

"Then I'll take an irrational one." She returned to her chair, sloshed back the remaining bourbon, and refilled her glass. "Tell me about Garrett."

"What about him?"

"I know the basic story. But what about you? What did he do to you?"

Now Sam stood. She walked to the deck rail, turned around, and propped one hip on it. "The folks who committed the murders all said that they had vividly colored dreams and visions. Each said they were powerless to resist the . . . I'm not sure what to call it . . . the urge I guess. Even Penelope Cochran, the girl I told you about. The leader of Garrett's satanic groupies."

"I remember."

"She had a dream. Very colorful. Then she took off, knife in hand, heading to kill someone. Even her lover Melissa Eriksson couldn't stop her."

"But I thought she did. Stop that is."

Sam shook her head. "No, Melissa didn't stop her. Penelope just suddenly fell out of the dream. Found herself far from where they had camped, in the middle of a neighborhood, Melissa pleading with her and crying. Freaked her out."

"I can relate to that."

"She said she couldn't resist the urge. That deep inside she knew it was wrong but couldn't stop. Said that if she hadn't snapped out of it she was sure she would have done something awful. Hell, even Sheriff Walker fell into some kind of trance and hit me over the head."

"But what about you?" Lucy asked. "Did he have any effect on you?"

Did he? Or had she simply been caught up in the collective madness that had permeated Mercer's Corner? Sam had never been able to sort that out and had never spoken to anyone other than Charlie about it. She retuned to her chair, leaning forward, elbows on knees, glass of bourbon cradled in both hands and stared at the floor as she spoke.

"That night in the desert. When I woke up, Garrett had stripped me, and hung me by my ankles from the cross beam of a mine entrance. He had a sacrificial table all set. Charlie and Nathan Klimek showed up and managed to distract Garrett long enough for me to unlock my cuffs with the key I had hidden in my cheek and slip out of the rope. Charlie got himself shot for it and Nathan took a knife in the shoulder but it gave me chance to fight back." She hesitated. She didn't want to go on with the story. Get into the parts she had tried for years to erase from her memory.

"And you managed to kill Garrett."

"Eventually."

"Tell me. The whole thing. I need to know."

"Why?"

"Somehow I think it might help me understand all of this."

Sam took a slug of bourbon and massaged one temple. "The world morphed into some multicolored cartoon. Not really a cartoon, since

Garrett had a knife and was prepared to kill me. Nothing cartoonish about that." She finished the bourbon and placed the glass on the table. "But as I stood there facing him across the fire he had built, I couldn't move. It was as if my entire being was frozen." She shook her head.

"And then?"

"I fought it. The colors seemed to fade and then intensify. Back and forth. When they faded I had control when they returned I was . . . I don't know . . . I guess helpless would be the word."

"What did you do?"

"I fought through it. Managed to slam a couple of hooks to Garrett's head. That seemed to break his spell."

"Spell?"

"Whatever the hell it was. Anyway, he ended up a crispy critter on his own fire."

"Amazing."

"Lucky."

"But you managed to take down Garrett after he had dispatched two men. One being the sheriff."

"They were more lovers than fighters," Sam said. "And I was a professional boxer back then."

That got a smile from Lucy.

"But I don't see how all that relates here," Sam said.

"This insanity started when I operated on John Scully, Senior. That's when I fainted. The first time. That's when everything went nutty. Sort of like you and Garrett."

"Except that Scully's dead. Even if Garrett had some kind of power it ended with his death."

Lucy sighed. "I know. But still something happened that day. Something I don't understand. But somewhere inside I feel that Scully is the key to this."

"Then let's dig a little deeper into the Scully clan."

"How? I don't think they'll be very forthcoming about their doings?"

"Let's start with Dwight Doucet. I'll give him a call and see if we can hook up with him. Maybe he knows something."

"If he'll talk to us."

"We'll just have to convince him."

"I don't want you beating up any of the citizens."

"Wouldn't dream of it."

❧

Felicia Scully stood just outside the door to her father's office and listened to the argument. Her father and grandmother had been at it for half an hour.

"You have to put an end to this," Miriam said. "Quickly. This kind of attention isn't helping us."

"I'm working on it," Scully said.

""That's comforting."

"You're not helping here, Mother."

"Look, this was a bad idea from the beginning. Your father was way off base on this. She wasn't ready. It was a gamble and it backfired. Not only is Lucy a loose cannon but everyone she touches goes berzerk."

"That was the plan. Pass along small doses of the power. Increase our influence exponentially."

"Exponentially? I'd say that was accomplished. These murders aren't just going to go away. They'll eventually trace all this back here."

"I don't see how."

"That's the problem, you don't see."

"Okay, Mother. What would you do?"

"Tie up the loose ends and sit tight."

"And exactly how would you do that?"

Felicia heard a vehicle pull up out front. She slipped into a closet just down the hall from the office, leaving the door cracked open. She watched as Eric and Elvin Dawson entered the office, pulling the door closed behind them. She slipped back down the hall and again loitered near the door.

"This is how," Miriam said.

"You called," Eric said.

"We need you boys to do a couple of things," Miriam said.

"What's going on here?" John asked.

"Since you don't seem able to fix this mess, I will," Miriam said. "The way I see it we have two problems. Lucy and Martha."

"And?"

"We need to set up a ceremony where we can take the power back from Lucy."

"And then what?"

"Give it back to you. Your father always intended to pass it on to you. That was the plan. But then he got that cockamamie idea of using Lucy."

"And now she's one of us," John said.

"How can you say that? She's no more part of this than the man in the moon,"

"She'll come around. Her grandmother was reluctant at one time, too."

"She's not like Martha. Martha was prepared. She's wasn't." A beat of silence followed and then Miriam continued. "But she has what we need. And we need to get it back."

John sighed. "Maybe you're right."

"Of course I'm right. But first we have to deal with Martha."

"She's senile, Doesn't remember anything."

"Even the most senile have lucid moments. We can't afford that risk."

"So what are you proposing?" John asked.

"That's where Eric and Elvin come in."

CHAPTER 42

"**M**r. Doucet?" Lucy shouted through the screen door.

No answer.

She and Sam stood on Dwight Doucet's front porch, a white two-person swing hanging on a pair of chains to their right, a large pot of roses flanked by two white wicker chairs to their left. Through the screen and the open front door, she saw a neatly decorated living room.

Lucy rapped on the door frame. "Mr. Doucet?"

Still nothing.

"What do you think" Lucy asked.

"Let's check around back," Sam said.

They found him, near a faded red barn, surrounded by two dozen chickens who fought over the dried corn he shoveled barehanded from a metal bucket and scattered on the ground, each handful raising a chorus of clucks, scratching feet, and rustling wings.

"Mr. Doucet?" Lucy said.

He looked up, startled for a beat, but recovered quickly. "Is it ten already?"

"A little after."

He dumped the remaining corn into a pile. The chickens descended on it. He hung the pail on a rusted nail near the open barn door. "Let's go inside."

After offering Sam and Lucy seats at his kitchen table, he washed his hands in the sink, drying them on a dish towel. "Can I get you something to drink? I have a pitcher of sweet tea in the fridge."

"No, thanks," Lucy said.

He sat down. "You want to talk about the Scullys?"

"If you don't mind."

"Why are you interested in all this ancient history?"

"My grandmother, Martha, Do you know her?"

"For many years."

"She's said a few things lately that don't make much sense. Of course, she's very senile now and most of the time she isn't exactly with it. In fact, she's pretty far out there."

"But?"

Lucy sighed. "I'm not sure. You might know that John, Senior died recently."

"I heard."

"He died on my operating table."

"I'm sorry."

"That's not it. We all lose patients. Particularly those as sick as Scully was. But when I told Martha about it, she became very agitated. Like she was afraid or something."

"I'll tell straight up, I'm not comfortable talking about the Scullys."

"Why?" Sam asked.

"They don't take kindly to folks gossiping about them."

"Nothing you say leaves this room," Lucy said.

He shrugged. "They always seem to find out." He glanced toward the window, his gaze unfocused. "But I guess I'm too old to worry about them now."

"Are you afraid of them?" Sam asked.

"Of course. You should be too."

"Why?"

"That's a question it'd be nice to ask Pete Grimm and Marvin Purdy."

"You don't think John Scully had anything to do with their murders do you?" Sam asked.

"Of course I do. Fact is, I have no doubt about it."

""Can you prove it?"

"Nope. Not anything that'd stand up. I just know it to be true."

"And you think talking to us would endanger your life?"

"Wouldn't surprise me none." He massaged his neck. "But like I said, at my age I guess I'm just a bit tired of being afraid of them."

"They ever threaten you?" Sam asked.

"The old man did. When I left the church he told me as much. Said that if I ever revealed anything about the church the Lord might strike me dead."

"With John, Senior being the lord?" Lucy asked.

He shrugged again. "That's what he thinks anyway."

"Why did you leave the church?" Sam asked.

He rested his forearms on the edge of the table and clasped his hands before him. "Me and old John knew each other forever. Since grade school. We were both members, actually deacons, in Billy Whitehurst's church." He looked at Lucy. "Your grandmother and your parents were members there."

"I know."

"Fact is, I remember you when you were no more than this high." He hovered a flattened hand about three feet above the floor. "Anyway, John took a trip up to West Virginia to visit some church up that way. Run by a fellow name of Rankin Sneed. Supposed to be gone a week but ended up staying a couple of months. Came back full of crazy ideas."

"Like what?"

"Sneed was a snake handler. Had some pretty odd beliefs. Seems John bought into them and tried to bring all that back to Whitehurst's congregation. Didn't sit well."

"Is that when Scully got into snake handling himself?"

He nodded. "Brought back a box filled with rattlers. Whitehurst wouldn't allow them in the church. Needless to say old John wasn't thrilled by that."

"And that led to Scully leaving the church?" Sam asked.

"Wasn't long after that. But it wasn't just the snakes. It seems that while John was up there, Sneed passed. John said Sneed had special powers. Said he passed those on to him. Said he had a direct line to God. That kind of crap." He smiled weakly. "Sorry."

"We've heard worse," Sam said, returning his smile.

Doucet stared off into space and spoke in an even and unemotional voice:

And he said unto them, Go ye into all the world, and preach the gospel to every creature.

He that believeth and is baptized shall be saved; but he that believeth not shall be damned.

And these signs shall follow them that believe; In my name shall they cast out devils; they shall speak with new tongues;

They shall take up serpents; and if they drink any deadly thing, it shall not hurt them; they shall lay hands on the sick, and they shall recover.

So then after the Lord had spoken unto them, he was received up into heaven, and sat on the right hand of God.

And they went forth, and preached everywhere, the Lord working with them, and confirming the word with signs following.

"That's from Gospel of Mark," Doucet said. "It became John's mantra."

Lucy glanced at Sam. "So we've heard."

"We all learned it. Used to recite it before every service." He offered a narrow smile, but his eyes carried a sadness. "Sort of like the Lord's Prayer we used to recite in school." He scratched an ear. "Course, the morons in Washington won't let you do that any more." He shook his head. "This world's a mess. Anyway, old John professed that he now had control of some God-given power. That anyone who didn't believe that was a heretic."

"Bet that didn't sit well with the congregation," Sam said.

"Mostly that's a fact. Some members bought in to it. Others didn't. Including Billy Whitehurst. So old John took a couple of dozen new true believers, as he called them, and moved on. Opened his own church."

"And Martha went with him," Lucy said, a statement, not a question.

"Your parents, too."

Sam scooted her chair forward and rested her elbows on the table. "Tell me more about this power he said he possessed."

"I take it you ladies already know a bit of it. About his interpretation of the Eden story. How the serpent was the real hero. The true savior of mankind."

"John, Junior enlightened us," Lucy said.

""Well there it is. He felt he could communicate directly with the Lord through the snakes. That he and he alone held the key to heaven."

"And you think this had something to do with the murders of Grimm and Purdy?" Sam asked.

"They both spoke out against Scully. I believe he silenced them. As I said, I have no doubts on that point."

"Just no proof?"

"Faith doesn't require proof. You just know."

"This is going to sound odd," Sam said. "But I'm sure you heard about the recent massacres in town."

He nodded. "Terrible."

"Do you think they might have anything to do with Scully?"

A flicker of surprise danced across his face. "I don't see how." Again, he scratched an ear. "You mean like maybe a revenge thing?" He looked at Lucy. "Did they also belong to Scully's church?"

"No. At least not that I know."

"Then I fail to see the connection. Or am I missing something here?"

Lucy hesitated, glancing at Sam, unsure how much to say.

Sam nodded saying, "Go ahead."

Lucy told him of her fainting during Scully's surgery and the other episodes and cold feelings she had experienced in the OR. Then she said, "William Nevers and Ronnie Draper were also my patients. Each had had surgery and each of them had post-op psychiatric complications."

"Psychiatric complications?"

"They became psychotic after surgery. And after they got home . . ."

"Oh, my. I never considered anything like that." His shoulders sagged and his head dropped forward. "So you're asking if maybe old man Scully passed something along to you and then through you on to these folks?"

Was that what she was asking? Could that be possible? No way.

"I'm not sure that's what I meant," Lucy said.

"Sure it is. You're afraid Scully . . . what's the word? . . . contaminated you in some way?"

Lucy stared at him but said nothing, her mind racing over recent events. She knew something wasn't right. But this? She started to protest but Sam laid a hand on her arm.

"Let's say that is what happened," Sam said. "Do you believe that's a possibility?"

He massaged his temples. "Look, I'm a religious man. I believe the Lord has power over all of us. He can make us do most anything if He wants. But I'm not sure Scully and the Lord are all that close. And I don't believe the Lord I know would allow any such thing."

Sam nodded. "Not sure I do either. But all this craziness began when Scully died."

"That's insane, isn't it?" Doucet asked.

"Yes it is," Lucy said.

Doucet stood and walked to the fridge. He pulled out a pitcher of tea. "Sure you won't have some?"

"We're fine," Lucy said.

He poured a glass, took several gulps, and returned to his seat. The sadness in his eyes deepened. "I'll tell you another thing. Scully killed his wife."

"That's something I considered," Sam said. "But I don't really know all the players here. Why do you think that?"

"Not think. Know." He took another gulp of tea. "She was bit by a rattler. Big one from I understand. Now she never touched those snakes. Deathly afraid of them. But somehow she got bit. He refused to take her to the doctor. Said the Lord would protect her from the poison. That and a little strychnine." He massaged his neck. "Old John used to drink it all the time. John, junior still does as far as I know. Part of that whole cockamamie religion Scully created. He said true believers were immune to snake poisons and strychnine, too. Said strychnine was the cure for snake bites."

"What killed her?" Sam asked. "The snake or the strychnine?"

"The snake for sure. That was after I left but some of the witnesses to her death said it was awful. Her arm swole all up and she commenced to vomiting and finally died. A good doctor could've saved her." More tea. "Now you tell me. Is that murder or not?"

CHAPTER 43

"**D**id Scully kill his wife?" Lucy stood looking down at Ty who sat behind his desk.

"What have you two been up to?" he asked.

"We visited Dwight Doucet," Lucy said. "He told us that he believes Scully used one of his snakes to kill her. Is that true?"

Ty picked up his phone and punched the com line button. Sam could hear it buzz somewhere down the hall. "Teri, do you know where Bump is?" Pause. "Thanks." He stood. "Let's go."

"Where?"

"Bump knows more about that case than I do. He's over at JT's." He held the door for them. "I suspect you ladies could use some Q anyway."

"I am hungry," Lucy said. "And Sam always is."

"Funny," Sam said.

"But true."

They walked the half block to JT's BBQ where they found Bump at a corner table, chatting with a tall thin man who wore a white apron over a plaid shirt and jeans. Bump introduced Sam to JT Dodd, the owner.

"NIce to meet you," JT said as he stood. Julie, the waitress, who had served them the last time Sam was here, walked up. "I'll leave you in Julie's capable hands," JT said.

"New hair do?" Lucy asked Julie. Julie's trade-mark short ponytail had given way to a severely-cropped, spiked arrangement that looked like a red version of Lucy's blonde do.

"I finally followed your lead." She forked her fingers through her hair. "This is more practical."

"And it looks great."

"Really? You think so? I wasn't sure."

"Once you get used to it, you'll love it," Lucy said.

"Cool. So what can I get you guys?"

They ordered, pulled pork sandwiches and sweat tea for everyone except Lucy who went for the barbecued chicken salad and water.

"What brings you guys here?" Bump asked.

"Looking for you," Ty said. He then nodded to Sam.

"We heard an interesting theory today," Sam said. "From Dwight Doucet."

"Like what?" Bump asked.

"He believes old man Scully killed his wife with a snake."

Bump leaned back, crossing his thick arms over his chest. "He ain't the only one to think along those lines. I've always believed that."

"What happened?"

"Verna, that was her name, got bit on her arm. Scully refused to take her to the hospital. Gave her some strychnine and prayed over her until the poison took her. Couple of days later. Pretty bad deal."

"Isn't that illegal?" Lucy asked. "Preventing someone from getting help?"

Bump nodded. "If he'd done it against her will I suppose so. But everyone said she didn't want no medical help."

"You believe that?" Sam asked.

"Guess I have to. I talked with a half dozen folks who saw her during that time and they all said the same thing."

"Rehearsed?"

Bump shrugged. "That'd be my guess."

"Couldn't you have forced her to get help?" Lucy asked.

"You ever try to take care of a Christian Scientist? Or try to give blood to a Jehovah's Witness?"

"Sure."

"And you couldn't, right?"

Lucy nodded.

"Same thing. It's one of those church and state deals."

"Ty?" It was JT. He stood behind the counter, phone in hand. "It's Teri Raines, over at your office. Says she tried your cell but didn't get you."

Ty stood, patting the pockets of his jeans. "I left it in the truck." He headed that way.

"And I take it none of them ever changed their story?" Sam asked Bump.

"Believe me, we tried. Scully got his dander all up about it. Said he'd sue the department if we kept harassing his church members."

"That might be a good way to smoke them out," Sam said, while keeping an eye on Ty who held the phone to his ear, brow wrinkled, jaw set. "Law suits open the doors to subpoenas and depositions. Most folks won't lie under oath even for their church."

"Maybe. But we didn't have the money to fend off such a suit."

Ty hung up the phone and approached them with long purposeful strides. "Let's go."

"What is it?"

"Something's going on over at Peter Finch's house."

Julie approached, carrying four plates.

"Sorry, Julie," Ty said. "We got to go."

"Want me to package this up for you?"

"No time."

୬ବ

Lucy sat in the back seat of Ty's Tahoe as he sped out of town and over the Crockett Bridge. She tried to tamp down the growing apprehension that rose in her chest. Please don't let this be another William Nevers or Ronnie Draper situation she silently prayed. But deep inside she knew this wouldn't go well. Why would she suspect anything else? With the way things had unfolded over the past week it really couldn't go any other way.

She half listened as Ty told them that a neighbor had called saying that she heard a commotion and a lot of shouting and what sounded like a war, her word, coming from inside the Finch home. As they approached Finch's, she saw an elderly woman, standing near the curb, waving them forward. Lucy recognized Esther McCumber. Lucy had operated on her husband nearly a year earlier.

Ty parked at the curb, Bump's truck just behind them. They all climbed out.

"What is it, Esther?" Ty asked.

"I'm so glad you're here. You too, Chief." She looked back toward Finch's house. "Somethings going on in there."

"Tell us," Bump said.

"I heard them yelling at each other. Peter and Dora. Then I heard what sounded like furniture breaking up. And glass breaking." She nodded toward the house. "That was fifteen minutes ago. Now it's all quiet."

"Did you see either of them?"

"No. I wasn't about to stick my nose into it. Whatever it is."

Bump looked at the house. "You go on back home and stay there," he said to Esther. Then to Ty, "I'll take the front. You go around back." He pulled his gun.

"I'll go with you," Sam said to Bump.

"I'll stay with Ty," Lucy said.

"You'll stay here, Lucy."

"Not a chance. He's my patient."

Ty pulled his weapon. "And this isn't a hospital. Stay here."

"What are you going to do? Shoot me if I don't?"

Ty sighed. "Then stay behind me."

She did. As they rounded the house she heard Bump fist the front door and shout, "Mr. Finch? It's Chief Whitworth."

Then she saw him. Peter Finch was on both knees in the middle of his backyard. Beside him laid the the bloodied body of his wife. He wore shorts, no shirt, his chest, arms, and face peppered with blood. He held an equally bloodied bat in his hands. He looked up.

"Stay way," he screamed. Then he looked at Lucy. "You. You did this to me."

"Mr. Finch, put the bat down and move away," Ty said. He held his weapon at his side, muzzle aimed at the ground.

Finch stared at him. He seemed confused.

"Now," Ty said.

"No." He stood and took a step toward them.

Ty raised his Glock. "Put it down."

"She did this. She's the evil one." Another step.

"Mr. Finch," Lucy said. "This isn't your fault."

"You're Goddamn right it isn't, you witch. You did this."

"Finch?" Ty said.

"No, she did this. She has to die. Don't you see? She did this to William Nevers and that kid. Now she's done it to me." His breath came in deep gasps, sweat glistening his chest, dragging the blood spatters down his chest and abdomen in long streaks. "She's a sorceress. She's pure evil." Another step forward.

"Stop now," Ty said.

"She has to die or she'll infect us all."

Bump and Sam came out the back door. Finch turned toward them. "Stay back."

"Mr. Finch," Lucy said. "Do what Ty says and let me check your wife. She's injured."

He laughed. It was explosive and his eyes were wild, pupils dilated. "You can't help her. She's dead."

No, no, no, Lucy screamed inside. "Then let me help you."

"Help me?" Another explosive laugh. "Don't you think you've done enough?"

"Take a deep breath," Ty said. "Drop the bat."

"No," he screamed and charged them, swinging the bat in wide arcs before him.

The twin explosions that erupted from Ty's gun caused Lucy to jump. Two red blossoms appeared on Finch's chest, one on either side of the midline scar from his bypass surgery, but he kept coming, the bat leading the way. Two more shots, also in his chest, and he staggered and fell facedown.

Lucy rushed past Ty. She knelt beside Finch, rolling him to his back. She checked his neck for a pulse but found none. She didn't hesitate, immediately beginning chest compressions. Blood flowed from his wounds and over her hands. She knew her efforts weren't going to work but she kept at it.

"Call the medics," Lucy said.

But Finch was gone long before they arrived.

CHAPTER 44

Lucy had slept fitfully the night before, the dreams that had abandoned her the past few nights back with a vengeance. The snakes larger and more aggressive. And more of them. When she finally dragged herself from bed, she mopped around all morning, doing little. Finally, Sam insisted that they get out of the house. Go downtown. Do some shopping. Saying she needed to buy a few things. That wasn't true but she followed Sam's lead. Shopping was something neither of them did very well. Not much practice. Lucy knew Sam felt that fashion was a scam, perpetrated by designers and manufacturers to make folks, particularly women, think that without the latest and coolest jeans, dresses, and of course shoes, their lives were incomplete. In high school, the crushing weight of peer pressure and the desire to be "like totally cool" led to catty remarks, feelings of inadequacy, and the type of parent-teen arguments that can fracture a family. She and Sam had talked about this entire dynamic many times.

For Lucy, she never had time to shop. Rather she knew what she needed, ran in some store to purchase it, ten minutes tops, and fled as quickly as possible. Fashion never affected her, never caused her to stalk the latest trends, simple being the operative word. Medical school, post-graduate training, a busy career that ate up eighty or more hours a week, left little time to dress well anyway. Not to mention that she spent half her life in surgical scrubs. Jeans and a couple of dresses for more formal events were all that hung in her closet and that was fine with her.

But wandering around town, visiting store after store, at least kept her mind occupied. Prevented her from dwelling on the fact that she had nothing else to do. For the first time in her life. The hospital, which had occupied so much of her life, was now off limits. Birnbaum had made it clear she was not welcome until "everything had resolved itself." Whatever the hell that meant. How could she fix something that made no sense?

Today a simple black dress that could be dressed up or down was her only purchase. For Sam, a new pair of New Balance running shoes and a pair of tee shirts covered her needs. Through the entire process, Lucy kept glancing at her watch, not wanting to be late and miss their meeting with Felicia Scully.

A meeting that raised more than a little apprehension in her.

She wasn't sure why, but somewhere deep inside she believed that Felicia held the key to understanding all that happened. She knew this wasn't rational thinking. How could a girl, really a child, be the keeper of the knowledge she needed? True, Felicia was an insider, knew the inner workings of the church, and probably had at least some insight into her father's and grandmother's beliefs, but what could she possibly tell Lucy that brought any clarity. Besides, Felicia was one of them.

Now, after dropping their purchases in the backseat floorboard of Sam's SUV, they stood in the parking lot of the Post Office, shaded by the shadow of the red brick building.

"She's late," Lucy said.

"Give her time," Sam said. "She's doing this on the sly so probably has to do a bit of maneuvering."

"Maybe she chickened out."

"She didn't." Sam nodded toward the building.

Lucy turned to see Felicia. She rounded the corner of the building, then hesitated. She walked slowly toward them.

"I thought it would just be you," she said to Sam.

"Why'd you think that?"

"The note was for you only."

"Is there a problem?" Lucy asked.

Felicia glanced over her shoulder and then back toward Lucy. "How do I know I can trust you?"

"Trust me with what?"

"That you won't tell my father that I'm here."

That made no sense. "Why would I do that?" Lucy asked.

"Because you're part of all that now."

Lucy looked at Sam. "Am I missing something here?"

"Not that I can see." Then to Felicia, Sam said, "Is she? Missing something?"

"They've pulled her in. In ways she might not even know. But she's inside now."

"What are you talking about?" Lucy asked.

"My grandfather had the gift. A very powerful gift. He was to pass it along to my father but something changed. I don't know what. But he passed it to you instead. You must know that."

Lucy felt the hair on her neck rise and a trickles of cold sweat collect between her breasts and along her spine. "I'm afraid I don't know what you're talking about."

Felicia sighed, and mumbled, more to herself, "In for penny, in for a pound." She glanced over her shoulder again.

"What are you afraid of?" Sam asked.

"I have a piano lesson at four. I told my dad I had some stuff to do at school so he dropped me there and will pick me up after my lesson. I sneaked over here to meet you. He has some business in town. I don't know where or with who, but if he sees me talking with you two, it'll be bad. Very bad."

"Maybe not."

"Let's move over there," Felicia said, and not waiting walked over to where two Dumpsters sat against the cinder block wall that guarded one side of the parking area. She stepped in between them. Sam and Lucy followed.

"You don't understand," Felicia said. "I can't really explain it. Let's just say we don't always agree."

"Sounds like the typical father-teenage daughter dynamic," Lucy said.

Felicia let out a short laugh. "Not even close." She fumbled in her purse, pulled out a pack of cigarettes and a blue plastic lighter. She extracted one and lit it. Lucy noticed her hands were shaking.

"I bet he wouldn't approve of that," Lucy said.

Felicia took a puff and let it out slowly. "I shouldn't be here."

Lucy laid a hand on her arm. "Relax. This is just between us."

"So you think. My father knows everything." Another puff.

"So what is this gift, or power, or whatever it is?" Sam asked.

"A direct line to God. Through the sacred serpent. It gives him control of some people."

Now Sam laughed. "You don't believe that do you?"

"Of course I do. I've seen it." She looked at Lucy. "You have, too."

"Are you talking about the recent murders?" Sam asked.

She nodded. "You don't think those were by accident do you?"

"Actually they were due to a known, though not common, medical problem," Lucy said.

"No, they weren't. I don't understand it all but I know my father and my grandmother were arguing about it the other night. Something about my grandfather making a decision that has now backfired."

"What decision?" Sam asked.

"Giving this power to her." Felicia nodded toward Lucy. She dropped the half-smoked cigarette and mashed it with her shoe. "My grandfather was The Keeper. He had the power and, as I said, he passed it to you."

Lucy felt a headache forming and massaged the back of her neck. "Okay, not that I'm buying it, but let's say he did. Why me?"

"Something about a deal between him and your grandmother."

"Martha? What does she have to do with this?"

Felicia stared at her for a beat. "You don't know, do you?"

"Know what?"

"Martha is your mother, not your grandmother."

"What?"

"And my grandfather is your father."

Lucy felt her lungs collapse. "That's insane. Not possible."

"It's true. I thought you knew."

A cold feeling swelled in Lucy's stomach, followed by dizziness. She grabbed the edge of the Dumpster for support.

Sam grabbed her arm. "You okay?"

Lucy beat down a wave of nausea and took a couple of deep slow breaths. "I'm fine."

"This is what you wanted to tell us?" Sam said. "That Lucy's parents aren't her real parents?"

"No. What I wanted to say is that you have to give it back. To my father."

Lucy stared at her as the cold feeling spread upward into her chest and then down each arm. Her hands ached as if dipped in ice water.

This was making less sense every minute. Was Felicia crazy? Maybe suffering from some paranoid delusion? Maybe even some form of schizophrenia? Or at least some religious idolatry. Yet, she showed no other signs. She was obviously oriented and not confused. Lucy wasn't a psychiatrist but she remembered her med school psych professor saying that one of the signs of schizophrenia is if you are talking to a schizophrenic you begin to think you're the crazy one. Some can make even the most outlandish ideas seem perfectly acceptable. This conversation qualified.

"I have nothing to give back," Lucy said.

"But you do. You're the new Keeper. But you were never prepared. Never trained. That's why it's all so out of control. You must give it back."

"Exactly how would she do that?" Sam asked.

Tears collected in Felicia's eyes. "I don't know. There's some kind of ritual but I've never seen it. I don't know anything about it. The only Keeper I've ever known was my grandfather." She looked at Lucy. "And now you."

"This all sounding pretty crazy," Lucy said.

Felicia sniffed back her tears and rubbed the palms of her hands in her eyes. "You're right. It's crazy. I shouldn't have come here. I shouldn't have said anything."

"Felicia, I'm not saying you're crazy. I just don't understand what you're saying."

"I've got to go." She brushed past them and into the lot.

"Felicia?" Lucy said.

But the girl didn't look back. She hurried across the lot and around the corner.

"What was that all about?" Lucy asked,

Sam shook her head. "I have no idea."

"I know who to ask."

"Martha?"

"Exactly."

"But she's so out of it I don't think she will be much help."

Lucy took a deep breath and let it out slowly. "I don't know who else to ask." Tears collected in her eyes. "But what she said isn't exactly wrong."

"Like what?"

"Something happened to me. When Scully senior died. Nothing has been right since then."

"But like you said, there's a perfectly logical medical explanation for all that's happened."

"Really? All these people going insane? Me fainting? It's like there's something in the water or something." Lucy started across the lot toward Main Street. "Let's go see Martha."

CHAPTER 45

"She's had a good day," Sue Cramer said. She was sitting in the nurse's station, working on a stack of charts. "She had a good lunch and even said a few things that almost made sense." She smiled at Lucy. "Almost."

"I need to talk with her about a couple of things so hopefully she's still with it."

"Good luck with that. These periods of even quasi lucidity are brief at best." Sue closed one chart and pulled another from the pile. "Let me know if you need anything."

Martha sat in her chair, back to them, facing her window, a loosely knit shawl draped over her frail shoulders. She didn't respond when Lucy pulled a chair around and sat facing her, Martha's gaze fixed on the window.

"How are you doing today?" Lucy asked.

No response.

"Sue tells me you've been very talkative today."

Nothing.

"Martha, look at me."

Martha's gaze bounced that way for a beat, but revealed no recognition. Then her attention returned to the window.

"I need to ask you some questions."

Did Martha's eyes narrow slightly? DId her shoulders tense slightly? Lucy couldn't be sure.

"We just had a chat with Felicia Scully. She said some pretty crazy things."

Martha's face definitely tightened.

"She said that you are my mother. Isn't that crazy?"

Martha begin to rock back and forth slightly. A small dollop of spittle collected at the corner of her mouth. Lucy grabbed a tissue from the table next to her and dabbed it away.

"Isn't that crazy?" she repeated.

Martha's rocking increased.

"And she said that John Senior is my father."

Now Martha begin to rock harder, her head wagging back and forth.

"Is that true? Are you really my mother?"

Martha's face contorted into a look of great pain. "No Scully. No Scully. No Scully."

Lucy grabbed her shoulders and stopped her gyrations. "Martha, look at me. Is that true?

Martha let out a deep, low moan followed by, "No Scully. No Scully."

"She said you and Scully had some sort of pact. Had to do with this special power he supposedly had. According to Felicia, it was supposed to be passed to John, Junior but for some reason he gave it to me. Do you know anything about that?"

"No, no, no." Martha's voice was strained and plaintiff as if in great pain.

"This all sounds preposterous to me but there have been a lot of odd happenings lately. I'm simply looking for an explanation. And the truth." She reached out and hooked a finger beneath Martha's chin, turning her head toward her. "Please try to concentrate. Try to remember."

Martha convulsed and tears welled in her eyes, magnifying them.

"You know the truth. It's in there somewhere. Try to dig it out. Please. It's important that I know."

Martha let out a long, agonizing wail. "Give it back," she screeched. "Give it back."

"Give what back?"

Martha suddenly looked at her, face drawn tightly over her boney cheeks. She clutched Lucy's arm, squeezing as if she were a life preserver and Martha was in danger of drowning. "You have to give it back."

"Tell me what it is. How do I give it back?"

Now Martha's entire body began contorting, her head snapping back and forth. Again she shrieked, "Give it back, It's not yours. Give it back."

"Is everything okay?" It was Sue, coming through the door and into the room. "I heard her screeching and figured she was getting all wound up again."

Before Lucy could say anything, Martha's screeching kicked up a few decibels. She began to writhe and try to get up from the chair. Sam grabbed her shoulders and held her down. Martha twisted and jerked and tried to escape.

"I'd better get some Ativan" Sue said.

Martha gave up her struggles and instead reached up, clutching Lucy's head with cold, hard fingers. She pulled her close, their noses only inches apart. "Give it back. It will destroy you. It's not yours. It's his. Give it back."

Sue appeared, syringe in hand.

"Just a second," Lucy said, and then to Martha, "What is it? What must I give back?"

But Martha was gone again. Her wails echoed in the room and she began to struggle against Sam, screaming,"No, no, no."

CHAPTER 46

.

S am stood near the door with Sue Cramer, her eyes watering as the scene unfolded before her. Lucy sat on the edge of Martha's bed, clutching her grandmother's limp hand. Lucy's head drooped forward and her shoulders convulsed with sobs.

The call had come thirty minutes earlier while she and Lucy sat at the kitchen table, sipping coffee, and planning the day. A few errands Lucy had neglected, the gym, and then lunch. Sounded like a good plan. Never happened. The call changed everything. Lucy had wanted to drive but Sam nixed that, saying she was in no condition. So they jumped into Sam's SUV and sped over to Wellstone Manor. Sue met them near the entrance and led them to Martha's room.

Sam knuckled a tear from one eye and then in a low voice asked, "When did you find her?"

"At breakfast. One of the girls from dietary brought in her food and found her unresponsive. She freaked out."

"Freaked out?"

"Sure did. I mean, we have deaths here from time to time. Comes with the population we serve. But most aren't Martha. She's an icon. Anyway she ran to me so I checked Martha. No doubt she was gone. She was cold to the touch so I suspect she died sometime in the night." Sue sighed. "In her sleep. All and all not a bad way to go."

Sam nodded. "That'd be my choice."

Sam remembered the day, many years ago, when she was only fourteen, when her mother had passed. Also in her sleep. FInally. Thankfully. After a bitter war with breast cancer. After the disease had taken her body and her soul. Had crushed her into a shell of who she was. The same could be said for Martha. Her dementia had left behind a different kind of shell.

Even expected deaths are unexpected. Sam had known her mother would die. Had known it would be soon. Yet, when it happened, it seemed sudden. Disorienting. Like everything had tilted at an odd angle. The theoretical, the possible, suddenly real. Preparing didn't make you prepared.

Guilt and recriminations. Things she had done that had vexed her mother. Things she had wanted to say but somehow never did. The simple telling her mother how much she loved her. How much she would miss her. But at that moment, when she sat next to her mother, holding her hand, her mind fixed on all the things she had done wrong. Nothing major, just the flexing her own newly found teenage muscles. When she, like every teenager, thought she knew it all. Had it all figured out. Her mother, of course, knew otherwise. Sitting there, willing her departed mother to know all she had left unsaid, the good moments seemed to slip away. Only the images of their conflicts formed in her head.

Sam knew that's where Lucy was. She had expected this day but didn't know it would be this particular day.

Lucy finally released Martha's hand and swiped the back of one of her own hands across her eyes. She took a deep breath, let it out slowly, and then stood. She turned to Sam, her eyes red and swollen, face drawn.

Sam walked around the bed and hugged her. Lucy seemed to sag against her.

"You okay?" Sam asked.

"No." She sniffed.

"I'm so sorry."

"And I'm so glad you're here." She hugged Sam more tightly and then broke the embrace. "I don't know what I'd do without you." Lucy's face screwed down as she suppressed another sob. "I should have been here."

"Had you known this would happen you would have. No one expects anymore of you."

"Still."

"Still nothing. I'm sure you've had patient's families say the same thing."

"Too often."

"And what did you tell them?" Lucy said nothing. "I'd bet you told them they had done all they could and to not carry any guilt with them. That Mother Nature didn't have a schedule."

"That's true."

"Then don't beat yourself up over this. Martha knew you loved her. And that you did all you could to make her life as comfortable as possible."

Lucy sighed, straightened her shoulders, and then wiped her eyes again, this time with her two palms. "I guess I should call the funeral home."

"Come on," Sue said. "You can use the phone in my office."

After they left, Sam stood over Martha. She remembered the Martha of years past. When she was bright, charming, and funny. When she spent hours painting. When she entertained guests with grace and elegance and gave deeply emotional speeches to schools and community groups and art museums. And now? Martha's corpse lay on the clean, white sheets, the top sheet and blanket snugged up to her chest. Her head lolled to one side, her mouth slightly open.

What a complete tragedy.

She turned to walk away but something caught her eye. She stopped.

She leaned over, bringing her face closer to Martha's. At first she saw nothing but as she moved her head slightly, changing the angle of her gaze, she saw it. No doubt. A bruise along the right side of her mouth.

What the hell?

She reached out and rolled down Martha's lower lip. Martha had been blessed with good teeth and, except for a single bridge lower left, she still retained all her own teeth.

The abrasions were readily visible. Abrasions from her teeth as someone had pressed something over her face. She carefully opened Martha's eyes. Several faint rusty red petechial hemorrhages dotted her white sclera and pale pink conjunctivae.

Jesus.

She quickly pushed the arms of Martha's nightgown up. The finger-shaped bruises that splotched both of Martha's upper arms suggested a very different story. Not one of a peaceful death during sleep.

Sam took a step back. She glanced toward the door, thankful Lucy and Sue hadn't returned. She scanned the room. All looked to be in order. Nothing out of place. Except a single pillow that lay on the floor, near the corner, beneath the window Martha loved to look out. She grasped one corner and picked it up. A whitish stain, flecked with tiny specks of blood, stood out against the stark white of the pillow. She carefully placed the pillow on the bedside table, stained side up.

Sam pulled her cell phone from her pocket and punched in17, the speed dial she had assigned to Ty's cell. He answered immediately.

"Can you get over here to the Wellstone?" Sam asked.

"Sure. What's going on?"

"Martha died."

"Jesus. How's Lucy?"

"Not well. But that's not why I called."

"Why then?"

"You need to see something."

"What?"

"You'll see when you get here."

"That sounds mysterious."

"Just get you butt in your truck and get over here."

"When you ask so nicely, how could I refuse."

He showed up in under ten minutes.

"Okay," Ty said as he walked into Martha's room. "What's this all about?"

Sam showed him what she had uncovered.

Ty pushed his hair back off his forehead. "What the hell is going on around here. Seems like we've had at least one murder every day."

"Well that took longer than I thought it . . ." Lucy said as she came into the room. She stopped mid-sentence when she saw Ty. "Ty? What brings you here?"

Ty glanced at Sam.

"She doesn't know any of this yet."

"Any of what?" Lucy looked from Sam to Ty and back to Sam.

Sam nodded toward Ty.

"I think Martha didn't simply pass in her sleep." The confusion on Lucy's face was apparent. "Looks like she was murdered."

Lucy paled and took a wobbly step back. "What are you talking about?"

Ty went through the evidence. Lucy sat in one of the chairs, her head forward, elbows on her knees, hands bunching her hair on either side. Her head shook slowly back and forth as he spoke. When he fell silent, she looked up.

"Who? Why?"

"I guess that's the million dollar question. Any ideas?"

Lucy hesitated a beat and then said, "Scully."

"Why would you think that?"

"Because somehow, I have no idea how, he's behind all this."

Ty looked at her but said nothing.

"Martha left the church. Not on a happy note either from what I can tell."

"That was a long time ago," Ty said. "Why would he decide to harm her now?"

"He's been trying to recruit me back into the church. Maybe he thought Martha was influencing me otherwise."

"That's seems like a stretch to me. I mean, she's . . . she was . . old and senile. Don't see how she could be a threat or a problem for him."

"Does anything make sense now?" Lucy said. "With all that's happened recently?"

Ty didn't look as if he was convinced. "I'll call Granville and we'll get her over to his office. Maybe he can shed some light on this."

Lucy stood. She looked at Sam. "Let's go."

"Where?"

"I have somewhere I need to be." With that she walked out of the room.

"Any idea what's that about?" Ty asked.

Sam shook her head. "None."

"Want me to tag along?"

"You take care of this. I'll go with her."

CHAPTER 47

"Do you think this is a good idea?" Sam asked.

"Probably not," Lucy said. "Just doing what I know you'd do."

"Which is?"

"Jump right in the middle of it."

"By confronting Scully?"

"Seems like a good place to start," Lucy said. "He's involved. I don't know how or why but he is."

"I won't argue with you there."

"So, it's time to get in his face."

"Grill. They call it getting into someone's grill now days."

"Whatever." Lucy stepped out of Sam's SUV, the gravel that covered the Eden's Gate parking area crunching beneath her shoes. "You have your gun, don't you?"

"Yes. But I don't particularly want to use it."

"You're getting soft."

"I didn't say I wouldn't. Just that I'd rather not."

"Then follow my lead."

"Yes, General Wagner."

Lucy shoved open the front door of the church and marched inside. Sam followed. They found Felicia in the chapel. On her knees, bent over a poster on the floor. She looked up.

"What's that?" Lucy asked as she and Sam approached.

"A poster for my Sunday School class this week."

The poster contained a picture of Jesus pasted in the upper left corner and numbered list written in elegant script with the bright blue marker Felicia held. It read:

The Attributes of Our Lord

1—Faithful
2—Compassionate
3—Kind
4--Foregving
5—Passive
6--

"Looks good," Sam said.

"The kids like posters and visuals. Helps them learn."

"Your father around?" Lucy asked.

"He and grandmother are in his office." She stood. "Come on. I'll take you back."

They followed Felicia down the hallway to a closed door along the left side. Lucy could hear voices inside. Felicia gave the door a rap and then eased it open slightly.

"Dr. Wagner and Sam are here."

Through the cracked door, Lucy saw Scully, sitting behind his desk. He stood.

"Please, show them in," Scully said.

Felicia pushed the door open and stepped aside. Mariam sat on a sofa along the far wall. Where Scully smiled at them, Mariam seemed to frown. Felicia excused herself, saying she had to finish her poster.

"Come in," Scully said. "I'm happy you dropped by."

"Probably not," Lucy said.

Scully seemed to recoil slightly. "What's wrong?"

"Martha's dead."

"I heard."

That wasn't what Lucy expected to hear. But then, if he was involved, of course he'd know.

"How'd you find out?" Sam asked.

"Our members keep us well informed. I got a phone call just a little while ago."

"From who?" Sam asked. "Those Watson clowns?"

Scully didn't flinch. "Can't really say."

"Of course you can't."

A brief glare toward Sam and then he looked at Lucy. "I'm sorry. Martha was a very special lady."

"She didn't just die," Lucy said. "She was murdered."

"Really? How do you know that?"

"It's called evidence," Sam said. "Most murderers aren't that smart so they leave stuff behind."

Lucy detected a slight flash of concern cross Scully's face. Didn't last long, his expression of false concern quickly reappearing.

"Who would do that?" Scully asked.

"I was going to ask you the same thing," Lucy said.

"I'm sure I don't know."

"I'm sure you don't," Sam said.

Scully's face hardened. "What exactly are you saying?"

Sam started to respond but Lucy cut her off. "That Martha was murdered. That I can't think of anyone who would want her dead. Except maybe you."

"Me? Why would I want that?"

"Let's see. You have been trying to pull me back into your little snake cult. Martha has been trying her best to warn me away. Now she's dead. Pretty easy to connect those dots."

Scully dropped back into his chair. "I'm shocked that you'd think that. We," he nodded toward Mariam, "loved Martha. Always have. We would never wish her harm."

"I'm having trouble with that," Lucy said. "There are a few things I don't understand."

"Such as?"

"For starters, was your father my father?"

"Yes."

"And Martha my mother?"

Scully nodded. "Also true." He glanced at Miriam. "Right?"

"It's true," Miriam said.

"Then who were the people I thought were my parents?"

Scully hesitated as if organizing his thoughts. "They were church members who agreed to raise you."

"Raise me? Why wouldn't Martha?"

"She did. After your parents untimely death."

"Untimely?" Sam asked.

"Maybe unexpected would be a better word."

"Was it?" Sam asked. "Unexpected?"

Another glare. "They died in a house fire. From a faulty heater if I remember correctly."

Sam shook her head. "Or so it seemed."

Now Scully offered a fatherly smile. "Perhaps you should check the police reports. You're a cop. Right? I'm sure you know how to read a police report."

"I just might do that."

"Do. Then you can stop these insinuations."

"Let's get back to Martha," Lucy said. "If she's my mother, why did she never tell me?"

Miriam sighed and Lucy looked her way. "Look at the big picture. My husband, your father, was the spiritual leader of the church. He founded it. And Martha was a pillar in the church. How would it look if they had a child out of wedlock?" When Lucy didn't respond, she continued. "The church was young then. Still trying to gain its footing. Such a scandal could have destroyed all John had worked for."

"You mean the snakes might have died from embarrassment?" Sam asked.

Miriam pushed herself off the sofa and stood. "You can demean this all you want, but my husband revealed the true word. The true power of the Lord. He was a good man and a true leader."

"Which brings up my next question" Lucy said. "What is this Keeper?"

Miriam took a step back, her calves bumping the sofa, causing her to waver a beat. She recovered and looked at her son.

"What do you mean?" Scully asked.

"I'm not saying I buy into any of this, but I've heard that your father was this mysterious Keeper. That he received this so called honor from some guy up in West Virginia." A crease of concern worked its way into Scully's forehead. "That it was to be passed to you but somehow was given to me. Do you believe that?"

Scully picked up a ball point pen from his desktop and began tapping it on the surface. Buying time. "My father was a spiritual leader. He learned a great deal from Reverend Rankin Sneed in West Virginia. But a Keeper? I'm afraid I've never heard that term."

"So your father didn't pass something on to me? When he died?"

"Passed on? Like what?"

"Like some evil power? Some ability to control others?"

Now Scully smiled openly. "Does that make any sense? That supernatural powers can simply be passed from person to person? That's crazy."

CHAPTER 48

Lucy grabbed the handle above the passenger door as Sam turned off the county highway on to an uneven and buckled blacktop, her Lexus SUV gyrating over its bumps and ruts. The road wound through a thick, regimented growth of loblolly pines, which thinned at a narrow bridge that spanned a shallow creek. The road then fell away and swung left before snaking back toward the creek.

"We're close." Lucy unfolded the hastily sketched map Felicia had slipped to her as they left the church and held it up so Sam could see it. Drawn with a bright blue marker: the creek a double wavy line, the road a single wiggle, and the bridge a rectangular box.

"Here is the bridge," Lucy said. "And we should be about here."

"Looks like the road parallels the creek a bit."

"More or less. Not sure how accurate this map is."

The road did follow the creek and after a few hundred yards butted right up against it.

"This looks like it," Lucy said.

Sam parked near a cluster of hickory trees and they climbed out. The creek here was shallow and wide, the water sliding over smooth, multi-colored rocks, the silence broken only by its trickling and the cooing of a pair of nearby doves. Lucy examined the note again. A large X marked the spot where they stood. At the top of the page Felicia's block printing said:

MEET ME HERE. 30 MINUTES.

"Any idea what she wants?" Lucy asked.

"I'd assume something about her father. Maybe her grandfather."

Lucy leaned against the SUV, arms crossed, palms gripping her elbows. "I hope so. This is all too crazy for words."

"No argument there." Sam picked up a smooth, reddish rock, examined it, and then tossed it into the creek.

"What do you make of what happened back there?" Lucy asked.

"About your parents?"

"That and this whole Keeper thing."

"I don't know. Maybe Felicia does."

Lucy glanced at her watch. "What if she doesn't come?"

"She will." Another rock, another toss into the creek. "Unless her parents catch her slipping away."

Lucy heard a rustling in the trees just across the creek and then Felicia appeared. She ducked beneath a sagging pine bough and into the open.

"I was afraid you wouldn't come," Felicia said. She tip-toed across the creek, settling each step firmly on a rock.

"Any trouble getting away?" Sam asked.

"No." She glanced back over her shoulder. "But I don't have much time."

"Why did you want to meet?" Lucy asked.

Felicia sighed. "So much is going on, I'm not even sure where to begin."

"Anywhere you want."

Felicia glanced up the creek, her gaze unfocused as if gathering her thoughts. Finally she spoke. "You said Martha was murdered. How do you know?"

"The evidence all points that way," Sam said.

"How?"

"I'd rather not say. Detective Everson is looking into it."

"What time did it happen?"

"Don't know for sure. Sometime between ten last night and early this morning. Why do you want to know?"

Felicia kicked at a loose rock. "My father was out last night. With the Watson brothers."

Lucy glanced at Sam. "Really?"

"He left around nine or thereabouts. I heard him come in around two."

"That unusual?" Sam asked. "For him to go out at night?"

"Not really. But he's almost never out that late."

"Were the Watsons with him when he came back?"

"I think so. It sounded like their truck that dropped him off."

"Do you think they had anything to do with Martha's death?" Sam asked.

"I don't know. Maybe."

"Maybe?" Lucy asked.

"Like I told you before. I overheard my father and grandmother talking the other day. Arguing mostly. Miriam was upset about this entire thing. Said that you should never have been made the Keeper. That it was my father's birthright."

"You believe all that? That you grandfather had some super power?"

"Absolutely." She kicked another rock into the creek. "I have no doubt about that."

"Why?"

"My grandfather had a way of manipulating people. I never saw it when I was younger, but looking back, he could bend people to his will."

"So could Charles Manson," Sam said. "And Jim Jones. Didn't mean they had special powers."

"This is different."

"How so?" Sam asked.

Felicia sighed. "I don't know. It's hard to explain." She worked a cuticle with her thumbnail. "He just had a way of getting people to do what he wanted."

"And you father? Does he have the same ability?"

"Not like granddad."

"So your father and grandmother were arguing," Lucy said. "About what specifically?"

"You. Martha."

They waited her out.

"Miriam said that you would never come around. Never be the true Keeper. That Martha was influencing you too much."

"Martha's wasn't in any position to influence anyone. She was very senile and made no sense most of the time."

Felicia shrugged. "I don't know nothing about that but Miriam was worried. Said that she had to be dealt with. My father said that he'd get the Watsons involved and everything would be alright."

"Did he say he would have them harm Martha?"

"Not really. But her name came up. As did yours." She looked at Sam. "Yours, too."

"In what context?" Sam asked.

"After they argued a bit, I got the sense that Miriam won out. That my father finally agreed that you and Martha were loose cannons. Dangerous to his cause. Father said he and the Watsons would make it all okay. Said he would get back what was rightly his. From you." Her gaze seemed to stab Lucy.

"Exactly how does that work?" Sam asked. "Let's say your father believes that Lucy is this Keeper, or whatever. That she was given this power. How does he propose to get it back, so to speak?"

"I told you. I don't know it works. I only know that it involves some ritual."

"Like burning leaves and chanting?" Sam asked

Felicia's face hardened and her eyes narrowed. "You shouldn't mock these things."

"Don't you think these things are a bit out there?" Sam asked. "Sort of don't pass the common sense test?"

"Religion never does. It's a matter of faith."

"Let's get back to your father," Lucy said. "Did he in any way threaten to do something to Martha?"

"Not in so many words, but I think his intentions were clear. He feared Martha knew too much. He feared Sam might find out too much. And he feared you might never take on the mantle my grandfather offered."

"And the only way to prevent Martha from talking just might be to kill her?" Sam asked.

"He didn't say that out right but with the Watsons involved anything's possible."

"I see." Lucy walked near the girl and looked her in the eye. "Do you believe that your father is capable of murder?"

"Of course I do. I believe he killed my mother."

"Do you have any proof?" Sam asked.

"Just what I overheard when he and Miriam were arguing. He said something like he might have to deal with you just as he had dealt with my mother."

"The snakes?" Lucy asked.

Felicia nodded.

"Would you testify to what you heard?" Sam asked.

"No way. My father would kill me."

"Literally?"

Felicia stared at Sam, then Lucy, and then at her feet.

"Why did you want to tell us all this?" Lucy asked. "What do you need?"

"I want out."

"Out?"

"Out. Away from both of them. My father is dangerous. I've known it for a long time. Ever since my mother died." She scrunched her face as if trying to prevent tears from escaping. Didn't work. Her eyes watered and a tear escaped down her cheek. She swiped it away. "I think I always knew he had something to do with her getting snake bit but I wasn't sure until the other day. Now I know."

"But you have no proof," Sam said.

Felicia shook her head.

"Where would you go?" Lucy asked.

She sniffed and again stared unfocused up the creek. "I have no idea."

"We can help you," Lucy said.

"Really? How?"

"There are ways," Sam said. "We can make you disappear and they will never know where you are."

Another sniff and a swipe of a hand across her nose. "You mean like witness protection?"

Sam laughed. "Maybe not quite that drastic, but we'll see."

"What now?" Lucy asked.

Felicia glanced back toward the trees she had come through. "I have to go. I just wanted to warn you."

"I'm glad you did." Lucy stepped forward and hugged her. "I know this took great courage for you to come here. You're a strong young lady. It's all going to be okay."

"I hope you're right but I have a very bad feeling." She broke the embrace.

"Don't do anything," Lucy said. "Don't say a word about this to anyone and go along with whatever your father says."

"And keep your eyes and ears open," Sam said.

Felicia hesitated a beat and then nodded. She turned, crossed the creek, and disappeared into the trees.

CHAPTER 49

L ucy found Martha's corpse unnerving. Not that she hadn't confronted many corpses in her career and, of course, had even seen Martha's earlier at Wellstone Manner. Stretched out in her bed. Like a deceased patient in the hospital. Calm and peaceful.

But this wasn't a patient. This was Martha. The woman who had raised her. Had taught her everything. And now she rested on a cold, metal dissection table, the overhead surgical lamps casting a harsh, flat light over her pale flesh. No way she could maintain a professional detachment here. It was all a bit disorienting.

Apparently Ty sensed her discomfort. He wrapped an arm around her shoulders.

"You okay?"

"No."

"It'll get better."

"I know." She sighed and looked across Martha's corpse to where Coroner Larry Granville stood. "What did you find?"

"Same thing Ty and Sam found." He pulled off his half glasses, folded them, and slipped them into the breast pocket of his white lab coat. "Petechiae in her eyes, a few in her throat, bruising inside her lips. And bruises on her upper arms consistent with someone restraining her."

"So she was murdered?" Sam asked.

"That'd be my guess. I haven't completed the autopsy yet but I don't expect to find anything internally that'd alter that opinion. I'd say she was held down and smothered by the pillow you found." He nodded toward Sam. "And the stain on the pillow was indeed saliva. I'll run a DNA analysis to make sure it's Martha's but I'd be surprised if it wasn't."

"Can we go someplace else?" Lucy asked. "Standing here talking across Martha's body is freaking me out."

"Let's grab some fresh air," Granville said.

He led them outside into the parking lot. They settled in the shade of a pair of maple trees near the entrance.

"This is better," Lucy said.

"Scully and the Watsons," Sam said. "They did this."

"We don't know that for sure," Lucy said.

"You mean like they were just out star gazing last night?"

Lucy shrugged. "I'm only saying that we don't know for sure that they did it."

"Am I missing something here?" Granville asked.

Sam told him and Ty of their conversation with Felicia.

"So Scully and the Watsons were together and out and about at the time of the murder?" Ty asked.

"If you believe Felicia," Sam said.

"Do you?" Ty asked. "Believe her?"

Sam nodded. "I do."

"Me, too," Lucy added.

"Why would she tell you guys that?" Ty asked.

"She wants to get away from her father and Miriam," Sam said.

"Don't most teenagers want that?" Granville asked.

"This is different," Sam said. "She believes that her father killed her mother."

"Not sure I'd argue with her there," Ty said.

"She also said that her father and Miriam consider Lucy and I problems."

"Gee, I've never heard that before," Ty said. "You two? Problems?"

"Funny," Sam said. "Felicia overheard them talking about Martha. And us. And now Martha ends up murdered."

"Apparently murdered," Granville said.

"Really?" Sam said. "What manner of death are you going to put on the certificate?"

Granville shrugged. "Unless I find something different, I'd say homicide."

"Then, there you go. And if they did kill Martha, Lucy and I could be on their agenda."

"Jesus," Lucy said. "That's all I need. Martha dead, my career in ruins, and now I have to worry about a crazy preacher and a pair of dirt balls." She shook her head. "Not to mention that I have the honor of carrying around some Keeper bullshit."

"Keeper?" Granville asked.

"I'd tell you, but you'd think I was crazy," Lucy said.

"Try me."

"Apparently Scully, Sr. got some supernatural power from a snake-handler named Sneed up in West Virginia. This Sneed character died while Scully was up there and apparently passed along this power to him. He calls it The Keeper."

"Sounds pretty woo-woo to me," Granville said.

"Me, too. Anyway, supposedly, when old John Scully died on my operating table he passed this crap along to me and then I passed it along to William Nevers, and Joseph Finch, and Ronnie Draper. Made them go crazy. Do what they did."

Granville nodded. "You believe that?"

"No. But I'm not sure I understand anything anymore." She looked at Granville. "Like who my parents are."

"What do you mean?"

"Felicia said that Old John was my father and Martha my mother. That the two people who I thought were my parents aren't."

"That young lady is just full of odd news," Granville said. "You sure this isn't all simply the wild imagination of a young girl?"

"Except that Nevers, Finch, and Draper did do all those awful killings. In a town where these things never happen."

"Don't they always say that?" Ty said. "That bad things never happen in this or that town? But bad things have to happen somewhere."

"You're quite the philosopher," Sam said.

Ty grinned. "You would doubt that?"

"I would," Lucy said and then to Granville. "I know how to solve that riddle. I want my parents bodies exhumed and DNA testing done."

"I don't think that's possible," Granville said.

"I'll pay for it."

"That's not the problem. Your parents were in a fire. Bad one from what I understand. I imagine the corpses were significantly damaged. And then there is all those decades in the ground. The odds of getting usable DNA would be fairly remote."

"But possible?"

"Anything's possible. But it's very unlikely."

"I'm willing to take that chance."

Granville nodded. "There's an easier way."

"Like?"

"Let's say we dug up your parents and did find good DNA. Let's say it proved they weren't your parents. Where would you be?"

"Confused."

"True. But you still wouldn't know who your parents are."

"If it matched I would."

"That's correct. But from what Felicia Scully said they wouldn't match so you'd still be at square one. But I have both Martha's and John Scully's DNA. From their autopsies. I'll do a paternity match and see if what Felicia says is true. And that wouldn't require digging anyone up."

"That makes sense."

Granville nodded and hesitated a beat. "Are you sure you want to know?"

"Why wouldn't I?"

"Sometimes it's best to let sleeping dogs lie."

"Not here. I have to know."

Granville sighed. "Okay. Let me take a buccal smear from you and I'll get on it. Probably have something tomorrow."

"Meanwhile, I'll go have a chat with Scully and the Watson brothers," Ty said. "See if they have an alibi for last night."

"Each other," Sam said. "They'll vouch for each other."

Ty smiled. "Might have to crack a couple of coconuts."

"Count me in," Sam said.

CHAPTER 50

"**N**o, you're not," Sam said.

"Yes, I am," Lucy responded. "This is my life. I want to look him in the face."

"I don't want you anywhere near Scully or the Watson brothers."

"But it's okay for you?"

Sam patted her jacket pocket. The one that held her .357. "I'm armed."

"Then, I'll stay behind you, but I'm coming with you."

Sam looked at Ty. "Can you talk some sense into her?"

"Lucy . . ."

"Don't Lucy me."

Sam saw tears collect in Lucy's eyes even as her chin elevated and her fists balled at her side. The tough Lucy. The defiant Lucy. Also the scared Lucy.

Sam hugged her. Lucy tried to slip from her grasp but Sam held on.

"Listen to me." She spoke quietly, her mouth near Lucy's ear. "This is a police matter. And it can get tricky. I don't want us to have to watch out for you while we just might need to cover each other's backs." She felt Lucy's shoulders sag as she gave up her struggles.

"But I want to hear it from his mouth. I want him to lie to my face."

"He already did. And he will again."

"But . . ."

"But there is nothing to gain here. No need for you to be near him."
Sam released her embrace and grabbed Lucy by the shoulders, looking her
in the eye. "You said you had a bunch of paperwork to do at your office
today, so go do that. We'll go see Scully."

Lucy nodded. "You're right."

"I know."

"Don't go all bitchy."

"Just trying to keep up with you."

That got a soft laugh. "Okay. You win."

Twenty minutes later, Ty wheeled his black Tahoe into Eden's Gate
parking area and slid into the gap between a gray Chevy sedan and the
Watson brother's truck. Ty had arranged for back up in the form of two
uniformed officers. She and Ty had left them a few hundred yards down
the hill, their cruiser parked in a turn out just off the road. Hopefully they
wouldn't be needed but where the Watsons were concerned, Sam guessed
anything was possible.

Sam pulled her weapon from her jacket pocket as she stepped from the
truck. She popped it open, spun the cylinder, making sure each chamber
held a round, and snapped it closed. She settled it back into her pocket.
"How you want to play this?"

"Low key. Just a few questions. Think you can do that?"

"Why would you ask that?"

"Sam Cody, if I've learned anything about you, it's that you like to stir
things up."

"Can't catch the bad guys unless you shake the tree."

Ty laughed and shook his head. "Just don't knock the tree down. Or
shoot anyone."

"I won't." She smiled. "Unless they need it."

"Not much comfort there."

The front door to the church opened, framing Scully, the Watson brothers in the shadows behind him, Elvin peeking over his left shoulder.

"Detective Everson, what brings you by?"

Ty walked toward him, Sam at his shoulder. Scully stepped outside, the Watsons followed, flanking him, Eric with a smirk on his face.

"Ms. Cody," Scully nodded as he addressed her. "You're spending a lot time up here on the hill today."

"Why not? It's lovely up here."

He smiled. "Where's Lucy?"

"She had work to do."

"Really?" Scully adopted a look of mock surprise. "I heard she had lost her hospital privileges."

Sam shrugged. "She still has work to do."

He hesitated as if he expected her to elaborate but when she didn't he asked, "So what can I do for you?"

"Wondering where you might've been last night?" Ty asked. "Say between ten and two. Thereabouts."

"Why?"

"Just wondering."

He smiled. "I never knew you to wonder without a good reason."

"That's mostly true but sometimes I just wonder. Like now. So where were you?" He waved a hand toward them. "All of you."

"We had a meeting."

"What kind of meeting?"

"Church business."

Ty swiped his hair back from his forehead. "I see."

"Where did this meeting take place?" Sam asked.

"Around."

"Care to narrow it down a little?"

Scully gave her a patronizing smile. "Not really."

"Why so late?" Ty asked. "What was so important that it required a middle of the night get together?"

"I'm not at liberty to discuss church business with you or anyone else."

"I suspect that's your right."

"Sure is."

"What about you?" Sam directed the question to Elvin. "Where were you two?"

Elvin offered a slanted smirk of a smile. "Same place."

Sam wanted to whack the arrogance off his face but instead she smiled back. "Tending to the Lord's business, were you?"

"You might say that."

"Did the Lord have any business over at Wellstone Manor?"

Scully's eyes hardened but before he could respond, Eric jumped in. "He could've if He'd been of a mind to. He's everywhere and knows all."

Sam gave him a look of mock confusion. "I thought that was Santa Claus."

"Ms. Cody," Scully said, "your sarcasm might seem cute to you, but I assure you the Lord does not take kindly to mockery."

"I wasn't talking to Him."

"And I can assure you, I don't care for such mockery either."

"Sorry to offend your sensibilities, but shoving a pillow into the face of a helpless woman and smothering her does that to me. I'm funny that way."

"Perhaps a little too funny?"

"Yeah. Maybe you're a little too funny for your own good," Eric said.

Sam detected a slight flinch from Scully but kept her gaze locked on Eric. "That a threat?" Sam hooked her thumbs on her belt and cocked her head to one side.

"Of course not," Scully said. "Eric was merely stating a fact."

"So you think I'm funny? I'm flattered. I always wanted to do stand up."

Scully's jaw tightened as he stared at Sam. He then turned to Ty. "If there isn't anything else, I have work to do."

"Just to be clear," Ty said, "each of you was at some meeting from ten until two or so?"

"That's tight," Elvin said. "We all was."

"And you'll each swear to that? If necessary?"

"Sure will," Scully said. "And if you need more folks to say the same we can get that too."

Ty nodded, and gave a brief two-finger salute. "Have a nice day."

CHAPTER 51

S am had absolutely no doubt that Martha's murder came at the hands of John Scully and the Watson brothers. They had the holy trinity: motive, means, and opportunity.

Homicide investigators use a simple formula: How plus why equals who.

The how is the means and opportunity. In cop-speak the *modus operandi* or MO. The when, where, and how of the killing. These are the meat and potatoes of homicide investigations and are usually easy to determine. Are the killer, or killers, capable of doing the deed? Of gaining access to the victim? Do they have a solid alibi that says they were anywhere but where they were? The scene of the murder.

Details like the time, place, and method often direct the investigation toward the perpetrator. For example, did the murder occur during the day or in the dead of night? At the victim's work or home, indoors or outdoors? Did the killer use a gun, a knife, or a poison? How did the killer plan and execute the crime? How did he reach the victim? How did he gather and then dispose of what he needed to commit the act? How did he approach and depart the scene undetected? How did he know when the victim would be alone and vulnerable? Where was he supposed to be and how did he cover those tracks? What or who is his alibi?

It's flaws in these steps that often trip up killers.

On the other hand, the why, the motive, can be a bit muddy.

But it's the motive that's most crucial. Murders don't happen in a vacuum. There is always a reason. Usually a very transparent one. People kill people they know. People they have some relationship with. And the motive arises from this relationship. Jealously, greed, revenge, to cover another crime. Even serial killers have a why. Might not make sense to most folks but it makes perfect sense to them. Gary Ridgeway, The Green River Killer, murdered nearly fifty, maybe more, Seattle-area prostitutes because he hated hookers and wanted to rid the world of them. Sick and twisted, but absolutely rational to him.

No doubt Scully and the Watsons were capable of killing, particularly an elderly, defenseless woman, and Martha's room wouldn't be very difficult to get into. No alarms or guards, unlocked windows and doors, and a minimal night-shift staff. Scully and the Watsons definitely had the means and the opportunity.

The why? For Scully, Martha had become a threat. Of sorts. He wanted control over Lucy and this mysterious Keeper crap, that Sam would dismiss out of hand had it not been for her encounter with Richard Earl Garrett. After Garrett, anything was possible. Regardless, Scully saw Martha as a obstacle and that's really all that mattered. His motive only had to make sense to him.

And perhaps Martha knew too much. Even if it was locked in her failing brain, it was still in there. And it just might find its way out. Scully couldn't afford that.

These thoughts occupied Sam's mind as she ran along the edge of the two-lane blacktop that had become her favorite running trail. The morning was cool, the sky clear, and the ground fog sparse except where it collected and thickened in the low lying areas. As usual, a squadron of crows seemed to follow her, flitting through the trees that lined the right side of the road, circling overhead, and cawing, sometimes as if harmonizing and at others times as if arguing. Right now arguing won the day their collective racket was harsh and discordant.

That's when she heard the truck engine. Close behind her. She eased on the shoulder and looked back.

The Watsons pulled up along side her.

"Thought we might find you here," Eric said.

Sam could smell the aroma of marijuana wafting through the open window. She stopped. Elvin hit the brakes, the tires emitting a sharp squeak as the truck came to a standstill.

"I see you guys are getting your usual early morning start."

"We're always up early."

She waved a hand as if shooing away a fly, or an odor. "That's not eactly what I meant."

Eric laughed. He held up a half smoked joint. "Better than orange juice for busting up the conwebs." He extended it toward her. "Want some?"

"I'll stick with OJ."

He shrugged. "Don't know what you're missing. This is good stuff." He passed the joint to his brother who took a hit.

"You boys have a nice day."

She jogged away but the truck moved up beside her, keeping pace.

"We meant what we said yesterday," Eric said.

"About what?"

"Don't go sticking your nose into church business."

She stopped again. The truck did, too.

"Are you saying that Martha's murder was church business?"

That seemed to surprise Eric and he fumbled for a response. "No. I mean. We told you you we didn't have nothing to do with that."

"Let's just say I'm skeptical."

"You can be that all you want but if I was you I'd be careful."

"Why do you feel the need to threaten everyone? Don't you see that threats only make you seem more guilty."

"You need some manners." He reached into the small cargo area behind the seats and pulled out a coiled rope. "Maybe we should simply hog tie your ass and explain how things are to you."

"I understand you two aren't the brightest bulbs in the chandelier so let me give you some advice. Don't try anything stupid. People only get away with so much stupidity and I suspect you guys have done a lot of stupid in your life. Sort of living on borrowed time." She smiled at them. "Take care." Again she jogged away.

The truck loped along behind her. These guys were becoming annoying. Then the truck moved up beside her yet again. As she looked toward them, the lasso fell around her shoulders and suddenly tightened across her chest, trapping her arms to her side. The truck sped up, forcing her to run with it or be dragged.

Elvin, twisted in his seat, both arms out the window, clutching the rope, laughing. "Good day for a run isn't it? Think you can keep up?"

The truck's speed increased slightly, Sam now in a hard run. She had to do something. She managed to slip her arms free but the rope was now around her waist. Before Eric could react, she grasped the rope with both hands, dug in her heels, and came to a stop. The rope jerked free of Eric's grasp. Good thing he was stoned and his reflexes were slowed, his grip weakened. She loosened the noose and stepped out of it. The truck stopped and Elvin jumped out.

"Not so fast. Missy," he said as he came toward her. "Guess we're going to have to do this the hard way."

The hard way? Sam actually loved the hard way. She closed on him quickly, not giving him time to think, set his feet, react to her attack in any meaningful way.

The voice of her old trainer, Jimmy Ryker, echoed in her head: *Hit first, hit hard, and keep hitting until they don't move anymore.* Sounded like a good plan.

The left hook was perfect, the straight right hand better. The hook staggered Eric, the right put him down. She heard the gear shift slam into park and the driver's door pop open. She stepped over Eric, who lay on the ground glassy eyed and moaning, and met Elvin head on as he circled in front of the truck. From the surprised look on his face, not exactly what he was expecting. Probably thought she'd run. Took two lefts and right took Eric down, too.

Time to leave.

She knew they wouldn't be down long and she was three miles from town, from help. She scanned the horizon, looking for some place to hide or at least get them on foot where she had the advantage. She saw no refuge so she ran, hard, straight ahead, along the edge of the asphalt, trying put as much distance between her and them as possible. She didn't suspect either could run very far without collapsing. Particularly at the rate she was now moving.

She managed to get a couple of hundred yards down the road before the truck's engine roared to life, the tires squealing as they grabbed the pavement. To her left, a dirt and gravel road branched off the county highway and knifed through a large field of waist-high, bright-green, regimented rows of corn. She veered that way, the road quickly descending into the ground fog. Not dense enough to hide her completely but maybe enough to slow them down. With luck maybe they'd miscalculate and slide off into one of the ditches that hugged either side.

She kicked up her pace, now moving flat out. Her lungs screamed for oxygen; her legs burned. The road was rutted and more than once she lost her balance, but managed to stay upright. The road descended deeper into the fog. She had no idea where it led but she knew it wasn't back toward town. She would have to worry about that later. Right now escape to anywhere trumped everything else.

The fog magnified the crunch of the truck's tires turning onto the gravel. It sounded as if they were right on top of her, but she still had a good hundred yard lead. They closed. Now she reached the rise in the road that lifted her above the fog. She looked back. The truck now only fifty yards behind her, the cab also above the fog, Eric pointing toward her, Elvin working the steering wheel. She veered right, off the road, and into the corn.

She glanced back again, this time seeing that the truck had stopped. Eric had climbed out, a rifle in one hand. These guys were serious.

Move it, Sam.

She kicked into an even higher gear and cut to her left, diagonally across the rows, toward a patch of trees. The corn stalks seemed to clutch at her legs, slowing her progress, the trees now only fifty yards in front of her. The crack of the rifle, the whizzing of the bullet, and the snapping of a stalk to her left jerked her head around. Elvin was laughing and pointing, Eric leveling the rifle in her direction. Sam dropped to all fours and began a bear-crawl sprint toward the trees. Twenty yards. Another pop-snap, this time the bullet well to her right. She stayed low, her hands and the toes of her shoes digging into the soft dirt. As she neared the tree line another pop. The bullet thumped against the tree in front of her. She rose to her feet and ran, the trees enveloping her. Two more pops. Bullets slapped leaves above and far to her left. They apparently could no longer see her and were firing randomly, hoping to get lucky. She ran deeper into the trees before she stopped, gasping for breath while trying to listen for footsteps above her raspy breathing. She heard nothing. Sweat glazed her face and chest, a trickle running down her nose.

Surely they were on foot, moving her way. She wiped sweat from her face with her shirt and looked around, every direction looking the same.

Trees and more trees. Which way could she go to get past them without being seen and make her way back toward town?

A pair of squirrels scurried by, one with a hickory nut firmly grasped in his jaws, the other apparently trying to wrest it away.

Got a secret way back to town, guys?

They continued their squabble as they darted one way and then the other, ricocheting off trees, tails fully fluffed and jerking from side to side. And then they were gone.

She heard the doors of the Watson's truck slam shut and the engine roar to life again, followed by the sounds of gravel pinging against the undercarriage, moving away. Then a sharp squeal as the truck's tires lurched back onto the paved roadway. The sounds faded, the brothers apparently giving up the chase.

CHAPTER 52

"**W**hat the hell happened to you?" Ty asked as Sam walked into his office.

After the Watson clowns left, Sam had knocked some of the mud from her shoes and wiped her hands clean against a tree trunk. She wasn't very successful. Mud spatters covered her shirt, shorts, and legs, which splotched with a few red welts from the corn stalks. She worked her way from the trees, across a couple of farms, avoiding roads and giving farmhouses a wide berth, through a neighborhood, and finally into downtown Remington. Curious eyes followed her as she jogged to Ty's office.

"Did a little cross country running." She extended one arm, showing him the pair of red welts on her arm.

"What's that?"

"Running through a corn field and a few trees will do that."

"There's a story there, I bet."

"The Watson brothers."

Ty's forehead furrowed and his eyes narrowed. "Tell me."

She did.

"They actually tried to lasso you?"

"That and a few rounds over my head. But once I got off the road and into the trees they took off."

Ty pulled his cell phone from his pocket and flipped it open

"What are you doing?" Sam asked.

"Calling Bump. Get him to work on an arrest warrant for them."

Sam reached across and laid a hand on his arm. "Don't."

"Why not?"

"It won't do any good."

"The hell it won't."

"Think about it. My word against the two of them."

"But they tried to kill you."

"Maybe. Or maybe they simply wanted to scare me."

"A little excessive don't you think?"

"A little?"

"My point exactly."

"They'll have iron clad alibis. Each other and probably a dozen church members. Say they were no where near there. That I'm just making it up."

Ty dropped his phone on the table. "Not when I finish with them."

"I can handle myself," Sam said.

"Of that I have no doubt." He smiled. "But I'll have a chat with them anyway."

"No you won't."

"And why not?"

"I'd rather they believe they spooked me. Believe it's mission accomplished. If they think I ran to you for help they'll try something else I'm sure."

"They might anyway."

Sam shrugged. "I've dealt with worse. Remember I put in a couple of years on the streets of LA."

"Still, I'd feel better if they knew I was watching them."

"Some day you'll make someone a good daddy. But I don't need one."

That got a smile from him. "I've said it before and I'll say it again, you're a hard woman, Sam Cody."

"I'll take that as a compliment."

"I'm still going to go have a quality face time with them."

Sam sighed. "Then I'm going with you."

"I think not."

"I think so."

Ty looked her up and down. "Like that?"

"Maybe we could swing by Lucy's so I can shower and dress?"

Fortunately Sam managed to make it to the shower before running into Lucy. She didn't want to explain why she was covered with mud. It would only stress her more. After she showered, slipped on jeans and a tee shirt, she found Ty in the kitchen, his cell phone to his ear.

"Yeah," Ty said. "We're going to go talk with them." He listened a beat. "Not yet. Let me see what they have to say. I'll call you later." He closed the phone and slipped into the hip pocket of his jeans.

"Bump?" Sam asked.

"Yep. He wanted to put out an APB but I told him we'd handle it for now."

"Well, you two are becoming quite the item." It was Lucy.

"How so?"

"Morning , noon, night. Seems you two are always together."

"Funny," Sam said.

"So what are you up to this morning?" Lucy asked.

Sam gave Ty a look. One that said, "Don't say a word." He gave a slight nod.

"Maybe breakfast. Want to join us?"

Lucy shook her head. "I need to go by the office. Do all the paper work I didn't do yesterday. Maybe lunch?"

"I'll call," Sam said.

Sam removed her .357 from the waistband of her jeans, climbed into Ty's truck, and laid the weapon on the center console. Ty glanced at it but didn't say anything.

"Basic self-defense," Sam said.

"So I see."

"Unless you think I shouldn't carry."

"No problem. In fact if you weren't I'd suggest you did." He cranked the engine. "Just don't shoot anyone."

Sam gave him a mock pout. "You never let me have fun."

Ty shook his head and backed from Lucy's drive.

"So you don't want Lucy to know what happened this morning?"

"No. Not yet anyway. She has enough on her plate."

"Platter. A plate ain't big enough for all the crap in her life right now."

Their first stop was the church. No Eric and Elvin but Felicia and Miriam were there. They were planting red, white, and purple azaleas on either side of the church's entrance. Miriam stood, brushing dirt from the knees of her brown pants, and faced them as they parked and climbed from the truck. Felicia continued her work, glancing up at Sam, a sliver of concern in her eyes. Sam gave her a smile. Hopefully one that said her secret was safe.

"What brings you by this morning?" Miriam asked. She attempted to sound friendly, forced smile and all, but Sam detected more than a little contempt in her voice.

"Looking for Eric and Elvin," Ty said.

"They ain't here. Wish they were. We could use a little help digging."

"Any idea where they might be?"

"Probably home. Or out and about."

"More likely the later," Sam said.

Miriam looked at her but said nothing.

"What about John?" Ty asked. "He around?"

"Nope. Headed into town. Needed a few things from the hardware."

"When's he likely to be back?"

"In a while I suspect."

And that was that. Miriam wasn't going to give up anything.

Did she know what had happened this morning? Was she covering for the Watsons? Sam suspected the answer was yes on both counts.

Once they were headed west on the county road, Sam asked, "What do you think?"

"About what?"

"Miriam. You think she knows what happened today?"

"Wouldn't be surprised. She and John seem to be in the loop on just about everything." He turned off the highway onto a narrow, pocked and patched black top road, loose gravel pinging the truck's undercarriage. "The Watson's farm is just up here a piece."

"You think they'll be there?"

He grunted. "Doubt it. Probably took Miriam about a microsecond to call them after we left the church. If they were here, they'll've high tailed it by now."

They were. Gone, that is. All was quiet and the house locked up tight.

Back on the highway toward town, Ty asked, "Breakfast?"

"Thought you'd never ask."

CHAPTER 53

Lucy simply couldn't gather up the energy to go to her office. What would she do? Push papers around her desk? To what end? She had nothing that required her immediate attention and no surgeries to prepare for. Might never again. At least not here in Remington. She could see no way through this. No way to explain her patients spiraling into insanity and her inability to even stay upright in surgery. Not to mention that Birnbaum had her in a tight box. And he would squeeze her with everything he had. Vindictiveness, jealousy, and greed have no bounds.

Her career was over.

That thought struck her hard. Was it true? Was it even possible? Her entire life had been medicine. Years of school and training. Ninety percent of her waking hours over the past decade plus had been in one hospital or another. In ERs and ORs. High velocity, high intensity. Could she even live without that?

And what about her dreams? The snakes that crawled through her recurring nightmare? The dream that was yet again a nightly visitor? What were they all about? The only thing she knew for sure was that they started the same day John Scully died on her operating table.

She could grasp all this if it were something physical. Some spot on her MRI. A tumor. A stroke. Things that could be dealt with. Things she understood. But all this?

Not to mention Martha's murder. And Scully. And her parents.

Who were her parents? Scully and Martha? She wasn't sure she could buy that. But if they were, who was couple who died in the fire that gutted her childhood home? The people that were buried over at Shady Hill Cemetery? The people she had believed were her parents? Whose graves she and Martha had visited every Sunday? Who the hell were they?

How could Martha have lied to her for all those years? Knowing she was Lucy's mother and the couple in the graves were . . .what? Strangers? Caretakers selected by John Scully?

Was that why she had no real memories of them? DId she know, somewhere deep in her DNA, that they were shills? That there was no real parent-child connection?

This was enough to drive anyone crazy.

Maybe that was it. Maybe she was crazy. If Martha was indeed her mother, had she inherited Martha's schizophrenia gene? Had she been wired for this madness from conception? Predestined? It did run in families after all. The genetic substrate passed down from parent to child. Yet when she thought back over her life, there was no hint that this was the case. No symptoms or signs. At least none she could remember.

Which raised an age-old question: Do crazy folks know they're crazy? Are they aware that they are different? Or do they believe that everyone sees the same world they see, feels the same things they feel? She had no answer for that.

But even if she was sliding into Martha's world, into schizophrenia, how would that explain William Nevers, Joseph Finch, and Ronnie Draper?

It wouldn't. No way. At least no way her scientific mind could wrap itself around.

And the other explanation? The one offered by John Scully? And Felicia?

She couldn't buy into that either. Couldn't accept that this was some evil spirit that had been passed to her by the older Scully. Accepting that would indeed be crazy.

Hadn't Sam been caught in the same nightmare with Richard Earl Garrett? Widespread madness that spread through a community and defied understanding? Thinking back, she couldn't remember Sam ever coming down on one side of that debate or the other. Was it simply a case of mass hysteria or did Garrett really have some type of special power? Like Scully claimed. Sam had always hedged her answers whenever the subject came up. And Sam was the most level-headed and normal person she knew.

These were the thoughts that rattled around in her head as she made coffee, grabbed the morning newspaper from the front porch, and settled in a chair on her deck. She attempted to push these thoughts aside but she couldn't concentrate. She tried to read a front page article about a new park planned for the lake front but her mind wouldn't grab any of it. She reread the first paragraph four times and it still didn't register. She tossed the paper on the deck and stared out at the lake, the image blurred by the tears that collected in her eyes.

What the fuck is wrong with you, Lucy?

That's when the phone rang.

Twenty minutes later, Lucy turned into Remington Medical Center's emergency room parking lot. But the ER wasn't her destination. Neither was the hospital, nor her office on the third floor of the adjacent medical office building. Rather she was headed toward the first floor office of Coroner Larry Granville.

The call had been from Granville. The DNA was back. When she asked the results, he said it might be better if she dropped by. She argued, but he held firm. So here she was.

As soon as she entered the lot, she saw Ty's truck. Why were he and Sam here? Had Granville called them? Why? Moral support for what she was about the hear? She already knew it wouldn't be good news. Good news could be passed along over the phone; bad news required delivery face to face. The presence of Ty and Sam only reinforced that truth.

She parked next to Ty's truck but rather than stepping from her car, she sat there for several minutes, trying to calm her nerves. Her fingers trembled as she held them before her.

Some surgeon you are. Get a grip, Lucy.

Her hesitation surprised her. After Granville called, she had rushed to get dressed and ignored speed limits as she drove over. Eager to put this all to bed. Yet, now, as she sat there, she felt an apprehensive bubble expand in her chest. Not the empty, cold feeling that had interrupted so many of her surgeries, but a growing, angry tumor of anxiety.

Did she really want to know?

Quit being such as wimp, Lucy.

She stepped from her car, entered the office building through the side door, and walked down to Granville's office. The door stood open. Granville sat behind his desk, Ty and Sam on the sofa to his right.

"Am I late for the party?" Lucy asked. A weak smile is all she could muster.

"You're right on time," Granville said as he stood. "Please, have a seat." He indicted the empty chair that faced his desk.

She started to sit but couldn't. Too restless. Instead she stood behind the chair, her hands, now moist with perspiration, gripping its back.

"No. Just tell me."

Granville sighed as he picked up a single sheet of paper and handed it to her.

She scanned the words and numbers of the lab report. Such reports were a daily part of her life, but right now she could make no sense of it. She handed the page back to Granville.

"What does it say?"

Granville sat down heavily. "That Martha and John, Sr. are indeed your parents."

Even expecting them, the words hit her full on. A sharp intake of breath. A flutter in her chest. She felt faint, her hands clamping tightly on the chair back.

"You're sure?"

"No doubt."

Now she sat, head forward, elbows on her knees. "Fuck me."

Sam stood and moved over the where she sat, laying one hand on her shoulder. "Are you okay?"

"No." She stared at the floor. Her eyes watered. She took a deep breath and let it out slowly, then suddenly stood. "I need to walk." She turned toward the door.

"I'll go with you," Sam said.

"No," Lucy said, never looking back. "I need to be alone." As she reached the door, she sensed Sam moving to follow her, but Ty stood and grabbed her arm.

"Let her go," he said.

Outside, Lucy walked past her car, across the asphalt parking lot, and down the grassy hill that led toward town, two blocks away. Entering the downtown area, everything seemed different. Remington did not feel like the place where she had grown up. The courthouse, the bank, the library, the shops that lined the square, places that were so much a part of her life now seemed foreign. As if she had never been there before.

Was her entire life a lie? Why had Martha kept this secret from her? To protect her? From what?

Scully.

Martha what did you do?

CHAPTER 54

"Sorry I'm late," Ty said as soon as Sam opened the door to his knock.

"No problem."

"How is she?"

"Deep in the bottle."

"Really?"

"See for yourself."

She led Ty through house to the back deck where Lucy curled on a lounge chair, wrapped in a thin blanket, a glass of bourbon in her hand, a half-empty bottle of Blantons on the chair-side table.

"You okay?" Ty asked.

"Better now." She lifted the glass toward him. "Me and Mr. Blanton are getting along just fine."

"You think that's a good idea?"

"Best I could come up with but I'm open to suggestions."

"Go with us. Out for dinner."

"I don't think I'd be very good company right now."

He smiled. "We'll make allowances."

Lucy adjusted her position, sitting up a bit, drained her glass, and poured a generous refill. "I think I'll just hang here."

"Come on, Lucy. You don't need to be alone right now."

"Actually, I do. I have a lot to sort out."

"And maybe we can help," Sam said.

"Look, I love you both. And I appreciate what you're trying to do. But right now I have to think through all this and I need time to do that."

"And the bourbon helps?" Ty asked.

"Always does." Again she lifted the glass toward him. "I'm fine. You two get to your courting."

Sam frowned at her but didn't say anything.

"You sure?" Ty asked.

"I'm sure. Now you guys go have fun. I'll be here when you get back and maybe I'll have all this sorted out by then."

❧

"You sure she'll be okay?" Sam asked.

She sat across the table from Ty. They had decided on JT's BBQ, which was crowded but they managed a back corner table. Julie, JT's best waitress as far as Sam was concerned, had brought them the bourbons they had ordered before she began cleaning a nearby table.

"Lucy's tough," Ty said. "She'll get through this."

"I know. But I feel so guilty. Leaving her alone right now."

"It's what she wants."

"It's what she said. Not sure it's really what's she wants."

"She'll drink herself into a coma, sleep all night, and by tomorrow things will look better."

Sam shrugged. "Maybe."

"You're really worried, aren't you?"

Sam took a sip of bourbon. "I've never seen her quite like this."

"It's understandable, don't you think?" Ty said. "I mean how often do you lose your job, have a bunch of murders that you feel responsible for, and find out your parents aren't really your parents?"

"My point exactly. That'd knock anyone over. Even someone as tough as Lucy."

"True."

"That's why I feel guilty."

"What can I get you guys?" Julie was back. She pulled a pad from her apron pocket and a pencil from behind her ear where she had nestled it.

"I'm starving," Sam said. "I'll have the smoked tri-tip, mashed potatoes, and cole slaw."

Ty nodded. "I'll do the same."

After she left, Ty said, "Lucy is lucky to have a friend like you."

"I was just thinking the same thing about you." Sam raised her glass and clinked it against Ty's. "But in all honesty, I've always felt like the lucky one. To know her. She is so special."

"True that." He smiled.

Sam loved his smile. It took over his entire face, raising his cheeks, baring his white teeth, and narrowing his eyes to mere slits, deepening the crow's feet at their corners. He was handsome, masculine, soft-spoken. Everything Sam liked.

"You know," Ty said, "it's still hard for me to picture you as a boxer."

"Why?"

"First of all, you're too pretty."

"I bet you tell all the girls that."

"Just the ones who box."

"Oh, so there have been other pugilists in your life?"

Another of those smiles. "You're the first."

"And I bet you say that to all the girls, too."

He laughed. "You're on a roll."

"I have my moments."

"But back to you boxing. You aren't all muscular like most boxers. Even the women boxers I've seen. You're tall and lean."

"I'll take that as a complement."

"As it was intended."

"It helps to be fast on your feet. Saves a lot of pain."

"I imagine that's true."

Their food arrived and they began to eat. Unfortunately Darlene arrived, too.

"Well if it isn't the two love birds." Darlene said. "How completely fucking cozy."

She wore frayed jeans that looked two or three sizes to large and a lime green tee shirt that was equally oversized. Sam guessed they had both fit at one time. Before the Meth killed her appetite. And just about everything else. Except maybe her mean streak. Seemed to make that worse as Meth usually does. Darlene stood beside the table, fists balled against her hips, head cocked to one side, eyes glassy and unfocused. She wavered slightly.

"You know he's mine, honey," Darlene said when her gaze finally landed on Sam. "Always was. Always will be."

Ty scooted his chair back a couple of inches. "Go away, Darlene."

"Free country. I can come in here if I want." She sniffed and rubbed her nose with the heel of one hand.

"Not intoxicated, you can't. Now go on home and sleep it off or I'll take you in and have you drug tested. Then we'll go see the judge about you violating your court order."

"That's BS and you know it."

"Darlene, you were arrested for possession. Of crystal meth. That's a felony in case you forgot. The judge let you avoid jail time only because you went to that rehab program. Which from what I see didn't work so well."

"Fuck you, Ty."

"But if I take you in and you test positive, he might change his mind."

"That's just like you. Always threatening me with your badge."

"Really? Wasn't it me that talked the judge into letting you go to rehab and not jail. Told him you wouldn't do well in jail." He pushed his hair back from his forehead. "But I just might reconsider everything if you don't turn around and waltz your butt right out of here."

Darlene's jaw tightened and she glared at Ty.

Ty's jaw set hard. "Right now, Darlene."

She looked at Sam. "You can have this asshole, girlie." She turned, wavered a beat, and then marched through the tables and out the door.

"Sorry," Ty said.

"You have such a way with women."

"Not with that one." He scooted his chair back up to the table.

"She seems to track you down every time we're together."

"That's just the part you see. She comes into my office at least once a week to rant about something. Even drives by my house all the time."

"Sounds like you need a restraining order." Sam laughed.

"Wouldn't help. Darlene ain't much for following the rules."

They ate quietly for a few minutes before Ty asked, "How come you never got married?"

"After what just happened? I wonder."

Ty laughed. "Not everyone is like Darlene."

"Thank goodness."

"Seriously, why not?"

"Guess I never found the right person." She took a sip of bourbon. "Or maybe I'm just too picky."

"I guess I should be flattered that you're here then."

"It's the food," Sam said with a smile. "I'm here for the food."

"I'm crushed." He laid an open hand over his chest. "I thought it was me."

"Maybe a little. You are easy on the eye, as they say."

"As are you, Sam Cody. As are you."

After they finished their meal and paid the bill, they decided to walk around town. It was nearly ten and most of the stores had closed. Sam took Ty's arm. They said little, mostly window shopping and enjoying each other's company. Then while standing in front of an electronics store, looking at the array of gadgets in the window, Ty pulled her to him and kissed her. She kissed him back.

"Can I show you my etchings? Ty said. That smile again.

"Just your etchings?"

"We can start there."

"I don't know. What if Darlene showed up?"

"I just might shoot her."

"I wouldn't want to be responsible for that."

"You wouldn't, She's earned it."

"I believe it."

"Besides, I don't bite."

"Pity."

He laughed. "You are an enigma wrapped in a conundrum."

"That's what I was going for." She laughed.

"I have some very old, very small batch bourbon."

"You sweet talker." She smiled at an older couple that waked by and then looked back up into his eyes. "Okay. But let's go by and check on Lucy first."

"You got it."

CHAPTER 55

After Sam and Ty left, Lucy knocked back a couple of more bourbons, going through nearly two-thirds of the bottle, before she finally crawled into bed. The ceiling appeared warped and the walls seemed to slowly gyrate. Nausea crept into her throat and she feared she would vomit. She managed to hold it together and before long had drifted to sleep.

The dream arrived almost immediately. The snakes even larger and more aggressive. Dozens of them. A chorus of angry rattles assaulted her ears as their muscular bodies wound around her arms and legs. A couple of them kept striking at her, always just missing as she somehow managed to twist and turn from them. Her muscles ached and fatigue tugged at her. Then a very large rattler settled on her chest. Thick and heavy. Suffocating as if collapsing her chest.

Golden eyes with black vertical slits stared into hers. A thin black tongue probed the few inches of air between her face and its triangular head. She froze. Afraid to move or even to take a breath.

Then behind the snake, a face appeared. Fuzzy at first, but as it snapped into focus she found herself staring into the face of John Scully.

She recoiled, pressing her head deeply into the pillow.

"I wouldn't make any sudden moves if I was you," Scully said. "Old Jake here is a biter."

"Sure is."

Another voice. She cut her eyes to her left. Eric and Elvin Watson stood beside the bed.

"What the hell . . ." Lucy began.

"Wouldn't talk either," Scully said. "Jake can be an unpredictable cuss."

He picked up the snake from her chest and held it in front of her face. Close. The snake's tongue danced across her lips. Lucy felt her heart jump into her throat. She was now in full panic mode. Her instincts were to kick and bite and scratch and fight like hell, but that didn't seem like a wise move right now. Her mind raced, searching for some plan, some way out of this, finding nothing that even remotely had a chance of success.

"You listen up now, you hear?" Scully said. "I don't want to turn old Jake here loose on you. That'd complicate things a bit. But you best believe I damn sure will if I have to."

Lucy tried to look at Scully but couldn't pull her gaze away from the snake.

"Where's your friend Sam?"

"She's not here."

"That I know, Where is she and when will she be back?"

"I don't know."

"What we going to do?" Elvin asked.

"Deal with her later." Then to Lucy, "Now you'll be coming with us and I expect you to do so very quietly and peaceful like." He glanced at Eric. "And to make sure, Eric's got something for you." He nodded. "Go ahead."

Eric reached into his pocket and came out with a syringe. It was filled with a light yellow liquid. He removed the needle cap while Elvin pulled the comforter off Lucy's legs. He pressed her knee into the mattress, holding her leg firm. The stab of the needle into her thigh caused her to flinch. The snake jerked its head back, neck arched, as if preparing to strike. Lucy moaned.

"Let's give that a couple of minutes to work and then we'll get her out to the van," Scully said.

Lucy fought it, fought it hard, but knew she had no chance, The drug was already settling in her brain, making her lids heavy. Her arms and legs jellied. She wasn't sure what they had given her but suspected it was a sedative of some sort. Valium or one of its cohorts most likely. As her world began to collapse inward, she saw Scully pass the snake off to Elvin.

After what seemed only a few seconds but was more likely minutes, Scully said, "Let's get going."

Eric and Elvin sat her up on the side of the bed and then lifted her to her feet. She wobbled, her legs barely able to hold her.

"I'm going to be sick," Lucy said.

Eric and Elvin looked at Scully.

"Get her to the bathroom."

They did. It wasn't easy as they had to support most of her weight. Once inside, Lucy grabbed the sink, bent over it, and vomited.

"Jesus," Eric said, taking a step back.

"I'll go get the van ready," Scully said. "Drag her out back once she's finished."

Lucy heaved until her stomach was empty and then heaved some more. Finally her retching settled. She clumsily splashed water on her face.

"Let's go," Elvin said.

"Pee," Lucy said. "I've got to pee."

"Jesus Christ, you bitch, let's go."

"Please. I can't hold it much longer."

"Let her," Eric said. "I don't want her messing up the van."

Elvin sighed. "Hurry up."

Lucy steadied herself with one hand on the sink and prepared to sit on the commode. Her tongue felt thick and her voice soft and unsteady as she managed to get out, "A little privacy."

Elvin looked around apparently making sure she had no escape route and then said, "Make it quick."

He and Eric stepped out the door, pushing it almost closed, only a crack left. Once Lucy finished and flushed the toilet, the door swung open.

"No more BS. Let's get going."

They each grabbed an arm and directed her out the back door and to the van, where Scully stood, the rear door open. They pushed her into the back, Elvin climbing in after her.

Lucy looked up at Scully. "Why?" Her voice was now thick and weak. "Why are you doing this?"

"You got something that's mine. Something you never should've had. Now I'm going to take it back."

CHAPTER 56

Ty parked his truck in Lucy's driveway. Sam jumped out and headed toward the front, rummaging in her purse for the house key. Ty followed. When she inserted the key, she realized the door wasn't locked.

"Guess she forgot."

"Probably too drunk," Ty said.

"Probably."

Inside all was quiet. Sam quickly walked down the hall to Lucy's room. The door stood open, the room was dark, but Lucy wasn't in bed. She backtracked, finding Ty out on the back deck.

"She out here?" Sam asked.

Ty turned and looked at her. "She isn't zonked out?"

"Not in her bed." I'll check the other rooms."

"This door was standing open." Ty nodded toward the rear door.

"Maybe she's down at the dock."

They walked down the slope to the water's edge. No Lucy. Not on the dock and not in the boathouse. Back in the house Sam searched the other bedrooms, including hers. No Lucy. She returned to the kitchen as Ty came through the door that led to the garage.

"Her car's here," he said.

Sam then saw Lucy's purse, cell phone, and car keys on the kitchen counter. "I don't like this. Something's wrong."

"Let's not panic just yet." He started back down the hall, Sam followed. They opened every door, even closet doors, until they came back to Lucy's room. Ty flipped on the bathroom light and stuck his head inside.

"Shit."

"What?"

"You can panic now," Ty said.

He stepped aside and Sam walked past him. On the mirror, scrawled in red lipstick was one word: *SCULLY*.

The tires of Ty's truck squealed as he reversed out of the drive, spinning the steering wheel. They chirped again as he floored it, the engine roaring with all its horses. He had his cell phone to his ear.

"Bump. Lucy's been abducted. By Scully." He listened for a beat. "Yes, I'm sure. Meet us up at the church." He closed the phone and dropped it into the center console.

The dread that had been steadily building inside Sam now blossomed.

"Why would he take Lucy?" she asked.

"Same reason he killed Martha."

"If he harms Lucy I'll kill him myself."

"You might have to beat me to it."

The trip up the hill would have made NASCAR proud. Ty handled the huge truck like it was a Ferrari, sliding through turns, kicking up shoulder gravel, fishtailing a time or two. Sam held on while but found herself rocking back and forward as if trying to make the truck go even faster. Ty slid the truck to a sideways stop in front of the church. They stepped out into the cloud of dust he had kicked up.

They approached the front door, each holding a weapon.

The church was dark and quiet. Ty slammed a fist against the door. "Scully," he yelled. Nothing. He tried the door. Locked. Right here, right now, the Fourth Amendment didn't mean shit. Without hesitation, he took a step back and launched a shoulder into the door. The frame splintered and the door caved in, now hanging by only a single hinge.

"That ought to handle the separation of church and state," Sam said.

"This ain't no church. Not anymore."

The interior was completely dark. They searched every room and found no one. They walked back out to the front lot. Bump and a pair of uniformed officers stood next to Bump's truck. Another black and while pulled up and two more officers stepped out.

"What you got?" Bump asked.

"No one's here," Ty said. "Sam and I will take a couple of the guys and swing by Scully's place. Why don't you and the others head on over to see if the Watsons are home."

"You sure Lucy was taken?"

Sam told him what they had found at Lucy's, including Lucy's lipstick message.

"Very clever on her part."

"She's at least clever," Sam said. "And now she's in trouble. We have to find her."

"Let's get rolling," Ty said.

Fifteen minutes later they arrived at Scully's. The house, like the church, was locked up and dark. Ty called Bump. No one at the Watson place either.

Ty stood on Scully's front porch, looking out into the darkness, eyes narrowed, jaw set. "What now?"

"Scully believes that Lucy possesses this Keeper power."

"That's BS."

"To you. To me. But not so Scully. He believes it and that's all that matters."

"So?"

"Felicia told us that this power must be transferred in some kind of ritual. She didn't know much about it just that it was a big deal."

Ty brushed his hair back from his forehead. "They ain't doing it at the church so where the hell are they?"

"Don't know. But I bet they have another place where they hold ceremonies."

"Any idea where that might be?"

"None. But I know who does." Ty looked at her. "Dwight Doucet."

Ty hesitated a beat as if considering that and then said. "Let's pay him a visit."

CHAPTER 57

Lucy bounced in and out of consciousness. She was stretched out in the back of the van that gyrated over a rough road, bottoming out a few times. Through the side windows she saw only darkness, imprinted with the faint outlines of trees. She had no idea where she was but knew it was remote and isolated. Somewhere up in the hills far from town. Somewhere she'd never be found. She was on her own.

She attempted to sit up, but Elvin pushed her back down with a hand plastered against her chest.

"Lay down" he said. "We'll be there directly."

"Where?"

"Don't matter. But you'll see soon enough."

Lucy sensed the van turn downhill, the gyrations intensifying. She heard brush scraping one side of the van. The vehicle jerked to a stop. Then voices came at her. The rear doors popped open and several people stood there.

"Let's go," Elvin said.

He grabbed her arm and tugged her to a sitting position and then dragged her from the van. Lucy stood on wobbly legs and looked around. The van sat among three dozen other vehicles in a clearing just off a rutted dirt road that curved away into thick woods. Down a twenty-foot slope to her left, along the bank of a small creek, burned a bonfire of sorts. Its glow painted the crowd of thirty or so gathered nearby, each face expectantly turned up toward her.

Scully stepped up to her. "Won't be long now."

"The others will be her shortly," a voice said from behind her.

Scully rubbed his hands together. "Then we can get this done."

"Get what done?" Lucy asked.

"Take back what is mine."

"You can have it. Whatever it is."

"See, that's the basic problem here. You don't believe. You never believed. And as far as I can tell you never would. So here we are. To correct my father's mistake."

"Mistake? Is that what this is?"

"That's exactly what this is."

"No. This is insanity." Lucy glared at him. She clutched the van's rear door frame to maintain her balance. "You're insane." She looked down at the gathered faithful. "You're all insane."

Scully smiled. "True believers always seem insane to the faithless."

"Fine. So I'm faithless. What happens now?"

"As soon as everyone arrives we will prepare the sacrificial alter and I'll take back what's mine."

"Sacrifice? Are you crazy?"

"Unfortunately for you, that's what's required." Scully stepped close. She could feel his breath on her face as he spoke. He laid a hand on her shoulder. "This won't end well for you but then you should never have been a part of this in the first place."

"Like Martha? Is that why you killed her?"

"Martha became a threat. We couldn't risk her exposing everything."

"A threat? Martha was old and senile and schizophrenic. How could she possibly be a threat?"

"She had her lucid moments. Am I right?"

"Not that I ever saw."

"Well, maybe you're right, but I couldn't take that chance." He kicked a pebble from beneath his shoe. It skittered across the ground toward a nearby tree. "She told you you had been passed the power. Correct?"

"She also said I should give it back."

"And she shall get her wish."

Eric and Elvin each grabbed an arm and led Lucy down the slope, her legs not exactly steady, forcing them to help support her. Scully followed close behind. Soon they reached the warm penumbra of the fire and Elvin and Eric released their grips on her arms and joined the crowd that now faced her over the flames. Scully stood next to her.

"This is a very momentous occasion for our community," Scully said. "Tonight we will make things right again. Restore the Keeper's power to its rightful place."

"Amen," the faithful intoned.

Lucy scanned their faces. Each reflected the glow of the fire and carried that vacant look of religion gone wrong. Very wrong. She flashed on the old Sci Fi movie "Village of the Damned." Each of the people before her had the same vacuous expression. She recognized some of them, others she had never seen.

"Do you all truly buy into this crap?" Lucy said. "God doesn't go around handing off powers to people. Particularly a psycho like this." She jerked her head toward Scully. "Are you willing to be a part of this murder?"

"Murder?" Scully said. "Far from it. The Lord would never condone murder."

"My point exactly."

"This is a religious rite. And we both know He isn't averse to sacrifice. Did he not ask Abraham to sacrifice his own son?"

"But he didn't. He merely tested Abraham and when he passed the test He spared the son."

"Maybe he'll step up and save you, too." He smiled. "But I doubt it."

Tears welled in Lucy's eyes, blurring the faces, turning the glow of the fire into a fuzzy, yellow-orange smear. An oppressive feeling of doom settled on her shoulders followed by a wave of dizziness. She dropped to her knees, sobbing. She saw no way out of this. She couldn't fight or run. She could barely stand.

"There there," Scully said. He laid a hand on the top of her head.

"Why? Why me?"

"It was all pre-ordained. From the time of your birth."

Lucy looked up at him. "What?"

Scully grabbed one arm and lifted her to her feet. He turned her to face him, a steadying hand on one shoulder.

"Martha was once one of us. She and my father are your real parents. The couple you thought were your parents all these years were selected. By Martha."

"Martha?"

"She was in this from the get go."

"And my fake parents? Why would they agree to this?"

"They were one of us. At first. But they lost their faith."

"And you killed them, didn't you? In that fire."

"I didn't. I was a child. But my father knew they had to be sacrificed for the greater good."

Another sob racked her. "I don't understand."

"Of course you don't. You see, when you were born, Martha gave you to my father. Your father. You were to be groomed to become a church leader. Like Martha. But Martha lost her faith and we feared we had lost you, too.

But my father believed otherwise. And when you became a heart surgeon, he saw another path."

Lucy sniffed back her tears and stood. "Proving he was as crazy as you."

"Actually his plan was brilliant. It just might have worked but the fatal flaw was that you were never properly prepared to handle the responsibility. That was Martha's failure."

"That makes no sense."

He smiled. "You see, the power of the Keeper can only be transferred through direct contact with the heart. That's how he took the power from Rankin Sneed. Up in West Virginia. Rankin was old and eaten up with the cancer. He elected to sacrifice himself in order to pass the power to my father."

"So your father killed him?"

"Rankin chose his fate. As a true believer."

Another wave of dizziness grabbed her, causing her to waver again. Scully grabbed her elbow to support her, but she yanked it away.

"My father planned all this. When he collapsed outside the hospital? When you opened him up in a futile attempt to save a life that was already sacrificed? When you held his heart in your hands and he passed the power to you? He knew all this would happen."

"But if I was so unprepared, why did he give it to me?"

"You were in a very unique position. You handle hearts every day. He believed that if you passed along small bits of the power to your patients you could produce an army of believers. True believers. Believers that held the power of the church inside. Who would spread the word."

"That didn't work out very well."

He sighed. "True. Like you, they were unprepared. The power was too much for them. Overwhelmed their psyches. Drove them to madness. To unthinkable acts of violence. He never predicted such an outcome. How could he? How could anyone?"

"So much for the power of the Keeper."

"No one is immune from making errors in judgement. But tonight, when we slice you open and I take back what is mine, all will be made right."

"Unless it makes you crazy, too. Maybe crazier is a better word."

He smiled. "Except, I'm prepared. Have been for years."

CHAPTER 58

Ty banged a fist on Dwight Doucet's door with such force the entire house shook. They had discussed calling ahead but Ty decided it might be better to surprise him. Not give him a chance to run off and hide.

"You think he won't tell us what he knows?" Sam had asked.

"Maybe. Maybe not. We have a better chance if he doesn't have time to manufacture a story or conveniently go visit a relative in another state."

"I'll admit that when Lucy and I talked with him he was hesitant. At first anyway. Then he told us what he knew."

"Let's hope he's as forthcoming tonight."

Again Ty slammed a fist against the door. Sam heard movement inside. The porch light snapped on. The door opened and a sleepy, disheveled, and surprised Doucet opened the door.

"Ty? What's this about?" His gaze bounced to Sam and then back to Ty.

"A couple of questions."

"About what?"

"What is it?" A woman's voice from somewhere in the house. Sam guessed it was his wife, also concerned by this middle of the night intrusion.

"It's okay," Doucet said over his shoulder. "I got it."

"But . . "

"Go back to bed. Everything's okay."

Doucet wore pale blue pajamas beneath a gray terry cloth bathrobe. He stepped out on the porch, pulling the door closed behind him.

"Want to tell me what the hell this is all about?" he asked. He was now wide awake and his irritation was showing.

"Where does the church hold it's ceremonies?" Ty asked.

'What?"

Ty took a step forward, chest out, teeth clenched. He looked down at the smaller man and spoke in an even tone, emphasizing each word. "Where does the church hold special ceremonies?"

Confusion ravaged Doucet's face. "At the church. Where else?"

"Not services. Ceremonies. Special ceremonies."

Doucet glanced at Sam. "I told her, the other day, I don't want nothing to do with them."

Ty crossed his arms over his chest. "Then tell me what I need to know and we'll leave you be."

Doucet hesitated.

Sam reached out and touched Doucet's arm. "Scully took Lucy."

"What? Lucy Wagner?"

"Yes."

"Why?"

The confusion on his face was now joined with fear and that fear told Sam that he knew something. Maybe everything.

"I think you know why," Sam said.

He sighed and his head hung, gaze directed at his slippered feet. "Jesus. I never thought . . ."

"Tell me," Ty said.

When Doucet looked up, his now moist eyes glistened. "Is this about that Keeper BS?"

"Tell me," Ty said again, this time a bit more forceful.

"I've heard . . . through the grapevine . . . folks I still know from the church . . . that Scully believes Lucy has hijacked this power that he believes is his." He looked out toward a pair of maple trees near the driveway, their leaves silvered by the moonlight. "If he's taken Lucy, he's gone completely crazy."

"I agree with that," Sam said. "If he wants this power back, what does he have to do?"

Doucet massaged both temples and wagged his head back and forth. "This is unbelievable." He looked at Sam, his face tightening, eyes narrowing against the gathering tears. "Mind you, I've never seen such a ceremony. Fact is, I don't know anyone at the church who has. Not even Scully, Junior himself. But it's my understanding that the passing of the Keeper's power requires a sacrifice."

"As in killing Lucy?" Sam asked.

He nodded. "I know the transfer requires the handling of the giver's heart by the receiver."

Sam shook her head. "Giver? Receiver? Makes it sound like Christmas."

"That's really all I know about it," Doucet said.

"Where would such a thing take place?" Ty asked.

"If I tell you, they'll know."

"And if you don't, you'll be an accessory to murder. You can bet on that."

Again, Doucet hesitated. Sam could almost hear the wheels turning inside. A man trapped between doing the right thing and fear. A tough place to be but she knew they didn't have time for Dwight Doucet to work out his moral compass. She pulled her gun, pointing it down.

"I swear to God," she said, "if you don't tell us, I'll shoot you right here, right now."

His head jerked toward her, eyes wide.

"Lucy is family," Sam said. "Basically my only family. She's the closest thing to a sister I've ever had.'

His tears broke containment and he sobbed. He wiped his eyes with two balled fists. "The most likely place would be out in Stemmon's Hollar. You know where the dirt road turns off and drops down to Stemmon's Creek? Down there by the creek is where Scully's held services before." He sighed. "Nothing like this mind you."

Back in the truck, Ty called Bump. "Looks like they might've taken Lucy down to Stemmon's Hollar. Near the Creek. I don't think we want to go tear-assing in there so let's meet up at the bridge. That'll be a half mile from the site and we can sneak in that way." He listened for a beat. "See you there in twenty."

CHAPTER 59

D id Martha know this would be my fate?

Lucy lay naked and anchored to a makeshift alter. Actually a heavy oak table top stretched across a pair of sawhorses. Not very elegant even covered with a white satin sheet. But out here in the backwoods with a rag tag group of snake worshipers what could she expect? Certainly not silver candle holders with elegant tapers, holy water, and a pipe organ.

When Martha told her she had to give the power back, did she know that feat required her sacrifice? That Lucy's chest would be ripped open, giving Scully access to her heart? Was this the deal she made with John, Senior.?

She wanted to believe that Martha knew nothing about all this. That had she known, she would have protected Lucy from Scully. Would have told Lucy about her deal with Scully. Whatever that deal was. Part of her said that Martha must have known. That she was major player, an insider, in the church for many years. Someone that would know all the tenets and practices of this cult. The snakes, the speaking in tongues, and the need for sacrifice. But she also knew that Martha left the church and that her departure had been around the time John, Senior became the Keeper. Did she know that Scully had sacrificed Rankin Sneed to gain this power? She must have. Is that why she left?

Why didn't you tell me, Martha?

Stop it, Lucy.

There is no power. No Keeper. This is all the insanity of a inveterate sociopath. Nothing more.

The night air sent shivers through her—or was it fear?—and the hard table top dug into her shoulder blades and hips. The thick leather straps Scully had nailed to the table top stretched across her neck, wrists, and ankles and dug into her flesh. Her left foot protested with a paresthetic prickling. She could turn her head from side to side but rising from the table wasn't possible. If she attempted to sit up or to even lift her hips, the neck ligature clutched at her throat.

The glow from the fire lit the expectant faces of the group, which now numbered around forty. They had coalesced into small groups. Their soft murmuring was mostly unintelligible, Lucy only able to pick out a few words and phrases. She heard "glorious day," "savior," "power of the Lord," and from a child, "Mommy, when can we go home?"

Lucy found the child's voice disconcerting. Who would bring a child to something like this? Expose a young mind to such madness. The answer she knew was that religious zealotry often possessed no common sense.

Near the fire, she saw Scully huddled with the Watsons and two other men she didn't recognize. Elvin Watson stared at her. She could feel his gaze travel over her nude body.

Another chill traveled up her back. She turned her head to the right, the leather tugging at the skin of her neck, resisting her movements. There, carefully laid out on a table, also covered by a sheet of white satin, the instruments of her death were on display. A large butcher's knife, a long-handled bolt cutter, two smaller knives, a copper basin, and a stack of white hand towels.

It reminded her of the surgical tray she used in the OR on a daily basis. Or at least she had. Those days were gone. Her career over. Tears welled in her eyes. It seemed silly to distress over her career when she likely wouldn't see sunrise, much less the inside of an OR ever again. But if she was anything she was her career. A doctor, a surgeon, all she ever wanted to be. All the long hours she had invested in climbing that mountain. The thousands of procedures she had performed. The patients she had helped, the ones she had lost.

And now she was the patient. The sacrificial lamb in this medieval ritual.

She flashed on the day John Scully, Senior had died on her operating table. Her first episode of fainting. The beginning of this madness. Did Scully choose the hour of his own death? Ridiculous. No way he could have caused his own aortic dissection. And John, Junior saying so only underlined the depth of his own insanity.

Something brushed her arm, She jumped.

"There, there." It was Scully, looking down at her. He now wore a long white robe. "No need for tears. This is a glorious day."

"You'll have to excuse my not seeing it that way."

"But it is. As Rankin Sneed passed the Lord's power to my father and he to you, you will now complete the cycle and hand over the strength of His word to me. The rightful heir."

"I'm not exactly *handing* it over."

"So to speak."

"You're fucking crazy." She tried to sit but the neck strap compressed her throat.

"It might seem that way to you, but to us," he waved a hand toward the faithful, who now stood in a haphazard array behind him, "this is a seminal moment. A strengthening of our church and our bond with the Lord."

"Amen," the crowd murmured.

Scully circled her so that he stood to her right. He picked up the butcher's knife and held it over her. "This is the instrument of our deliverance. Just as Moses used his simple staff to liberate the Hebrews, to turn the water to blood, the bring down pestulence on the Egyptians, to part the waters, so too will this tool be our salvation."

"Praise Him and all His glory," the faithful proclaimed.

"So let us begin."

He replaced the knife on the table and then dipped his hands into the copper bowl. He turned toward her and beginning at her chest dripped the water down her body. It coldness caused her flinch.

"With this blessed water I cleanse your soul."

Twice more her dipped his hands and sprinkled her body. Then with one of the smaller knives he pricked his own left index finger. He let the blood dribble onto her chest, between her breasts.

"Bless her Lord and cleanse her so that this passage will be ordained."

Using his finger and the pooled blood, he painted a cross on her chest. The congregation shuffled forward, forming a circle around the sacrificial table. Lucy saw Miriam, Felicia, the Watson brothers, and two men she didn't know emerge from the crowd to her left. Each now wore a white robe similar to Scully's.

Scully then lifted the larger knife once again, cradled it in both hands, and held it skyward.

"Lord, bless this instrument and this congregation. Bless this passage of your power from the nonbeliever to your true servant."

"So shall it be," the faithful responded.

"Let us pray," Scully said.

CHAPTER 60

S am, Ty, and Bump lead the way along the banks of Stemmon's Creek, a half a dozen officers following. Thirty minutes earlier, they had gathered near the bridge and then descended a steep slope down to the gently flowing water. The plan was to quietly follow the creek to where hopefully Scully and his gang had taken Lucy.

"What if this isn't the place?" Sam whispered.

"Then we're screwed," Ty said.

"Don't say that."

"Nothing you weren't thinking."

"Thinking it and saying it out loud are two different things."

"Superstitious?"

"Seems appropriate about now."

The trees that lined the creek were densely packed, blocking out the moonlight, making walking on the loose rocks of the creek bed an exercise in concentration. Sam had less trouble than most, a byproduct of her almost daily runs over dried creek beds back home in the California desert. The silence was as thick as the forest, broken only by the sounds of boots scraping over the rocks and the occasional scurrying of small animals through the foliage.

On they moved, Sam's apprehension that they just might be in the wrong place growing with each step. Surely they should be close. Suddenly Ty stopped. He raised a hand. Everyone froze in place. Sam could hear voices. Chanting something she couldn't make out. Ty pointed ahead. Through the trees a faint glow appeared.

Ty turned and motioned everyone toward him. He spoke softly. "This is it. I figure another fifty yards or so." He tapped two of the officers on the chest. "You two go with Bump. Up the left side of the creek." They nodded. "You two," he indicted another pair of officers, "and Sam move to the right to flank them. The rest follow me on up the creek bank."

"What's the play?" Bump asked.

"Move quickly but quietly. Get as close as you can and on my signal we'll go in from three directions."

"You think they'll be armed?" one of the officers asked.

"You can bet Eric and Elvin are. Beyond that, who knows? Best to assume everyone is." He looked back toward the voices. "But let's be clear on this. You are authorized to use whatever force is necessary to bring this to the right conclusion. Any questions?"

No one said anything. "Check your weapons and get moving."

Sam pulled her .357 and moved into the trees, two of the uniforms following her. She weaved through the trees, the voices and the glow from the fire increasing as she closed in. Soon the fire and then the congregation came into view, through the last few trees that surrounded the clearing. She saw Lucy, nude, on a table. Scully stood over her, a large knife in his hand. She could now hear everything clearly.

"Lord, bless this congregation and your humble servant. Make me worthy of your trust."

"He is worthy, O' Lord," the crowd chanted.

Sam squatted and duck walked to the edge of the trees, settling among the low boughs of a cedar. She leveled her weapon, siting it on Scully.

"I am your instrument. Bless this passage of your benevolent power to your most devoted disciple."

Scully raised the knife high above his head. "With this instrument I take back what is mine."

Sam curled her finger around the trigger and locked her aim on the center of Scully's chest. She took a deep breath, let it out, and began to squeeze the trigger.

Then a loud pop, to her left. Scully jerked, dropped the knife, and clutched at his left arm. Ty charged from the trees, his gun leading the way.

"Don't anybody fucking move," he shouted.

The crowd gasped, hesitated a beat, and then began to scatter.

"I said don't fucking move," Ty said. He snapped off two more rounds over their heads. Everyone froze.

Almost everyone.

As Sam bolted from her hiding place and turned toward the table where Lucy lay, she saw Elvin run into the forest, shedding his robe along the way. Eric lifted his own robe and came up with a gun. He directed it toward her. Sam fired two rounds, both striking the center of his chest. He went down.

Chaos followed.

The crowd released a collective scream, some falling to the ground, others running up the hill toward their parked cars. Still others ran into the trees. Sam could hear them crashing through brush and splashing through the creek.

"Stop," Ty shouted.

Some did, holding their hands skyward, but most ignored him. One group continued up the slope. Two officers followed.

"Don't let anyone leave," Ty shouted after them.

"You shot my boy," Miriam screamed. She squatted beside Scully who sat on the ground, one hand clasped over his left bicep, blood oozing between his fingers.

Ty turned to her. "He'll live."

Miriam let out a high-pitched howl and scooped up the knife Scully had dropped. She stood facing Ty, the butcher's knife clasped firmly in her hand. She stepped around the table and staggered toward Ty.

"Miriam, put down the knife."

"You shot him. Like a dog." She raised the knife above her head and charged.

"Don't do it," Ty said.

She never wavered, closing on him with surprising speed, her face contorted by rage. He and the two officers with him fired at the same time. One bullet struck her in the right leg, the other two her chest. She stumbled and fell facedown.

Gunfire erupted from the trees. One of the uniforms went down. Everyone else dropped to prone positions.

Elvin. Sam fired two rounds into the trees where Elvin had taken a position. She saw him turn and disappear into the trees, firing twice more over his shoulder.

Sam hurried to the table where Lucy lay.

"You okay?" Sam asked as Ty walked up.

"Glad to see you." She tugged against her restraints. "Get me out of this."

Sam looked at the bindings. Scully had nailed them to the table. She yanked at the one over Lucy's right wrist but it wouldn't budge. She grabbed one of the knives and began cutting the leather straps. Once Lucy was free, Sam picked up the robe Elvin had jettisoned and handed it to her. Lucy slipped it on.

"I'll be back in a sec, Sam said.

"Where are you going?"

"Elvin."

Wait," Lucy said, but Sam was gone.

❧

Lucy examined Eric but he was beyond salvage. Nothing she could do. Based on the location of the two entry wounds in the center of his chest, Lucy knew they had struck Eric's heart. No pulse, no breathing, and pupil's fixed and dilated.

She walked to where Miriam lay. Blood leaked from her chest and from her open mouth. Her breathing was shallow and weak, more a series raspy wheezes. Carotid pulse barely palpable. Lucy ripped the robe off the old woman, wadded it, and applied pressure over her chest wounds. MIriam moaned and then coughed, wet and rattling, blood spraying over Lucy's robe.

"She alive?" Ty asked.

"Barely. We need to get her to the hospital."

"It'll take a while from here."

"She don't have a while."

"Her dying wouldn't be the worst thing that happened today."

"Ty, you know I'm not going to sit by and let that happen. So get a ambulance out here. Now."

Miriam gasped and then fell silent. Lucy checked her pulse again, now finding nothing. She began to perform CPR.

"And get them here as quick as you can," Lucy shot over her shoulder.

"I'm on it," one of the officers said. He pulled out his cell phone and dialed as he walked away.

"Where's Sam?" Ty asked.

"That way," Lucy pointed. "She went after Elvin."

CHAPTER 61

S am moved deeper into the trees, now dark, the glow from the fire fading. She stopped and listened, but heard nothing. No footfalls or splashing water or crashing brush. She spun in a circle. Which way? Would Elvin try to climb the hill to where many of the cars were parked or would he turn south, back toward town? The cars made the most sense. She suspected he'd want to get as far away as possible as fast as he could. She turned that way, but after taking only a few steps she heard the explosion of quail wings through the trees. Behind her. Must be Elvin. He had stumbled on a sleeping covey of Bob White's.

She turned and charged that way, gun in one hand, pushing tree limbs out of her way with the other. She reached the area where the covey had been, now hearing them scurrying through the underbrush to her right. No sign of Elvin. She hesitated, held her breath, and listened. At first she heard nothing and then footfalls, splashing in water. Elvin was headed downstream.

Sam guessed Stemmon's Creek, maybe thirty yards to her left, ran downhill toward Crockett Lake near town. Made sense that Elvin would use it as guidepost. She scrambled that way.

As she stepped into a clearing near the trickling water, a bullet thudded against a pine trunk to her left. Bark fragments showered her. She ducked behind another tree. It was too narrow to completely protect her but at least its sagging limbs provided some cover. Another shot, this one snapping a small limb above her head, showering her with pine needles.

Where the hell was he?

She dropped to her knees and bear crawled between two trees, settling beneath a larger one. She peered around the tree trunk. Through the array of pine needles she saw him. A hundred feet away, standing in the middle of the stream, legs spread for balance, gun leveled in her direction. Two more shots whizzed by above her head. Thankfully Elvin wasn't a very good shot. Then she heard the snap of an empty chamber.

Bingo.

Sam didn't hesitate. She charged him, splashing up the stream on a dead run. He squeezed the trigger twice more but with the same result. Sam stopped fifteen feet from Elvin.

"What's the matter? Run out of ammo?"

His eyes were wild, his gaze bouncing around as if looking for an escape route.

"An empty gun is just a rock," Sam said. "Not much help here is it?"

He hurled the gun at her. She ducked at it flew by her head, splashing into the creek behind her.

Elvin balled his fist at his sides and glared at her. "What are you going to do, shoot me?"

"I might."

"Then go ahead," he shrieked.

"And I might not."

"If you don't, I'll run."

"Where? You've got no place to go."

"I ain't just going to give up."

Sam smiled. "I hoped you'd say that." She stuffed her gun beneath her belt in back and walked directly toward him. He took a defensive posture.

As she closed the distance he started to say something but never got a chance. Sam popped him in the mouth with a straight right hand.

"Talking's over," she said.

She snapped a left jab into his nose. She felt it crack beneath her knuckles. Blood erupted.

"That was for the lasso."

Another jab to his left eye. "That's for shooting at me."

Still another another jab, followed by a right hook to his left temple and a left hook to his ribs. HIs breath escaped in a loud whoosh. She slammed another right, left, right into his ribs.

"That was for killing Martha."

Now she went after him. Rights and lefts. Mostly to his ribs, chest, shoulders, wanting to avoid his head. No knockout here. Not yet. Elvin needed a beating. She landed two dozen punches as he tried to defend himself. No chance there. The blows came from all angles. Finally, she released a wide left hook that landed flush on his jaw. He went down, hard, splashing face first into the water. Like a skydiver who's chute didn't open. He groaned and rolled to his back.

"And that was for Lucy, you fucking psycho." Sam stood over him looking down.

"Remind me to never piss you off."

She jerked her head around toward the voice behind her. Ty stood in the stream, the water eddying around his boots.

❧

Lucy continued CPR, compressing Miriam's chest with a rhythmic beat. Blood trickled from the woman's chest wounds and from her mouth. Her pupils were dilated and glassy, like polished black marbles, the reflection of the fire dead center as if the flame was within her eyes.

"I know CPR." A man's voice above her. She looked up but didn't recognize him. "You need some help?"

"You can take over here."

"Sure thing." He knelt on the other side of Miriam, interlaced his fingers, and began the same rhythmic pumping.

Lucy examined the woman, now seeing that her neck veins were distended like thick ropes. Tamponade. One of the bullets had nicked her heart, resulting in bleeding into the pericardium, the heart sac. As the blood accumulated, it compressed the heart, preventing it from pumping properly. Even CPR wouldn't fix this. Only opening the pericardium and relieving the pressure would.

"Keep going," Lucy said. She picked up the butcher's knife from where Miriam had dropped it. She looked at the man. "There's going to be a lot of blood."

The man said nothing but nodded as if to say go ahead. He removed his hands, ceasing his external cardiac massage.

Lucy drew the knife straight across Miriam's upper abdomen, just beneath the rib margins. There was no way she could cut through the breast bone with only this knife so the only viable approach was through the belly and the diaphragm. Miriam didn't react, a testament to just how far down the road to death she had traveled. Dark blood oozed from the long cut.

Lucy now inserted the knife more deeply into the the wound, feeling the tip against the muscular diaphragm. She made another horizontal cut. Her skilled fingers searched deeply into the wound, finding the pericardium where it sat above the diaphragm. Using the knife tip, she punctured it. Blood erupted, spreading over the knife and her hands. She tossed the knife aside and with her fingers extended the rent in the dying woman's pericardium completely. She reached inside. Miriam's heart settled into her grasp and she began to rhythmically squeeze it. The heart was soft an pliable. Miriam had lost too much blood and this wasn't going to help. She needed blood and she needed it right now.

"Doesn't look good," the man said.

That was an understatement.

The officer who had called for an ambulance walked up. He looked down and paled. Lucy feared he might faint. He finally managed to speak. "They said it'd be a good half hour."

"She doesn't have that long."

"It's what they said. The roads being what they are way out here."

No way Mariam could survive that long. She might not survive another two minutes. But Lucy really had no options. She could only continue internal cardiac massage and wait. And pray. Though she doubted prayer would help much here. If anyone had ever pissed off the Lord it would be Miriam and Scully. She doubted He would be so merciful as to bestow a miracle on old Miriam.

She continued the rhythmic squeezing.

Give it back.

Martha's voice echoed in her ears.

Give it back.

Could she? Was that even possible? Hadn't Scully said it required touching the heart to remove the Keeper's power? Would it work in reverse? And if so, how?

She looked around. No Scully. He had obviously already been arrested and taken away. Probably to the hospital. But even if he knew how to reverse the process she doubted he'd tell.

Now what?

Fatigue grew in her fingers so she decided to change hands. But before she could let go of Miriam's heart, a deep cold feeling swelled in her chest. She felt dizzy and a wave of nausea swept over her. The man who had helped her, who was still kneeling next to Miriam, looked at her and said something. She could see his lips move but only heard the sound of her own heavy heartbeat in her ears.

The bitter coldness spread down her arm and into her hand. It seemed to cramp, locking onto Miriam's heart.

Miriam's body lurched upward and her back arched, so that only her shoulders and heels contacted the ground. She shook. Her her eyes jerked open, the reflected fire in her black pupils expanding. Her mouth gaped open and a long slow breath wheezed out. Then all went limp and Miriam collapsed against the ground.

Lucy jerked her hand free.

The cold feeling evaporated and she began to cry.

CHAPTER 62

Over 200 people attended Martha's graveside funeral service beneath a clear blue sky and a warm sun. Several people spoke, including Lucy. Most praised Martha for being the great artist she was. Lucy echoed those sentiments but added how Martha was so instrumental in her upbringing. How Martha raised her after her parents' untimely death.

Lucy had decided not to bury Martha in the plot Martha had selected long ago. Next to Lucy's fake parents. Next to the two graves Lucy and Martha had so often visited, flowers in hand. Somehow it didn't seem right to place her in the same soil as the two innocent people who died for no reason other than being a convenient cover for Scully's plan. A couple who apparently woke up to the madness and tried to leave the cult but instead found themselves enveloped in a literal firestorm.

Was Martha part of the plan to murder them? Lucy had no way of knowing. She wanted to believe that Martha was not involved but with everything else—like Martha promising Lucy to old John Scully and never telling Lucy the truth about who her real parents were—she couldn't convince herself of that fact. Common sense dictated that she must have known. Agree with it or not Martha had let all this happen. Had she just refused, had she simply told the truth, all of this could have been avoided. The murders, the infection of Lucy with whatever the hell it was, the passing of the contamination on to others.

Lucy chastised herself for thinking that way. There was no power. No infection. Not possible.

But she couldn't deny that since last night, since she failed to save Miriam, since whatever happened out in the woods near that sacrificial table, she felt . . . What? Relief? Not a strong enough word. Safe? Yes but more than that. Cured, healed? From what? Whole. That's the word. She felt as if she had been restored to her previous self.

No doubt her thinking was clearer, more focused. The depressing fog that had surrounded her had evaporated as surely as the morning ground fog that so often collected in the low areas around Remington faded under the glare of the sun.

But the truth was she had no idea what had happened last night. Didn't know how to process all that happened. She wasn't sure she would ever know but she was damn sure she was going to swing by the jail and have a chat with Scully about it.

She stood graveside, watching Martha's pewter metal casket descend into the dark rectangular hole. Sam held her hand, Ty snugged against her other shoulder, Bump next to him. The casket abruptly scraped the bottom, the thick nylon straps that had suspended it falling slack.

Lucy swallowed hard.

Sam squeezed her hand. "You okay?"

She squeezed back. "I'm fine."

The mourners began to break up, most moving toward the line of vehicles parked along the road that looped through Shady Hill Cemetery. Many stopped to offer condolences to Lucy, using the cliched phrases that always accompanied such occasions:

"So sorry for your loss."

"Things will look better in a few days."

"If you need anything, just ask."

Other than the two overalled workers charged with finishing the burial, they were the last to leave the gravesite. They walked down the gentle slope to where Sam's SUV and Bump's truck were parked. Lucy turned and watched the two men toss shovels of dirt into the grave. She sighed.

"I guess that's that," Lucy said.

"I'm sorry," Sam said.

"It is what it is. It hurts but I'll get over it."

"I know."

Lucy looked at Ty. "I want to talk with Scully."

"Why?"

"I have a few questions for him."

Ty nodded. "I'm sure you do. We all do. But, I'm not sure now is the time."

"It's the perfect time," Lucy said. "Before he concocts some story or talks to a lawyer."

"Said he didn't want no lawyer," Bump said. "Said the Lord was all he needed."

"Then there should be no problem with me talking with him," Lucy said.

Ty brushed his hair back from his forehead. "Okay. I don't see any harm in it." He looked at Bump. "You?"

He waved a hand. "No problem."

Lucy climbed in the backseat of Sam's SUV, Ty riding shotgun. They followed Bump out of the cemetery's main gate and turned toward town.

"How many did you end up arresting last night," Sam asked.

"Scully, Elvin, and three of the church elders. Everyone else we let go on home. Of course I told them not to leave the county since we would drop by for chat at some time." He laughed and looked at Sam. "You sure did a number on Elvin."

"Good."

"Three broken ribs, jaw fracture, and a crack in his left eye bone."

"Nothing he didn't deserve."

"True." He looked out the window. "I'd of shot him."

"Crossed my mind," Sam said. "But beating him was much more fun."

"What about Felicia?" Lucy asked.

Ty twisted in the seat, looking at her over his shoulder. "She going to stay with a couple Bump knows until we figure things out."

"She okay with that?"

"Seemed so. But she's still afraid of her father. That's for sure."

"She seems like a good kid," Lucy said. "I hope is all works out for her."

The Remington jail was a two-story, gray concrete structure that sat just behind the police station, a fenced rec yard filling the narrow gap between the two buildings. Ty led them out station's locked rear door and across the yard, mostly dirt with a few patches of sickly grass, to where the uniformed duty guard unlocked the solid metal entry door for them.

"Thanks, Will," Ty said as he walked inside.

"No problem."

The guard was mid-thirties, overweight, with fine blonde hair already thinning and receding above his soft blue eyes. Lucy noticed his name tag read, "Lt. Will Proctor." Inside was a good twenty degrees cooler than outside as if someone had clicked the AC on high.

To her left, Lucy saw another guard sitting at a desk, thumbing through a copy of *Sports Illustrated*. He was older, maybe sixty or so, and painfully thin. He looked up and, without saying a word, pressed a large red button on the wall. A section of the bars that separated the eight cells, two down and six up, from the guards area, buzzed and slid open. Will stepped inside and turned, waiting for Ty, Sam, and Lucy to follow. The door then whirred closed, ending with a sharp snap as the locking mechanism engaged. Will tested it with a tug and satisfied the door was secure, motioned toward the stairs to their right.

"He's upstairs," Will said. "Number six."

Lucy led the way, Sam and Ty behind her, Will bringing up the rear. As she climbed, she heard Will say, "Middle cell on the right."

Lucy turned down the corridor, past an empty cell, to Scully's. He lay on a bunk against the far wall and appeared to be asleep. An open Bible lay on his chest. Then she saw the blood. Several arching sprays covered the bed, Scully's clothing, and the wall behind his bed. A large gelatinous maroon pancake of blood covered the floor, beneath Scully's dangling right arm

"Oh my God," she said. She yanked on the bars. "Open this."

Will glanced into the cell, took in a sharp breath, and hurried back down the hall to an intercom box on the wall near the top of the stairs. He thumbed the button. "Open number six. Now."

The cell door vibrated open and Lucy rushed in. Now she could see that Scully's face was ghostly pale. She checked for a pulse but that wasn't really necessary. The coldness of his skin told the story.

"Jesus," Ty said.

Lucy lifted Scully's dangling arm. His wrist had been slashed. Not crosswise but rather in a six-inch gash that extended up the radial artery. This was no amateur effort, no gesture designed to garner sympathy, as was the case in many suicide attempts. This was the real deal. He knew exactly what he was doing. Knew that cutting along the artery's axis would prevent spasm, would make the blood loss rapid and complete.

"Look," Sam said. She pointed toward the right side wall.

"What the hell?" Ty said.

Lucy let Scully's arm drop and moved that way. The bloody writing on the cinderblock wall was splotchy. Obviously done by Scully with his finger.

And he said unto them, Go ye into all the world, and preach the gospel to every creature.

He that believeth and is baptized shall be saved; but he that believeth not shall be damned.

And these signs shall follow them that believe; In my name shall they cast out devils; they shall speak with new tongues;

They shall take up serpents; and if they drink any deadly thing, it shall not hurt them; they shall lay hands on the sick, and they shall recover.

So then after the Lord had spoken unto them, he was received up into heaven, and sat on the right hand of God.

And they went forth, and preached everywhere, the Lord working with them, and confirming the word with signs following.

Amen.

Mark16:15-20

"Unbelievable." Sam said. "He wrote that in his own blood."

"Sure looks that way," Ty said.

Something wasn't right. Lucy turned toward Scully's corpse. The sprays over the walls and bedding, the pool beside his cot, the nasty gash in his right wrist. He would have been unable to stand and function within minutes of slashing his own wrist and would have completely bled out very quickly. No way he could have done all this after he cut his wrist. She lifted his left hand. His index finger was a bloody stump, bone exposed.

"Does that mean what I think it means?" Ty asked.

Lucy dropped the hand and nodded. "He wore his finger to the bone writing out his last will and testament."

CHAPTER 63

Lucy, Sam, and Ty sat on Lucy's deck, sipping whiskey. Earlier, Ty had suggested that they go out somewhere to dinner. To relax and put the past couple of weeks behind them. Lucy declined so Ty picked up a couple of pizzas and fresh bottle of Blanton's bourbon and they gathered at Lucy's kitchen table. The pizzas didn't last long and afterwards they migrated outside to enjoy the evening and finish off the bourbon.

"So what do you think?" Ty asked Sam.

"About what?"

"About all of this. You have some experience with this woo woo stuff."

"Woo woo stuff?" Lucy asked.

Ty shrugged. "You know what I mean."

"I think I don't have a clue." She sipped from her bourbon. "I've never been able to explain Richard Earl Garrett so I doubt I'll ever be able to explain this either."

"Lucy?" Ty asked.

"I agree with Sam. I don't think this will ever make sense." She forked her fingers through her hair. "I'm just glad it's over."

"Is it? Over?"

Lucy looked at Ty. 'What do you mean?"

"I'm not sure exactly. It's just that if this so called power is real, where is it? Where did it go?"

"It died with Miriam," Lucy said.

"Did it?"

DId it? Lucy suspected that was the million dollar question. Did she pass the whatever it was to the dying woman? Was it indeed extinguished with her death? Or was it still out there searching for another host. Like some parasite. Looking for a symbiotic partner.

Jesus, Lucy.

"Look, I don't believe there was some mystical power in the first place. It was all some bogus religious myth."

Again Ty shrugged. "Hope you're right."

"I am."

But was she? The truth was that she didn't understand any of what had happened. She couldn't get her head around why she had fainted in surgery or had so many episodes of that cold and dizzy sensation. Not to mention her nightmares. Or why so many of her patients had gone psycho and committed such atrocious acts. Hadn't each of them said she had put something inside them? Didn't Ronnie Draper try to cut open his own chest to get whatever it was out? Wasn't that what Scully said? That his father had passed the power to Lucy for the sole purpose of her passing small doses along to her patients?

Lucy drained her glass and placed it on the deck. She leaned forward, propping her elbows on her knees. Moonlight reflected off the calm lake in a long silver slash.

"All I really know is that I feel better. Back to my old self. Before, besides the dizziness and the fainting and the nightmares, I felt out of it. Like everything was behind some gauzy curtain." She straightened and looked at Ty and then Sam. "But the moment Miriam passed it seemed as though the fog lifted. Like some weight had been removed." She shook her head. "I don't know how else to explain it."

"What now?" Sam asked.

Lucy snatched up the rapidly emptying bottle of Blanton's. "More bourbon."

"That seems to cure everything," Sam said.

Sam held out her glass and Lucy refilled it, along with her own. She handed the bottle to Ty and he poured the final inch into his own glass.

"But tomorrow morning I'm going to have a chat with Birnbaum. Get my privileges back and get to work."

"What if he balks?" Sam asked.

"That's why I'm taking you with me."

Sam touched her glass to Lucy's. "Looking forward to it."

Lucy laughed. "Of course you are."

ABOUT THE AUTHOR

D. P. Lyle is the Macavity and Benjamin Franklin Silver Award winning and Edgar, Agatha, Anthony, Scribe, and USA Best Book Award nominated author of both non-fiction and fiction (the *Dub Walker* and *Samantha Cody* thriller series and the Royal Pains media tie-in series). Along with Jan Burke, he is the co-host of Crime and Science Radio. He has served as story consultant to many novelists and screenwriters of shows such as *Law & Order, CSI: Miami, Diagnosis Murder, Monk, Judging Amy, Peacemakers, Cold Case, House, Medium, Women's Murder Club, 1-800-Missing, The Glades,* and *Pretty Little Liars.*

Website: dplylemd.com
Blog: writersforensicsblog.wordpress.com
FB Page: facebook.com/DPLyle
Crime and Science Radio: dplylemd.com/DPLyleMD/Crime_%26_
Science_Radio.html

Reputation Books